FADING LIGHTS

Other Books by

Ryan D Gebhart

The Jewel of Life

Splendor of Dawn

Hidden Within

FADING LIGHTS

PART THREE

OF

THE JEWEL OF LIFE

RYAN D GEBHART

Hardcover ISBN 978-1-7326355-5-5

Paperback ISBN 978-1-7326355-6-2

Distributed by Ingram Publisher Services

Printed in the United States of America

Cover design by Fiona Jayde Media

To Chris,

for walking with me through

one door and out the other.

Table of Contents

Acknowledgements

Fading Lights is centered on the virtue of justice. My books were never intended to comment on the political atmosphere in the real world beyond its pages, but it is difficult to maintain that value, especially following the passing of US Supreme Court Justice Ruth Bader Ginsburg. This acknowledgment, in my own small way, largely belongs to her as she strived to uphold our highest ideals of equality under the law. Like so many others, I am a beneficiary of Justice Ginsburg's long fight for justice. She was fighting for my rights before I even knew I wanted them—before I even allowed myself to dream of them.

Before I appreciated Justice Ruth Bader Ginsburg, much of my own understanding of justice came by way of the ancient Greeks, passed down to me by my cherished professors at the Catholic University of America. I'm partly expecting them to send me a grade on a singular paragraph at the end of this book. I feel so fortunate to have been able to read and study the likes of Plato and Aristotle under their careful guidance. I am the richer for receiving the philosophical education that I did, even though I'm still paying off those pesky student loans.

I offer my sincerest gratitude to the readers who have been following Devlyn's journey, along with the many other characters who are very dear to me. This story started in a small chapel in Philadelphia—West Philadelphia to be precise. At that time, I never imagined that that small spark of creativity had enough charge to create an entire world, leading to a seven part series of novels and more. The world expands just a little bit more with every page of my many yellow notepads, with each book peeling back the shroud over this fantasy world just a little further. So, thank you, dear readers. Thank you for your continued support and your reviews asking for more. I honestly couldn't keep this story suppressed and unwritten if I tried!

When I finally started the publishing process with *Splendor of Dawn*, I was fortunate to be introduced to my very talented editor, Micheline Brodeur. I can't thank you enough for polishing this next story, often, and necessarily, with a sand grinder! Thank you for your patience and the care you have given to this story and to me.

Fading Lights was written well before *Splendor of Dawn* and *Hidden Within* were published, but I only started the publishing process after completing my thesis and receiving my master's degree in architecture in December of 2019. I first starting writing it in 2015 and writing it helped me through a difficult and distressful transition in my life, which even led to shingles. This book saw me through one job, returning to seminary twice, unemployment, and eventually a decision to return to my first love, architecture, to seek a master's degree, making a full circle in my academic career. I cannot thank my parents and sister enough, along with the rest of my expanding family and friends, for being with me during that time and not losing faith in me. Your love and encouragement mean the world to me. It truly pains me during this pandemic that we cannot spend more time together. I love you all very much.

Ryan D Gebhart

18 September 2020

Skrein Sea
PERRIEN
PARENDIOT
Wooded Hills of Thellion
Gneal
Undol
Renyl
Mount Verinie
Lake Soesindol
Septyl
Asenthyl
The Verrien Mountains
Oern
Belina Watch
Cyrillean Pass
Cyril
Selma
Lews Wood
Ortyl
KRYSEN
Verenth
Evenn
EVELLION
Stellanter
River Ethion
Audun
Delmira Wood
The Eldin Wood
Overen
Brunst
Plains of Mindale
Hamil
Wexly
Binton
Farenton
The Purged Desert of Dwonia
MINDALE
Jopht
Ashton Wood
River Znasl
River Znasl
New Castle
Freitor
YANIL
Dwotas Gap
Houlk Wood
Nyner
Nuntol
The Shadow Mountains
Lankor
Dornal Marsh
Mount Cyngol
Kinzdol Island
Howling
Zorik
Tempestien Sea

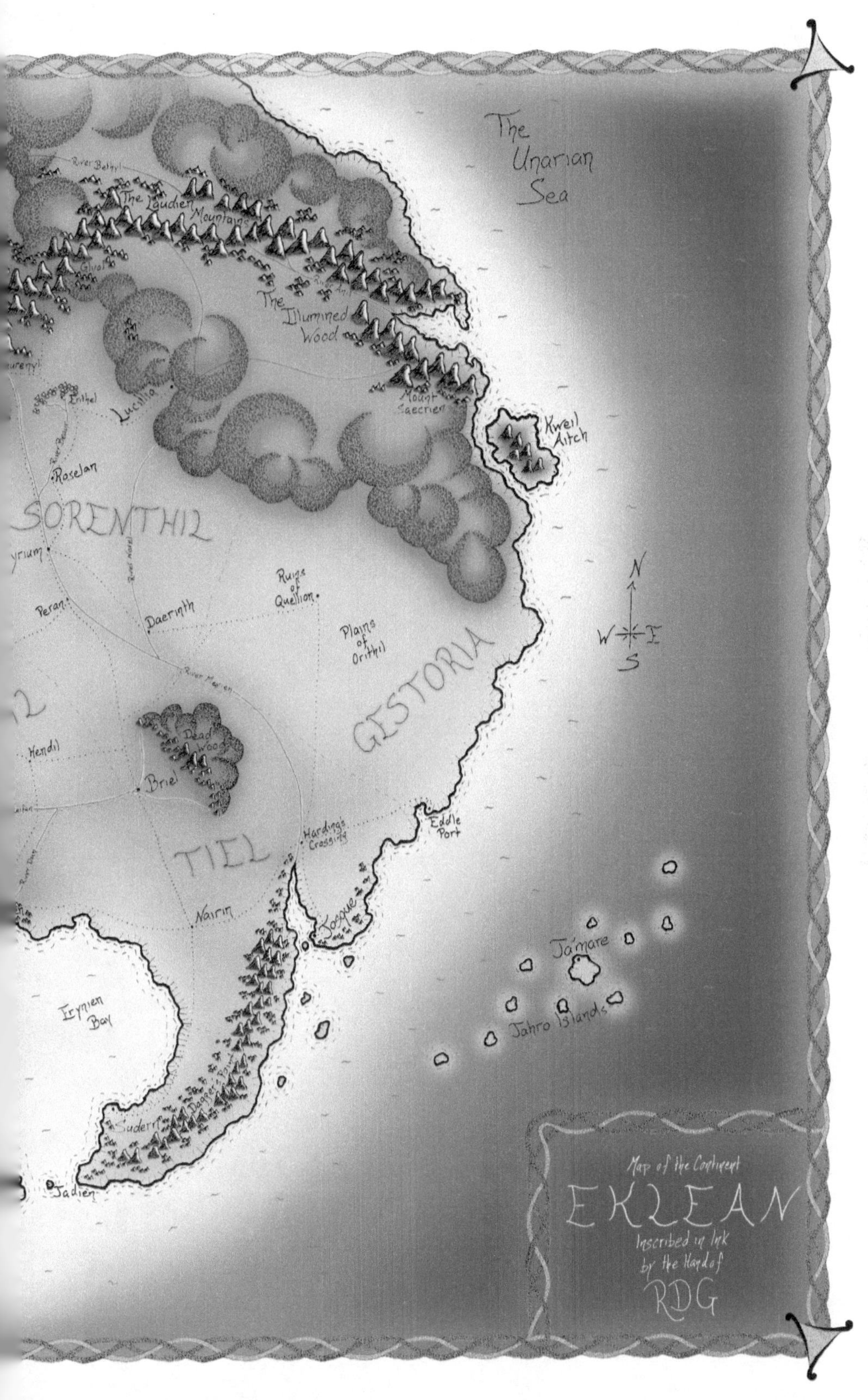

The Unarian Sea
River Bethyl
The Laudien Mountains
Gluath
The Illumined Wood
Mount Saecrien
Kweil Aitch
Enthel
Lucellia
Urenyl
Raselan
SORENTHIL
yrium
River Morel
Ruins of Quellion
Peran
Daerinth
Plains of Orithil
GESTORIA
River Maren
12
Dead Wood
Hendil
Briel
Eddle Port
Harding's Crossing
TIEL
Nairin
Losque
River Day
Irynien Bay
Ja'mare
Dooper's Pass
Suderin
Jahro Islands
Jadien
N
W E
S
Map of the Continent
EKLEAN
Inscribed in Ink
by the Hand of
RDG

DUST AND DISCRIMINATION

Vine Vaerin sat in her cozy chair in the library of the manor home she shared with her husband Clyde, waiting impatiently for him to return from their vineyards. Clyde and the workers were eagerly preparing for autumn harvest of the grapes that became the famous Cor'leran Blue ice wine. Vine couldn't understand why Clyde had to involve himself so much with the day-to-day upkeep of the vineyards. After all, she didn't do anything in the vineyards, and they functioned just fine without her. Surely, the grapes would manage without Clyde's constant attention. For half a heartbeat, her thoughts wandering as she waited, Vine considered walking over to the abbey school to visit her brother Entiel. The walk was not a short one and if it hadn't been for the hot Reventh sun, that thought might have lasted longer. Naturally, she could arrange a carriage to carry her out from Cor'lera and to her brother's abbey school on the village's outskirts, but those carriages were so stuffy this time of year.

No, she thought, *much better to wait for Clyde.*

Shifting on the rose velvet cushion of the chair, Vine reached for one of her favorite candies in a silver bowl on the small table beside her. She still could not believe the delicious sweets came from the likes of Walei's shop. *Such an odd man,* she thought as she popped one—not the first this afternoon—into her mouth. The problem with the candies was how quickly they disappeared. Another quickly followed and it too disappeared.

Vine's gaze followed the various leather spines of Clyde's books around the library. She recognized that she shared many traits with her husband, but his love for his books was not one of them. He guarded them jealously. Most of the spines' lettering had faded, but Clyde had seen to it that the gold leaf had been reapplied to the most worn. One tome's spine never dulled, however, a book that Vine had read more than any other. Truly, the book that described House Vaerin's ancestry was the only sort of book that caught her interest and it was kept on a shelf well above the height of any child. Not that they had any young children with sticky fingers around anymore.

But seeing it reminded Vine that her eldest son, Sam, was considering asking that woman, the daughter of one of the men who worked at their vineyard, for her hand in marriage. No one was good enough for her Sam. He could have at least fallen in love with someone from a better family. What sort of a dowry could the family of a vineyard worker provide? Vine shuddered at the thought of welcoming them into her home. She'd never get their stink out of the wood paneling. To make matters worse, neither Clyde nor her brother, Entiel, saw the union as an issue. All they cared about was whether Perrien blood flowed through a potential bride's veins. Not so much for her sake, but for Sam's sake and his future children.

Entiel should have known better. He knew very well that her union with Clyde of House Vaerin was the only reason their family had flourished so. Lex would have never received his first appointment in the military if not for her marriage with Clyde. And Entiel likely would not have become the abbey school's abbot either. *Foolish men.* Vine scoffed at the idea that men thought they made the world spin.

Vine stood, grabbed another candy as she rose and popped it in her mouth. Naturally, that one also disappeared too fast, so she grabbed two more before walking out of the library and into their wood-paneled hall. She passed the grand staircase, quick to notice dust accumulating between the wood spindles. Lenna was going to get an earful the next time Vine saw her. Vine paid her maid good money. The woman would have to look good and hard before another family would pay her a silver jent a week, and even harder if Vine decided to let her go. No one in

Cor'lera would hire her after hearing how neglectful she was. That woman had no idea how fortunate she was. Just like the men in Vine's life, Lenna never seemed to appreciate what Vine had done for her.

Apart from the now restored Cor Inn, there wasn't a single building in Cor'lera, inside or outside the original wooden defensive wall, that could rival Vaerin Manor. Not only was it the largest private home in the entire village on either side of the wall, it also carried the prestigious weight of House Vaerin. The dated, refurbished inn couldn't compare with Vaerin Manor, even if it was slightly larger than Vine's home. Vine abhorred her neighbors for building their own homes so close to her property. Because of them, she would never be able to expand her manor house.

And as if her neighbors weren't mean enough, that Arlyn, a supposed ei'ceuril from Ceurenyl, had ruined her reputation by restoring that wretched inn. Why he'd felt the need to return to Cor'lera after all those years away made Vine want to scream. She didn't care that Arlyn had been born at that inn or that with Evellyn's disappearance, he had a legal right to that property. He should have left it well alone. But no, he'd had the debris cleaned out, the walls washed, and the floors swept. He had even started to fly that wretched flag with a purple doe on a beige field above the blasted inn. Vine had recognized the flag immediately. Clyde had a book illustrating every Eklean standard, and that one had belonged to an independent Parendior. And if that wasn't enough, it seemed that there were dozens of traitorous Cor'leran families who had stashed away their flags when Perrien had conquered their country— passing their contraband treasure down through the generations. That flag now flew over dozens of homes and even over the village gates, just as it had a century ago.

The Cor Inn was the least of the reasons that Vine swore off anything to do with Arlyn. He might be Evellyn's only surviving sibling, but he had no right marching into Cor'lera three years ago and then setting up a resistance against her brother while the village's elite had been celebrating Lex's return at a party at the abbey school. Lex should've found a way to burn the wooden wall around the inner village when her Alex was whisked away in the dead of night by that ei'ana witch. Naturally, she blamed Devlyn as well, since she was sure he had led Alex astray. Vine had only recently discovered how that corrupt ei'ceuril Arlyn had managed to hold off her brother and Perrien's military. He had been and probably still was teaching some of those women with elven blood how to wield. Fortunately, they were probably all gone from Cor'lera now, following the treasonous ruffians to who knew where!

Vine didn't care that the walls surrounding inner Cor'lera were allegedly woven from the Illumined Wood, and that there was some sort of connection between that forest and the Lucillians living in her village. Whatever it was, they had managed to hold off Perrien soldiers from breaching the village walls, walls that should have been an easy target—a shepherd could've breached those walls since they were neither tall nor constructed of stone. But against all odds, the wooden walls stood whole and uncharred under an enchantment put in place due to Arlyn's leadership. That enchantment had been up for a year and Vine's store of Walei's candies were nearly depleted, since no one who had been outside the wall after the enchantment had gone up—everyone who was anyone, and who also lived in the outer village—had been able to go into the older part of the village. Without notice to those who had been unable to visit the shops and merchants within the wall, Arlyn had removed the enchantment once he decided the village was safe from further Perrien aggression, but Vine had yet to go to Walei's to see if she could replenish her candy stocks. Instead, she sent Lenna's son to fetch them for her.

With the thought of the wall, Vine scoffed in the direction of the original defensive wall and found herself looking forward to the completion of the stone wall which would encompass the newer part of the village. Because of Cor'lera's growth over the past century, the placement of the new wall took into account continued expansion and would cut through farmland well beyond the current village limits.

Crossing the hall, Vine went into the parlor and peered out the window past her lavender floral drapes. The street on which Vaerin Manor stood was still in shambles. Ruffians had passed through on their way to the inner village and Cor Inn, where they had stayed for a month, and then gone on their way again, taking her Alex with them! Even though they were slightly better than half the people native to Cor'lera, people diluted with filthy elven blood, the newcomers were still ruffians, nonetheless. Every one of them had been gathered from one farm or another across southern Parendior along the way to Cor'lera. Their departure had brought a huge sense of relief to Vine, especially since they had taken along those she considered a stain on Cor'lera, including Arlyn. Not just those tainted with elven blood and pointy ears, but full-blooded humans who were sympathetic to them. How anyone could align themselves with Lucillians was beyond her. It seemed that just about every Parendian was fed up with the Perrien Council and eager to fly that purple flag again. The next time she saw her Alex, she was going to have to have a very difficult conversation with him.

How her little boy got himself involved infuriated her to no end. Ei'ceuril or not, Entiel deserved all the blame! Surely her brother had to know the consequences of sending their nephew, Devlyn, to her home to play with her Alex at such a young age. The cousins had become quick friends and even insisted on sharing a room together at Entiel's abbey school, which her fool of a brother had actually allowed. Three years ago, when Vine had discovered that her son had gone off with her nephew and that pointy-eared, red-haired woman, she had nearly thrown her brother from the tallest tower at his abbey school. Granted, none of those towers were tall enough to cause the harm she wanted. Vine was half tempted to drag Entiel all the way to Gneal just to toss him from one of the castle's towers. Surely, those towers had to be tall enough. Instead, she had settled for not inviting him back into her home since Alex's disappearance.

Sighing, Vine watched a grandmotherly woman sweeping the cobbled street outside. *Certainly took her long enough*, she thought. Every street was filthy—mud and dust everywhere! Just looking out the window made her feel dirty, although not as dirty as talk of a Perrien resistance. The reminder made her want to spit, even if that was something she abhorred and would never do. But certainly, something those ruffians would do. She prayed that her son wouldn't adopt more of their bad habits. Just the thought of her Alex spitting made Vine cringe, and again, want to spit herself.

She had no doubt that those ruffians would be killed by Perrien's military. No one stood against Perrien's grey coursers. If not for her other brother's status as a general, she would have feared for her Alex. But instead, she figured Lex would simply find her rebellious son involved with the wrong crowd, give him a good beating, and send him home to his mother for a proper spanking. Whatever Lex did to Alex would pale next to what she intended for her wayward son the next time she saw him.

Her hatred for those with elven blood had increased when Alex had returned, just over a month ago, after having gone missing for years only to spew nonsense at her and the rest of their family. It had been and still was deplorable, and she was thankful that the meeting with Alex had not taken place in the manor. They'd met in the inner village square, which wasn't an appropriate place for such a conversation either, but she certainly wasn't going to allow such thoughts into her home! Just thinking of the stench it would leave on her wood paneling made her shiver. How anyone she was related to could think such a way was disgusting—especially her own son! Granted, her Alex wasn't the first of her family to like those pointy-eared vermin. How her brother Dolan ever got involved with that pointy-eared woman was beyond her. Vine knew that he had never recovered from his first wife's passing in childbirth, but to then settle for a Lucillian! Vine had only invited Dolan and Evellyn to her home once. She still swore she could smell the filth left by Evellyn. Wood paneling simply absorbed the worst scents and remained tarnished forever. No matter how much she had paid her maids over the years, they could never remove the scent.

Evellyn was part of the reason Vine had become so prudent about who she permitted in her home. To say nothing of what others would think of such filth entering her manor house. House Vaerin was above all that. House Vaerin was an example all Cor'lera looked up to. If she allowed those with revolutionary ideas into her manor house, or worse, those with elven blood, it would not be long until other prominent families did the same. Mayor Folt already flirted with the Lucillians more than she cared for or thought proper. Cor'lera would return to the dark days before Perrien had welcomed Parendior into its kingdom. How Parendior had ever managed before Perrien's guidance bewildered Vine. *Clyde should really consider replacing that mayor—such a weak man*, she thought.

Stepping away from the window, Vine noted dust collecting on the windowsill's corner. Lenna would hear of this too. The drapes would have to be cleaned as well. Vine turned to leave the parlor just as the door creaked open in the adjacent vestibule. *Finally*, she thought.

"Watching Moira sweep the streets again?" asked Clyde from the parlor's threshold.

"She waited an entire week this time. Really, what took her so long? Those ruffians left with our son a week ago."

"Last I checked, no one set up a fund to pay Moira for her service." Clyde turned away.

"Why pay someone to do what they're already doing?" Vine spoke to Clyde's back as she followed him to the library. The parlor was much more inviting, but when Clyde was home, she spent most of her time with her husband in their library. He complained that it was too small, and his father should have built it larger, but Vine was relieved he hadn't. It was one of the few things she appreciated about her late father-in-law. There were too many books on those shelves already, collecting dust. If Clyde had more shelving space, he wouldn't give his current collection space to breathe. Oh no, rather, he would clutter the entire space further. If Vine had allowed him, he would come home from the market or from Walei's shop with a new tome every week.

"Honestly, I feel a bit bad for her. Her only son left with those rebels, took his wife and two children with him too. What sort of band of miscreants has our son involved himself in? I've never heard of a military force taking spouses and children along for the ride."

"Sounds terribly dangerous." Vine eyed the candies in the silver dish. *No, not yet.* "But I wouldn't classify that group as a military force, honestly. They're more of a farce. They won't stand a chance against Perrien soldiers."

"Still, you should write to your brother, tell him to keep an eye out for Alex if there's an actual engagement. Wouldn't want our son getting confused for a rebel and their assured ill fate," said Clyde, his back now to Vine, his eyes scanning the packed shelves of books. "A Perrien resistance though…makes you think, doesn't it?" Vine knew which book held his attention. His head tilted up, eyes looking directly at it.

"Don't tell me you have sympathies for them as well? This entire village has lost its mind!" Vine popped a candy into her mouth. Its sweetness consumed her. "Did you see the farm equipment they took with them? Do they expect they'll stand a chance against the Perrien military with farm equipment? If you decide to join them, are you going to take your pruning shears with you as your weapon?"

"I'll be sure to take my own farming equipment rather than the rusted tools at your brother's school, that's for sure."

"My brother was never known to take an interest in agriculture. I'm sure the other ei'ceuril there are like-minded."

"The place is worse off now without our nephew taking care of their tools. I'm surprised Entiel hasn't found another indentured servant to replace Devlyn yet. Your brother could learn something from the native Cor'lerans; I certainly have. They take pride in their trade and treat their tools with the same care as you give our glass dishware."

"Our glassware isn't going anywhere near those rebels and neither is our farming equipment. Do you want our vineyard to fail overnight?"

"You know very well I have little love for that Perrien Council. If it wasn't for their predecessors, I would have been born in Gneal."

"You speak treason, and you know it."

"To the council, yes, but not as a son of Gneal." Clyde slumped his shoulders and turned to face Vine. "There is only one person toward whom I can truly be treasonous."

There's that stupid smile! thought Vine, feeling her knees go weak. "You'll beg for a swift execution if you're ever treasonous toward me! One which would never be granted—that type of treason needs a proper, drawn-out punishment."

Clyde's eyes now matched his stupid smile. Vine did love his clear blue eyes. No one had eyes as blue as those of the members of House Vaerin. They went so well with his blond hair, true marks of a Perrien. Naturally, she shared the same features, as did all their children, although her eyes could not compare with the clarity and beauty of his.

"Promise me one thing?" he asked.

"You're hardly in the position to request anything." Vine tried not to look into his eyes—he knew very well that his eyes were her weakness.

"My dear Vinessia…" Clyde was the only scoundrel of a man she'd ever permitted to use her full name. She'd even boxed her brothers' ears when they were young, just as she had every other fool man who had sought her hand in marriage and mangled her name in doing so. But other than her parents, only her Clyde pronounced her name correctly and without a hint of mockery in his voice.

Vine raised a single eyebrow.

"Invite our son inside our home the next time he visits and don't try to send him immediately back to your brother's school."

Vine pursed her lips. "Only if he doesn't insist on bringing any of…*them* with him. I won't have our wood paneling reeking from those with elven blood. I can still smell that Evellyn."

"Speaking of your sister-in-law, have you been to see what Arlyn has managed to do with that old inn?"

"There aren't enough maids in all Eklean to get rid of all those cobwebs, to say nothing of the mountains of dust there." Vine's fingers found the silver candy dish again as her anger flared. The worst part about all those ruffians passing through Cor'lera was the amount of business that restored inn had received. It had been at full capacity for an entire month—she had heard that they actually had to turn people away. Her lips pursed with distaste despite the swiftly melting sweetness in her mouth.

GATHERING

A large wagon filled to the brim with weaponized farm equipment rumbled past a startled Alex, a sturdy wheel narrowly missing his toes. Lost in thought about the ever-growing Parendior uprising, he hadn't been paying attention to what was going on around him, risking getting trampled. From what he'd seen as he stepped away from the wagon, even the infamous vineyards of Cor'lera had lent tools to the cause. While Alex appreciated the extra resources, he didn't see how a pair of pruning shears would benefit the Perrien resistance.

Parendian smiths knew little about forging weapons, but they were no novices when it came to their anvils. Hammers clanged throughout the day when the caravan was not on the move, and well into the evenings when it stopped. At least, until someone hollered for them to quiet. Often, it was a mother with a screaming infant who yelled at the blacksmiths. While the humans noisily made weapons of iron, the elves focused their energy on the much quieter crafting of bows and arrows.

The transitory camp bustled with activity—wagons creaked, horses neighed, and people hollered at each other. Few were trained soldiers. Most had devoted their lives to the land as farmers and had only recently picked up a spear or sword for the first time in their lives. Alex knew everyone from Cor'lera by name or at least recognized their faces. He was even getting to know many of the Parendians from other villages who had joined the growing army over the weeks and months. Every one of them intended to push Perrien back across the Arvil.

Alex was still awed every time he took note of how many Cor'lerans had joined the resistance. Those with elven blood had offered their support first. They were not merely humans with diluted elven blood, as Alex and Devlyn had grown up believing, but true elves. And not just any elves—they were Luminari, like Devlyn. When Reia and Sara had told the elves about the raising of the Protection of the Wood in Lucillia, the implications of that event for all Luminari left them in no doubt as to whether they would support the resistance. This war wasn't just a battle against Perrien, but a battle against the Erynien Empire. The Luminari knew what they had lost at the hands of Erynor—not just their kingdom and resplendent cities, but their immortality and freedom. They would never be Erynor's slaves again.

The rest of the Cor'lerans had been quick to show their support too, which didn't surprise Alex. The humans and elves native to Cor'lera had once been part of the independent land known as Parendior. No one had reigned over this humble land of farmers and village folk since the time of Thellion. Each village tended their land and they were spread out far enough apart that it was considered a significant journey to travel to the next closest village. The loose-knit communities had made Parendior an easy target when Perrien had invaded a century ago to claim the vast country of rolling hills and plains as part of its own kingdom. The acquisition had doubled Perrien's landmass and the conquerors had swiftly implemented a tax that no farmer could reasonably afford.

Alex had expected Parendians to join the resistance against Perrien, but he had never in his wildest dreams expected Perriens from Cor'lera to bolster their numbers. Many had been shut out of the walled interior of Cor'lera when the native villagers rose to defend themselves against a squadron of Perrien soldiers, soldiers led by Alex's Uncle Lex just three short years ago. That was when Velaria had managed to convince Devlyn and him to follow her across every land known to man! Alex remembered that day vividly. Velaria had given an account of Devlyn's family and the night that Devlyn had become an orphan, a tale not known by a single resident of Cor'lera. Lex was aware of that story, since he had played a great part in it, but he'd kept those details and his fratricide to himself. Instead, he had lied to the entire village, telling everyone that Devlyn's family members were criminals, turning them into pariahs.

Not everyone had left Cor'lera with the newly formed Perrien resistance army. Over half the villagers remained to protect it from those who would attempt to make the village their own.

Two months ago, when Alex and his companions had first reached Cor'lera after traveling from Binton, he had been delighted to find the boards removed from the windows and doors of the Cor Inn, a sight he had never seen. A flag with a purple doe on a beige field flew above the restored inn. Alex had wanted to tell Devlyn about the changes at the inn, but even if he could have managed to find a messenger bird, there was no telling where his cousin was. Locating Devlyn was the bigger issue. Alex hadn't seen him in months, not since they'd parted company after the events in Binton, Devlyn off to who knows where with Velaria, Ellendren, Andrew, and Viren while Alex had headed for Pariendor with Oliver, Sara, Reia, and Abbie, raising a rebel force as they moved along.

Once they'd reached Cor'lera, Alex had been relieved to discover not only the inn restored, but the village still standing after his Uncle Lex's assault. Although Velaria had assured Devlyn and Alex of just that, shortly after they had left three years ago, Alex had trusted little that came from her mouth in those days. Even now, he still took everything she said with a hint of skepticism, despite and perhaps especially because she was now the Chair of Azurelle. But as she'd said, Arlyn had managed to protect the village, and not a single casualty had been reported, other than his Uncle Lex's pride.

Alex's own family had refused to listen to anything he'd tried to say, the only time he had seen them when he'd first returned to Cor'lera. When his mother had realized that he was with the "ruffians" at the Cor Inn, she hadn't even invited him into their family home. Lex was still involved in Perrien's lengthy campaign in Evellion and Abbot Entiel had refused to leave the safety of the abbey school. His mother was fiercely loyal to her brothers and refused to believe that they were involved in any wrongdoing. Arlyn and his revolutionary flag deserved the blame.

Alex had known very little about Devlyn's uncle Arlyn, only that he was an ei'ceuril steward and a kien wielder, an untrained kien wielder.

Fortunately, Arlyn hadn't attempted to use his wielding to protect the village. With his lack of control, he just as likely as Lex would have burnt the village down. Rather, he'd been able to provide instructions and guidance for the women capable of wielding on how to protect Cor'lera.

However, Alex had learned that Arlyn no longer avoided wielding, claiming that a woman named Clara had come to their small village—conveniently, she'd gone by the time Alex had reached Cor'lera so he couldn't verify the truth of that—and taught Arlyn how to control his wielding. The village's kiara wielders had also benefited from Clara's instruction, their abilities having improved to the point that after only three years of wielding, and perhaps a month of training under Clara, Reia and Sara were in awe of their skill. Arlyn maintained that Clara was an ei'ceuril—a steward even, a fact that Alex doubted. He had visited the Temple of Ceur dozens of times as a student at Gwilnor Academy, mainly to visit Devlyn, and not once had he met a female steward, let alone heard mention of one. Although, hearing of a female steward was much less concerning than hearing that another man wielded, something that Alex still held as not proper. That it was Arlyn made it just barely acceptable. Alex still questioned Gwilnor Academy's willingness to start training kien wielders again. Surely, they'd realize their mistake soon.

In the month since the growing rebel army had left Cor'lera, their westward pace was slow, and it slowed even more with every village they passed. They spent a few days at each, speaking with the village leaders, and without fail, every village bolstered the rebel numbers with people willing to join the growing force, increasing the size of the caravan and further slowing their pace.

Distracted by another passing wagon, Alex at first didn't notice a small child approach. The boy looked familiar, although he was no more than ten years old, and, much like Devlyn's brother Liam, it was difficult to tell whether he was an elf or a human. His ears were pointed, but in a rounded point, not as extreme as others, and his eyes shared the emerald fading to silver characteristic of the elves, but were also rounded, like human eyes. The boy extended his arm, offering a rolled parchment to Alex and looking briefly into his eyes before quickly looking down to his feet.

"What's your name?" asked Alex, taking the proffered parchment.

The boy hesitated a moment before looking up to answer. "Aen, sir, uh, general, I mean, my lord." He looked back to his feet.

"I'm no lord," Alex responded automatically. It was annoying how quickly people had started to address him as lord once he had started gathering an army to resist Perrien. He wasn't the only one who had come to Parendior for that purpose and officially, he was still just a student at Gwilnor Academy. He hadn't even been knighted yet. But for some reason, no one addressed the others as though they were nobles. Granted, Reia and Sara were ei'ana and Oliver was a Septyl knight. And Abbie Wintyr was whatever Abbie Wintyr was! "Aen? Sounds elvish."

"It is, sir, general, uh, not lord. My momma insisted on it; she's an elf, I'm only half. My papa's human. People didn't used to like him, but now they do. I don't know why; he hasn't changed or anything." Aen once again glanced up at Alex then looked shyly to his feet. "How come you're not a lord? Everybody says you are."

Alex grinned, taking a liking to Aen. "Lords are born; you can't simply become one."

"Why not? I think you're a lord, and so does everybody here. You should let them call you lord. People like having nice lords and ladies, not like the mean ones across the river," Aen said, gathering confidence as he spoke, and Alex couldn't stop the laugh that popped out at the image of the mean lords and ladies of Perrien.

"What's funny?"

"You're a good kid." Alex avoided a direct answer. "How would you like to deliver all my messages in the camp? You can be my personal page."

The boy grinned, showing all his teeth, some of which were missing. The grin quickly faded, then Aen asked, "If I'm your page, can I still learn to be a knight like you?"

"I'm not a knight—not yet." Alex laughed again. "But I can help you train when you're old enough. You can even become my squire one day. How does that sound?" Alex asked, getting ahead of himself.

Aen wore a determined expression. "All right but promise that I can be your squire when I'm old enough. When you're a real knight and it's ok for people to call you lord," said Aen earnestly, putting out his small hand to shake in agreement. Alex tried hard not to grin, because Aen's seriousness was quite amusing, and shook Aen's hand. "Now that I'm your official head page now, you really should read that. The woman who gave it to me said it was from someone important; very important."

Unfolding the parchment, Alex saw a golden symbol, one he'd never seen before, at the top of the message. It looked like a bird—in fact, it looked like Aliel.

Alex,

I'm in Myrium and the invading Tieli and Torsillian armies have been defeated. I'm not sure how much you've heard, but Aren murdered the Sorenth queen and Myranda is now the Queen of Sorenthil. I'm a full Phaedryn now. It happened while I was fighting Aren, and I almost died, but the transformation happened just in time to save my life. I'm worried about what Erynor will throw at us next. Shadow elves are the least of our problems. The Eldinari agreed to leave the Eldin Wood and help Everin. Velaria said that you're gathering an army; if Perrien's forces are pushed from the Cyrillean Pass, they'll fortify themselves in Gneal. You need to get there first. Take the city and get as much local support as possible. Depose the Council; Erynor has them all in his pocket. I'll try to fly out to you sometime, but I'm not sure when. I'm to return to Gwilnor for additional studies.

- Devlyn

Alex only read the letter once and was a little confused by some of it but was also left transfixed by Devlyn's request that he conquer Gneal before Perrien's forces returned. His intention was only to bolster Parendior's defenses to protect it from Perrien, pushing their forces back across the Arvil. He'd never even considered taking the fight into Perrien, let alone to their capital. *We might as well dig our own graves before crossing the Arvil. Good thing we have all those spades from the farms.*

Aen had been watching Alex read through the letter. "What's it say?" he asked, his concern evident, even for a ten-year-old.

Alex hadn't needed to see the name at the bottom to know who had sent it. He knew Devlyn better than most, and his handwriting was unmistakable. There was nothing special about it, only that it was Devlyn's, and how the message had made it to him was a mystery. "Sorry, Aen," he said. "It's a lot to take in."

"Really?" asked Aen. "It doesn't look like a long letter. I've written things twice as long. Once, I had to write something at least three times that! Momma 'sisted. But my hand hurt after."

It was impossible to suppress a grin, when not a moment ago he had been on the verge of cursing his cousin's name. "I'll have to tell you about it later. Now, I have to talk to some people."

"I can get them for you. It's my job. And I can run fast."

"Oh, that would be great. Tell Arlyn, Sara, Reia, and Oliver that I received a letter from Devlyn, and that I need to talk to them about it. You'd better tell Abbie too—she'll cut me in my sleep if I don't involve her." Aen ran off, barely waiting for Alex to finish speaking.

And as Aen raced off, Alex just stood there, the letter clutched in his hand. Devlyn was no king, not even a lord, yet he gave orders as though he was. He read through the crumpled letter once more, hoping to make sense out of it. Not the actual message, that was quite clear, but that his cousin had assumed that he could give Alex military instructions, tasking him with an invasion.

Alex started walking, lost in thought about the changes in Devlyn. He'd never shown any interest in leadership or politics; in fact, Alex had always been under the impression that Devlyn would defer any kind of responsibility to nearly anyone else. So, this new Devlyn who gave him orders to conquer a city was quite a different Devlyn than the one Alex had grown up with. Odder yet was Devlyn's asking him to charge head-first into an offensive battle. The more he thought about it, the more likely he thought the letter had been dictated by Velaria. *Devlyn would never ask me to do something like that,* Alex mused, relieved to have puzzled it out.

Satisfied with his conclusion, Alex looked around, surprised to find himself on the far side of where he needed to be. He turned around and headed to his tent, recalling that he should have told Aen where to have the others meet him. Even as he had that thought, another came. *Why would Velaria dictate the letter and have Devlyn sign it, rather than just write it herself?* Alex reread the end of the letter. *Fly? What type of magic makes a person fly? Even elves can't fly.*

When he reached his tent, he found Aen rocking back and forth from toes to heels at the tent's opening. "I found them all. They're waiting inside," Aen said with a broad-toothed grin.

"Um, thanks," Alex replied, shocked at Aen's efficiency as a page. Opening the flap, Alex found everyone he'd asked for jammed inside; Arlyn stood between Reia and Sara next to the cot where Oliver sat on the end, while Abbie stood in a corner by a small desk. They all looked to Alex and Aen, who had followed Alex in, making the tent even more cramped.

"You really should consult us prior to appointing someone as your page," Reia said as she eyed Aen, half hidden behind Alex. "Surely we could have found someone older and a little less persistent for your errand boy."

Alex glanced back, catching Aen giving the ei'ana a funny look.

"I don't know," said Arlyn. "I like the lad. After all, he did precisely what that occupation requires. He even got us here before Alex. Most impressive." Reia's expression said she didn't agree.

"I would talk with his parents before sending him on any more errands," Sara suggested kindly.

"And you should remind him that you are not a lord, and not even a king would dare to summon ei'ana in such a manner. Our presence may be requested, but never demanded," said Reia. Aen took offense, stepping out from behind Alex.

"He is too a lord!" he insisted, his eyes hard. Alex wanted to laugh, but one look at Reia told him he would regret it.

"I have," Alex said instead, "in fact, I've told everyone here that I'm not. But the more I tell them that, the more they say it."

"I remember learning that before kings or queens laid claim to any throne, the people would name certain individuals as their leaders, deeming that they possessed the qualities necessary for such a position," said Oliver. "Considering Parendior has no nobles nor recognizes Perrien's authority, the people of Parendior have every right to elevate one of their own to nobility. After all, there isn't a person in this camp who hasn't named Alex their lord."

Alex rolled his eyes but Aen's lit up. "So, he *is* a lord."

"I suppose he is," Arlyn agreed.

"That's so neat! Can I tell everyone now? Please?"

"You are his page, not his herald," Reia chided, eyeing Aen as she walked over to the boy. The air inside the tent started to whirl, the water in the goblets bubbled, the ground rumbled, and a ball of fire appeared above her palm. "Tell me, Aen Finamarc, son of Edward Finamarc. Do you promise to never repeat what you hear within this tent, or at any other meeting?"

Aen nodded even as he tucked most of himself safely behind Alex again, his head peeking out from just below Alex's elbow.

"Do you promise to be loyal to your new lord, and swear him fealty, even in the face of his enemies?" Again, Aen nodded.

"Reia, you're scaring the boy," said Sara.

The air in the room stilled, the water calmed, the ground stabilized, and the flame vanished in a puff of smoke. Reia took her attention from the boy and sat down at the small desk, causing Abbie to shift slightly toward the opposite corner by the tent opening.

"I wasn't scared," Aen said, no longer hiding behind Alex, but still close by.

A hint of a grin came to Reia's face. "I think you'll make a fine page. With luck, you won't take too long to grow up. I bet you'll make a better knight than a page," she added, no longer looking at the boy. If she had been, she could have counted all his missing teeth at the mention of such a possibility. "Unfortunate that you're so loyal to Alex; Septyl would have been very pleased to have gained a student like you. Now then, Lord Alexander Vaerin, if you would, please tell us why we've been summoned." The distraction of the discussion around his elevation to lord had made Alex almost forget the letter. With the reminder came a desire to throttle Devlyn the next time he saw him. "Right, well, I received a letter from Devlyn, who says he's a full Phaedryn now, whatever that means, and that Myranda Lariviere is the Queen of Sorenthil because Aren killed her mother, and that Myrium is no longer under siege. Also, he wants us to continue expanding our army here and take Gneal while it is under-protected."

Waiting for the gasps of shock from everyone at all the news and the absurd idea of taking Gneal, he was left disappointed when no one seemed to object.

"Clever," Oliver commented, lost inside his own strategic mind.

"So, you all think this is a good idea? Not ludicrous?" asked Alex.

"It's far from ludicrous. I assume he wants us to take the city before Perrien's army needs to retreat from Everin," said Oliver. "Is there a reason he believes they *will* need to retreat?"

"Oh, right, I forgot something," said Alex. "Devlyn says the Eldinari are joining our cause and will be going to help Everin." Alex lowered the parchment. "And what exactly is an Eldinari?"

"Did you learn nothing at Gwilnor Academy?" chided Reia. Arlyn's astonishment was clear.

"I never thought I'd live to see the day!"

AWARENESS

Wind rushed across Devlyn's bare skin as he dove toward the hidden valley on the outskirts of Ceurenyl. He was nearly home again.

Throughout the entire past month when he'd still been in Myrium after the epic events that included his emergence as a Phaedryn and the ending of the siege, he had not found any clothing capable of withstanding the transformation with Aliel. Dozens of fine pieces of extremely expensive items had been destroyed in the testing process, and he still was uncomfortably naked when bonded fully as a Phaedryn with Aliel. And it wasn't as if he could ask other Phaedryn what to do about staying clad, so the search for transformation-proof clothing continued. When he thought about it, thought about how he was *naked,* he was embarrassed, almost ashamed, but when he didn't think about it, just *was* a Phaedryn, it felt wonderful.

They'd stayed in Myrium for a month after the siege ended. Skirmishes orchestrated by shadow elves who refused to accept defeat or flee the area had continued to plague the countryside. While they had no longer possessed the strength or numbers to threaten the city known as the Jewel of the River, they had focused their energies toward ravaging Myrium's satellite villages. With each skirmish, a horn had sounded requesting help from the capital.

Since Devlyn and Aliel were the best suited to dispose of the shadow elves, they had quickly bonded as a Phaedryn, Devlyn's body transforming in mere seconds. Wings of golden light sprang from his shoulder blades, his vision took on Aliel's lighted sight, and his muscles expanded, not in size but in capacity. His hair was not long enough for him to see it for himself, but Viren had commented that it looked as if Anaweh had spun golden threads of light into his scalp. He could see his own skin though—everyone saw that—and it took on a luminous quality, disintegrating his clothing in the process, leaving his entire body visible for anyone to see.

That had been only one of his concerns, since he also had to deal with the soldiers accompanying each of the remaining shadow elves in the raids on the villages. Devlyn had learned that most of the soldiers were forced to attack and kill as many villagers as possible. If the soldiers refused, the shadow elves threatened to consume the souls of their loved ones, preferably in front of the recalcitrant soldiers.

At first, Devlyn had taken no thought about how to deal with the soldiers. If they attacked him, he swiftly incapacitated them. There was no telling what they could or would do if given the chance. But as the skirmishes persisted, Devlyn had overheard a Sorenth knight joking with another about one of the Torsillian soldiers begging for his life, swearing that he had joined in the raid only because he was being manipulated by a shadow elf.

Devlyn had doubted that every enemy soldier was being coerced to attack the Sorenth—some soldiers enjoyed the violence and mayhem—but once he'd understood that not all of them were willing participants, he no longer felt certain about what to do when a soldier surrendered. He knew that if their positions were swapped, the soldiers would not think twice before removing his head from his neck, and he shivered at that thought. While he had only managed to incapacitate a few shadow elves, he'd never had a moral dilemma about it, feeling some relief when he watched the consumed souls, stolen to lengthen the shadow elf's own wretched life, float away to peace whenever a shadow elf was killed.

The skirmishes dwindled with every passing week and Myrium's dungeons filled with enemy soldiers who had willingly surrendered. Queen Myranda was confident that they had uprooted the remaining shadow elves. Either they had been defeated or their masters had finally called them away. Devlyn remained concerned at the thought of Erynor commanding his shadow elves to retreat. From what he knew of the Erynien Emperor, retreat was never an option; if Erynor had in fact called for them to pull back, he was planning to use them in some other fashion.

If not for Devlyn's daily lessons with Velaria, Alethea, and Viren, Erynor's intentions would have kept him awake at night. Fortunately, not a day had passed over the past month in Myrium when he had not been pushed to his limits—physically, mentally, and spiritually. Velaria and Alethea had kept his mind fully occupied with sessions in wielding, history, philosophy, and his least favorite, awareness. Alethea had also insisted that he spend at least an hour in meditation with her. Then, at the end of every day, Viren had urged him to spend time learning the fine art of handling a sword, mentioning that he had never heard of a Lorenthien who could not use one. All that training was exhausting.

The lessons had been suspended once Myranda felt assured that Sorenthil was once again safe. Lines of communication had reopened between the crown and Sorenth nobility, although there still were decisions to be made about the Prince of Daerinth's secession. With Sorenthil's reclaimed stability, Myranda offered her gratitude one last time before saying farewell to Myrium's allies. The Eldinari star wardens had returned to the Eldin Wood, the majority of the Blue Dragon Flight had left with a recovered Rusyl, and Devlyn, Velaria, Ellendren, Alethea, Wyn, Viren, and Andrew had flown toward Ceurenyl.

For Devlyn, the two-day flight to Ceurenyl was a wonderful experience, naked or not. He spent each day bonded with Aliel, flying through the bright sky and low hanging clouds as a Phaedryn. He felt revitalized since leaving Myrium. Being fully bonded with Aliel was the best feeling in the world—nothing in all Teraeniel could compare to it. Sure, he spent hours on end flying, but his body never tired of the repetitive motion of flapping his wings. *His* wings!

It still felt like a dream that he and Aliel had finally fully bonded. Devlyn turned his head to glimpse a golden wing aloft in the air current—*his* golden wing—and felt the air, felt it wanting to guide him—to hold him—as if it was its sacred duty to do so.

Devlyn grinned at the incredible sensation rushing through him. *No need to hide your joy*, Aliel conveyed and needing no further permission, a strong exuberant laugh burst forth from deep down. It felt good to laugh. He knew Erynor and his shadow elves were going to make his life, and all Eklean's, miserable in the future, but they had just won a major victory for Sorenthil, and he was finally a full Phaedryn, and all of it was just *amazing!* His lips parted as the autumn wind rushed against his face, and with no warning, he swallowed a bug.

Coughing and spluttering, he heard a jovial whistle from behind or beside him. It didn't matter, but in his joy, he had forgotten that he was not flying to Ceurenyl alone. But not even the bug he'd just swallowed could dampen his spirits. The reminder that someone was paying attention was embarrassing though. He was not comfortable with being seen naked, and to make it worse, it was impossible to cover himself while flying. Whenever he tried to use his hands to provide some sort of coverage between his legs, he would lose balance and almost fall hundreds, if not thousands of feet to the ground.

"Look at those red cheeks," hollered Wyn from atop Eolwn, his black and grey griffin, and let loose a second whistle. Viren ignored the younger elves and soared through the skies on one of the free blue dragons who had helped defend Myrium, Andrew holding on behind for his dear life.

"You'd better be referring to my face!" Devlyn was the only one who didn't laugh at his comment. While he wished he could have flown by himself, he did need someone to accompany him to carry his clothing. He refused to sit around camp with the others while bonded with Aliel—his unclothed state in the proximity of the fully-clothed others was far too uncomfortable. Especially when Ellendren was present. And he would certainly need at least a pair of trousers once he reached Gwilnor. He wasn't going to walk around school naked! When they had first left Myrium, Devlyn had been relieved to no end that the women had agreed to wait an hour after the men each day so he could move out of sight, hand his clothes over to Wyn and bond with Aliel to fly off.

Enough of his clothing had turned to ash in the past weeks; he wanted to be careful with what remained, until he could find a better solution.

As they flew on toward Ceurenyl, he again wondered why it was necessary to return to Gwilnor Academy. Now that he'd become a Phaedryn, he wasn't returning to continue his studies to become an ei'ana or an ei'ceuril; he belonged to neither. While he didn't pretend that there wasn't useful information to be gained from his various classes and accepted that he still had quite a bit to learn from his favorite art of wielding class, he saw little reason to return to the school that was meant for ei'ana and knights.

He *was* happy that he and Aliel were returning to Gwilnor though. The castle had become his home. He had friends there, and even family. Several months had passed since he had last seen his brother and he was eager to find out how Liam's studies at Gwilnor were going as a student wielder.

Also, Ceurenyl was the only Krysenthien city that had not been consumed in the Shroud. It felt right, as a Luminari, to live in that city, more right even than Lucillia, home to the majority of the Luminari. He had an odd relationship with Gwilnor castle; it was not his favorite building in the world, especially after seeing the palaces of Mar'anathyl in the Skyland of Luminare. Gwilnor castle was no competition to those, and according to Alethea, even Mar'anathyl paled next to Arenthyl. It was impossible to grasp how anything could surpass what he'd seen of Mar'anathyl through those memories, but doubting Alethea was never a wise idea.

While he looked forward to returning to Ceurenyl, returning to the temple city also meant that he had to formally declare that he would not continue his studies as an ei'ceuril. Only the Ceurtriarch, Ealyndol Roendryn, could release Devlyn from that commitment. Other ei'ceuril could probably facilitate the task in the Ceurtriarch's name, and most likely had official roles to do just that within the temple's hierarchy. However, most students were not mentioned by a fourteen-hundred-year-old prophecy spoken by Lucillia herself.

Devlyn had never been comfortable with becoming an ei'ceuril. It just didn't feel right, had never felt right. The prophecy must have been misinterpreted somehow, for even though he was now sure that his destiny was not becoming an ei'ceuril, he had no intention of dying any time soon, and absolutely refused the notion of ever causing doom to Teraeniel. He was determined to discover a different path. Whatever it was, he would have to figure out what it meant to give of himself fully.

Devlyn landed elegantly in the grassy valley and felt the thud of the dragon carrying Viren and Andrew landing nearby, sending tremors through the ground from his impressive weight. It was quite a contrast to Wyn's griffin landing right after with no more than the sound of wings rustling. When Devlyn and Aliel withdrew from one another, becoming two separate physical entities once again, Devlyn's sight dimmed, but the contrast was not as distinct as it once had been. He was beginning to experience the world differently. He could feel it within his heart as it made itself known through the rest of his body.

A bundle struck his left shoulder from behind. "Just in case you wanted them," said Wyn.

Just as Devlyn had one leg in his trousers, Yelaris, carrying Velaria and Ellendren, landed with another thud beside the other blue dragon. Alethea's griffin alit next to her. They were supposed to be an hour behind—he wasn't half dressed yet!

"You need to become more comfortable with yourself," Alethea instructed yet again as Devlyn hastily shoved his other leg into his trousers and pulled them up. "Have you learned nothing?"

"I swear I have," said Devlyn, "but, that doesn't mean everyone in Ceurenyl needs to see, um…all of me."

"That is precisely what should happen."

"I know, I know. I need to show and express my interior through my exterior."

"Weren't we also shy when we were their ages?" Viren commented.

"I'm much older than he," said Wyn, sticking his chest out slightly.

"You forget that mortals age differently. You didn't begin your studies until you saw at least a hundred fifty winters," reminded Alethea. "You're more of an age than you think."

"True, but I've also spent well over a hundred thirty years since."

"Still a youth," Viren said with a chuckle. "But, so was I when I was knighted a Guardian."

Desperate to leave the subject of comfort levels and bare skin, Devlyn led the others through the valley toward the cave that concealed a secret tunnel into the Temple of Ceur, a tunnel that let into his very own apartment. The dragons and griffins remained in the valley, content to soak in the warm Reventh sun.

As he walked, Devlyn gave thought to when he should schedule a meeting with the Ceurtriarch. He had to tell Ealyndol sooner than later that he would be ending his novitiate before taking any of the ei'ceuril vows. Playing through the potential scenario in his mind, he felt it would be unwise to make the announcement immediately after his prolonged absence. Not that his time away was uncalled for; Ealyndol had been involved in the decision for Devlyn to leave the city after all. Since leaving the temple under the cover of night, he had met a plethora of individuals willing to stand up to Erynor and protect the free people of Eklean. And there was his invaluable time in the Eldin Wood. He didn't think that he and Aliel would have bonded as they did while defending Myrium if they had not gone there, met the Eldinari, and learned more about his elven background. It was also at Stellantis that Devlyn had met one of the enthiel, Boriel, who had given him one of the seven lucilliae that formed Ceurendol—the Jewel of Life. Devlyn now had two lucilliae. He'd received the first, a violet one, from Queen Vernal Roendryn—who with her husband, King Harnyl Roendryn, were the Aryl of Lucillia—and it contained the faith of the Luminari. The second, an indigo gem, held the prudence of the Luminari.

The small group would have walked blindly through the dark tunnel if not for Aliel's presence. They could have wielded a globe of light, but it would have extinguished the moment they passed through the temple's ward. Devlyn knew that there was a wield in place that prevented anyone from wielding within the temple, and he had passed through it many times before without being conscious of it, but this time, he could sense it just in front of him. He paused, held his hands up to touch it, while pressing into the erendinth.

"I nearly forgot about that old wield," Alethea said as she too inspected it. "You sense it now, don't you? It's the first time you've noticed it, isn't it?"

"Um, yeah," said Devlyn, not sure how he felt about having previously walked unaware straight through something that was now so obvious. "Who put it there?"

"Aldarch Theseryn, the first Ceurtriarch. No other ei'ceuril would have been able to manage a wield of that magnitude. The other aldarchs could have done so, but they never understood why Theseryn would choose to step down from his near deific station to found the Ei'ceuril. He left his sanctum on Aldinare, Thas'thallas, and his followers remained true to him, but none remained here on Eklean and Theseryn eventually transitioned to Lumaeniel, the only aldarch to leave this world for the next.

"With all the benefits of wielding, Theseryn also knew that it could be used as a weapon. He had the foresight to place this wield around the temple to prevent any potential bloodshed."

They all crossed Theseryn's ward and instantly, Devlyn felt himself cut off from the erendinth. He felt its presence, but the further he walked through the secret passageway, the more distant it became.

"Everyone, stop," said Alethea. "Well, only Devlyn, really. Everyone else can continue to the temple if you would like, you too, Aliel. This is the perfect place to practice."

They shrugged their shoulders, not entirely sure of what the ancient elf had in store for Devlyn, but simply went on, leaving the two behind in the secret passage, cut off from wielding. Aliel followed them to Devlyn's apartment, lighting the way for them. Once the phoenix was gone, the tunnel grew dark again, but with Devlyn's changing sight, he had no problem seeing. That is, until Alethea covered his eyes with a long piece of cloth and tied it behind his head.

Panic quickly overtook him. *What's she playing at?*

"Now, I want you to walk to your apartment."

Grumbling at the absurd exercise. Devlyn extended his arms,

feeling for the rough stone walls. Taking several carefully placed steps toward his apartment, Devlyn walked blindly onward.

Thump.

"What was that?" Alethea asked, as though she didn't know exactly what had happened.

"My head meeting rock. I couldn't see the lowered ceiling," grumbled Devlyn. He pressed his hand to his forehead to soothe the injury, because somehow that made it hurt less. Well, he thought it did.

"You didn't know that rock was there?"

"How could I? I can't see a single thing with this blindfold on and it's not like I can wield to feel the stone," Devlyn replied, his irritation escalating.

"Good. Stop where you are, I need to show you something while you're unable to wield and see." Devlyn turned to Alethea, at least where he thought she stood; he wasn't aware that he faced the rough wall of the tunnel rather than Alethea.

"Our eyes are not the only way of sensing that which is around us; all of who we are connects with our surroundings. And no, it has nothing to do with wielding. We've talked about this before. Now, press your hand against the stone nearest you."

Devlyn felt the slick stone, thick with moisture against his palm. Touching the stone helped to orient himself, and he realized that his ears had not deceived him—he wasn't facing Alethea after all.

"The touch is familiar, yes?"

"It's just like any other rock." Devlyn was annoyed at having to practice yet something else when he really just wanted to be with his friends, and enjoying the comfort of his apartment.

"Right, now remove your hand and try to feel the rock there without touching it."

"How am I supposed to do that if I can't wield?"

"By using your inner sense. Become aware of your surroundings. Not with your external senses, but with your interior ones. Feel the stone surrounding you, pressing in on all sides." Alethea paused, and gave Devlyn a moment to digest what she had said. "Now try. And don't forget, it's not wielding."

Devlyn reached out, wanting to press into the erendinth, to follow the same process to discover his surroundings, but he was still in the limits of the temple and could not. He thought of how he reached out to Aliel; there was no wielding involved, but something inside him went beyond, seeking the phoenix's life force.

So, he quieted his mind and focused on what surrounded him. He recalled his sessions with Alethea in the Eldin Wood, where she would have him do something similar. Here, it was different. It was easier to sense trees bursting with life, sensing their own awareness. The stone of this tunnel was cold and dead; if it had ever been alive. Alethea insisted that, at one time, all stone was alive—just like the sleepy trees had once been much more interactive with the elves.

The area pulsed and a brief glimpse filled his mind. It was not an image, but a sensation. In that sudden phenomenon, he *felt* the stone inches above his head, the stone that his forehead had met just moments ago, jutting downward, and the vast depth of the tunnel, including the distance they still had to walk. It reminded Devlyn of pressing into terys, yet it was distinctly different. It emitted a dim presence—the faintest shadow compared to when he wielded terys.

"Good."

"Thanks." Devlyn was still not sure whether he was happy with Alethea's teaching methods; maybe Ellendren was right about Gwilnor Academy and their standardization. "Hold on, how could you tell I managed it?"

"Did you not sense me?" asked Alethea.

Thinking back, Devlyn did recall that some sort of presence had come from the old elf, emanating from her body, but he had barely paid any attention to it, not knowing that he should.

"When our eyes are open, are we not aware that someone else with eyes can also see? We cannot see from their perspective, but we know that they are seeing something from their point of view. Much is the same with the inner sense; our bodies give off an aura of sorts, just as one who wields has a different aura depending on what erendinth they wield, and whether they wield kien or kiara. Our inner sense allows us to glimpse people's auras. Those who do not use that inner sense have a faded quality, as if they are asleep. There are some whose inner sense is so strong that they are aware of every minor detail about a person simply by drawing near to them."

Remembering the centaur, Oreniel, Devlyn asked, "Do the centaurs have access to this inner sense?"

Alethea chuckled. "Every creature has an inner sense, both anadel and anacordel. Even the cordel, wild beasts and plants, have it, the upper crust of Teraeniel once had it, before the rocks and dirt faded due to ignorance and abuse.

"Remember, like any other part of your body, it's a muscle. If neglected, it weakens. Think what would happen if you never used your arms and legs. Would they not become fragile and sluggish? To strengthen them, you must use them and exercise them. Only then, will you know what they are capable of. Such is the same with the inner sense; it's not an innate ability. One needs to use it, to exercise it, for it to grow strong. Never underestimate the importance of meditation," Alethea said, removing the blindfold, indicating it was time they joined the others. When they opened the door to the secret entrance to Devlyn's apartment in the Temple of Ceur, Devlyn's eyes darted to the sofa that he very much wanted to lie down on. His temple apartment was just the same as he had left it, and while he had expected to find Velaria, Ellendren, Andrew, Wyn, Viren, and Aliel waiting for him and Alethea, he had not expected to see Therril sitting on that sofa, grinning broadly at him. How the old ei'ceuril had known that Devlyn would return today was beyond his understanding, but not beyond his expectations of Therril. He was funny like that—always knowing something before anyone told him. Devlyn suspected that Alethea and Therril had some of the strongest inner senses currently in existence—certainly in Ceurenyl.

"Oh, is it good to see you safe and whole again!" Therril smiled broadly to Devlyn, but only glancing at Alethea.

Devlyn returned Therril's smile; it had been a very long time, and something about the old ei'ceuril's demeanor made Ceurenyl feel like home.

"While I would very much like to take part in this reunion, these old bones are very tired," said Alethea. "Tell me, Velaria, will accommodations be made available in the castle for Wyn and me?"

"Of course, and I'd be delighted to escort you to the current Emradiel wing of the castle. I can only imagine how delighted they'll be to see you and learn of Father Phendien's imminent return."

"I'm sure some of them will be. I trust you'll arrange a meeting with the other Chairs for me?"

"It's my first priority, after arranging accommodations for you and Wyn."

"I'd better join you; I have to let Mother Paurel know that I've returned to resume my studies," said Ellendren. "And poor Laureniel left in those stables all that time. I do hope the stable hands were good to her. Would you mind if we stopped at the castle stables first?"

"Not at all." Velaria smiled her small smile, as if she had already planned on doing just that.

"I have to report back to the castle as well. I'm not looking forward to informing my lieutenant that Oliver won't be returning anytime soon," said Andrew, scratching his back. "In case I don't see you again soon, Sir Viren, I know the Septyl knights would be delighted if you would share your experience and expertise with us. No one could best Sir Oliver with a sword—no one. We've all grown up with the tales of the Guardian knights, those legends inspired many of us to join the Septyl knights in the first place. And no one living remembers how to craft armor like yours; the technique has long been lost."

"I'll visit the Knight's Tower and speak to the captains after Devlyn gets settled back here. Unfortunately, I know very little how the Luminari smiths crafted our armor, but I can say that the technique is not entirely lost."

"Thank you, Sir Viren." Andrew saluted. "Though you'll find us mostly in the North Tower now."

"Viren, will you be taking up residence with Devlyn here in the temple?" asked Velaria.

"I will. There does seem to be more bedchambers than any one student would ever need."

"Quite out of the ordinary, I assure you," said Therril.

"Devlyn, Aliel, Viren, Therril, until next time," said Alethea, not waiting another moment to head toward the exit, trailed by Velaria, Ellendren, Wyn, and Andrew. That Alethea knew exactly how to leave the apartment made Devlyn think that she had visited it before. She knew exactly which door led to the decoy novice chamber and Devlyn wondered whether her knowing was more than just her highly tuned inner sense.

The door closed behind them—the door that looked like a mirror on the opposite side—and Devlyn smiled again at Therril, knowing his theoreticals magister would insist on hearing every detail about their journey. Doubtless, he had already heard of the fiasco at Binton and its exploded gate, as well as the Sorenth victory at Myrium. News of events such as those traveled quickly.

Devlyn spared no details as he recounted everything, fully aware that Therril would insist he fill any holes, both intentional and unintentional. Before Devlyn could even finish recounting the events—he had just told Therril of the failed excursion outside Myrium's walls—Therril looked deeply into Devlyn's eyes.

"They've changed. And that's not all that has changed, is it?" In the pause following Therril's comment, Devlyn remembered that incredible first experience bonding fully with Aliel.

"Good, and about time," Therril added.

"Do I have to report to anyone that I'm back?" asked Devlyn, only just remembering that Ellendren and Andrew had left almost immediately to do just that.

"I'll take care of all that, besides, I doubt you'll stay here much longer anyway."

Devlyn's guilty expression wobbled between a smile and a frown.

"Hmmm?" Therril's voice sung the drawn-out inquiry.

New Appointments

Exhausted students filled Magister Yvonne Kardol's warm classroom. The stagnant air tempted the students to close their heavy eyelids. Devlyn was not exempt from the late afternoon lethargy in the stuffy classroom. Burning a fire in the hearth during Kyrenth was completely unreasonable. Summer had only just officially ended, and the weather was still very warm with the start of the autumn term. Devlyn had difficulty thinking clearly and struggled to pay attention to the newly appointed magister. Apparently, she preferred the heat and humidity. Growing up in Yanil will do that to a person.

Magister Yvonne Kardol was near Velaria's age and the youngest magister at Gwilnor Academy; not even the temple had magisters that young. Yvonne was also an Albien wise one. Each School only had seven wise ones—holding two such prestigious positions at her age was unheard of for an ei'ana. Her impressive talent had provided her with the ability to rise quickly through the Albien School's hierarchy.

After only two weeks of attendance in the new magister's class, Devlyn already knew he was going to have difficulty concentrating. He found her lectures incredibly dry at times, and the magister's appearance made paying attention all the more difficult. Devlyn had already found himself lost in her mesmerizing eyes on several occasions, two deep pools of brown complementing her radiant caramel skin, framed by long raven hair. He'd also discovered that she had a vicious temper that flared all too quickly when stirred.

After Hannah had been named Chancellor of Gwilnor Academy,

she had appointed Yvonne as the new magister of the highly coveted art of wielding class. It was one of the few classes that ei'ana, other than Albiens and Azurelles, volunteered to teach. Devlyn had half expected to find Hannah still teaching the course in addition to her new responsibilities. The magisters at Gwilnor rarely left their academic roles, so rarely in fact, that no current student at Gwilnor had ever experienced a new magister. Yvonne was the first. And because of Yvonne, Devlyn desperately missed Hannah's lessons and hoped that none of the other magisters would be replaced. Devlyn even wanted Ethyl's very boring and very monotone history class to remain just as it had been for who knew exactly how long.

The newly appointed magister spoke with a distinguished voice and her vocabulary too often necessitated the use of a dictionary, taking away precious time that could have been spent learning complex wields. Devlyn never bothered looking up the words; he took notes like the rest of the class but thought it a waste of time to bother with every detail Yvonne lectured about. She structured her classes so that one week was spent lecturing about a specific wield or erendinth, and the following was a practicum week, where they attempted the wield she had described in exhaustive detail the previous week. Devlyn had learned that their homework over each fortnight revolved around researching the wield they were learning, culminating in a lengthy essay about it.

Devlyn found her methods less than ideal. Perhaps if her assigned readings were relevant and described how to wield rather than providing a history and known uses for the wield, Devlyn might have learned something. He had yet to receive any grade above common marks and had even earned his first bad marks. Not a single student had earned the coveted foremost mark, and only one student so far had been given an exceptional mark. Devlyn hoped that the practicum section would balance his grades out. Recovering from a bad mark this early in the term was a difficult task, but at least he hadn't received an awful mark.

Although Gwilnor Academy had begun to accept and teach kien wielders, Devlyn was the only one advanced enough for this section. When Chancellor Hannah had taught the course, he had been the only kien wielder in the entire school and had received his highest marks from her. She had even given him the foremost mark of her class for one term, something Ellendren had not been pleased about. Yvonne however, was not impressed with Devlyn's particular aptitude, and graded based on knowledge of a specific wield, not its application. Following his first lecture with Yvonne, Devlyn told Alethea about it. With only fifteen minutes of instruction from Alethea, Devlyn would become proficient at the wield Yvonne had spent two hours lecturing about.

Today, Yvonne continued with the lectures she'd given last week about how to breathe under water, which meant they would spend the second half of this class finally practicing the wield.

Without warning, Yvonne slammed her book shut. Devlyn had been about to fall asleep, but now his heart raced at the sudden, violent sound of the closing of the magister's book.

"I want everyone to remain in their seats." Yvonne peered across the classroom. "Each student will come to the front as they are called; not sooner or later. You will have one chance to perform the wield required of you and you will be graded on that performance. Cassandra, you are first."

Cassandra's grey eyes glanced nervously over her shoulder. She clearly did not want to go first and took her time standing before walking to the front of the classroom where an impatient Yvonne waited.

Once Cassandra reached the front of the class, Yvonne formed a simple wield that lifted water from the nearby cauldron in a large globule and then encased Cassandra's head. The suddenness of the water cutting off her oxygen caused Cassandra to quickly close her eyes in panic.

Tears might have been forming at the corner of her horrified eyes, but it was impossible to tell. Her blonde hair floated in the watery sphere, and she began a clumsy wield that would return oxygen to her lungs following the instructions from Yvonne's lecture. A small bubble of air began to form near her mouth. It was difficult to tell what happened next as Cassandra lost control of the small air pocket she had wielded, but it suddenly popped in the water and escaped, leaving Cassandra even more anxious.

Yvonne stood emotionless next to Cassandra, watching the girl struggle to use her hands to push the water away from her mouth and nose. As much as she tried, the water would not budge. Devlyn and the other students began whispering amongst themselves, one girl even demanding that Yvonne release Cassandra from the water which was beginning to suffocate her. The students only grew more demanding as her face turned blue.

"Stop it!" Devlyn yelled over the other students. "She can't breathe."

Yvonne shot a fiery glare at Devlyn before waving a hand to return the water to the cauldron. Cassandra fell to her hands and knees the instant she was free of the water, as if it also had kept her from collapsing. She panted hard, sucking air back into deprived lungs; wet hair clung to her head.

"Of course, she couldn't breathe," said Yvonne. "What do you think is the point of this wield, if not to learn how to breathe under water?"

The answer was obvious, but Devlyn didn't dare to respond.

"Now, since Devlyn has volunteered the intention of this exercise, he will be next to exemplify the wield."

Devlyn stood and stared at Yvonne as he walked toward the front. He did not like this woman. *How could Hannah entrust someone this awful with teaching?* When he reached the front, he did not turn to the rest of the class but kept his eyes on Yvonne. He struggled to avoid showing his frustration to the magister. Her eyes were still stunningly beautiful, but he no longer got lost in them. Whatever he had previously felt about the magister's beauty had significantly altered.

"Turn and face the class."

The harsh tones of her voice made his skin crawl, but he did as she commanded. He did not see the wield or the water globule rising from the cauldron but had expected it to sever his source of oxygen. More shocking than not being able to breathe though was the temperature of the water; it was freezing. *How could anything in this furnace of a classroom be so cold?*

Devlyn pressed himself into the necessary erendinth, aerys and aquaeys; he could even feel Yvonne's wield. It was a simple one that he could easily remove. But if he'd not had an explanation of the required wield from Alethea, he didn't think he would have known how to form the wield in the first place. It was not about creating or drawing air into the water, but rather, *pulling* it from the water, and using the water, not the air, to form a barrier around the pocket of air. Without the barrier around the air pocket, the air would try to escape the water. If the wielder prevented the air from escaping using only aerys, the air bubble would break apart and disperse. Devlyn assumed that that's what had happened with Cassandra.

Forming the wield, he pulled oxygen from the water and began to wield aquaeys to form a barrier. But Magister Yvonne interfered with his wielding, dissolving the expanding pocket of air as he formed it. His initial nervousness turned to anger as the more he tried, the more she interfered. How could interference like that encourage the students to even try to perfect the wield? How could it even be allowed? Yvonne was also remarkably strong for a kiara wielder who had no interaction with a kien wielder. *How had she become so strong?* Kiara wielders required kien wielders, just as kien wielders needed kiara wielders. Neither could reach their potential without the other.

Devlyn formed several of the same wields simultaneously to give himself air, but Yvonne unraveled every single one. Time was running out, and his anxiety grew. Of course, Aliel was in the classroom, and considering Yvonne's strength and her success at unraveling his wields, he and Aliel bonded slightly. He couldn't bond fully, since he still had not found clothing immune to his transformation. But with Aliel's added strength, he easily formed the necessary wield, and oxygen returned to his lungs. The instant he completed the wield, making it powerful enough that Magister Yvonne could not overwhelm him, she returned the water to her cauldron, spun Devlyn around, and slapped him full across the face. Devlyn's bond to Aliel snapped away from the shock.

"Never again will you attempt that. That bird is banned from my classroom." Yvonne's eyes blazed with anger and she looked as if she was ready to kill him. "As if being an elya wasn't advantage enough."

He wanted to touch his face, more astonished by the unexpected assault than by her interference with his wielding. "I have permission from Mother Velaria to bond with Aliel," Devlyn said through gritted teeth. As if he needed permission to be a Phaedryn.

"The Chair of Azurelle is not the Chancellor of Gwilnor, nor does her authority over Gwilnor Academy go beyond granting admittance. You will not join with that bird in my classroom. Is that understood?"

Devlyn vaguely remembered that the involvement of the Seven Chairs with Gwilnor was limited to admitting students, and that the actual power at Gwilnor lay with the chancellor. "Yes, Magister."

"Return to your seat."

The rest of the students took their turns to practice the wield, and not surprisingly, no one succeeded, each one returning to her seat with her head soaked, gasping for breath. Devlyn sulked in his seat, arms crossed mutinously across his chest. Even Aliel seemed subdued by the events. When the class ended, Yvonne instructed them to read a hundred pages about aquaeys. Relieved to finally leave the overheated classroom but still seething, Devlyn stalked to the dining hall for a late lunch. Yvonne's classes had the tendency to extend past the standard time allotment, which was just another irritant in a growing list of negative aspects of the newest magister's classes, as she consistently ignored the chiming Arenthylean bells marking the end of her class.

He grabbed a sandwich and a bowl of hot soup, even though he was still sweating from being in Yvonne's classroom—the chilling effects of having his head soaked in freezing water had long worn off. The dining hall was emptying as many of the students had finished their lunches. Devlyn intended to find a seat and eat by himself; he was in no mood to socialize. As he looked around for not just an empty seat but a secluded spot, Liam signaled him over. *Should have gone to one of the smaller dining rooms*, he thought, knowing that Aliel was aware of his thoughts.

It will be good for you to spend time in amiable company, Aliel conveyed.

She's awful. I can't believe they permit her teaching methods, Devlyn conveyed as he made his way to Liam and Jaerol. They were sitting by themselves in the middle of a long table with half-eaten sandwiches in front of them.

"Hey, Devlyn," Liam said with a big smile.

"Hi," Devlyn replied dully, unintentionally contrasting Liam's cheery mood. He was happy to see his brother—technically, his half-brother, for they had different mothers, but that didn't matter.

"Er, what's your problem?" Jaerol was surprised at Devlyn's tone.

"Yvonne."

"Oh," Liam responded, perfectly understanding Devlyn's reaction. "How many students did she nearly kill this time?"

"Better yet, how'd she *do* it this time?" Jaerol asked.

"She tried to drown the entire class," Devlyn said and when his stomach rumbled, took a quick bite of his sandwich before continuining. "No matter how well a student was doing with the wield, she prevented everyone from accomplishing it. So, I bonded with Aliel and successfully performed the wield."

"I bet she didn't fancy that. She doesn't like losing, especially to students. Did she ban you from doing it again?" asked Jaerol.

"Well, yeah, how'd you know?"

Jaerol looked quickly at Liam, seeming to ask whether Liam wanted to tell the story. Liam simply shrugged his shoulders, so Jaerol went on.

"During one of our classes with the esteemed magister, the wield she asked everyone to perform was impossible to find any information on, leaving every student at a loss as to how to accomplish it. So, when it was my turn to exemplify this unknown wield, I chose a different one that had the same effect. As you might imagine, she was not at all pleased with it, and banned me from performing anything but what was part of the lesson. Even though the wield I chose was much simpler and easily outmaneuvered her."

"I thought the whole reason you returned to Gwilnor was to learn as a Phaedryn," Liam commented. "It might be worth talking to Chancellor Hannah about Aliel and bonding for wields."

"I guess it couldn't hurt. But I've been in Ceurenyl for over two weeks now, and I still haven't had the chance to speak with the Ceurtri-arch about releasing me from the Ei'ceuril. I should probably see to that first."

"Most likely, but that's not the only thing you have to explain," Jaerol said, glancing between the two brothers with his arms crossed.

"Sorry?"

"What our dear Jaerol is referring to," said Liam, now smiling toward Jaerol, "is this business you briefly mentioned last week about Da and the Eldinari."

Devlyn had only had the opportunity to mention in passing that their father was not a Telvin. "Well apparently, Abbott Entiel was right, Da never was related to him. The Telvin family adopted him as a toddler. His actual mother is an Eldinari, named Leienya Lierafen, and his father a Cyndinari. But, because of the Cyndinari blood, he was not gifted with immortality as were the other Eldinari, so his family thought it a kindness to send him to live a life with mortals."

"I always did wonder why Da didn't look anything like the Telvin's. I mean, he was the only one of them who had black hair with a tint of red, wasn't he? All his siblings have blond hair. To say nothing of his darker complexion."

While Liam had a contemplative expression and reacted to the news well, Jaerol took the news differently. "Is anything known about the Cyndinari who fathered your da?"

"I never learned his name, only that the union between him and the Eldinari was not consensual."

"I figured as much."

"You're not all bad," said Liam, elbowing Jaerol in his ribs.

Jaerol forced a smile and steered the topic away from his kin. "Still, it's pretty good luck finding yourself belonging to House Lierafen. Their aryl is the closest thing to a monarch that the Eldinari would ever permit—wartime will do that. Do you know when the Eldinari will arrive at the castle? We've been invited by ei'ana and ei'ceuril alike to several conferences at the temple discussing ways to oversee and regulate such a momentous arrival. There's even a symposium planned for the end of the month."

The news of the Eldinari rejoining the populace of Eklean had had an explosive effect in Ceurenyl. Ei'ana and ei'ceuril pontificated on how their reintegration would occur, and whether it would benefit Eklean as a whole. Neither group ruled out the potential negative consequences that the reclusive elves could have on the rest of the continent. Many argued that a civilization cut off for fifteen hundred years simply could not reintegrate successfully, each having changed in different ways.

"Most of the ei'ana here are alarmed over the number of ei'ana among the Eldinari, and not just about the kiara wielders, but the fact that there's an equal number of kien wielders," Liam said. "When it had become widely known that Tiera Weldon was not the true Chair of Emradiel—that the appointment was held by Phendien, an Eldinari kien wielder—outlandish specualations started to circulate through the castle.

"It seems like every ei'ana and her mother are demanding explanations from the Emradiel School. I've even overheard some ei'ana declare that the Emradiel School had broken their trust by concealing something so pivotal as an unacknowledged substitute Chair," Jaerol added.

"I thought the Emradiel hierarchy had alleviated the nerves in the castle," Devlyn said, hastily swallowing a bite of his sandwhich.

"To an extent," started Liam, before Jaerol interrupted.

"Some ei'ana went so far as to say that not a single student was truly enrolled at Gwilnor since Phendien had secluded himself in the Eldin Wood with the other Eldinari, while others went even further to declare that the only true Emradiel ei'ana were the ones in the Eldin Wood, since all seven Chairs are required to accept new students to Gwilnor Academy and only the Chair could accept a newly professed ei'ana into their respective Schools. Tiera ensured everyone, that she, and every other woman who had sat in Phendien's stead, had held full authority."

"You make it sound like Ceurenyl is about to implode," Liam said, gawking at Jaerol. "Many of the larger community are still unsettled, but the uproar has faded, and people in Ceurenyl are genuinely looking forward to the return of the true Chair of Emradiel. The Emradiel School is planning a banquet for his return, a celebration with the full support of the other Chairs."

Devlyn finished his lunch quickly while Liam and Jaerol chatted about some of the things they'd learned while he'd been away and provided gossipy details about various events. Done eating, Devlyn stood to return his plate and and utensils to the counter and caught sight of a downcast Kevn walking away from the buffet table toward a vacant table with a sandwich, his head bent and his arms pulled in tight to his body.

"Kevn?" Devlyn called, closing the distance between them. Surprisingly, Kevn had not noticed Liam, Jaerol, and himself at their long wooden table. Most of them were vacant at this point; nearly everyone had already eaten and gone on to other things.

"Oh, sorry," Kevn replied, barely acknowledging Devlyn.

"Everything all right?"

"I've been better," said Kevn with a quick glance at Devlyn, as they joined Liam and Jaerol at their table.

"We should be going—Magister Kai assigned a lengthy essay last week on the political structure and tensions in Briel. We'll meet up later; see you guys," Liam said, picking up on Kevn's distaste for company.

"I just had a meeting with Chancellor Hannah. She insisted that I visit her office today without giving me any indication as to why she wanted to see me." Kevn told Devlyn, still not looking at him.

"And?"

"She wants me to attend Yvonne's classes."

"So, they're going to let you become an ei'ana?"

"It's possible, but I don't want to learn how to wield," said Kevn, finally lifting his head. "All I want is to be left alone with my research; I don't want to get involved with this crazy war that's brewing across Eklean. I just want to be left with my books and scrolls, not fight shadow elves or worse, the Deathless."

"You could become an Albien," suggested Devlyn. "They practically live in the library. And think about it, if you did learn to wield, you could help me remove the Shroud and be one of the first to enter Septyl in over fourteen hundred years." Devlyn whispered the last part, looking around to make sure no one could overhear.

Kevn looked at Devlyn with a raised brow. It seemed as though he wanted to argue, to call Devlyn's bluff and say that it was impossible, but beyond opening and closing his mouth once, he didn't say anything.

"You've said it yourself, Septyl has the largest library in the world," Devlyn tried. "Where better to lose yourself in your studies than there?"

Kevn kept his mouth closed and just ate his lunch, looking up from his sandwich briefly every now and then until he finished his lunch and stood to leave. "I'll consider it. One thousand four hundred seventy-three years, to be exact," he said, rising and waving a hand at the door to indicate he intended to leave the dining hall.

"Is anything else bothering you? Talk of libraries always makes you smile."

"It's nothing; I have to go."

Devlyn wanted to tell his friend to go read something; it always seemed to balance him. But, Kevn was gone before Devlyn had completed half the thought.

RELEASED

Ceurtriarch Ealyndol Roendryn, High Archsteward and Arbiter of the Light, sat across from Devlyn and Aliel, his tired eyes steady on them. Devlyn felt those eyes peering into his being—reading him like a book. Uncomfortable with the Ceurtriarch's gaze, he tried to avoid fidgeting. The desk separating the two of them was suddenly much more interesting and Devlyn's eyes drifted to its intricate carvings. If Aliel had not been in the office with him, he doubted he would have had the confidence to tell the Ceurtriarch that he wished to be released from his ei'ceuril novitiate.

"Tell me, Devlyn, is it true?" Ealyndol asked when the lengthening silence was starting to be uncomfortable. He sounded old and more somber than usual.

Ever since his return to Ceurenyl, Devlyn had spent a great deal of his time thinking about how he might best communicate his thoughts, feelings, and desires related to his new status as a Phaedryn to Ealyndol. The Ceurtriarch had always been kind and nurturing to Devlyn; never pressuring him in his studies or discernment with the ei'ceuril. He had even been supportive of Devlyn leaving Ceurenyl, knowing full well that Velaria had intended to seek assistance from the Eldinari.

At Ealyndol's question, Devlyn looked into the Ceurtriarch's silver to green eyes, hoping to discover there the right thing to say. The wood grain of the desk certainly held no answers. He didn't know how to tell someone he cared for and admired that he was going to leave his order in the wake of turbulent change. There were no words to express what he wanted to say. He tried going through the foreign words and phrases he could remember from his language classes, but not even they seemed adequate. *It would be easier to convey it to him*, he thought, recalling how simple it was to express to Aliel what he needed without having to waste any time trying to find the right words. He wished that Alethea would increase the pace of his training in communicating telepathically with others, even though he knew he was the only reason he wasn't learning any faster, not Alethea or her training.

"It's hard to explain," Devlyn started, using a filler phrase to buy himself more time. "It's just that, I don't think I'm meant to be an ei'ceuril. And I don't think I'm meant to be an ei'ana either; I'm a Phaedryn. Sure, all three can wield, but they're all very different. By becoming an ei'ceuril, it's like trying to fit something round through a square slot. Sure, it's possible, but the only way to manage it, is forcing it through, damaging both the round object and the square slot."

Devlyn waited for Ealyndol's response. The silence nagged at him. Did what he had finally said make any sense? There was nothing round or square about an ei'ceuril or a Phaedryn.

"I see," Ealyndol eventually replied, still staring into Devlyn's eyes. "Is there anything or anyone that is drawing you away from us?"

"I'm sorry?" asked Devlyn, not understanding what the Ceurtriarch meant.

"Most young men decide to abandon their studies with the Ei'ceuril because the thought of not marrying someone is too burdensome. Your relationship with the young Lucillian princess is not unknown to us here, Devlyn. Few of our young novices would remain among us if they had the opportunity to court Princess Ellendren Roendryn." Ealyndol reclined in his straight-backed chair, as much as it allowed, and even then, he still had better posture than Devlyn.

"Well, I do have feelings for her, but that's not why I'm leaving. I'm a Phaedryn and don't take this the wrong way, but the only reason I agreed to join the ei'ceuril in the first place was because of a prophecy's interpretation. I'm sorry, but it doesn't make any sense; it just doesn't. There are other ways for me to give my life, other than becoming an ei'ceuril or dying."

"If you are decided, I will not bind you to the temple." The words came slowly from Ealyndol, making Devlyn think that he wanted to retract them. As he spoke, the Ceurtriarch rose and came around the desk to stand next to Devlyn, who also stood in respect. "Mother Velaria has always felt so; she never thought it wise for you to join the ei'ceuril. She also believed we were misinterpreting the prophecy. We have spoken at length since you entered the Illumined Wood. I will not say that I'm not disappointed, because I am sad to see you leave us; you could have accomplished wonders that have not been seen among the ei'ceuril since before the fall of Krysenthiel." Ealyndol paused a moment to take a breath—a deep and heavy sigh. "Devlyn, son of Evellyn and Dolan Telvin, I, Ceurtriarch Ealyndol, High Archsteward and Arbiter of the Light, release you from the Order of Ei'ceuril and the Temple of Ceur. May the Light ever dwell in your heart."

His voice was strained, as if to speak that statement caused physical pain. The opposite reaction occurred in Devlyn. A sense of relief coursed through his body, his fingertips tingling. Once those words were spoken, Devlyn's body loosened, as if an invisible rope that had bound him was now untied.

Ealyndol returned to his seat, pressing his palms against the desktop as he sat, the unpleasant meeting finally over.

"There's something else I've learned since leaving Ceurenyl," Devlyn said, unintentionally dragging out this encounter as he too sat back down. Ealyndol raised a single eyebrow before reclining back into his straight-backed chair.

"My father does not belong to the Telvin family; they adopted him at the request of his true family, well, his maternal side, that is," said Devlyn. "His mother, my grandmother, Leienya Lierafen, is an Eldinari. His father is an unknown Cyndinari; Leienya never spoke his name. Because of the mixed elven blood, the immortal life from his mother did not pass on to him and House Lierafen thought it most prudent for my father to live and die with a mortal family beyond the Eldin Wood."

Ealyndol listened attentively. "A kindness, perhaps. If your father had not been murdered, he would have passed long before his peers were considered adolescents should he have remained in the Eldin Wood."

"And," Devlyn hesitated, taking a deep breath before continuing, "through my mother, I am not only the descendent of Lucillia, but also of House Lorenthien. An unbroken line from youngest child, to youngest child."

"Your name is…" Ealyndol breathed the unfinished question. His gentle expression washed away with the realization of the enormity of what a living Lorenthien entailed. And not just one, but four, assuming Devlyn's mother was still alive; her brother, Aryln, in Parendior; and with Leilyn safe in the Illumined Wood.

"…is Devlyn Lorenthien."

"How is that possible?" whispered Ealyndol, stunned at the revelation. "Erynor wiped out every descendant of that House. He spared no one."

"Feolyn married Gwendolyn, daughter to Oblivyn and Ellyn; Oblivyn did not know he was a Lorenthien, for his father and mother, Garethyn and Ulienne, were enslaved when he was an infant. Neither were crowned after Garethyn's parents were killed—Faerndryn and Ithendryl, the last Exalted Aryl of Krysenthiel to sit upon the Crystal Throne. Erynor tortured the heir and his wife by separating them from their infant child, passing off Oblivyn as a child born out of wedlock," said Devlyn, shocked as the words poured from his mouth. *Where did all that come from?*

"How do you know this?" Ealyndol whispered.

"I…I don't know," Devlyn answered. No one had told him these details before. Not even Alethea had mentioned it when she spoke to Devlyn about his ancestry. "Alethea told me that this sort of thing could be buried in my memories. But I don't understand it."

"Intriguing. I will have to speak with this Alethea. And in the meantime, I strongly recommend that you continue to use the Telvin name," said Ealyndol, lapsing into quiet thought. Devlyn moved as though to leave, but the Ceurtriarch lifted a hand to indicate he still had something to say. "There is one other point of business we must discuss.

Since you are no longer with the ei'ceuril, it would be inappropriate for you to remain in residence here."

It took Devlyn a moment to register what the Ceurtriarch's words meant. It made sense, after all the only reason he had moved into the temple in the first place was because of his novitiate with the ei'ceuril.

"So, do I return to the dormitories at Gwilnor?"

"I doubt Chancellor Hannah would permit a student living outside the castle walls. Even though you are not there to become an ei'ana or a Septyl knight," Ealyndol offered with a cautionary smile. "Do be sure to visit from time to time. I have enjoyed our meetings and would be delighted to be part of what is to come. Before I forget, a woman by the name of Clara has taken up residence in the temple. I believe you know her."

"Abbess Clara?"

"Yes, the Poor Lady has returned to the Temple of Ceur. It seems you are not the only lost treasure to return to us."

Devlyn thanked the Ceurtriarch for his kind words as he stood and was almost out the door when Ealyndol cleared his throat.

"Before you go, Devlyn, make sure to try on the spare clothing in your bedchamber. I've heard that you've had some difficulties in finding adequate clothing for your transformation. If I'm not mistaken, the Phaedryn who once resided in your room never removed his belongings. You are welcome to them. Perhaps you will have better luck with them."

Devlyn's mind leapt at the thought of clothing that would not turn to ash every time he and Aliel bonded. The very idea excited him, even though Alethea insisted that he had to be more comfortable in his own skin. *I'll just have to be comfortable with myself fully clothed*, he thought, relieved he would not have to worry about others seeing more of him than they ought to and already had.

Viren had waited for Devlyn and Aliel outside the Ceurtriarch's quarters in the Chamber of Light. Devlyn noticed that he had not moved a single step after Devlyn had gone into the Ceurtriarch's office.

Devlyn told Viren about his meeting with the Ceurtriarch as they walked toward Devlyn's soon-to-be-vacated apartment, making sure to stay along the rim of the Chamber of Light. Although Devlyn would have enjoyed floating there for the rest of the day, he did not have the time; he had to pack his belongings and try on the items Ealyndol had mentioned, not to mention write an essay for Yvonne's class and translate part of an ancient Luminari codex from Old Aelish for Nynthel's languages class.

He recalled that when he had first moved into the Temple of Ceur, he had noticed the exquisite garments in the wardrobe, but since he was studying with the ei'ceuril, he had been permitted to wear only the white robes of his station—the itchy white robes he currently wore.

If he remembered correctly, the wardrobe held four separate outfits that were clearly not ei'ceuril robes. He had thought of trying them on before, but since they did not belong to him and he had no idea whose they were, or how old they were, he never tested them. They had to be ancient indeed if they were last owned by another Phaedryn. What sort of fabric could survive that long? *They'll most likely disintegrate the second I take them off their hangers*, he conveyed to Aliel, who merely sent back soothing feelings.

Entering the apartment which no longer belonged to him, Devlyn headed directly to the bedchamber, Viren only a few paces behind. He opened the wardrobe's wooden door and was relieved to see four different outfits of various styles and colors hanging there. He reached for the one that had beautiful gold threadwork over dark blues and light greys and held the outfit at arm's length to see it fully.

"That's lierathnil; a silky fabric spun from the kryseniels, the golden lotuses that once blanketed the landscape of Krysenthiel," said Viren before Devlyn could form his own opinion of it. "I can't believe they were left untouched all this time."

"They're what?" Devlyn stared blankly at Viren.

"Extremely expensive," Viren replied, not removing his eyes from the outfit. "Whoever once lived here was a very wealthy elf. Lierathnil is resistant to the effects of the transformation that takes place between an elf and phoenix. Every Phaedryn had at least one set. The first set was gifted by the order; every Phaedryn would contribute to purchasing one for the newest member. If they ever wanted more, they had to provide the necessary funds on their own. Each set cost around five hundred lumols. And those were the cheap ones."

Devlyn converted the currency exchange. "That's fifteen hundred crowns! Each!" He nearly dropped the outfit at the news, suddenly feeling very heavy. He had two lumols in his pouch with the two lucilliae and he had thought that was a small fortune! He couldn't fathom owning five hundred of the opaque gold-like coins especially since that would buy only one outfit.

"Only wealthy elves possessed multiple sets. To own four required a small fortune that not even some kings and queens today would have."

"Did only the Phaedryn wear these?" Devlyn now held the garments more carefully.

"Not at all. To wear clothing made of lierathnil was a sign of wealth. Every young Luminari dreamt of purchasing at least one item, even if it was just a scarf," said Viren. "Go on, see if it fits."

The lierathnil was unlike any fabric Devlyn was accustomed to. It felt as though it would slip between his fingers, as if the material was spun out of water and into an incorporeal fabric. Each set included a robe—rather a long jacket really—a pair of complementing trousers, and a tunic. Some had sashes and others had buttoms. The robe he picked was open down the front and was held closed at the waist by an intricate golden clasp of two outstretched wings that entwined when the clasp was fastened. The clasp looked familiar.

"Is it lumaryl?"

"It certainly is. That's the Order of Phaedryn's emblem."

Without wasting any time, Devlyn tore his itchy white ei'ceuril robe off and shoved his legs into the dark grey pants, followed by the indigo tunic with gold threadwork. The lierathnil was unlike anything he had ever worn before; it was exceptionally light, and the fabric seemed to barely touch his skin. It felt like a cloud suspended about his body. And it wasn't an itchy robe either. He wore actual trousers.

Viren held the long outer garment open by the shoulders, helping Devlyn put his arms through the sleeves easily.

With the lumaryl clasp fastened, Devlyn turned to face Viren and stretched his arms out. "Well? How do I look?"

"As if Krysenthiel had never fallen and Ithendryl's heir, Ei'ethil Devlyn Lorenthien, had been born a prince in Arenthyl's palace."

Devlyn felt Aliel just beyond his own consciousness, as he always was. Nothing was conveyed, but Devlyn was not alone in his curiosity about the durability of the clothing. With an apologetic look at Viren, Devlyn and Aliel went to the balcony before touching that quiet light within their hearts. A fleeting thought at the wealth draped across his skin nagged at him. But that thought vanished and Devlyn felt his spirit explode outward in a burst of color and light as he stepped outside and onto the balcony. He was no longer aware of where his being stopped and Aliel's began. Somehow, the fabric allowed his wings to appear, and his vision sharpened as he looked over the edge of the balcony toward the mountains north of Ceurenyl.

A smiling Viren—a rare sight—waited in the doorway separating the balcony from the apartment. Devlyn thought he saw a glimmer of poorly concealed pride in the Guardian's eyes.

Looking down at himself, Devlyn extended his arms and saw that every garment he wore remained intact following the transformation. Devlyn's joy was equally shared by Aliel.

Well, we can't just stand here, Aliel conveyed and Devlyn took one powerful step and lept over the edge of the balcony and dove down the sheer walls of the temple and toward the craggy ravine below. The precipice plummeted well below the temple before rising again into another mountain.

Wind rushed past his face as air tried to fill and spread his wings. Devlyn could feel through their every fiber that the air wanted to carry him upward and away from the ground. As Devlyn plummeted toward the bottom of the craggy ravine, he at last opened both wings in a wondrous display of light. They caught him in the air and carried him up.

He flapped his wings only twice before he found himself just below the magnificent glittering dome of the temple. Half domes of considerably less girth revolved around the larger central dome, buttressing the temple's enormity.

With a third flap, he rose above the great dome and looked down not just on the Temple of Ceur, but the entire city of Ceurenyl. The temple rested atop the highest point of the city, on the slopes of the mountain that defined its northern boundary. Sloping away from the temple on the same mountain lay the rest of Ceurenyl, including the impressive castle that was Gwilnor Academy.

Having to return to the castle as a resident again stirred a dilemma in Devlyn. He certainly looked forward to living closer to his friends again, but that also meant he would be subject to ei'ana again. For the most part, he admired the Ei'ana of Septyl, however, since returning to Ceurenyl, he had grown increasingly aware of a shift in Gwilnor Academy, especially with Yvonne as the new magister of the art of wielding.

Deliberately deciding to not worry himself, he resolved, with Aliel's encouragement, to enjoy this flight above the city. Not even the sight of the Shroud, hungrily clawing toward the city, bothered him. It was impossible to ignore, but there was nothing he could do about it at present.

With his improved Phaedryn sight and hearing, Devlyn first heard and then observed people on the streets below watching him soar above their heads. They called out his name and congratulated him.

Their enthusiasm helped distract him from having to return to the castle, so that it wasn't until the Arenthylean bells tolled for a second time since he and Aliel had leapt from the balcony, that he was reminded of just how long they had been flying.

By the time he returned to the apartment's balcony—an apartment that was no longer his—he saw Viren, sitting quietly with his eyes closed, just inside the still opened balcony door. Knowing that he still had to pack his belongings and move them and himself into the castle, he and Aliel withdrew from one another. For Devlyn, that withdrawal was the worst part. No other experience compared to being bonded as a Phaedryn.

As soon as they had separated, Devlyn looked at his body and saw that he still wore the beautiful lierathnil garments. However, he was acutely aware that he had somehow lost his small clothes. They were not woven of lierathnil and had disintegrated in the tranformation. As Devlyn walked into the apartment, Viren stood.

"Are you ready to move on?"

"As soon as I'm done packing. I'll be quick."

"No need. I saw to it while you were out. All your belongings are safely on their way to Gwilnor. Did you expect me to just sit around and patiently wait for you to return?"

Devlyn's initial relief dissipated as soon as he remembered the two lucilliae and two lumols tucked inside a pouch still concealed in the ei'ceuril robe. Devlyn scanned the room for his discarded robe, looking to the corners, the couches, and other surfaces. In his eagerness to test the new garments, he had completely forgotten about the jewels. Ellendren would throttle him if she ever found out. That would be inevitable if they ended up lost. His heartbeat quickened and his fingers grew sweaty.

"I would not allow anyone to take something so precious." Viren supplied, noting Devlyn's sudden panic. He pulled the pouch from his own pocket and handed it to Devlyn.

Opening the pouch to confirm its contents, relief washed across Devlyn as the gentle violet and indigo glows filled his vision. Devlyn patted his outer garment for signs of a proper pocket. Opening his robe, he found a slit on the inside fabric near his chest and slipped the pouch safely inside the hidden pocket. Viren shared a quick smile with him and tilted his head toward the door.

Taking only the time to also collect his coin purse and tucking it into his trousers pocket, Devlyn, Aliel, and Viren left the apartment and made their way out of the temple and toward the castle. Passing through the Chamber of Light again, Devlyn recalled what Clara had told him he would have to do in order to wield Lumenys. He'd have to get to that soon.

When they reached Gwilnor, Devlyn realized that he didn't know where they should go. As his sworn protector, Viren had been staying with him at the temple apartment, but nothing else had been arranged and Devlyn felt foolish for not telling any of the Chairs or magisters that he intended to discontinue his studies with the ei'ceuril. Velaria knew that he intended to do so, but he hadn't told her when he would speak to Ealyndol, not realizing the consequences to his living quarters. Would he have to sleep in an inn for a few nights? He felt his coin purse, wondering if he could afford it. Speaking to the chancellor was the obvious choice. After all, she was in charge of Gwilnor Academy, while the rest of the ei'ana residing there were only there due to the inconvenience of the city of Septyl being inaccessible in the Shroud. Not even the Seven Chairs could truly call the castle their home.

Gwilnor's main entry remained barred, which was an enormous inconvenience, as the chancellor's office was in the central tower, directly above the main entrance hall. They were forced to walk past the curved plaza with the curious pointed arches and across the bridge to the quad, framed by the southern wing of the castle. Few students were about at present and Devlyn passed through the castle with no interruptions. They were soon standing outside the chancellor's office in the central tower overlooking the castle's main entrance. Devlyn gave a single knock on the beautifully carved wooden door. As he waited for an answer, he followed the door's intricate details, the carvings telling some sort of story. Devlyn wondered if it had anything to do with the founding of Gwilnor or Septyl. Before he could take in all the images, Chancellor Hannah opened the door.

"Why, hello there Devlyn, Aliel, and Viren," she said, her voice filled with warmth and sincerity. "To what do I owe the pleasure of your visit?" Viren responded to the greeting with a simple nod.

"Good afternoon, Chancellor," said Devlyn. "I was hoping to speak with you briefly."

"But of course. Come right on in. You'll have to excuse my sloppiness; business as chancellor has been quite hectic now that the Eldinari are returning to our world. Logistics and what not. The castle is vast, but will it be large enough for a population that does not die? I suppose that was the norm at one point, but we also had the palace-city of Septyl, didn't we?"

Devlyn looked through the widening door curious about the chancellor's *mess* and saw a pristine office. The surfaces actually sparkled.

As Devlyn and Aliel followed the chancellor into her office, Viren nodded to him once and stayed in the stair hall. Devlyn closed the door behind him, not knowing why the Guardian knight preferred to remain outside.

Hannah walked over to her desk, closed a single book and straightened several stray parchments. "Now, isn't that better," sighed Hannah. "Please, have a seat, Devlyn."

Sitting on one of two beautiful chairs opposite the desk, Devlyn said, "There's been a change in my, um, station."

"Has it anything to do with your beautiful new outfit?" Hannah asked, holding his eyes, waiting to weigh and judge his every word. "I highly doubt the ei'ceuril would ever abandon their white robes."

"I met with Ceurtriarch Ealyndol this morning, and he has released me from my commitment with the Ei'ceuril. Since I am no longer studying with them, I was informed that it would be improper for me to continue residing in the temple." Devlyn felt a tightness in his chest. He hadn't realized that he had been concerned about telling Hannah that he was no longer with the Ei'ceuril. He respected her, and it was more difficult than he initially had anticipated.

Devlyn sat uncomfortably in the plush armchair, waiting for Hannah's response. *What if she won't take me back?* Devlyn again felt his coin purse and wondered how expensive inns were.

"What of the prophecy?" Hannah folded her hands atop her pristine desk, unblinking.

Wishing that she asked anything but that, Devlyn gulped. "I think it was misinterpreted."

"And, you've reinterpreted it?" Hannah rose a questioning eyebrow.

"Well…no. But it doesn't make sense. It just doesn't fit together."

Devlyn waited for Hannah to say something, anything. But she remained quiet for a few seconds that seemed to stretch forever but was probably truly no more than half a minute, while he continued to sit with his chest tight with tension. "Mother Velaria believes the same," he added, hoping to gain some credibility.

"Well, I have no intention of validating *your* decision, as it is your decision," said Hannah without removing her gaze from Devlyn, not even for an instant as she broke into a smile. With the smile, the tension in Devlyn's chest released, and in his relief, he ignored a sense of disquiet that he picked up from Aliel. "That said, I for one am very delighted that you've returned to the castle and you are very much welcome here. And, as it turns out, Mother Velaria did brief me on your likely return to us."

"Now, we had better find adequate chambers for you and Aliel. And Sir Viren as well, I suppose. You'll remain in the castle, of course. We can't have students living out in the city; not only because of our rules here, but it's far too dangerous out there nowadays," said Hannah as she stood, inviting Devlyn to do the same. "Actually, I've been meaning to speak with you about the city's safety. Aliel could provide us with a unique advantage of patrolling the city, especially at night time, without any shadow elves or servants of Shadow being the wiser. It doesn't have to be all the time, but now that you're a student wielder here again, I would consider paying for your tuition here in exchange for Aliel's nightly surveillance. How does that sound? Certainly, a better use of Aliel's talents than disrupting Yvonne's classroom."

Devlyn reddened at the mention of the art of wielding class, but more importantly he hadn't yet thought of how he was going to pay for Gwilnor's tuition of a crown per term again. He'd had an arrangement with the previous chancellor, who simply couldn't accept Devlyn's lumols in payment. And while Devlyn did have one golden crown in his coin purse along with several silver jents, they wouldn't last much longer than a single term. Because of his own excitement at being able to have his tuition paid for without having to spend his few coins, Devlyn barely noticed Aliel's hesitancy through their bond. Still, Aliel did not object outright.

"That's very generous of you," said Devlyn, expecting that she would change her mind and rescind the offter.

"Oh, splendid! Then consider it a deal." Hannah strode past Devlyn and to the exit.

Devlyn and Aliel collected Viren from the stair hall and followed the chancellor down the long spiral stair to the entry hall and through the corridors of the castle. She walked swiftly, slowing only to acknowledge everyone they passed with a warm smile. She did not lead them to the North Tower, home to the male dormitories, but in the opposite direction, causing Devlyn some bewilderment.

"Excuse me, Chancellor, but where are we going? I thought I was supposed to live in the North Tower," Devlyn asked when they crossed the bridge back to the castle's southern wing, the Dragon Tower looming above their heads.

"Oh, that will never do," said Hannah not slowing her swift pace.

They went up two stories of the marble stairs in the Dragon Tower, and down a long corridor, passing an open room to the left. Devlyn caught a glimpse of the quad and realized he had never visited this wing of the castle before.

As if hearing his thoughts—something that Devlyn had grown increasingly concerned about since meeting Alethea—Hannah supplied, "This wing of the castle once belonged to the Emradiel School, at least before the Eldinari left to seclude themselves in their forest." Devlyn caught a hint of disapproval in her tone, but before he could think what that might mean, the chancellor went on. "It's been abandoned ever since. The Emradiels who were not Eldinari moved to a smaller wing after that. Keeping the entire castle at functioning capacity is extremely expensive. I imagine the Emradiels will reclaim this space, once the Eldinari return, of course, since there will be more of them now. But you'll be in the South Tower, where our guest quarters used to be for visiting ei'ana and potential students. I've decided it best if you take up residence there. That way, you won't be bothered more than necessary; I doubt half the castle's residents have even made their way through the abandoned corridors there."

SUNKEN THOUGHTS

A brisk wind swept through the open window into Devlyn's extensive new quarters in the castle, rustling the velvet draperies hanging along either side of the pointed arched window. The last time he had lived in the castle, his room could only fit a tiny bed and desk. Now, his accommodations were large enough that the bed and the desk each had their own room. In fact, Devlyn's new apartment had a solar with a perch for Aliel and a balcony, a study, and three adjacent bed chambers, one of which Viren had claimed. The apartment even had its own private lavatory, a true luxury.

His apartment was halfway up the tower and looked west over Ceurenyl and into the Shroud beyond. The grey murkiness of the month of Kyrenth was intensified by the gloom in the city. Unusually for the first month of autumn, the sun barely appeared, and when a few rays of sunlight did fall onto Ceurenyl, the Shroud considerably dampened its reach.

He had moved back into the castle a week ago, and Hannah was right, no one bothered him while he was in his rooms in the South Tower. In fact, no one seemed to be aware that the mostly empty tower now had three occupants. There were the occasional wanderers but Devlyn suspected they were either lost or searching desperately for one of the many secret passages scattered throughout Gwilnor. Only once had someone tried to force their way through Devlyn's door, presumably in hopes of uncovering at least one of the castle's many secrets.

Hannah had impressed the importance of maintaining a low profile, even from his friends at the school. She seemed concerned that other students would grow jealous if they saw Devlyn's luxurious living conditions. While Devlyn would have liked to invite friends, and especially Ellendren to visit him, he did have the small satisfaction of knowing that Trethien had no idea where he resided. *I wonder if he knows about Elle and me? Do I even know what we are? More than friends, that's for sure.*

To reach his quarters in the isolated tower, he had to pass the abandoned Emradiel wing, coated with centuries worth of dust and cobwebs. None of the ei'ana at Gwilnor recalled the wing framing a portion of the quad ever being used. Its vacant lancet windows had looked down over the quad for the past millennium without a single servant or student in detention being assigned to scrub the glass clean and sweep out the rooms. Grime layered the once translucent glass, making it near impossible to see through, and Devlyn and Viren walked carefully to his apartment past the vacant spaces to avoid raising the sneeze-inducing layers of dust. Aliel chose to disappear as they approached the tower and would greet Devlyn from his perch in the solar the minute the door opened into the apartment.

But the apartment itself had been spotless, all surfaces and windows gleaming when they'd moved in. Hannah must have anticipated his return to the castle. Perhaps Velaria had discussed it with her sooner than he'd thought. Otherwise, how else would the chancellor have seen to the apartment's thorough cleaning in anticipation of Devlyn's move out of the Temple of Ceur? He couldn't find a single cobweb—not even in the groin vaulting above. Devlyn didn't want to know how long it had taken to clean the grime and cobwebs—perhaps the erendinth had been wielded to get it this clean.

While he was relieved that he didn't have to move back into the boys' dormitories in the North Tower, the size and opulence of his new apartment was beyond anything he had ever expected. Not even his rooms in the temple had been this remarkable. Before Hannah had left them, he'd expressed his doubts about the appropriateness of the space for a student, even one that housed a phoenix and a Guardian knight. Her response remained fresh in his mind. Chancellor Hannah had said that he was very important and deserved every luxury Gwilnor could provide. And even though he was still a student wielder, as she repeatedly reminded him, since he was not going to become an ei'ana, there was no need for him to remain strictly within the same program.

Devlyn lounged in his soft feathered bed and allowed his mind to wander as the cool breeze washed over him where he lay on top of the bedcovers. Ceurenyl was never a hot city, but even that wind seemed too cold for this time of year. The first month of autumn was ending, but the first snow was still at least a month away. Somehow, that breeze made the first snowfall feel imminent.

Devlyn knew better than to allow his mind to stray at night; it made drifting to sleep very difficult. Closing his eyes once more with the intent of falling asleep and entering Somnaeniel, Devlyn allowed the weariness of his body to influence his state of mind. It was certainly a long and eventful Uraen. His class load that day had been exhausting. Ethyl had given her history class an exam on Brieli-Tieli relations, Jayna taught a complex series of equations and how they were related to the larger world in her algorithms class, and he'd sat through another of Magister Yvonne's frustrating classes. His only respite that day had been Therril's theoreticals class, although Therril's classes always required Devlyn's complete attention. He wanted nothing more than to rest, both his mind and body. But only his body would receive that luxury tonight.

Abbie and Eagan Wintyr had continuously assured him that his mind received just as much benefit from entering the World-in-Between as it would while truly sleeping. They insisted that the experience was akin to a normal dream. He didn't agree, but weariness continued to wash over him and his mind grew foggy as his eyelids became heavy.

Abbie and Eagan were eager to teach Devlyn how to enter Somnaeniel on his own. Ever since his return to Ceurenyl, it had become their main priority, especially since neither of them were anywhere physically nearby. With his last grasp of consciousness, he focused his mind on that place which was very much like the world he walked while awake, yet definitively other.

An ability unique to those visiting Somnaeniel was shifting, moving from one place to another instantly. Eagan had told him that to enter the World-in-Between, he had to perform a similar action, yet it was important to not commit yourself entirely.

With his eyelids closed and on the final verge of sleep, he willed himself into Somnaeniel, his desire loose in his mind so that it wasn't complete willingness, just as Eagan had instructed.

His consciousness began to slip from his control as he faded into slumber.

Either a single second passed, an hour, or an eternity, impossible to discern from in the Dream, yet there he stood in that surreal realm, wholly the same, yet wholly different as his body slept in his bed at Gwilnor. Standing in a reflection of his apartment in Somnaeniel were Abbie and Eagan, both waiting for who knows how long for Devlyn to arrive.

"Better," said Eagan. Devlyn knew that was the closest thing to a compliment he would ever get from the Druid of Kweil Aitch. "You must practice more often. Every night. You should be able to lie down to sleep and enter the Dream immediately."

Without instruction, Devlyn shifted from the castle to a wet plain overlooking the city of Lankor. This wasn't the first time he had shifted to this location and neither would it be his last.

He wanted to learn everything he could about this southern city. The Kingdom of Yanil was Erynor's proudest supporter and wielding the erendinth in every shape and form was outlawed there. He knew their wielders were routinely sent to a prison camp west of the capital, along the River Eindol, forced to produce weapons for Yanil and by extension, the Erynien Empire's shadow elves. It was said that if anyone in the camps was caught wielding, a shadow elf would immediately consume their soul. If Yanilean soldiers came across an adult wielder outside the camps, someone who had managed to evade slavery until discovery, the soldiers would not hesitate to execute them. That they had managed to live freely made them less willing to become subservient and more of a liability to the prison camps.

Ferinn's words at the feast celebrating the end of the siege of Myrium rang through his mind. The merpeople were aware of a lucilliae, one of the seven which formed Ceurendol, the Jewel of Life, in Lankor Bay, lying in the ruins of the Drowned City, a precursor to present day Lankor. If Ferinn spoke true, then the possibility existed for Devlyn to retrieve a third lucilliae from right under Erynor's nose.

The entire landscape surrounding Lankor reminded Devlyn of a swampy mire. It looked as though, if he truly traveled here, and if he took ten steps to either side of the road, he would sink in the mud. The few trees he could see stood isolated, and little other vegetation was noticeable, making him wonder where the large city farmed its food.

As before when he'd come here, Somnaeniel's sky swirled ominously with dark grey clouds, threatening to unleash a horrendous storm. Devlyn made sure to keep his gaze on the ground and not the sky. Alethea's warning about the puddles of black ooze haphazardly scattered across Somnaeniel forced his constant vigilance. He didn't understand how the small pools manifested death, but he didn't intend to find out on his own either.

"Can we shift into the city?" Devlyn wanted to learn more about Yanil's capital and the books he had read concerning it simply weren't as helpful as actually walking the city's streets.

"I would not," answered Eagan. "It's difficult to say how proficient our enemy has become in the Dream. It's possible for one in the Dream to be aware of another's presence in a specific area. The more attention you place on Lankor, the more will your arrival be anticipated."

Devlyn wanted to argue. How was he supposed to navigate the city when he arrived if he could not begin learning its layout now?

"Besides, it's not the city you need to concern yourself over, but the Drowned City in Lankor Bay," Abbie pointed out.

She was right. Devlyn grumbled about how often she was right as he prepared to shift to another perspective. Before he could though, his surroundings dimmed, and Eagan and Abbie vanished. He was suddenly surrounded by hundreds of men of various races, but mostly elves and humans. Some wore expensive finery, others plainer robes, and still others simple trousers and shirts. Iron chains at their wrists and ankles bound them in place, not one able to move more than a step.

Then, one by one, the chains fell, and the man would disappear in a puff of smoke, leaving only the broken chains behind. Only a third still had chains still in place, and those chains too disappeared, although the men did not.

Devlyn sprang upright in his bed, a cold sweat covering his skin and blankets in a tangled mess around him. The dream was too vivid for him to return to sleep. He knew Abbie would scold him later for not returning and explaining why he had disappeared without warning, not that it had been intentional. The thought that she could not scold him in person was a relief since she was still with Alex somewhere in Parendior. Perhaps she and Eagan knew that he'd had another vision. Moving over to the side of the bed, Devlyn sat, forearms hugging his knees, thinking of what just happened.

He didn't recognize any of the men in the dream, yet even though he couldn't identify any of them, he felt a kinship with them. Devlyn thought through different scenarios, trying to determine what the vision could reveal, knowing the importance of interpreting the dream or vision. The many chains made him think of Erynor, reinforcing his dominance by enslaving any who resisted him. It made sense, but he doubted that that was the true interpretation. Somewhere in his gut, he knew it was wrong, just as he'd known for sure that Queen Karina Lariviere of Sorenthil had been killed by Aren.

After a while, his mind went blank and he couldn't imagine any more interpretations. He also knew that it was unlikely that he would fall asleep again. The vision had been too vivid for him to ease back to sleep.

The first hour of the morning, marking the rising of the sun, was still hours off and the inaudible Arenthylean bells would not wake anyone in the city until the break of dawn. Rather than lie in bed thinking about the dream, Devlyn walked over to the large, pointed, arched window and looked over the city and into the Shroud. A breeze washed through the open window and across his bare chest, still coated in sweat from the dream. Goosebumps tingled across his skin.

His sight was definitely changing. Before he and Aliel fully bonded, he would have never been able to see as clearly as he saw now, especially while the sun slept. Yet, now he could even see a cat stalking through the city streets, hunting an early breakfast—he should not be able to see that.

Aliel's amusement passed through their bond as Devlyn marveled over his increased ability to see. *Every time we bond, your eyes will change until Teraeniel will see the golden eyes of the Phaedryn again,* Aliel conveyed, his pride in the development evident.

How do we get rid of the Shroud?

It was wrought by anacordel; it can be eliminated by anacordel.

Not the best advice he'd ever received, but Devlyn appreciated the reminder that it was possible, even though he had no idea how to do it. *Any idea who those men from the vision are?*

I didn't recognize them. But I agree with you, I don't think they're currently slaves, conveyed Aliel.

Turning from the bed chamber window, Devlyn went out into the expansive solar. Like all the pieces in the apartment, the furniture was finely crafted, and the fabric covering it was more exquisite than anything he had ever sat on. In fact, he rarely sat on any of the furniture, worried he would ruin them just by sitting on the chairs or sofas. The walls of his apartment were stone, just as the rest of the castle's interior, yet unlike most of the castle walls, these were covered in historic tapestries, tapestries that dated back thousands of years. None exhibited the Skylands, at least none that Devlyn could determine were of the Skylands. Most displayed beautiful landscapes that stretched from small rolling hillocks to towering jagged mountain ranges and from small quiet streams to expansive roaring seas.

His favorite tapestry was a finely detailed depiction of Eklean that hung in his study; it showed the entire continent, including the entirety of the Purged Desert of Dwonia. Most maps only showed a small fraction of the land west of Dwota's Gap. Yet, oddly enough, the artist who had woven this tapestry had not depicted it as a dry desert, but rather as sprawling green plains. Granted, it was not as green as the lands east of Dwota's Gap, but it certainly was not a desert. The tapestry even included part of a land Devlyn had never seen west of Dwonia. It was separated by a small sea and embroidered in silver thread on the small sliver of land was 'Qien Dynasty.'

Devlyn knew that the world was bigger than Eklean, his visits to Somnaeniel exemplified that, but none of his acquaintances ever mentioned a time when the entire world interacted. He wanted to know why communication had ceased between the continents. Erynor was likely to blame.

Placing his fingers on the embroidery, Devlyn felt the writing of the threaded letters, moving his fingers slowly toward the shore of that land and the body of water separating the two continents, titled the Misty Sea. As he did, he was shocked to see the depiction move to follow his touch. Not only could he see the small sliver of land with the peninsula jutting out into the sea, but now, the entire coastland along with a mountain range and several cities appeared. Fine lines divided the land, each labeled as a kingdom within the Qien Dynasty. The lands east of Dwota's Gap were no longer visible once the landscape on the tapestry shifted.

He must have let out a yelp, for Viren entered the room with a determined expression, his hand grasping the pommel of his translucent sword. Like Devlyn, he wore only his small clothes since he had undoubtedly been sleeping moments before. Devlyn suddenly felt self-conscious about his teenage body next to Viren's muscled form. The older elf certainly could not be considered burly, not like humans or dwarves after all. But his chiseled physique reminded Devlyn that he needed to visit the knights' training grounds more often. Viren scanned the study, then joined Devlyn in front of the tapestry, his sword arm slackening, and said, "I didn't realize there were any of these here."

"What is it?"

Viren raised an eyebrow at the obvious answer before speaking. "A map."

That much was evident and an irritable sensation arose in Devlyn.

"It shows the entire world, every continent, every kingdom, every city, and every landscape. That is, as it was when it was woven." Viren drew closer to the large tapestry and placed two hands on the fabric before swiping them toward each other. The fabric of the tapestry condensed, and simultaneously revealed a globe-like representation covered with three continents. With his left hand, Viren swished to the left on the tapestry, rotating the entire image until it slowed on the other side of the world. With both hands, rather than swipe inward, he pushed them apart, increasing the size of a specific location on the tapestry map.

"That's incredible!" said Devlyn, thoroughly impressed. "How's a simple tapestry of ordinary thread capable of doing all that?"

"Simple? Ordinary thread? You're lucky I'm no weaver. They would scold your ears raw. The same thread and fabric that make up your new garments is woven in this tapestry: lierathnil. I doubt the chancellor knew what treasure this room held. The weavers who crafted your robes and these tapestries are wielders; the entire project is accomplished through various wields to create the fluidity of it."

"So, I can see the whole world on this map?"

"Yes," Viren replied, crossing his arms.

Devlyn grinned and stepped closer to the map, and with one hand swiped across the landscape of a continent called Daereneth. He kept swiping northward and eastward until the map showed Dwonia, before crossing the Shadow Mountains and through the lands of Yanil. Slowing his pace, he focused on the bay leading to Lankor, pushing his hands apart on the fabric. The larger Lankor grew on the tapestry, the more bewildered Devlyn became. The city stood on the shores of the bay and along the River Eindol.

It was wrong.

Devlyn pushed his hands apart along the fabric, searching for the two other rivers, but they met further upstream. Ever since Ferinn had told him of the lucilliae hidden in Lankor, he had studied maps of the city whenever he had the opportunity. The occasions had been rare. But according to every map he'd examined, the floating city had one river run right through the center, and two other rivers on either side, near its borders. Nothing of the city on the tapestry map matched his studies.

"What you see on the tapestry is how Lankor once stood, before it was drowned by Erynor's use of Nauto's Wrath," said Viren to Devlyn's confused expression. "How that vile elf managed such power, I'll never understand."

"What is Nauto's wrath?"

"Nauto is an anadel—one of the enthiel bound to Theniel, Lady of the Seas. Nauto guides the human kingdoms living along Eklean's southern coast," said Viren. "I had only just been inducted into the Order of the Guardian Knights when Erynor was scheming and gaining allies. One of the first kingdoms he went to was Yanil, a powerful kingdom that shared no love for Evellion or Myrium yet held no hostility toward Krysenthiel. Our kingdom had brought prosperity and stability to all Eklean—the Yanileans had no desire to stir the waters. They originally refused Erynor when he sought their allegiance, telling their southern neighbor they had no desire to interact in the affairs of elves. That infuriated the emperor, and he unleashed Nauto's Wrath on them, bringing upon the unsuspecting Yanileans a tsunami of devastating proportions. The waters rose to such a height from the unnatural nautical activity, that the sea claimed the soft sandy landscape, burying the capital city beneath Lankor Bay. Our more sensitive kin felt the tremendous loss of life that day, not understanding why the anadel would so harm his own people. Lankor Bay never returned to its previous depth, the surrounding farmlands irredeemable. Shortly after the catastrophe, Erynor returned and pledged to rebuild their beloved home if they pledged themselves to his Erynien Empire."

"Why would they do that after he destroyed their city?"

"They did not know that he was behind the destruction. The Yanileans, to this day, place the blame on their wielders. They saw Erynor as a savior, not a menace. He kept true to his word and rebuilt Lankor above the Drowned City on either side of the Eindol as it entered Lankor Bay, two floating peninsulas, shaped by the three rivers merging into the bay. It's a nasty place I hear. If you do intend to go there, never let them discover who you are."

Devlyn gazed at the map before him: the layout of the very place where one of the lucilliae lay buried. How he was supposed to retrieve something lying on the bay's floor was beyond him, but as he looked at the map depicting what had once been Lankor, he knew it was possible.

REACQUAINTED

Devlyn stormed out of Yvonne's classroom, stalking past a group of huddled students and toward the dining hall. He didn't notice Ellendren waiting until she had hurried past the same group of huddled students to catch up to him and put a hand on his arm to slow him down.

"Is something wrong?"

On the verge of shaking off her touch, Devlyn stopped and turned at her voice. She looked every bit the ei'ana, even though she was still several years away from professing the Ei'ana Counsels. His heart skipped a beat at seeing her so unexpectedly, and his anger abated without completely fading. She held her head level, her silver and green eyes captivating his own. In his opinion, no one compared to how beautiful she was. Yet, not even she could dissipate his current rage toward the Ei'ana of Septyl in general and one woman in particular.

"More like someone," he replied through gritted teeth.

"You still aren't getting along with Magister Yvonne?"

"How is anyone supposed to get along with that witch!"

Slap.

It came without warning, but Ellendren stood firm with her arms crossed staring coldly into his eyes. His cheek stung, and the pain lingered as a red mark bloomed there.

Of all the words he could have used, Devlyn understood that he shouldn't have used that one. In fact, he hadn't intended to either; it just sort of slipped out. "I'm sorry—it's just that she knows exactly how to push me beyond my limits, embarrass me in front of the entire class, and denigrate me as if I had no claim to dignity or decency."

"What did she do this time?" asked Ellendren, without indicating that she'd heard the apology.

"She called me out in front of everyone, saying that people like me think we're better than the rest, and can wear anything we want to class." Devlyn gestured to his lierathnil clothing. "Not one other magister had any issue with it."

"I was going to compliment you. It is very nice." Her tone was kinder—softer. "Noble, even. Funny how something over a thousand years old—perhaps several thousand—is still fashionable."

"Thanks," said Devlyn. "She went on a tirade that lasted fifteen minutes. And to make matters worse, when she was finally done yelling at me, she ordered me to display my privileged power with a wield we're not scheduled to learn for another two months!"

"Were you able to do it?"

"Of course not, I've never even heard of this wield," said Devlyn as he pulled a book from his bag and opened it to page four hundred seventy-two and watched Ellendren's eyes skim over the page.

"This doesn't say anything about how to actually perform the wield." She flipped to the next page and the one after that. "I haven't had the best interactions with her either, but this is absurd."

"Welcome to the new and improved art of wielding class."

"How are you supposed to learn how to wield if the book doesn't mention anything about what exactly you are supposed to do?"

"I've been wondering the same ever since I started her class. Would you believe I was actually looking forward to it when we returned to Ceurenyl?"

With a light shake of her head, Ellendren pulled him forward. "Come on, let's get you away from this classroom. What of your other classes? You've always enjoyed Kai's politics class."

"They're going fine—honestly, I think the other magisters are taking sympathy on student wielders. Nynthel has been handing out exceptional marks like candy. I barely managed common marks in her languages class before. And I know that my Aelish hasn't improved past decent marks."

"Well, that's certainly encouraging," Ellendren said. As they walked along the dimly lit corridor, she took a small box wrapped in colored paper out of a pocket in her robe. "This is for you. I thought it might brighten your spirits."

"Does this mean you think I'm special?" Devlyn accepted the small package with a sideways smirk.

"It must, even though you haven't given me anything," said Ellendren, without so much as hinting at any irritation.

A guilty smile quickly followed. Devlyn almost missed a step forward as he wracked his brain. "Hold on, what's the occasion?" Devlyn asked, knowing he would soon regret asking. He had planned on purchasing a book for her, but the cost of any book he thought she would find interesting had quickly dashed that idea and he had instead settled on a bouquet of yellow chrysanthemums. Viren suggested any other flower would be more appropriate, unless Devlyn truly intended to convey slighted love. All that he had wanted to do was do something nice for her, but apparently, he was more likely to offend her with a simple gesture of yellow flowers. It had not occurred to him that each flower had a specific meaning. He returned to the book idea; he could probably afford at least one volume with the two lumols he carried. But then he rethought that; something told him he shouldn't spend them, as if they were more valuable than any book he might come across.

"No occasion, just because."

Devlyn sighed in relief, grateful he hadn't forgotten something important, and pleased that they'd been thinking along the same lines. Still, he hadn't actually bought her a gift, just thought of it. *So much for being considerate*, he thought.

"That doesn't mean you shouldn't give me something too."

Enjoying the teasing, Devlyn shook the package once before ripping the paper off while still walking.

"No, be careful, don't shake it!"

He paused, offering an apologetic smile before returning to the package. With the paper crumpled over the edge of the small box, he lifted the lid to find a small translucent figurine. Alabaster perhaps? "Where did you get this?" Devlyn stared at the familiar figurine of a phoenix wrapped in flames. Devlyn rotated the figurine in his fingers, it felt familiar—it felt like his two lumols. *Is it lumaryl?* It had to be—nothing held that golden inner light.

"Do you not like it?" Ellendren sounded disappointed. "I couldn't resist buying it for you—it called out to me. It also reminded me of Aliel."

"No, it's not that, I really like it. It's just that, I've seen this before—at a small shop in Cor'lera."

"Oh, isn't that curious? The shop I purchased it from has the most unique items." Ellendren looked from the trinket up into Devlyn's changing eyes. "I can take you to the shop now if you want. It was closed for the longest time. Fiona and I used to love looking through the odd items sold there. She was actually the one who noticed it opened again."

"Could you?" asked Devlyn, taking a moment to remember his day's schedule. His private lessons were devoted entirely to Alethea now, and he only met with her in the mornings before lessons, leaving the rest of his day open after classes.

"Of course," said Ellendren with a beaming smile on her face. He could not help but kiss her on her cheek, blushing immediately after. "Before I forget, I've been asked to join the Vyoletryn team."

"Their team? What team?"

"I keep forgetting you haven't completed a full year at Gwilnor. Their team for the Erendinth Games of course! They're held every three years. Every School of Septyl has a team and they compete in a year-long tournament. The other two years serve as preparatory years. Anyway, after a student wielder chooses their School, they are eligible to compete in the Erendinth Games. They practice fairly frequently."

"Congratulations. I know you've mentioned it before, but what do the Erendinth Games entail again?" Devlyn remembered something about having to use the different erendinth to play the game, but that was it.

"Where was your mind wandering to when I explained it to you?"

teased Ellendren. She knew very well where his mind had been the last time she'd described the Erendinth Games. Fortunately, it had ended with their first kiss, although it also led to their first squabble.

"Well, each School has its own team of seven players and there are seven different colored balls scattered along the field's circumference with seven reciprocal colorful goals in the middle of the field—three in the inner ring, and four on the outer. Each ball and goal represent an erendinth and only that erendinth can influence that ball or goal. No one can remember the last time all seven balls were in play—since no one has been able to wield the transcendental erendinth. Once the Vyolet-ryn team found out that I could wield animys and umbrys, they quickly brought me on their team, eager for the advantage. They didn't even have a try out. They've always had a formidable team, but they haven't won the School Cup in over two decades."

"That sounds like fun. Where's the field?"

"You've never seen the stadium when looking down from the south wing of the castle? The circular arena with benches along the outer rim."

"That's a stadium? I thought that was a park. I did think the lack of trees and the raised benches odd though. But I never thought twice about it. Since leaving Cor'lera, I've seen more peculiar things than I'd ever imagined."

Devlyn felt Ellendren staring at him in disbelief. However, the thought of a game sounded fun, and he wanted to play. "Can you teach me sometime?"

"Sure. Like I said, I'll be practicing quite a bit, so perhaps after a scheduled practice one evening?"

Excited at the prospect of learning a wielding game, Devlyn followed Ellendren out of the castle and across the two bridges over the two streams and toward the city. The knights standing guard eyed them grudgingly as they exited the castle and onto the quad.

"Don't we need an escort to leave the castle?" Devlyn glanced over his shoulder at the knights.

"Hannah's lifted some of the security measures since she became chancellor, citing the Sorenth victory as reason for doing so."

The further away from Gwilnor Ellendren led him from the castle, the better Devlyn felt. Putting physical distance between himself and Yvonne soothed him. Not even the mountain-sized load of required reading mattered anymore; he doubted he'd get through half of it. All his stress remained safely in the castle, waiting for his return.

Thinking about Yvonne made playing the Erendinth Games more appealing by the second.

Devlyn's fingers tingled as he watched Ellendren's hand swing past her body as they walked. Were they allowed to hold hands yet? Could he simply grab her hand without asking? Were they far enough away from the castle? His eyes kept darting between her hand and the city street and all the passersby. Just as Devlyn looked away from her hand again, he felt her figners find and entangle his own. He heard his heart beating loudly and hoped she did not hear it as well.

Ellendren strode through the city, weaving between streets and side streets. She seemed to know Ceurenyl just as well as her native Lucillia, smiling and nodding to people they passed. Devlyn wondered if they recognized her for who she was or if they were just polite to Gwilnor's students. Ceurenyl remained overcrowded due to the Sorenth refugees who remained in Ceurenyl despite the return of peace there. Many found the prospect of returning to their homeland daunting, especially since the winter months would soon begin. No one wanted to travel through mountain passes with the prospect of snow.

Ellendren stopped at a plaza near the city walls, situated between the castle and the city gates which still had not been repaired. The vast weight of the stones used to construct the gate still lay in ruins, despite constant efforts to restore the gate and provide defense to the city once more. So far, every ei'ana who attempted to wield the large stone blocks back into place was met with stone that refused to budge, no matter her strength.

A large shop window filled with an assortment of bright curious objects stood out amidst the other buildings. Walking toward the green-painted wooden door, Devlyn pushed it open, causing the bell that hung inside above the door to ring.

Just as in the shop in Cor'lera, cluttered shelves covered the walls of the shop, and the tables scattered throughout were equally laden, with boxes beneath for extra storage.

"I'll be with you in just a moment, take your time browsing," hollered a familiar voice from a back room.

Devlyn wasn't interested in browsing, since he was quite familiar with the foreign trinkets this shop sold. He went straight to the back door, and called out, "I was wondering if you still sold those candies my aunt likes so much." It was only then that he remembered that his Aunt Vine, was not actually his aunt at all.

The sound of hurried shuffling came from the back room, no reply, just movement and the sound of boxes toppling over as someone clumsily pushed past. When the handle turned, Devlyn stepped away as the whole door swung open with Walei's not-too-narrow body now filling the doorway.

"Ah hah! Look at you!" cried Walei, wrapping his large arms around Devlyn's torso, forcing the air from his lungs in the process. Loosening his grip, and allowing Devlyn to inhale, Walei took hold of his shoulders, and held him at arms' length to look directly into his eyes, now almost level with each other, with a serious expression in his own. "They're changing."

"I know." Not a day passed when his eyes did not grow more golden in appearance. It was not a great change, and it was only noticeable if someone looked into his eyes, which fortunately did not occur all that frequently. They still had a trace of his original silver to green. "That's not all either." Gently caressing the bond connecting him to Aliel, Devlyn felt the phoenix soaring above the city.

Since Yvonne's insistence that Devlyn not bond with Aliel during her lessons, they had decided it best that the phoenix avoid attending those classes altogether. Which meant, that while Devlyn experienced a living nightmare, Aliel spent the morning enjoying a wondrous flight high above the city. They had taken Hannah's tuition exemption seriously, and Aliel preferred the open sky over the sealed castle anytime.

There's someone I want you to meet, conveyed Devlyn.

Not a second passed before the phoenix appeared in a flash of light that bathed the entire small shop.

"Light be blessed!" Walei's eyes sprung open. "Devlyn, how is this possible? Not a single phoenix has been seen for over a thousand years, not since Erynor saw to it that that dragon of his consumed every last one of them."

"Aliel was unhatched," said Devlyn. "The only phoenix who was then not yet born, and then carefully watched over by a hundred Guardian knights in their mountain keep."

"And he chose you! I didn't realize phoenix could lay eggs," said Walei, before his voice lowered to a whisper. "Have you? Did you? I mean, you know what I mean."

Devlyn nodded as a smirk crept to his lips, unable to hide his excitement.

"Do you actually have wings? Can you fly as all the legends said the Phaedryn did?"

"It's incredible, Walei, it's unlike anything I've ever experienced." Devlyn couldn't stop grinning. "By the way, this is…" Walei didn't let Devlyn finish.

"No need for introductions; the princess has been coming to my shop for quite some time now." Walei bowed his head toward Ellendren. "Although, I will say, it had been a while since she'd come to my shop. I had no intentions of staying away from Ceurenyl as long as I did. I typically alternate between the two shops every few months. It's been over two and a half years since my last return, I'll have to stay here at least an extra month or two to make sure everything is in order and take inventory. I would have come back sooner, but, well, you remember how you left Cor'lera. I was there so long that my wares were nearly depleted. Not that that kept that aunt of yours from getting her candies. I honestly don't know how she manages it! The walled part of the village was barred, no one in, no one out for almost a year after Arlyn raised that enchantment. Those Perrien soldiers are a nasty piece of work. That ei'ceuril uncle of yours, Arlyn, told the soldiers that if they tried to enter, the wielders he'd trained would fry them alive. Anyway, my supply of those candies steadily decreased over the entire duration, since a child of about twelve routinely came to the shop, buying large quantities of them."

"She must have been determined to have them," said Ellendren.

"That's not the half of it," cried Walei. "You should have seen her when her darling son arrived in town. The gates were open by then and the Perrien soldiers were long gone, although Arlyn still kept the gates heavily guarded. Anyway, since Alex returned with two ei'ana, a knight, a wild red-headed girl, and a sizeable militia, your aunt took it upon herself to try to remove him from their company and send him back to the abbey school."

"I bet her heart nearly gave out when she realized who he was with!" laughed Devlyn before explaining. "She isn't the biggest supporter of Lucillians; to her, they're not elves, there are no such things as elves anymore; they died thousands of years ago. Also, she despises wielders. If she had it her way, all Eklean would lock up their wielders and threaten them with death if they even so much as thought about wielding. Just like they do in Yanil."

"That's horrible. Why does she feel so strongly against us?" Ellendren asked.

"It's hard to say," replied Walei. "She shares her brothers' sentiments, only, her brothers are worse than she is. Lex will undoubtedly give the Lucillian Alliance a run for its money! As personally awful as he is, he is a proven general. I think she might be softening up though. Before I left, I saw her give a package to Alex, and then giving him a huge hug and scurrying to her home outside the village walls. Alex was about to lead a small army west toward the River Arvil to challenge Perrien's influence in Parendior, while gathering as many supporters as possible. I think for the first time in her life, she's going to disagree with her brothers. And a good thing too!" Hearing about Alex and his family jogged Devlyn's memory.

"I forgot to mention something," he said. "I'm not actually a Telvin. My da was born of an Eldinari, conceived in a heinous act of violence by a Cyndinari. Because of the Cyndinari blood, the immortal life of the Eldinari did not pass to him. So, the Lierafen family sent him to live amongst the Telvins, who were apparently at one time a respectable family. At least that's what I'm told."

"What an odd twist of fate. And thank the Light! You don't have to go around calling yourself Devlyn Telvin anymore." Walei shifted his weight. "So, the dynamic duo are not cousins after all. That will certainly delight Abbot Entiel. He's been researching relentlessly, since you both disappeared with Mother Velaria, trying to disconnect his family's honorable name from any tarnish from those with vile pointy ears. His words of course."

Devlyn could see Ellendren's desire to understand the Telvin family's hatred of Lucillians and wielders. Not particularly eager to discuss the political climate he'd grown up in, Devlyn shifted the conversation away from the Telvins. "Is Fei here?" he asked. "It would be great to see her again."

"My daughter stayed back in Cor'lera to watch over the shop and the village. Why she puts up with me I'll never know! An ei'ana watching over her father's shop! I've never heard of such nonsense before."

"What? She's an ei'ana!"

"Of course, she is, and she was incredibly helpful to Arlyn, teaching other women how to wield and all. Why do you think I have a shop here in Ceurenyl? Because of the temperate weather? Ha!" bellowed Walei, slapping his knee.

"What School does she belong to?" asked Ellendren.

"Vyoletryn. I'm also an observant of the same School, but don't mention that to anyone. I'm not half as useful when people know that bit of news."

Devlyn continued talking with Walei about Cor'lera and its current state, shocked to hear that they had begun constructing a new wall to surround all the buildings outside the current one, this one of stone. Was it possible that the divided village was finally uniting, both humans and elves alike? And not just the humans who had always lived in eastern Parendior but also many of the more recent transplants, those taking advantage of the unique grape vines native to Cor'lera, producing the popular Cor'leran Blue ice wine. Most of the conflict had arisen from the latter group of humans, native to the original boundary of Perrien, west of the Arvil.

The afternoon quickly turned to evening as they chatted and the sun had begun to drop when Ellendren reminded Devlyn that they were still under curfew.

Walei refused to let them leave without accepting a small package of candies.

––––––––––

By the time they had returned to the castle, the quad was crowded with griffins. Loose feathers and fur billowed through the grand arch as Devlyn and Ellendren crossed beneath it. Devlyn had completely forgotten that the first wave of Eldinari were slated to return to Gwilnor that afternoon. He still had not begun his assignments for Yvonne's class. Granted, it was not the only class that Devlyn had homework for, but if he failed to complete Yvonne's homework, he would fall victim to her ridicule once again. Not a single lesson passed that did not include Yvonne tearing him down. As much as it felt like she had it out for him, Yvonne tormented her other students as well, but Devlyn certainly received most of the abuse.

Just as he and Ellendren pushed through the griffins, Wyn brushed through the entry. He had apparently been waiting for them.

"Hey, Wyn," Devlyn greeted him with a smile, still elated from spending the afternoon with Walei. "There must be over a hundred griffins here."

"These aren't even all of them—the stablehands have ushered most into the castle stable already. Alethea sent me looking for you hours ago. No one seemed to know where you had disappeared to, not even Viren. Don't expect him to be in a good mood when you see him later."

It hadn't occurred to Devlyn that Viren, and many others as well, would be concerned about his lengthy absence, even though Viren typically went everywhere with him. Wyn was right though, Viren would not be pleased about not being able to find him for an entire afternoon. "Where's Alethea now?"

"Have you completely forgotten about the banquet? The dining hall is cleared of its long tables and Father Phendien has already been received by the other Chairs. I've never seen the dining hall so crowded before! Every ei'ana, knight, student, and servant has managed to squeeze inside. We'll be lucky if we can get past the entry!"

Wyn didn't wait for them to follow but turned on his heels and started at a quick walk through the castle, leaving Devlyn, Ellendren, and Aliel to follow behind. Devlyn had never seen Wyn so excited before. He had only been away from the larger Eldinari populace for a matter of months.

After crossing the entire length of the castle, they reached the dining hall, which had students spilling out past the entry and into the corridor beyond. Wyn glared at Devlyn for making him late for the banquet. Devlyn tried to apologize, but Wyn just shouldered through the crowded entry as Aliel disappeared from the crowd. While the dining hall was certainly large and its rafters soared high over their heads, Devlyn had learned that phoenix preferred less cramped spaces.

Devlyn and Ellendren followed Wyn and the path he had carved out of the masses. If they were not quick, the effort Wyn had taken to open a pathway would diffuse as the huddled bodies would fuse back together, forming a wall that Wyn had somehow managed to penetrate.

The further into the dining hall they pushed, the more evidence Devlyn saw of the new arrivals. A sole elf in shades of green with ebony hair stood out next to the multitude of elves with light brown hair and even more so next to the smattering of humans. Yet, the elves with the distinct darker hair and skin tone, became more common the deeper into the dining hall Wyn led Devlyn and Ellendren. While Devlyn knew that a significant number of Eldinari were to come to the castle, he did not know what their status would be. Would the ei'ana in the Eldin Wood send students to Gwilnor? Or would they send the more established ei'ana beyond their borders? He doubted the former was likely. When all the elves were immortal, they learned how to wield in a very different manner. A mere decade of education would serve only as an introductory course for those who had the luxury of aging slowly. While he and Wyn appeared the same age, Wyn was well over two hundred years old. None of his formation had been spent in a typical classroom.

And indeed, the more Eldinari that Devlyn saw in the dining hall, the older they all appeared. It was impossible to know their age for certain, but none looked young enough to be students. Most had probably seen a thousand winters pass by. How many had lived through the Ceurendol War?

The high table at the front of the dining hall typically only sat magisters, and when the rare feast occurred, the Seven Chairs. Today, however, the high table saw many Eldinari. Father Phendien Shendielle, Chair of Emradiel, had brought with him his most trusted advisor, Lyrin Allandis, who had served as an Emradiel wise one as long as Wyn could remember. Devlyn recognized several Eldinari aryls seated among the dignitaries. This reunion meant more than the Eldinari ei'ana simply returning from their secluded forest. Devlyn could practically hear Ellendren buzzing in his head about the political implications of the Eldinari venturing past their forest home.

"Did you know the aryls would come?" Devlyn asked.

"I had no idea," Ellendren said, blushing at the reminder of her last encounter with them. As the daughter of the current Aryl of Lucillia, as well as the crowned princess of Lucillia, Ellendren had shared her not so subtle opinion on the Eldinari hiding in their forest.

Wyn was out of earshot and kept pushing forward to the high table. It was only when Devlyn recognized Dalenya and Fendryl, Aryl of Lierafen, and Devlyn's and Wyn's great-great-grandparents, that he understood Wyn's impatience. Devlyn had only learned of his connection with House Lierafen several months ago, but it was the first time he could remember being welcomed into a family—his family.

Devlyn quicked his pace, now mimicking Wyn's eagerness.

The high table rose three steps on a dais and extra seats had been brought to accommodate the additional guests.

"Ei'terel, Ei'denai," Devlyn and Wyn said together as they inclined their heads in a bow, Ellendren repeated the greeting a few steps behind them.

Dalenya and Fendryl both smiled to their younger family members. "It is good to see you both well," said Dalenya.

"Our House's star wardens reported some marvelous accomplishments at Myrium," Fendryl said, looking intently into Devlyn's eyes. "I see they did not exaggerate."

Devlyn still was not accustomed to people staring so deeply into his changing eyes.

"Will you be staying here at the castle?" asked Ellendren.

"Regretably, no," said Dalenya. "We came only for the welcome banquet. It's been so long since we've had diplomatic relations with the kingdoms outside our forest. But other than the aryls and a small guard, the rest of the Eldinari will remain. Many have longed to return to Gwilnor Academy, and even more still long to return to Septyl."

"With the exception of Velaria, none of the other Chairs or magisters were able to recognize us as aryls. Truly, I doubted Velaria and the other Chairs expected us to accept the invitation. There was a bit a scramble to bring more seats to the high table when we came in," said Fendryl, extending his elbows a few inches to emphasize just how crowded the high table was.

"Ellendren, do you know of any Luminari aryls currently outside Lucillia? We're terribly sorry that we cannot pass through the Protection of the Wood to meet with the Aryl of Lucillia in person," said Dalenya, pointedly not commenting on the prerequisite for the protection being in place.

"There are towns and villages up and down the Illumined Wood, but I don't think any of the Luminari aryls were outside Lucillia when the Protection of the Wood was raised. I could be wrong, but I've learned nothing to suggest otherwise. As for my parents, the Aryl of Lucillia, their fate is unknown." Her chin dipped as her sight drifted to her feet. "The Protection of the Wood demands a heavy price."

"That is a shame and please, accept our sincerest condolences."

"Well, don't spend the evening speaking with us. These types of feasts are rare occurences, go enjoy yourselves," said Fendryl.

Devlyn, Wyn, and Ellendren all bowed and melted back into the larger crowd. Ellendren did not want to dwell on Lucillia and her parents, knowing what the Protection of the Wood had cost her mother.

Distressed

Thenaen was the only day of the week where Kevn had the opportunity to rest from his daily chores and he had decided early that morning that there were two things he really had to do. The first was to visit the temple gardens to collect his thoughts—he was exhausted, sore, and even angry. Worse, he felt like a sponge wrung dry and then left in the Purged Desert of Dwonia. The second was to correct the mistake he had made in returning to the Temple of Ceur to resume his studies with the order of Ei'ceuril. He should not have acted so rashly when Hannah pressured him to learn how to wield. He had always felt guilty about leaving the ei'ceuril four years ago; they were like a family to him. The pressure from Hannah on top of that guilt had driven him to make a very hasty, very poor decision. Kevn hadn't even told his friends at Gwilnor that he was leaving. But he certainly had not expected his freedom to be so limited.

Instead of resuming classes with the other students at the temple, Kevn had been sent to serve a probationary period with the temple servants. His first action when he had returned to the temple two months ago was to visit Homas, the steward responsible for admitting the boys who intended to become ei'ceuril. Steward Homas had informed Kevn that he needed to understand the seriousness of his actions. Kevn had grumbled inwardly at being forced to help clean the massive temple— the kitchens being the worst part—but his grumbling transformed to all-out fury when he had learned that he would not be compensated for his labor. His back still ached from hauling cast iron cauldrons to the kitchens from a distant storeroom several days ago. According to Homas, it was part of his penance. Kevn wasn't familiar with any precedent where returning students were punished for coming back to the temple. As if the chores weren't bad enough, Kevn's direct superior, Steward Lacus, restricted Kevn from spending any time with his old classmates. Instead, whenever Kevn had free time, Lacus filled it with needless personal chores and errands. The unrelenting schedule often found Kevn falling asleep during his daily meditations, which resulted in Lacus pointedly taking note of the transgressions.

Kevn's mind now lingered on the cold Orenth breeze outside in the temple gardens. The last month of autumn was nearing its end and the first light snowfall had dusted the city two weeks ago. He had been waiting long enough that his face no longer stung from the wind's piercing chill, but even so, he would have preferred to still be strolling through the temple's gardens than sitting in this small uncomfortable chair in an anteroom with no windows. The chair was far too small for anyone over the age of twelve, especially for a sixteen-year-old like Kevn. Typically, the chair was only ever used once, when students first came to join the ei'ceuril as children. For Kevn, though, this was not the first occasion when he'd anxiously awaited while sitting in this particular chair. He had been only ten, that first time, and then twelve the second time when he'd asked to leave, and his body had been better proportioned to the small chair in the room with no windows. And he had not noticed the size of the chair two months ago, when Homas had ushered Kevn into his office so quickly that he didn't have time to consider the size of the chair.

Once again—for the *fourth* time—he sat in the windowless room, staring at a wall that, in his opinion should have a window. *Every room needs a window*, he thought as he stared at the unadorned wall, hoping a hole would appear to allow a breeze in to freshen the stale air. Part of him wanted to go outside and march right back to Gwilnor. The castle had some of the largest windows he had ever seen for a building constructed entirely of stone. And countless grand windows lined the Temple of Ceur's thick stone walls, but given its colossal structure, much of the interior spaces and subterranean levels had no natural light.

When he had made his way from the temple gardens and through the temple corridors to the small office, Kevn had rehearsed exactly what he intended to say. He was exhausted, his mind was jumbled, and he doubted he could utter a single composed sentence. The probation and accompanying restrictions were not conducive to fostering the reverence appropriate for a temple student. He still felt bitter about missing last month's banquet to celebrate the Eldinari returning to Gwilnor Academy.

Kevn had immediately readjusted to the temple's schedule, a routine not easily forgotten. It felt like an age ago when he had first studied among the ei'ceuril with every intention of professing their vows. He'd been with them two years when, suddenly and without much warning, he had informed Steward Homas that he wanted to leave to study at Gwilnor instead. Steward Homas' responsibilities were limited to admitting the young boys who wished to join the order of Ei'ceuril, and on very rare occasions, to administering their dismissal if they chose to leave the temple before completing their studies. And now Kevn wanted to do just that for a second time, which was probably unheard of. It had already been rather difficult when he'd asked to return only two months ago, resulting in his current probation.

Just as his thoughts turned once again to fleeing the difficult conversation to come, the door opposite him finally opened and Steward Homas signaled Kevn to come into the office.

Steward Homas' office was larger than the poky anteroom, but certainly not large in comparison to some of the offices occupied by more prestigious wise ones.

The ei'ceuril sat behind his desk and stared blankly at Kevn, waiting for him to begin the conversation since Kevn had requested the meeting. But Kevn simply waited; silence never bothered him, in fact, he typically preferred it. Why everyone felt the need to share their thoughts aloud all the time was quite curious to him. Some of what he unintentionally overheard was incredibly personal and the amount of information other students shared with each other was shocking.

Kevn's gaze darted to the window, relieved to look at something—

anything—other than the patiently waiting Steward Homas. He did not want to even have the conversation, let alone begin it. He just wanted his dismissal from the ei'ceuril to happen and skip everything in between. Couldn't he just sign a piece of parchment and leave?

The steward maintained his gaze on Kevn, making him squirm in his seat. The silence was becoming too much, even for Kevn, and just as his lips parted to finally speak, Homas cleared his throat. "Do you recall, just before you decided to leave us the last time, what I told you?"

He did. It was impossible to forget those haunting words. Impossible to not feel them within his very being as they still echoed and tormented him, despite his best efforts to ignore them over the past four years. And when he had finally stopped ignoring them, he'd made the mistake of returning to the temple. "That you believed I was making a mistake in leaving."

"You are not a foolish young man, Kevn Weyvien. Much less irrational than some of the others who came here when you first did and who've remained. Yet they *did* remain. I cannot say that I entirely understand your reasoning for leaving us four years ago. I have my suspicions. But I will not question you about that. What I ask you to explain is what you desire from me today."

Kevn looked down at his hands fidgeting with the itchy white fabric. He wanted nothing more than to leave Steward Homas's office and this itchy robe behind. *Why does he have to make this more difficult than it already is? He knows perfectly well why I came here*, he thought.

He felt the ei'ceuril's gaze hold him. A gentle gaze, yet properly held with judgment. Kevn felt his mouth open a second time, and it seemed like it was acting on its own volition. He heard words form, creating a sentence—not the request he had planned. He was shocked by what he heard himself say. He spoke of how, nearly every night since he'd returned two months ago, he found himself curled up in bed telling himself that he was going to leave and go back to Gwilnor until he finished his studies, and then, he would leave Ceurenyl forever to return to Lucillia. Well, that was assuming that Erynor had lost his war by then and everything had returned to normal.

He spoke of how the ei'ceuril had certainly been accommodating, and that they'd spoken many words of welcome, yet he'd felt in his heart that he was not actually welcomed among them. There was an incredible sense that they were ei'ceuril and he was not. Nor would he ever become one. An impenetrable barrier had been erected between him and them. It was a very different sensation than what he'd felt at his initial entrance. When he'd first arrived at the temple as a child, he had received more words of support and encouragement than he knew what to do with. But this time, he'd felt nothing but discouragement. He felt like an orphan who had run away from his adoptive family, and when he had returned, that family did not want him back.

The words that had come out of his mouth were not the ones he'd intended to say; the request to leave was not made. Instead, he'd spoken of his desire to feel that he belonged and was valued. Steward Homas had simply let Kevn pour it all out, looking at Kevn for a long space of time until finally, Homas stood. Kevn was not sure whether he should stand as well, since he wasn't sure he was finished speaking—he hadn't yet asked to leave but then Steward Homas asked him to stand as well. Kevn felt like a coward for not speaking his real desire and his stomach twisted in knots.

"It is good that you have come to me with your concerns, and that you have decided to stay with us this time. I am sorry you have experienced such discouragement; it was never the intention, but you know how some of the ei'ceuril can be. I could not be happier that you are with us again, brother. You will soon be returning to your studies, I am sure. I will speak with Lacus personally to ensure that."

Kevn's body trembled slightly at the ei'ceuril's words and he felt his eyes moisten at being called brother for the first time in over four years. He had not expected to have a personal connection to the title. Despite the relief that came from the steward's words, Kevn knew this would not make anything better. His depression and exhaustion would continue to worsen. But it would take too much effort to try to explain when he himself wasn't sure what he wanted or needed. Steward Homas had thought Kevn needed to vent, and had allowed it, but the steward also believed that Kevn belonged among the ei'ceuril.

Kevn turned to leave, a jaw-breaking yawn he couldn't prevent causing the steward to frown as he closed the door behind him. His lungs seemed to close, and his chest heaved with a familiar tightness; his skin prickled with an ever-present rash. His body was once again reflecting the anxiety he'd always felt when he wore the white ei'ceuril robes. None of the healers at the temple had ever given him a reason for his anxiety—it surely wasn't the fault of the ei'ceuril or due to living in the temple. But neither could those same healers explain why Kevn's body had healed after he had left the ei'ceuril and enrolled at Gwilnor Academy.

Medicine and healing did not interest Kevn. He tended to stay away from that section of Gwilnor's vast library. He didn't need to research poultices and medicinal maladies to know why his body had stabilized when he was at Gwilnor.

Since coming back to the temple, the symptoms had returned. Like last time, none of the ei'ceuril could explain it. Not a single healer was willing to propose that it could reflect the turmoil Kevn felt at returning to the temple. Returning was a mistake. They weren't willing to admit that perhaps Kevn was not suited to become an ei'ceuril. Steward Homas was wrong; he did not belong here in the temple as an ei'ceuril.

Kevn walked aimlessly through the temple, his arms wrapped around his chest. The touch calmed him. Just as he decided he would return to his own chambers, he recognized Aaron at the far end of the corridor. Aaron wore his white ei'ceuril robes proudly, and unlike most of the ei'ceuril wearing those robes, Aaron seemed to shine in his. The robes were not intended to heighten—let alone compliment—someone's physical appearance, but they did just that for Aaron Roendryn. Clearly, Aaron belonged here. The Lucillian prince wore his new station as steward exceptionally well.

Aaron beamed at Kevn, who waved politely in response. Kevn hoped Aaron hadn't seen him hugging himself in the empty corridor. It was embarrassing enough that he'd returned to the ei'ceuril after leaving four years ago. Fortunately, Aaron had been away during most of that time in the Illumined Wood for his Return, the final phase of initiation to become an ei'ceuril steward. He too had dealt with his own doubts, so much so, that Aaron had almost remained in the Illumined Wood, never to return to the temple.

"Peace of the Light to you," said Aaron.

"And to you." Kevn forced a smile.

"What's wrong?" Aaron's elated expression dimmed. He could see past Kevn's façade.

"It's nothing." Kevn kept his eyes on the floor.

"It's fine if you don't want to tell me, but I hope you're not also telling yourself that you're fine."

Kevn held his breath. For a split second he considered telling Aaron about his meeting with Homas. Kevn had always admired Aaron. The Lucillian prince had been one of the first people in the temple to offer any warmth or comfort to Kevn when he had first come to the temple as a child. Everyone else had seemed so cold, so aloof to Kevn. As if the stone walls weren't cold enough! It was worse now, especially since he was working as an indentured servant.

Kaeyth and Taen had been the exception. Shortly after Kevn returned to the temple and before Steward Lacus had restricted his interactions with his friends, Kaeyth had insisted on Kevn joining them in their secret chapel which was really just a broom closet.

Both Kaeyth and Taen, like the rest of Kevn's former classmates, had spoken their vows. When he was still at Gwilnor, he had realized that he was the only one of that group to not have spoken the Ei'ceuril vows. It was a large part of why he was back in the temple. He had felt a driving force within, almost pulling him back to the temple. Yanking him there against his will to be more precise. *So much for free will.*

"You seem exhausted, Kevn. Are you sleeping enough? I've lost track of how many times you've yawned since we've been standing here."

"I fall asleep the moment my head hits the pillow. Quite the miracle considering how thin it is. It's just, well, they've been working me hard since I've returned. Not the reunion I'd envisioned." Kevn tilted his head down toward his shoulder. He wished he could bury himself in the darkness of his arm.

"How so?" Aaron nudged him gently and started at a walk again.

Kevn looked about the corridor; he'd been wandering aimlessly, and didn't know exactly which part of the temple they were in. By the looks of this corridor, they were at least five levels below the Chamber of Light, lower even than Steward Homas' antechamber. The entire temple had a refined simplicity, yet the further one traveled from the Chamber of Light, the less ornate the architecture became. The expressive columns found on the main level shamed the wider pilasters set in the walls below. These were still beautiful and magnificent, yet the time and attention given to the ones above overshadowed the ones below. Kevn knew that money wasn't the reason. The temple architects had intended to show hierarchy. Nothing could outshine the Chamber of Light—that was physically impossible.

Kevn still hadn't answered Aaron's question. His legs were growing weary from walking and the cloudy opaque walls kept Kevn's attention divided. Kevn thought he could see his reflection in the depths of the opaque walls, as was customary, but whenever he turned to focus on them, all he could see was the milky wall that seemed to fade into nothingness. The walls of the Temple of Ceur unnerved him.

But Kevn felt his confidence returning, a drumming feeling building inside. He felt ready and able to answer Aaron. His time in the temple had not been what he had expected.

Just as he opened his mouth to speak, he heard a faint clanging sound. The drumming sensation did not come from inside but echoed through the corridors ahead. "Do you hear that?" Kevn asked, distracted from answering Aaron's question.

"It sounds like swords. Hasn't there been unrest with the lay votaries in the lowest levels of the temple? Those kien wielders restricted to the temple who've never joined the ei'ceuril or temple knights?"

"There's been rumors, but I thought the temple knights had everything under control."

Aaron turned away from the direction they'd been heading and down the corridor. "Well, whatever it is, it's not coming from the training rooms; those chambers are on the other side of the temple. Come on."

Aaron quickened his pace and Kevn had to run to keep up.

They rushed down the corridor as the sound of metal on metal intensified. The distinct clash of swords smashing against swords and shields filled their ears, and they could also hear men yelling.

A temple knight stood at the intersection ahead. Kevn couldn't see any movement behind him. The fighting must still be a few corridors away and perhaps on a lower level too. The temple knight looked hopeful at seeing Aaron, since everyone in the temple knew that Aaron could wield kien with control. But the optimism faded quickly. "You can't wield here; quickly, run back and warn those above that there's a revolt on the lowest levels and tell the ei'ceuril to lock themselves in their chambers. Get to the Chamber of Light and warn the Ceurtriarch!"

Kevn wanted to argue but the temple knight was right. Not only could Aaron not wield here, but they had no weapons either, leaving them completely defenseless.

The temple knight didn't wait for their response, just rushed on toward the fighting.

The sound of clashing steel grew louder.

"Quick, let's get to the Ceurtriarch," said Aaron.

BROKEN PROTOCOL

Kevn and Aaron hurried through the temple corridors toward the Ceurtriarch's apartment, yelling to everyone they passed that there was fighting on the lower levels, and to stay away from there. Temple knights were rushing past them toward the conflict. The news of the fighting below seemed to have spread before them. Nearly every door was shut tightly. They continued to yell the warning, nonetheless.

In their hurry, and not watching where he was going, Kevn turned a corner and collided with a surprised Kaeyth. The two fell to the floor tangled together. "What's the rush?" Kaeyth asked, obviously unaware of any problems. Taen reached out to help him up.

"There's fighting in the lower levels." Aaron answered as he helped Kevn stand.

"The lay votaries? What harm could they possibly do? It's not like they can wield down there. And the only weapons in the whole temple belong to the temple knights," replied Kaeyth, rubbing his head where it had met the floor. A bruise was already beginning to show.

"I'm not sure how, but whoever's fighting down there have swords, we heard steel clashing on steel. Come on, we have to warn Ealyndol," said Aaron, tugging at Kevn.

Kaeyth and Taen shared a look that clearly said there were flaws in Aaron's story, but followed Aaron and Kevn instead of continuing on their way.

"How could the men in the lower levels get swords?" Kaeyth asked. "It's not like any of the temple knights would hand out their own weapons."

"You don't think there are servants of Shadow in the temple, do you?" Taen glanced over his shoulder, shuddering in the process.

"I'll keep you safe, little Taen." Kaeyth flashed his dagger.

"You still have that!"

"And you're lucky I do. But that doesn't answer how they managed to get into the temple. I thought anyone with ill intent would collapse when passing through the Chamber of Light."

Aaron froze. "Unless if they didn't pass through it at all." All the color drained from his face.

"How's that even possible? How could they simply appear inside the Temple of Ceur?" asked Kevn, just avoiding bumping into the stock-still Aaron. Aaron's obvious fear was shocking, but not as shocking as his words.

"A seguian."

The reality washed over Kevn. That was not possible. Wielding inside the Temple of Ceur was not possible.

"The Erynien Empire captured a minum who was trying to bring my sister back from her novitiate about a year ago. Ellendren told me that she had watched Aren, the Dark Phaedryn, pierce the minum with tenebrys. I can't believe it, but Erynor must have broken the minum's resolve." Aaron darted away.

"Are you trying to say that Erynor forced the minum to open a seguian into the temple? I thought wielding was impossible inside the temple," Kaeyth yelled after the departing Aaron.

"Seguians aren't connected to the erendinth. They're something else completely," answered Kevn, and then he, Kaeyeth, and Taen dashed after Aaron. Kevn didn't quite understand what seguians were, but he did know that the Time Wardens did not need a wield to open one.

Aaron's white ei'ceuril robes billowed behind him, and the only noise in the now-vacant corridor came from their racing footsteps. Kevn tried to imagine the repercussions of servants of Shadow inside the temple.

Kevn tried to catch Aaron, but the prince's speed was unlike anything Kevn could have imagined him capable of. Not even Kaeyth could match Aaron's haste. Aaron had disappeared ahead by the time Kevn, Kaeyth, and Taen reached the entrance to the Chamber of Light. A sense of relief washed over Kevn when he saw that extra temple knights guarded the doors to the chamber. They looked flustered, presumably from Aaron pushing past. Kevn didn't think that Aaron had stopped to utter the required words to enter the sacred chamber.

The knights recognized them easily enough but refused to allow anyone else into the chamber without following the proper protocol.

"I am not worthy to enter into such splendor, but by the will of Anaweh, the Creating Light," they recited in unison.

The temple knights grudgingly parted, and Kevn wondered if they knew what was happening below; they had to. As always, the incredible light inside was blinding and awe inspiring, but they quickly reached the far side of the Chamber of Light where they found the doors leading to the Ceurtriarch's quarters ajar. Kevn assumed that Aaron had left them open as he rushed past to warn Ealyndol Roendryn, his great-uncle. The three slipped into the foyer between the Chamber of Light and the antechamber to the Ceurtriarch's apartment and came to a full stop at the sight in front of them. Shocked gasps followed, and Kevn's heart skipped a beat.

Kaeyth turned to Taen, "Quick, tell the knights at the entrance." Kaeyth knelt beside the two collapsed knights just inside the door. Their throats had been slit open and they lay in pools of their own blood. The sight paralyzed Kevn. They were in the Chamber of Light. Blood had been spilled on holy ground. How was that even possible? Any form of violence was supposedly impossible in the Chamber of Light. Whoever had committed the desecration should have fallen to the floor, incapacitated by simply conceiving such a crime.

Kevn pushed himself forward, unable to look at the ruined bodies any longer. Stepping past the doors to the antechamber, Kevn found several more bodies strewn across the entryway. Some were temple knights, others ei'ceuril. The far doors to the Ceurtriarch's office stood ajar and

Kevn made his way past the bodies and assorted pieces of furniture strewn about.

A weeping Aaron knelt with his back to the office door, obstructing Kevn's view as he approached. Kevn gasped and covered his mouth in shock at the sight of Ceurtriarch Ealyndol Roendryn, High Archsteward and Arbiter of the Light slouched on the floor with his back against his desk, a bloodied dagger protruding from his chest. His eyes were still open, and he managed slow, difficult breaths.

"Would you…" said Ealyndol, struggling to speak, "open the doors." He took several strained gasps between each word. There was no doubting what the Ceurtriarch wanted.

Kevn quickly returned to the entry where Kaeyeth and Taen hovered, and pushed the doors wide open, then the doors to the Chamber of Light beyond.

"Can one of you find a healer?" he asked, and with a quick nod, Kaeyeth went. Taen followed Kevn back to Aaron's side.

"You will…have to…" Ealyndol struggled to say.

"We're here now, we'll help you." Tears rolled down Aaron's face as he looked at the severely wounded Ceurtriarch.

Ealyndol simply shook his head slightly. The light from the opened doors bathed his slight form; a tiny smile came to his pale face. Looking into Aaron's eyes, and pointing toward the doorway weakly, he managed to say, "Through the portal…is hope endured…tell Devlyn." Ealyndol's eyes glazed over.

"I promise," said Aaron, then he repeated the Ceurtriarch's words.

Despite the soothing light, it was clear that speaking was causing Ealyndol incredible pain; Kevn thought he shouldn't try, but it wasn't his place to say so.

Ealyndol's eyes focused, looking directly into Aaron's. "Be at peace, my son…Do not be afraid, Aaron," he said. When he paused, Aaron tried to tell him not to talk, to preserve his strength, Ealyndol pressed on.

"Already, can I feel Anaweh's gentle call. It is written in one of the older scrolls…that in times of doubt and strife…the Ceurtriarch can appoint a successor of unquestionable dignity without the wise ones electing the successor."

Kevn had never heard of such a thing, and evidently neither had Aaron, considering the shock on his face. *What scroll is that hidden in?* thought Kevn.

"Who do you wish me to inform of your selection?" asked Aaron, his tears still falling freely as death gained a stronger grasp over the Ceurtriarch.

Ealyndol's mouth moved periodically as he tried to speak but Kevn couldn't hear any words. Then Ealyndol raised his right hand toward Aaron, and as he did, a burst of light shot from it and pierced Aaron's chest just where his heart lay. The whole room glowed in the light that passed from Ealyndol to Aaron.

When the light began to fade, so did Ealyndol. His eyes closed and a slight smile hovered on his slackening face.

Taen, watching the transfer, began to sing a hymn. Kevn had never heard it before it, but somehow, he knew it was appropriate—the passing of a great office from one to another.

Temple knights, wise ones, and archstewards began rushing into the room which got more and more crowded as every archsteward who saw to the spiritual welfare of Eklean's metropolises came to see for himself. Chaos ensued, and it became nearly impossible to make out anything anyone was saying, although Kevn did hear some casting blame on Kevn and Aaron without rhyme or reason. Taen and Kaeyeth had wisely left the Ceurtriarch's quarters to wait in the Chamber of Light.

Speaking loudly over the noise of the gathered ei'ceuril, a senior temple knight said, "Quiet, everyone. We need to sort out what's happened. And we need room to deal with those taken from us so violently." The room quietened, and a few of the ei'cueril had the wherewithal to look chastened. "I would appreciate it if only the most senior of you remained, while we seek answers." After some murmuring, and shuffling, and hand waving, most of the ei'curil cleared the room, leaving only a dozen or so archstewards and wise ones in the room. The knight turned to Kevn and Aaron.

"Tell us exactly what happened and why you came here." He

spoke in a level tone, and the archstewards and wise ones quieted themselves to listen. They too wanted answers.

Aaron still knelt beside Ealyndol, visibly in shock and willing to let Kevn speak for both. Kevn kept his eyes on the knight, finding it easier to describe what had happened if he didn't look at everyone. He told them of how they had heard the fighting in the lower levels and had come to warn the Ceurtriarch, and how they had found him severely wounded in his quarters, and a dozen or so temple knights and ei'ceuril already dead just outside the office.

The listeners were quiet at first, weighing and judging Kevn's words, then stirring in agitation at the magnitude of the events. The temple knight who was leading the questioning raised a hand to ask for silence.

"He did something before he died," said Kevn, nearly starting them going again. He paused to wait for them to completely quiet and looked toward Aaron. It was apparently too lengthy a pause for one of the elderly archstewards.

"We don't have all day," the impatient archsteward snapped. "As I'm sure you're aware, the temple is in complete upheaval and we are without a Ceurtriarch." Kevn recognized the Archsteward of Briel, an all but useless role now as all correspondence with Briel had ceased two decades prior. Not that any of the other archstewards had a significant role beyond letters and welcoming the stray pilgrim to the temple. As untrained kien wielders, they were not allowed to leave the temple.

Aaron's head came up and he leveled his gaze at the Archsteward of Briel. "He named a successor," said Aaron, his courage returning. Kevn was relieved, feeling that this news should come from Aaron himself. Kevn had said enough. After all, he wasn't the one named as Ealyndol's successor.

Every head in the crowded office turned to Aaron. This was important and each one wanted to hear the young ei'ceuril correctly.

"Such authority belongs with the wise ones. A Ceurtriarch cannot name his own successor; there is no precedent," said a scowling wise one.

The elderly Archsteward of Farenton stood near the Ceurtriarch's desk, calmly perusing the contents on it, perhaps seeking to unveil Ealyndol's final thoughts. Brushing loose parchment to the side, he picked up an unrolled scroll that rasped against his wispy white beard. "I beg your forgiveness, Josthiel, but this scroll claims otherwise," said the Farenton archsteward, rustling the pile of parchments.

He handed the scroll to Josthiel, who quickly scanned the lettering.

"And who did Ealyndol name?" asked the Farenton archsteward, brushing aside the interruption.

Kevn looked from the archsteward back to Aaron, hoping Aaron would continue the tale so that Kevn wouldn't have to repeat what Ealyndol had said.

"Me." The room was so quiet, Kevn could hear hushed shuffling beyond the Ceurtriarch's quarters.

The Farenton archsteward now looked at Aaron very differently. He was no longer simply looking at the great-nephew of their deceased Ceurtriarch nor an elven prince.

"This is not possible," Josthiel muttered as he read over the scroll.

The other archstewards and wise ones in the room began crowding Josthiel, asking to see and read the scroll themselves.

The temple knights in the room were more interested in dealing with the aftermath of the violence than who had been named Ceurtriarch or what might happen next. It was not their place to intervene in temple politics, especially when the most senior members were involved. The one who had led the questioning looked like he'd rather they all removed themselves to some other place to continue the discussion.

"Only the wise ones are raised to Ceurtriarch, and custom has seen only archstewards elevated to that position. And he hasn't been a steward for an entire year yet!" one of the wise ones stated.

"Neither of which are required. Customs are not law," said the Archsteward of Erithel, grinning as he spoke. He seemed pleased to avoid the customary politicking that went with the selection of a new Ceurtriarch. "I'm sure Aaron will make a fine Ceurtriarch. It will be interesting to live in an era where the Ceurtriarch can control the erendinth. Such has not happened for far too long I believe. If I didn't know better, Josthiel, I would assume the only reason you're upset is because now you don't have the opportunity to sway our minds to raise you to the office bestowed upon Aaron."

The single comment was akin to a small flame in a bale of hay; not a single wise one let it pass, and the bickering renewed. As they continued to squabble, what held Kevn's mind was what might be going on in the lower levels of the temple. What about the lay votaries—the untrained kien wielders who dwelt there?

"Has the fighting stopped?" Kevn interrupted, tired of the temple's hierarchy unseemly squabbling, when Ealyndol's body still lay in the room, a dagger embedded in his chest. He looked toward the temple knight who had earlier asked for an explanation of what he and Aaron had seen. There was a strained quality about him. "What's happened?"

The office quieted, everyone looked expectantly at the temple knight.

"The confusion in the lower levels ended just as quickly as it began. There are more casualties in this office than there are in the levels below. I'm of the opinion that those we fought did not intend a lengthy conflict. It seems some of the men confined below are still loyal to the ei'ceuril, despite how badly they've been treated over the years. It is difficult to spend your days with no particular purpose."

Josthiel made an impatient noise, wanting the temple knight to conclude his report swiftly so that the more important discussion of the Ceurtriarch's successor might resume.

"How did they get in? Was it a seguian?" asked Aaron. All heads turned to him; many gawked in astonishment, sharing the opinion that that was not possible.

Shaking his head before replying, the temple knight seemed to have finally received the missing piece to the puzzle. "That would explain it. I don't know how to tell you, um, your holiness, but they must have gone through the seguian."

"Yes, I assumed that they entered and left the temple through the seguian, but what did they do, besides cause a commotion? Was it only a diversion to assassinate the Ceurtriarch?"

"It very well might have been part of the reason. But you misunderstand. They're gone. The men in the lower levels, at least two thirds of them, are gone. They must've gone through the seguian to wherever it led," said the temple knight.

It finally clicked. The reality struck Kevn hard. As if the death of Ealyndol was not enough, hundreds of kien wielders had disappeared from the temple and were now under Erynor's protection. "Have the ei'ana been notified?" asked Aaron.

The temple knights looked uncomfortably toward the ei'ceuril, hoping that they had sent some form of message to Gwilnor Academy.

Understanding that no message had gone, Aaron said, "Now would be a good time to inform the Seven Chairs of Septyl that Erynor has liberated hundreds of kien wielders to serve in his ranks."

"Listen here, you might have received a recommendation for elevation to Ealyndol's office, but you have no authority to give orders to temple knights," said Josthiel, resentful to see another speak with authority that he clearly felt should belong to someone more senior, like himself.

Aaron had been speaking from where he knelt next to Ealyndol. His eyes were red from the tears that had fallen from them, yet he looked more determined than anything else as he rose to his feet.

"We have just been attacked, Ealyndol's corpse is not yet cold, and you question *my* authority?" Aaron looked at the temple knight before continuing. "Send a message to Gwilnor, immediately, make certain that it reaches every Chair—send seven of your knights if you have to. And have every corner of the temple searched. I want to know how many kien wielders are still in the temple, and when you find them, I want them brought into the Chamber of Light for examination."

The temple knights immediately left the Ceurtriarch's quarters, happy to have someone provide clear orders. Other than Josthiel and a handful of those likeminded, the ei'ceuril still in the room appeared pleased and relieved that Aaron was assuming control.

"Ealyndol might have named you his successor, but it is not yet finalized. We must study this scroll and determine its validity before we can accept such a radical motion against tradition, and proceed with the installation ceremony," said Josthiel with a strained voice. "Whether for you *or* another." It was clear that all he wanted was to gain some time to discover a flaw in what Ealyndol had done, and in that time, garner the required support for his own election.

"Tell us," said the Farenton archsteward. "When Ealyndol named you his successor, did anything happen?"

Aaron concentrated on the events at that harrowing time.

"It was just before he passed. He wanted the doors to the Chamber of Light open. After Kevn opened them, he pointed his hand toward my chest; a beam of light sprang from it and struck my heart—I felt it strike. The room grew to such a luminosity that I could barely distinguish one form from another. I could feel a vibrancy within my heart; there was another present—someone wholly different than myself. So much more, yet simpler at the same time. I was asked if I would serve; I said yes. I was asked if I would submit; again, I said yes. Lastly, I was asked if I would spread Light through every land and heart, scattering any and all Darkness; I said yes."

Kevn felt moved to bend his knee, and he was not alone; every archsteward and wise one fell to one knee and bowed their heads to Aaron.

The eldest was the first to speak. "Under your service, do I serve. With your submittal, do I submit. Through your willingness, will I also spread the Light and scatter the Darkness," he said, bowing even lower to the floor, nearly prostrating himself.

The others soon followed, each reciting the same phrase, and seeing that every archsteward and wise one spoke the words, Josthiel too bent his knee to join in what became a chant.

ALEXANDRIA

An early snow had covered the fallen leaves, turning the landscape white. It was not the first snowfall this Orenth, the last official month of autumn, nor would it be the last time, but it promised that the winter months to come would be bitter, cold, and likely bring much more snow. Alex wondered when he would next see the bare ground.

It also gave him more confidence in his decision and subsequent insistence, that they spend Kyrenth and Vespenth pushing westward. The newest soldiers—former farmers for the most part—had wanted to stay in Cor'lera longer, to ensure that their families and lands were prepared for the coming winter. While that was no surprise, the majority of the Parendian recruits had thought the same. The impending winter months simply provided an excuse. No matter that all of them were here because they believed it was time to do something about the Perrien Council, most were unused to the constant travel, and had gotten comfortable with their daily routines.

In Alex's lifetime, he had only heard of a few people traveling willingly from Cor'lera, and other than some of the merchants like Walei, they were typically winery owners whose purpose in traveling was to distribute the Cor'leran Blue. Alex was still amazed, shocked even, to have discovered that the famous ice wine had tripled in profit for its producers since he and Devlyn had snuck out of Cor'lera's abbey school in the night. It definitely had not been on his mind nearly three years ago when he'd stood with Velaria and Devlyn on the same bridge where he now stood in the chill wind, his cloak pulled tightly around his body.

The uncertain times and all the traveling had left many of the new soldiers and rebels easily irritated, and Alex had decided to remove himself from the midst of yet another squabble over something that might have been let slide if the participants had been at home. He had climbed to the crest of Aewen Bridge, adjacent to where the rebel forces had set up camp and settled in for the winter. Beneath the bridge's glassy surface flowed the River Arvil, dividing Parendior from Perrien. Alex looked west across the landscape, imagining the logistics required to transport several thousand soldiers, including horses, and wagons full of supplies. It was daunting.

At one moment, he was left in awe at the amount of support, the sheer numbers of those who had decided to join the Perrien resistance, yet in the next moment, he felt overwhelmed by the vast numbers surrounding him. He sighed in relief that a stabilized camp had been set up after crossing all Parendior's hilly terrain. The entire makeshift army was happy about that, squabbles notwithstanding. No one wanted to travel through Perrien or Parendior during the winter.

Marching an entire army through the hill country was difficult enough. Alex didn't want to consider what the conditions would be like once the heavy snows started to fill in the valleys. The current powdery snow on the ground was not much more than a chilly nuisance.

Several weeks had already passed since they had reached Aewen Bridge, and already superstitions were spreading about the Wooded Hills of Thellion due north. The rumors first originated from Parendians and Perriens who lived in small secluded villages in the northern territory, and swore that those wooded hills were haunted. Alex had heard someone claim that a witch summoned the ghosts of Elothkar to stalk amidst those trees.

During those weeks, more Parendians had flowed into the camp despite their distaste for traveling. What was of great concern to Alex though, is that it meant they also brought their innate desire to settle, and already, despite their superstitions about the Wooded Hills of Thellion, makeshift houses were being constructed, along with some wooden barns and stables.

Shortly after reaching Aewen Bridge, Alex had tried to prevent one family from building a home for themselves—they had already begun disassembling their wagon for construction materials. This was a *military* camp—a *temporary* camp! Alex had hoped that the ei'ana would help in deterring any construction, but rather than try to talk anyone out of it, the ei'ana went so far as to suggest naming the new settlement Alexandria. Alex quickly rebuked anyone who dared to say the name aloud, and insisted that they were at Aewen Bridge, and in a transitory camp. It was already enough to stomach being called Lord Alexander at every turn!

Despite his constant efforts to quell the naming of the growing settlement, he kept coming across scrolls soliciting more aid from the countryside, asking for able volunteers to join their fellow Parendians at Alexandria. He hated the idea that new recruits would arrive thinking that this place had been named in his honor. At that point, how many wagons would have been stripped apart and turned into houses?

As he brooded over the growing settlement, he caught sight of Aen jogging up the bridge toward him, his determination evident as he moved up the arc of the bridge. In fact, Aen exuded excitement. *At least he doesn't think the forest is haunted*, Alex thought.

Alex couldn't begin to think what might cause that excitement, since as soon as his official page was within shouting distance, he was calling out. "You're needed at once! There's an elf lady that came from the north and she wants to speak to the person in charge." A panting Aen stopped next to him, and Alex tried to take in what Aen's words meant, just as Aen gasped out, "My Lord." Past his irritation at the title he still refused to accept, Alex responded.

"Who is she? Does anyone know her?"

"Come on, she's waiting!" Aen yanked Alex's hand, refusing to wait.

"Is she the witch everyone is scared of? Did she bring her ghosts with her too?" Alex asked as Aen shot him a challenging glare.

"She is *not* a witch and she's pretty. Witches aren't pretty like her." Whoever this woman was, she had certainly made an impression on Aen. The boy pulled Alex through others who'd gathered on the bridge to look at the water below until they reached the eastern bank, where the settlement, no, the *camp* not called Alexandria, stood. Alex heard people whisper about the witch of the Wooded Hills of Thellion. Apparently, this woman or witch had not arrived in secret.

Once there, Aen pulled Alex north toward the brink of the make-shift buildings where a small crowd had gathered to observe Reia and Sara standing proudly next to Arlyn who was speaking with a peculiarly dressed elf of incredible beauty. *Definitely not a witch,* he thought. Alex had seen some odd fashions in his travels, but none were similar to the dress worn by this woman. It looked as though it was made of a single piece of silvery fabric that wove about her body, falling elegantly from her shoulders down to her toes. Silver hair draped over her shoulders, making it difficult to discern where the dress's fabric began and her hair ended. It didn't seem to be a warm dress, but she didn't seem to feel the cold.

Alex bent low and asked again, "Aen, who is she?"

"My Life did not pass to my children nor to theirs, but the blood in my veins flowed through them just the same, as it does in yours, Alexander Vaerin," said the elf. It seemed that she had remarkable hearing as well as the famed elven long-sightedness.

In his surprise, Alex nearly missed the intent of her words. He thought he had heard correctly, but what she said was not possible. "I'm sorry, but I must have misheard you."

"You need not doubt your own ears," said the elf. She stood tall and elegant, far more elegant than any other ei'ana, elf or human, Alex had ever seen. "My name is Aewen."

"Just like the bridge?" Aen asked, enthusiastic, but suddenly embarrassed by his voice falling into the silence, his ears turning a vivid red. The beautiful elf smiled.

"Nay, young one, the bridge was named for me."

"Truly, ma'am, you are the elf the bridge was named for?" asked Sara, sharing Aen's excitement. Aewen spoke to Alex again.

"I was once wed to the first King of Thellion, King Thellion I, himself. I mothered many children, and they too had many children. Countless generations followed until seven siblings each governed a portion of their father's kingdom before he passed. Evellion was the eldest and heir to the throne, but Dennion was the middle child, always jealous of his eldest brother, and joined his siblings to rebel against Evellion. Alexander, you are Dennion's descendent."

"Um, excuse me," Alex said, then came to a stop.

What else has history forgotten? asked a voice in Alex's mind. *Does it name the Lady of the hallowed halls of Elothkar as a witch? Do I also summon the specters of Elothkar's deceased?*

Alex's eyes flashed wide open and his mouth gaped in shock. Those were not *his* thoughts speaking in the privacy of his mind.

"I come to implore you to prevent your followers from felling the ilithae trees of the Wooded Hills of Thellion to the north. They are a memorial to Thellion, gifted by my elven kin after the civil war tore it asunder. Aldarch Gael came down from her sanctuary, Quel'anir, and planted the grove herself. The trees are also the last remembrance of the Skyland of Aldinare. In their pride, the Aldinari could not imagine anything taking their home and lifestyle away from them, and in their arrogance, lost everything. Vespiel has not stirred since."

Happy to not address everything that Aewen was saying, Alex narrowed his attention on her request. "I couldn't be happier to prevent the continued construction of this place." Alex smiled at the thought of telling everyone who had come to Aewen Bridge that they had to stop building their new settlement or else they would anger the witch of the haunted forest. Limiting the availability of fresh wood would keep it from growing into a true town.

"You misunderstand," Aewen replied, "I think it's appropriate that this land is being cultivated once more. I only implore that it is not done to the detriment of the ilithae trees."

"Forgive me, my lady, but how do you recommend our people build a settlement if not from wood?" asked Arlyn.

"Are you not a wielder, an ei'ceuril? Are not these women ei'ana? Surely there are others here as well." Aewen's questions were met with an uncomfortable silence as she took in Arlyn and the ei'ana's embarrassed expressions.

"There are a few among us," Reia broke the silence just before it became unbearable under Aewen's questioning gaze. "But I do not understand what wielding has to do with construction."

Aewen did not answer, but after a brief pause, the ground began to tremble. Aen drew close to Sara, who placed a comforting arm around the young boy's shoulders.

From the unbroken ground around them rose individual threads that spun together to join in an expanding form around the group who stood mesmerized by the marvelous creation as it unfolded. Alex's eyes flashed from one form to another as the interweaving threads formed stone walls, ceilings, and even solid floors beneath their feet. Each thread lanced outward and about. Soon, portals lined the walls to serve as windows and doors, the windows at the same massive scale as the doors. Columns, pilasters, and buttresses sprung from the threads and wove into the walls. Some of the magical threads had created a magnificent glass dome to enclose the expansive space.

Aen was the first to speak. "Wow, how many of these can you make?"

"As many as Alexandria requires."

"This reminds me of the Temple of Ceur, on a much smaller scale, mind you, but there is an unshakable likeness," remarked Arlyn as he studied the building.

"That is a place I would delight in beholding once more. Since you seem to have forgotten much of history, I will tell you that Aldarch Theseryn veered from the path of the pantheon, and desired to remind the mortals of this land below of Anaweh. Aldarch Lerathel agreed to assist Theseryn in his endeavor and wove an architectural design unrivaled in Aldinare. The newly founded Ei'ceuril, all of whom were once pledged to Aldarch Theseryn, sought out every stone of Teraeniel to create a temple that no other building could match. With the aid of Lerathel and the ei'ceuril, Theseryn directed their combined abilities in shaping that marvelous place," said Aewen.

"Of course, we were foolish to think that it was the work of the Luminari; their involvement in these lands below did not begin until the founding of Gwilnor Academy," said Arlyn.

The focus on the Temple of Ceur that was well out of their reach baffled Alex. He stared up at the crystal dome now sheltering him and the others from the snow, and considered the advantages of having a permanent settlement—as much as he wanted to avoid one—and the protection offered by stone buildings against the elements already warmed him, especially with the first of Estlenth only weeks away, marking the beginning of winter.

There was also the possibility of confrontation should they be discovered in the north. News of the Perrien resistance entrenched on the River Arvil would not take long to reach the Perrien Council. Stone buildings with thick walls far surpassed any defensive plan they currently had in place.

The possibilities continued to unfurl before his eyes as he not only imagined buildings springing from the ground, but also protective walls, gates, and even turrets to keep watch from. Alex immediately imagined archers atop battlements, protected by castellations. He only half paid attention to the conversation as he fantasized over what might became of the settlement at Aewen Bridge. The morale of the soldiers would also improve if they slept in buildings, rather than in tents with only thin canvas separating them from the cold. With endless possibilities, his ears caught a key phrase which drew him back to reality.

"Absolutely not," Alex objected. His enjoyable lapse into fantasy faded, his brow set and his eyes stern when he'd caught words that indicated the discussion had turned to training more wielders. "Under no circumstances will you scour through our ranks and diminish their numbers to place everyone here at greater risk than we already are."

"Under what authority do you presume you can prevent us from training wielders?" questioned Reia, hands on her hips. She was a fierce woman who typically reserved that intensity for strategy.

"Technically, he has no authority to determine this," said Sara. "The training and acceptability of kien and kiara wielders belongs to the Seven Chairs of Septyl alone."

"And when, dare I ask, did you get their blessing?" demanded Alex.

"Such blessing is only required for formal education at Gwilnor," said Sara, making Alex wish she did not possess the encyclopedic knowledge common to the Albiens, given that she belonged to Auburnis. Arguing with Sara was impossible.

Alex felt trapped; he knew he could not prevent ei'ana from training others and if Arlyn agreed with them, he was doomed. He would have a better chance at reversing the flow of the River Arvil than changing an ei'ana's mind.

"Balance must return," said Aewen. She had been standing patiently by as the others had discussed the possibilities afforded by a solid, defensible structure. "There are certain to be men among your numbers who will have a predisposition to wield, and I am certain that with a gathering this large, there are bound to be some who have an innate ability, especially those from Cor'lera with the blood of the Luminari running through their veins, particularly those of a singular noble house. They will begin to wield whether they intend to or not."

The thought of one of his soldiers beginning to wield in the middle of the night terrified Alex. All he could imagine was one of the large barrack tents overstuffed with soldiers and their gear catching ablaze as an individual accidentally wielded fire for the first time. Alex well remembered Devlyn wielding for the first time in the Queen of Evellion's sitting room and causing the door to smash against Alex's nose. When he realized that his hand had unintentionally risen to his nose, he feigned scratching it—relieved that there hadn't been any permanent damage. He'd always thought he had an attractive nose.

A week later, the small settlement had transformed under Aewen's guidance—the so-called witch of the Wooded Hills of Thellion. The soldiers had stopped using that title once they slept in a permanent building. Instead, she was now known as Lady Aewen, Queen of Thellion and queen of their hearts—Lady of the Wooded Hills of Thellion. Stone buildings wielded from the very stone of Parendior sat on the edge of the River Arvil with the approach to the east end of Aewen Bridge at its center, the rest of the settlement radiating east. Alex knew that it was only a matter of time before the same construction started on the other side of the river in Perrien. *So much for simply pushing Perrien forces out of Parendior,* thought Alex. *We're going to take it over.*

The buildings were unlike the one that Aewen had wielded; Aewen might have brought about the first one, but Alex had overheard Sara explain to Aen that the buildings took their form from the one wielding them into existence. Reia and Sara were accustomed to a different style of architecture than Aewen's. Because Reia and Sara had both spent the majority of their lives at Gwilnor Academy, the buildings they wielded took on a style similar to Gwilnor, which even Alex had grown to admire. It certainly was not his preferred style, but the defensive opportunities it provided were incalculable. And since they were in Parendior where the humans shared their own views of how their new town should look, those same wielders melded the different architectural styles into one. People started calling the style Alexandrian, making Alex groan whenever he heard the reference. Not only was there a blasted city named after him, but now an architectural style with his name had been born overnight.

When Aewen had offered to provide as many dwellings as needed, Alex hadn't understood that she did not intend to wield them herself, which when he thought about it, was a good thing, otherwise the growing settlement would have consisted of hundreds of domed structures. At least it wouldn't have been called Alexandrian!

Aewen never remained at the settlement overnight. Without fail, when the sun began to set, she would leave Alexandria and walk north toward the Wooded Hills of Thellion to the ruins of Elothkar. In Alex's opinion, that was a waste of time. Even though he didn't approve of her combing through the soldiers seeking wielders, both male and female, she could have devoted a much larger portion of her time to doing so if she just stayed in Alexandria. It would be better still if she raised a resilient defensive wall around the growing settlement.

Alex sat reading reports from Oliver at a simple wooden desk in his own apartment in one of the newly wielded buildings. It was one of the larger buildings and had a tower that offered a better vantage point than the highest point of Aewen Bridge. Well defended, it even had arrow slits in the walls, added at Alex's request, to help with its defense. In every sense of the word, the building was a castle. It was not a large castle, no where near even a small part of Gwilnor, but since the ei'ana had left the castle yard large enough for it to grow, who knew just how large it would be one day.

Alex had asked Arlyn to take up residence in the small keep. The ei'ceuril's wisdom and guidance was greatly appreciated. It also helped that Arlyn was Devlyn's uncle and native to Cor'lera, therefore trusted by the Parendians. Arlyn was one of them, just as Alex was.

After Arlyn moved in, Reia and Sara insisted that they also belonged in the castle, leading to an additional wing wielded from the ground as well as a chapel for Arlyn. He was an ei'ceuril steward after all. Naturally, Aen was also a resident and had taken on duties common to squires. Of course, he still maintained his responsibilities as a page, but he was a highly driven boy, intent on becoming a knight when he was old enough. In his mind, the first step was becoming a squire, which placed Aen constantly around Alex, who was not yet a knight himself.

As Alex read through reports, Aen sat quietly with his head buried in a book. "Do you think it's true?" he asked without giving Alex any indication of what he meant.

"What's that?"

"What Aewen said last week. About you and Dennion."

"I doubt it." *Not this again*, thought Alex, suppressing a groan.

"Why would she lie about it?"

"Couldn't say."

"I don't think she lies." Aen no longer looked at his book. "I think you should be king. Your family is from Perrien; you said so yourself. And it says here that the last king was forced out of power by that nasty council. And the name of their House was Vaerin! A branch of House Dennion. I'm trying to find out what happened to that king and his queen."

"All right let me see that book. And there could be hundreds of different Vaerins," said Alex, reading the title in bold print, *The Strength of the People.*

"It's about the Perrien Council overthrowing Perrien's monarchy and nobility. All the original council members were merchants of some sort," said Aen, proud with himself for remembering what he read. "Do you think the reason it doesn't say what happened to the last monarchy is because they don't know where they went? I think they went to Cor'lera and I think you should be the next king. King Alexander of House Vaerin!"

Alex brushed his hands through his blond hair, suddenly regretting his decision to allow a ten-year-old boy to constantly remain nearby. "Could you imagine that? Me strutting about wearing heavy furs and all! Even if your theory is right, I have older brothers and sisters, and our parents are still alive and well. They would have first claim to any throne. But I doubt the Perrien Council is going anywhere willingly." Alex couldn't help but think of the influx of Perriens to Cor'lera over the past century. He glanced at the shelf holding a pair of pruning shears, emblazoned with a double 'V' for Vaerin Vineyard. Alex had always thought that his father was a clever man, but if Alex's mother ever found out that he had sent some of their farm equipment to support the war effort, he would likely end up sleeping on the village streets. As he spoke, Aen came to stand next to Alex's desk with his elbows resting on the surface.

"But isn't that why we're going to Gneal?"

LIGHT ETERNAL

Devlyn stood in the Chamber of Light, waiting for Ealyndol's funeral to begin, his lierathnil garments in stark contrast to the white robes of the ei'ceuril. He was uncomfortable to be among so many ei'ceuril, many of whom still considered Devlyn a quitter for leaving the temple and their order. They were also aware of the prophecy, and his leaving meant that they thought he had doomed all Teraeniel. Their glances at him were not welcoming him back into their midst, no matter how solemn the occasion.

A full seven days of mourning had followed Ealyndol's passing while the body of Ceurtriarch Ealyndol Roendryn, High Archsteward and Arbiter of the Light lay in state in the Chamber of Light. Throughout the entire time, melancholic bells had tolled across Ceurenyl—even the Arenthylean Bells had been hushed in his honor. Devlyn was quite dependent on the Arenthylean Bells, and lost track of time which might have been unfortunate if lessons had not been cancelled for the duration of those seven days of mourning.

The funeral bier had rested in front of the Ceurtriarch's quarters and long lines of the city's inhabitants had formed around the vast circumference of the holy space so they could pay their respects. A rotation of young ei'ceuril and temple knights had stood vigil beside Ealyndol's remains. On first seeing the Ceurtriarch's funeral bier, Devlyn had mistaken it for a new altar. The Ceurtriach rested on a low pillowed bed between four lacelike columns rising twenty feet into the air to hold aloft a thin baldachin of intricate stonework. Sculpted roses and other flowers vined up the supporting columns, and wreathed across the baldachin, swooping down in wide girths.

It was only when Devlyn's eyes left the bier's lofty height that he noticed poles attached to the base of the bier. The entire contraption was intended to be lifted and moved—even the thin columns and baldachin. Devlyn tried to keep his jaw from dropping out of respect for Ealyndol and on account of the hundreds of people filling the Chamber of Light.

It appeared that everyone in Ceurenyl and beyond had come to the Temple of Ceur for the funeral at dusk on the seventh day of mourning. They filled the temple past its capacity. Every side chapel radiating around the Chamber of Light had standing room only and even then, people still spilled out into the adjacent corridors. This evening, the rarely used interior balconies were lined with dignitaries and people too important to be squished among the masses below.

Devlyn noted a few crowns amidst those gathered up above. How they had managed the logistics of traveling to Ceurenyl in a week with all Eklean threatened by Erynor's war left Devlyn baffled. *Perhaps a seguian?* Pain pierced Devlyn's heart at the thought. A seguian had facilitated access to Ealyndol and his assassination. Without a seguian, Ealyndol would still be alive.

Devlyn was not amongst those on the balconies. He had been given a place of honor, one that accommodated Aliel and Viren. He was someone of note, due to his status as a Phaedryn, but he wasn't a monarch, so the seneschal of the temple had placed Devlyn as close to the funeral bier as possible, in front of the Ceurtriarch's quarters. It wasn't so close that he stood in front of any of the Seven Chairs in attendance, or any of the wise ones. Whoever the seneschal was, he had ranked Devlyn's importance the same as an ei'ceuril or ei'ana, but since he was the only Phaedryn, he had been positioned directly behind the ei'ana wise ones where he could easily be seen by the mourners who cast glances at the mythical phoenix, a creature long believed extinct. Devlyn would have liked to be able to pay his respects to Ellendren, but she was with Mother Paurel, very close to the bier. For them, Ealyndol had been not just the Ceurtriarch, but family.

Devlyn glanced again at the impressive bier. Ealyandol's body lay as if on a cushioned bed, He didn't appear dead, only asleep, wearing his richest ceremonial vestments. Gold threadwork scrolled across the hem and great swaths meant to imitate the Creating Light's beams of light cascaded from his neck to his feet.

Devlyn bit back tears, not wanting to cry in front of the assembled crowd. But when Viren placed a comforting hand on Devlyn's shoulder, the touch was too much and Devlyn felt salty tears streak down his cheeks.

The hushed whispers that filled the sacred space broke off when deep sonorous bells announced the start of the Ceurtriarch's funeral. Behind the bier, the doors to the Ceurtriarch's quarters opened wide. Hundreds of ei'ceuril in ceremonial vestments processed out of the doors in a slow march, two by two. Devlyn recognized a handful of them as they passed. Although he had lived in the temple as a novice for a time, there were many ei'ceuril that Devlyn had never seen.

The solemn procession was led by the youngest and lowest of the ei'ceuril hierarchy, singing a hymn that filled the entire Chamber of Light with a somber melody. They took places on the benches that had been placed in rows in the empty area around the bier. The young ones were followed by elders and higher-ranking wise ones who seemed to number in the hundreds. It took a full hour before a dozen or so archstewards finally followed the long line to their individual seats, the procession as slow and as measured as the non-stop chanting of the hymn. Finally, Aaron, in his rich vestments as the new Ceurtriarch, entered the chamber behind the archstewards to take his seat in a chair that was better described as a throne. Younger ei'ceuril stood by to help the archstewards and Ceurtriarch with their heavy vestments so they could sit.

While each of the individual chairs for the archstewards was finely crafted, the Ceurtriarch's chair outshone the others. It was crafted from a cloudy silvery material that reminded Devlyn of lumaryl, but the color was all wrong.

"Viren," he whispered, "is that aldaryl?"

"Yes. I'm surprised you recognized it."

It was only its resemblance to lumaryl that had made Devlyn think so. He guessed it belonged to the Skylands. He knew it wasn't eldaryl, as he had seen that in the Eldin Wood, and it was unlikely to be cyndaryl. Great whorls of vines covered the sides of the aldaryl chair, giving way to cascading beams of sculpted light, radiating from a sun at the head of the chair. It rose well over Aaron's own head and everyone gathered could see the sculpted sun, emitting a light of its own.

The ritual stretched on with chants and prayers. Ealyndol's relatives, many of them wearing the white ei'ceuril robes under decorative vestments, rose to say their final farewells. They knelt on either side of the bier, along the two long poles. Mother Paurel, closest to Ealyndol's head, wept silently next to Aaron and Ellendren, Aaron's arm wrapped around his sister. All the Roendryn kin wept.

Then the archstewards followed a similar ritual, though not as many of them were weeping, as they chanted a solemn prayer, also kneeling around the bier.

Then Aaron returned to the bier when the archstewards returned to their seats, approaching not as Ealyndol's great nephew, but as the newly elevated Ceurtriarch. He rested his open palms on Ealyndol's temples, spoke an inaudible prayer, then led the entire assembly in a final chant. The hymn rose slowly at first, intensifying as the entire space filled with its harmony.

Four ei'ceuril, one of them Kaeyth, and four temple knights approached either side of the bier. They bent to grasp the poles and in unison, gently lifted the funeral bier. Devlyn held his breath as the top-heavy construction was lifted off the ground. It swayed slightly, but the men carrying it were clearly chosen for their strength, and it stabilized.

The light in the center of the chamber intensified then thrummed in unison with the hymn. The ushers carried the bier toward the center of the Chamber of Light. It was impossible to see through the luminosity of the chamber and the bier and ushers disappeared into that light. Devlyn half expected them to start floating since it was not uncommon to see ei'ceuril bobbing up and down as they hovered near the center of the chamber. Perhaps that was the reason for the heavy bier—to keep the ushers grounded.

The chanting slowed and the empty bier and ushers returned from the center of the chamber. Ealyndol's empty garments remained, his body vanished. Not enough time had passed for the ushers to undress the corpse and return the garments precisely to how they had been positioned. They simply walked into the light and walked back. Devlyn tried not to gawk at the sight of the vacant vestments.

The ushers returned the bier to its resting place and the recession began starting with the youngest and lowest ranking ei'ceuril.

BALANCE

Devlyn felt very out of place in his straight-backed and not-very-comfortable chair at the large round table in the Temple of Ceur. He sat in the same chair as everyone else around the table, except Aaron's—well, Ceurtriarch Aaron Roendryn's—chair. That chair had a sunburst cresting the top of it, and it towered over every other chair around the table. It was not the throne of aldaryl that had been used at the funeral a week ago. This one was crafted of wood, like the rest of the chairs, but the sunburst upped the grandeur, and clearly identified it as the Ceurtriarch's chair and therefore the head of the round table.

Ceurtriarch Aaron Roendryn sat at apparent ease in the chair, and while Devlyn hadn't studied the ei'ceuril histories as thoroughly as he should have, he was certain that Aaron had to be the youngest elf to ever occupy the chair as Ceurtriarch.

Aaron sat tall and confident, leading the current meeting—*could it drag on any longer?* Devlyn thought and shifted to ease his numbing parts—which concerned the merging of the studies of the temple's kien wielders with Gwilnor's ei'ana students. Facts and statistics were provided, boosted by the new Ceurtriarch's suspicion that if the lay votaries who had vanished from the temple had been given an opportunity to study and learn to control their wielding, they would never have willingly left in the first place.

Velaria was a quick supporter of the merge, as she shared similar suspicions over the disappearance of the temple's kien wielders. The rest of the Seven Chairs held varied opinions although none were as supportive as Velaria, and there were a couple who outright rejected the merge.

Luckily, a few archstewards and wise ones among the ei'ceuril thought as Aaron did, otherwise he would have been alone in his desire to reintegrate kien wielders with kiara wielders at Gwilnor. The vast majority of the ei'ceuril present refused the possibility, convinced that wielding kien only led to chaos and destruction. Trusting a kien wielder outside the protection of the temple's ward was not an option for them. The discussion had been lengthy, and loud.

"Balance is finally returning. There is no reason to restrain kien wielders to the temple any longer," Clara said calmly from her seat beside Aaron. She had already spoken exhaustively about how it had once been normal for both male and female students to study with the ei'ceuril and become stewards, something that had not occurred during the lifetime of any of the present ei'ceuril.

None of the wise ones knew how to rank her authority in their hierarchy. As far as they were concerned, the female stewards were thought to have all passed from existence. Her small monastery, hidden in the Ashton Wood, was the only known settlement of female stewards, something which had only very recently become common knowledge in the Temple of Ceur. Most of them refused to accept it or considered it scandalous. And while she did not look like it, she was the oldest ei'ceuril in the room. Devlyn would never ask, but he suspected she might even be older than Alethea. She too had been born on the Skylands and had even known Francesco, a human whose simplicity had strongly influenced Mainor Auburnis, one of the founders of Septyl.

"We must follow precedent," started the Brieli archsteward, one of the few wise ones who dared challenge Clara, emboldened by his title. "Ceurtriarch Ealyndol made ensuring the safety and wellbeing of Eklean his top priority. He would never recklessly release untrained kien wielders."

Aaron clasped his hands in front of his face, just below his eyes as Devlyn's own attention drifted at what promised to be a lengthy tirade. He stifled another yawn, attempting to hide his boredom.

Devlyn still could not believe Ealyndol had died. He had certainly lived a long life, but as Devlyn had so recently spoken with him, it seemed impossible that the person he still thought of as the Ceurtriarch was no longer around.

Unfortunately, despite Aaron's quick donning of his new mantle, Ceurenyl was in upheaval. Ealyndol's assassination had led to cries of outrage not only from every corner of the city, but beyond, to other parts of Eklean. Blame for Ealyndol's death was cast at any likely suspect. Even Devlyn had received a share of the accusations, despite being nowhere near the Temple of Ceur at the time Ealyndol had been murdered. Accusations had also been flung at the new Ceurtriarch since Aaron was not only present at the moment of Ealyndol's passing, but only Kevn, a lowly student with the ei'ceuril, had also been there to bear witness to Ealyndol naming Aaron his successor.

No one could say for certain where the rumors had begun or on what basis they were founded, but everyone seated at the table with Devlyn was aware that the rumors strained any sense of community remaining in Ceurenyl. Brawls routinely broke out in taverns and inns over the unorthodox succession, since everyone had an opinion and many felt that there should have been more thought given by the wise ones as to a successor.

Ceurenyl was a peculiar city. There was no reigning nobility, nor was it liege to any crown. The people of Ceurenyl felt deeply connected to their Ceurtriarch, much like the rest of the world's faithful to the Creating Light, but this city did not just depend on the Ceurtriarch for spiritual guidance. Their livelihoods and safety were also at stake. The Ceurtriarch was responsible for the protection and wellbeing of the entire city. Depending on the competency of the Ceurtriarch, the city either thrived or plummeted into disorder and chaos, which was something that had certainly occurred over the past millennium.

Steps had been taken to deal with security since the assassination. More guards patrolled the city, and more temple knights than had ever been assigned before were now not only stationed outside Aaron's new quarters, a small detail stood inside as well, since Ealyndol's murder had taken place in his own chambers. Despite the ongoing general unrest concerning Aaron's succession, he had been given full authority as Ceurtriarch. And as the new Ceurtriarch, he had ensured that Devlyn was included in these round table meetings. Devlyn was not just the only Phaedryn, but he was also the first kien wielder capable of wielding with control accepted into Gwilnor Academy. It didn't matter to Aaron that Devlyn was only fifteen years old and still learning the limits of his powers. Unfortunately, this meeting seemed more interested in mimicking the shape of the round table with its circular logic. Devlyn stifled another yawn.

His attentiveness perked up as his past tutor, Dorien, spoke. "The reason men with the ability to wield were first placed in the Temple of Ceur was because of their inability to control the erendinth and the destruction they caused when not confined. To freely allow them, not only to refine their ability, but become stronger in the erendinth is utterly irresponsible, and I will not support such a merge," he said. Many of the others banged on the table in approval and the noise level went up as comments flew across the room while Aaron maintained a calm demeanor.

Devlyn was concerned. If he were the new Ceurtriarch, he would have fired back, yet Aaron sat patiently and waited for the commotion to settle down before speaking.

"You forget, Dorien, such irresponsible kien wielders have already been loosed upon Eklean. They can now be found with Erynor, who continues to welcome more wielders by the hour—plucking them from unsuspecting villages, whether they wish to go or not," another wise one said when the noise abated somewhat. "If we do not permit the men still in the lower levels of the temple to train, we will not win this war. We might as well welcome back the shadow elves with open arms through our still-ruined gate. In fact, we must encourage them to train their abilities to better resist the Erynien Empire. Forgive me, honored Chairs of Septyl, but kiara wielders will not be sufficient in the battles to come. We have already seen that our lack of balance means we are easily overpowered."

Phendien sat among the Chairs, dignified in his robes of varying shades of green, customary of the Emradiel School. The wise one who had just spoken must have forgotten that the Chair of Emradiel was in fact a man. This was the first meeting between the ei'ceuril and the ei'ana that Phendien had attended, having arrived only shortly before Ealyndol's assassination. He leaned forward a little, to catch the eyes of the group around the table.

"Balance must return to these lands east of the Vespien Mountains." Phendien's gaze now fell on the most vocal protestors against the proposed merger. "Septyl cannot stand upon a single leg. The longer we refuse to teach kien wielders, the more likely will Septyl crumble beneath her lop-sided weight. The Seven Schools will perish into forgotten legends, and only the Tenebrae School will survive with Erynor as their Chair and Emperor. Every day that passes without specific steps to regain Balance will only leave us more susceptible to fading into history, never to resurface again. The Eldinari have not left their seclusion only to disappear into the pages of history."

Indistinct scoffs came from the greater gathering scattered throughout the room. Devlyn tried to identify the speakers of the various insults, but there were too many people in the room to be sure of any specific one.

"Do not be absurd," said Josthiel. "I refuse to believe that the Tenebrae School is anything more than a myth. It's a blatant threat from ancient days and nothing more."

"And what of Erynor? Is he also a myth to you? Do you think that Erynor could draw breath without resurfacing the Tenebrae School?" Velaria kept her steady gaze on Josthiel.

"Are you convinced of this?" Mother Paurel asked from beside Velaria who responded with an emphatic nod while maintaining eye contact with Josthiel. He squirmed a bit under her relentless stare.

"Very well. I wish it was not so, but as you said, with Erynor's influence, there are undoubtedly ei'ana bound to that abominable school which wishes to dominate all others. Sadly, and for quite some time now, I too have suspected, have told myself, that this possibility exists. I also told myself that it was not possible. However, I have come to believe that they are well entrenched amidst our numbers," said Paurel.

"If such a School exists, how, dare I ask, do you imagine you will uproot them from their hiding places in your castle?" asked Dorien.

Devlyn felt the room turn to ice as every Chair glared at the ei'ceuril wise one.

"That's enough, Dorien," Aaron cut in with a look just as cold and threatening. Before Dorien could argue with the young Ceurtriarch, Aaron went on. "It appears that we have few options. Either we maintain our current policy which restricts kien wielders from leaving the temple, a policy that is quickly becoming obsolete, considering it's possible for kien wielders to learn control again—I myself am proof of that—or we fill Gwilnor with those men who remain in the lower levels. Any ei'ceuril also capable of wielding can learn to hone their untapped ability at Gwilnor Academy."

Aaron looked around the table, making brief eye contact with those seated there. Devlyn saw some quickly avoid Aaron's look, while others held his gaze.

Mother Paurel rose, straightening her back slowly as she stood to her full height. Until the return of Father Phendien, she had been the most senior Chair and so was speaker on behalf of the Seven Chairs of Septyl. Phendien had refused the appointment, citing that his absence would make him a poor speaker.

"Do we, the Seven Chairs of Septyl, revoke the ordinance of the sixty-eighth year of the Fourth Age, the seven thousand nine hundred twenty-fifth year of the Third Era? Do we, the Seven Chairs of Septyl, accept once again our responsibility to kien wielders and admit them to Gwilnor Academy, to study our histories and theories, practice and refine the art of wielding kien, in anticipation of either living peacefully without harm to themselves and others, or joining us as sons and brother ei'ana?"

Mother Paurel remained standing, awaiting the other Chairs to voice their decisions.

Velaria and Phendien stood together, neither holding any reservations about kien wielders learning to wield. The risks and challenges were known, yet they both agreed whole-heartedly that Septyl's harmony was pivotal. Balance had to be restored between kien and kiara.

The other Chairs slowly stood as well, first Selenya, Chair of Albien, then Agnelle, Chair of Auburnis, and with an infinitesimal pause Loretta, Chair of Crimsyn. Loretta wore a remorseful expression, as if she fundamentally disagreed, but chose to go along without any prompting from the other Chairs.

Firmly on her seat was Mother Melanie Birkwell, Chair of Arantiulyn. Devlyn did not know her very well, having only seen her briefly in the corridors of Gwilnor. Like her predecessor Lenora, she too was human. Unlike Lenora who had been a native of Ceurenyl, Melanie was from Mindale and had grown up in its largest city, Farenton.

"Forgive my hesitance," she said. "But, I cannot in good conscience agree to these rash actions. After all, the only reason I stand in this position is because a kien wielder murdered my predecessor."

Paurel did not hesitate to respond. "My dear Mother, there are many reasons why I believe our acceptance of kien wielders is necessary, but that one is why I believe it is paramount. Mother Lenora wasn't just killed by a kien wielder; the abomination that killed her was a shadow elf. And if it wasn't for the recent events here at the temple, he would still be a prisoner here."

"There must be another solution. I understand the necessity for such actions, but the thought of men wielding freely once again troubles me. Forgive me, I know that we now have a few fine young men learning the art of kien, but there's no telling what might come to pass with unchecked admission of many more potential kien wielders into Gwilnor. Especially when it comes to an area that our magisters have no training for."

A hushed murmur spread through the room as those assembled agreed with the Chair of Arantiulyn. Devlyn could tell that Paurel wanted to say something to comfort the younger Chair, but Melanie's reasoning was solid. Gwilnor Academy was unequipped to accommodate a large number of kien wielders and support and safeguard their training.

"Perhaps we can assist with that," said Phendien.

"What do you recommend, Father?" Paurel asked.

"I understand that a new magister has been assigned to teach the art of wielding. I would not suggest removing her from her post, but perhaps an addition to that class would be most prudent, to meet the growing needs of Gwilnor. I have in mind two Eldinari ei'ana, a brother and sister who once taught at Gwilnor, before our withdrawal. I believe that if asked, they would consider returning to their teaching positions. They are excellent magisters and have continued to train wielders all these years in the Eldin Wood."

A moment passed where everyone gathered seemed to consider the proposition. Melanie looked up toward Phendien and then Paurel. "I would feel much more comfortable if that were the case." Melanie stood to join the other Chairs who had remained standing.

"Are we agreed?" asked the Chair of Vyoletryn. In unison, every Chair of Septyl responded positively. "Ceurtriarch Aaron Roendryn, do you as High Archsteward and Arbiter of the Light bless this revision and release unto us the responsibility of kien wielders?"

When Aaron stood, his head rose to the center of the carved sun at the top of the chair behind him and it looked as though the carved beams cascaded from him and not the chair. As the Ceurtriarch, Aaron alone held the final decision among the ei'ceuril. There would be no vote among the archstewards and lower ranking wise ones.

"May Anaweh, the Creating Light, bless this joyous occasion and guide the hearts of every wielder." Aaron made an odd gesture with his hand toward the Seven Chairs, and as he did, a luminous quality filled the chamber.

It was not a blinding light, but Devlyn was finding it more and more difficult to judge the brightness of various lights since he and Aliel had bonded fully together. It did not last long, only long enough to bathe everyone present, and it indicated that the meeting was over.

The room began to empty and Devlyn overheard the archstewards speaking amongst themselves, both positively and critically about the decision. Devlyn lingered, wanting to speak to Phendien.

As the room emptied, Phendien also dawdled for a moment before approaching Aaron. "Perhaps we live in the days when lumenys is to be wielded from the Temple of Ceur once more," he said, referring to the light that had bathed the meeting attendees.

"Truthfully, I have no idea how I did it. I don't even think I had any control over it. It just happened," said Aaron, staring at his hands, still somewhat awed by the sudden appearance of the light.

"Never neglect the power held within words. Too many here believe that the erendinth are powers to be controlled—they were part of this world long before the Children drew their first breath. The erendinth are as old as creation itself."

"Would you be willing to instruct us in wielding lumenys?" Devlyn asked, drawing closer to the Chair of Emradiel and the young Ceurtriarch.

"It is beyond the realm of teaching. Surely, Alethea has taught you this," said Phendien. "Do not try to force it; you will only delay your progress. Allow it to happen to you—it is pure gift."

"Thank you for your wisdom," said Aaron, choosing words that were nowhere near the ones in Devlyn's mind.

Phendien inclined his head in appreciation and started for the door.

"Before you go," said Devlyn, remembering the reason he stayed behind in the first place. "Would I have met these two magisters you mentioned?"

"Not likely. They belong to the Lesser House Glaeda, grandchildren of the current Aryl of Glaeda. They rarely spent time in Stellantis, preferring the dwelling of their kin in the northern reaches of the Eldin Wood, Glaethyl. Myrah belongs to the Albien School and devoted her entire life to study and education, choosing not to marry. Fyreh on the other hand, married young for an elf and every couple of centuries or so, he and his wife add another elf to the Glaeda family. He belongs to the Azurelles and is an outgoing ei'ana with a passion for teaching. Before we withdrew to the Eldin Wood, he had taught several classes for the Azurelles.

"When will you ask them to come to Gwilnor?" asked Devlyn.

"I have no authority over them or their position at Gwilnor. Remember, they became ei'ana long before we withdrew from the rest of the world, and they were not restricted in their choice of which School to join. Also, the decision to invite them to teach belongs to the chancellor alone."

As Devlyn was about to follow Phendien out the door, Aaron caught his arm.

"Before he died," Aaron blinked away a tear, still holding Devlyn's arm. "Ealyndol asked me to tell you something."

Devlyn swallowed. He sorely missed Ealyndol and the suddenness of his assassination pained him, but he was afraid that whatever message the deceased Ceurtriarch had for Devlyn revolved around the prophecy.

"He said, 'through the Portal, is hope endured.'"

DISTANT RELATIONS

Devlyn studied the lierathnil map on the wall of the study in his apartment, staring at the sunken city of Lankor, which according to this old map, was not sunken at all. Broad tree-lined avenues wove across the silken tapestry with majestic public buildings dotting either side of the grand streets. On a table near the tapestry were several newer maps of Yanil that showed the current city of Lankor. Some of the maps were quite old, and only showed the first stage of the city's construction as a single floating peninsula east of the River Eindol. Other maps showed its current state, two prongs separated by the River Eindol and a keep wedged between the two.

From history lessons with Magister Ethyl, Devlyn recalled that after their original city was lost to Nauto's Wrath, the Yanilians had built the new city so that a catastrophe like that would never claim their home again. They were a people of the sea—they would not be bested by it again. Ethyl refused to mention where they had mined the floating stone. Perhaps if he had completed his research on the city, he might have discovered it for himself. *Elle will know*, he thought, but she rarely had the time for questions these days.

Ever since she had joined the Vyoletryn's erendinth team, half of her evenings were devoted to training with her teammates. Vyoletryn's first practice match was only a few weeks away and they were up against Emradiel and Crimsyn. The real games would not be played until after the new year began in Marenth, still three months away. But the seven teams wasted little time as they prepared through the autumn and winter months.

Luckily, Ellendren was with the others in the adjacent solar, and as Devlyn examined the ancient city, conversation buzzed from the other room. He had excused himself from the others to examine the maps again. He needed more time to study them, even after the first guests had arrived.

Wyn and Alethea had arrived early that Saraen morning, as they did every Saraen morning. Alethea used that scheduled time to train Devlyn and Wyn together, often running through wielding exercises, but rather than wielding this morning, she'd had them perform breathing exercises for well over an hour. That had only ended when Velaria and Ellendren had arrived, which was a surprise to Devlyn since neither gave a reason for their unexpected visit to Devlyn's secluded apartment in the South Tower.

Devlyn's heart leapt as Ellendren walked through the door, but instantly regretted that the others were also in his apartment. He didn't know what he would say to her if they were alone, maybe comment on how much he liked her silky gold and silver hair. Did she like people complimenting her hair? It's not like she had done anything to make her hair that color. Maybe he should focus more on how good of a wielder she was, or her soon-to-be success playing the Erendinth Games. Either way, all of that would have to wait. He did hope that she noticed the lumaryl phoenix resting on the mantelpiece.

Then, as if there weren't enough people visiting, Therril arrived last, and immediately questioned why no one had bothered to tell him that there was a lucilliae at the bottom of Lankor Bay. So, it seemed that someone had called a meeting and forgot to tell Devlyn that it was going to be held in his apartment. And, it would be about going to retrieve another lucilliae. *About time.* They discussed various suggestions for how they might attempt to do so, until Devlyn had stepped away from the already lengthy meeting, needing to reexamine the maps of Lankor.

Devlyn renewed his focus on the maps. The current city had minimal roads. Instead, hundreds of canals dictated the cityscape, and many bridges spanned the canals. After one last comparing look between the old and new cities, Devlyn spun away and rejoined the others in the solar.

"This is impossible." Devlyn pushed both hands through his hair. "How are we supposed to go into a city that bans wielders without them discovering who we are. It's not as if we can fly in without them noticing a Phaedryn or a dragon. Or can we?" Devlyn rose a questioning eyebrow to Alethea. She sat nearest the fireplace, picking grapes from a bowl on her lap. Devlyn still wasn't positive about the full extent of her abilities—or his own for that matter.

Everyone in the room knew why Devlyn wanted, better yet needed, to go to Lankor. They not only knew, they intended to participate in retrieving the lucilliae buried in the waters beneath the current city of Lankor.

"No, they are both far too noticeable," answered Wyn, scratching his chin. "There are alternatives, though. I know it's not customary, but it might be permissible to use griffins."

"They are, without a doubt, far less noticeable," said Viren, considering the implications of such a tactic. "We might go unseen if we arrive after nightfall."

"True, but that is something they would expect. They know the Eldinari have abandoned their seclusion. They will be watching for griffins," Therril said.

"Only if they know we are coming," said Alethea.

"What makes you think they don't know?" Therril returned.

"We have given them no reason to suspect that we have interest in visiting Lankor."

"What if they know what lies hidden in that watery grave? What if they are concealing something else there that they do not want the Lucillian Alliance to acquire? At least, what's left of the alliance."

"You're speaking foolishness, spitting out reasons to avoid the use of our griffins." Alethea placed the now empty bowl on the small table beside her.

"Just because one nearly took my arm off when we were younger and tolerated each other, does not mean I'm afraid of those beasts you call dignified."

Everyone in the room stared openmouthed at the two elderly elves arguing back and forth. "Sorry to interrupt, but how do you know each other?" asked Ellendren, calming the room with her gentle inquiry. "It's been on my mind ever since I saw you two together that first time in the temple when we returned to Ceurenyl."

"My apologies for this bickering, Princess," said Therril, attempting to rein in his temper. "I've kept a secret for quite some time, one more fragile than Velaria's Cyndinari ancestry. I suppose I have kept it unspoken long enough; but take care not to spread it across all Eklean." The old elf took a deep breath before speaking again. "Many in Ceurenyl believe me to be an incredibly old elf, however none know exactly how old I am. Which, let me assure you, is quite old." Therril chortled in his typical fashion, quickly forgetting his spat with Alethea.

"How old are you exactly?" asked Wyn, a heightened sense of reverence evident.

"Let's see here," said Therril, eyes rolling up to the ceiling as he calculated his age. "I was born during the Second Age of the Third Era, after the elves left their Skylands, which might I add, makes me at least several thousand years younger than Alethea here," said Therril, with a nod in feigned reverence at her. Alethea responded with an accusatory expression for the *younger* elf.

"That would have been 1538 of the Second Age, or 4772 of the Third Era, if you prefer. That would have allowed four thousand two hundred ninety-seven autumns to pass since my birth."

Alethea was the only one in the room who was not astonished by Therril's age. "They did not understand what you said; whether that was intentional on your part or not, I will not say. But say plainly what you're not and do not leave it there," said Alethea. "And I have seen twelve thousand five hundred twenty-eight *winters*, which among the civilized warrants respect." Alethea's age made Devlyn shiver. He couldn't grasp how a body could endure for so many years. And she still looked younger than Therril! No wrinkles on her smooth face, and only her white hair hinting at her advanced age.

"Oh, very well, you old busybody! What my dear *elder* is trying to point out, is that I have not explained *who* I am. Before you ask how it was possible for me to reach such an advanced age without the Jewel of Life, it's because my Life was never connected to it. I count the years with the passing of each autumn, as does every other Aldinari. My parents were among the minority rescued from the Skyland of Aldinare when it was lost—consumed by the Darkness. And, while we're at it, the second bit that my dear *elder* is referring to has never been spoken aloud. Not once did I permit those words to escape my mouth, not even to my own sons."

Devlyn thought he heard the ancient elf right. *But, he's an ei'ceuril, they can't have children. Was there once a custom for ei'ceruil to marry and have children?* He didn't say anything, and with a quick look around noted that he was not the only one thinking it.

"Before Krysenthiel fell, I was an ei'ana of the Auburnis School. When the Shroud blanketed that blessed realm, I was trapped with all my Aldinari kin in Arenthyl. We made a home in the Grotto of Verakryl, the Tree of Life, but as the years passed, we learned that we could safely explore the city, but only if we did not veer from the roots of the Tree of Life. They protected us from the Shroud, and despite our inability to leave, we lived without want. As time passed, I began to have dreams of a young woman, a Luminari as it turned out. She claimed my heart from the first moment. Her determination brought her to Arenthyl, with the sole purpose of retrieving a lucilliae, the jewel of faith, which had remained there when the Luminari had been dragged away in chains.

"She did not remain long in Arenthyl, but it was long enough for unexpected love to blossom between us. An Aldinari ei'ceuril married us before her departure." As he spoke of the woman, a smile lit Therril's features. "I knew that if I left with her, she would die in what to me would be no more than a breath, leaving me to live the rest of my days alone. My kin also knew this, so with their counsel, I remained in Arenthyl. And so it was; not a year passed before she breathed her last, but as she died, she came to me in a vision in her last moments and I saw the birth of our children, twin boys. They were beautiful and looked every bit like their mother.

"If it were not for them, I would have remained in Arenthyl, but I could not abandon them as orphans. I sought the advice of the Aldinari ei'ana and ei'ceuril still in Arenthyl hoping they could suggest a way to escape the Shroud. They told me I would likely die. I didn't care—I had to leave. With a complex wield, I began my journey east from Arenthyl across the now-frozen lake.

"I felt my body age and my wielding weaken. I thought I would die before I reached the land beyond the frozen crystal blossoms of Krysenthiel. But, with Anaweh's help, the sun at last touched my skin for the first time in over two hundred years. Yet, I paid a terrible price." Therril looked at his shriveled hands. "I was in my prime when I began my traverse. The passage aged my body and my ability to wield was sucked from my very being into the Shroud, feeding it and giving it strength. And let me tell you, I was quite the handsome formidable young elf back then and still would be if I had never left." Therril's slight levity lightened the mood and a quiet moment passed before Therril went on.

"I found the Luminari caring for my sons. They were treated with such tenderness; it was as if their mother had never left them. Because of the great changes wrought to my appearance by passing through the Shroud, I withheld my identity and my origins from everyone, especially my sons. I let the legend of what was to come breathe into their identity."

"You never told your sons who you were?" asked Devlyn, unable to bear the thought of never knowing his own father.

"They knew me, and they might have guessed my identity; the heart recognizes things the mind is blind to. But they never told me that they knew. I looked much as I do now, an old elf. I did not want to disrupt their authority by informing them that they had more than Luminari blood in their veins. If they had discovered the truth, it would have raised questions with answers that the recently liberated Luminari were not ready to hear."

"Your story matches another; one that is well known to my family. The woman you spoke of," said Ellendren, connecting the dots more quickly than Devlyn, "her name was Lucillia, wasn't it? No one ever knew Roendryn and Feolyn's father; Lucillia never told anyone his name nor even spoke of him before she sacrificed her life."

Therril smiled in ecstatic joy. "Never a name so beautiful; never an elf who so reflected the beauty of the lucilliae she was named after. She never needed the jewel of faith which remained in Arenthyl; her faith was greater and had no equal. She risked her life so that she might return it to her still-enslaved people. Where she found the courage, I'll never know. But, in the moments of her passing to Lumaeniel, she sung her prophecy to me."

"That would make you," Devlyn muttered, finally tying the pieces together, "our ancestor." Speaking the thought was overwhelming. How could such a thing be possible. It was too unimaginable to even grasp.

Therril smiled. "I told you when we first met how much you looked like your father, but I was not speaking of Dolan, but of your distant forefather, my son, Feolyn. Granted you bear a stronger resemblance to Feolyn's bride."

"That also means we have Aldinari blood running through our veins. I always wondered why my family had hair so light," said Ellendren as she held up her arms to look at the veins on the underside of her pale forearms.

"And if my mother was both Luminari and Aldinari, and my father was both Eldinari and Cyndinari, then my sister and I are of every elven kindred." Devlyn's astonishment grew by the second. Only several months had passed since he'd discovered his father's mixed heritage, and less than three years ago, he'd learned that he was an elf, and not just a human with elven blood, as had been deceitfully told in Cor'lera.

"It's about time you riddled that out," said Therril. "Haven't you ever wondered why your features were slightly different? Even among the elves in Cor'lera. Your skin tone and hair are most telling. I mean look at your hair; you have the brown of the Luminari, a bit of red from the Cyndinari, some blond, what mine used to look like, and even some black from the Eldinari. The Luminari always had golden brown hair, but yours has a distinctive quality not found on any elf that once lived on Luminare. And your skin tone is incredibly unique, I doubt there's another like it, other than your sister of course."

Devlyn turned to look at himself in the mirror on the opposite wall, as if seeing himself for the first time. It was odd how it was different. Remembering the picture that Lex had stolen in Cor'lera, outside of the Cor Inn, he remembered that even though he saw a lot of himself in his mother, there were differences.

"It's also the reason, you, Ellendren, and your family, descendents of Roendryn, have lighter features, common to the Aldinari," said Alethea. "However, Devlyn, while you come from every elven kin, you are above all a Luminari, as you well know by now, of House Lorenthien. A covenant was created between the Luminari and the phoenix long ago, one which saw the rise of the Phaedryn. The phoenix bonded themselves in service to the Luminari and their descendants; Aliel would have gone to no other anacordel. His allegiance belongs to the elves of the Rising Sun. Certain blood lines are incredibly strong, and none are known to outshine the Lorenthien line."

While Devlyn had indeed known his lineage for a while now, it was obvious that he had forgotten to mention that bit of information to Ellendren, for she turned on him quicker than a shadow elf could wield tenebrys. Noting her reaction but choosing to not entertain the brewing dispute, even though he found it amusing, Therril said, "I wondered when you might find out. How long have you known?"

Racking his mind to remember when he had found out, it finally came to him. "While we were in the Eldin Wood, during my first session with Alethea," said Devlyn, resurfacing memories of Mar'anathyl. It was only after he'd spoken that he wished he'd said he could not remember. Ellendren was hurt, clear from the look of betrayal on her face. Then it shifted, and she crossed her arms and her expression made Devlyn's blood turn cold.

"Have you unveiled the connection yet?" asked Alethea.

Devlyn nodded although he still could not explain how he'd discovered it. The words and understanding about his ancestors had simply spilled out after he'd told Ealyndol about his decision to leave the ei'ceuril.

The pit in his stomach deepened at the thought. If he responded honestly, Ellendren would never forgive him for not telling her. Looking at her with his most apologetic expression, he outlined his antecedents. "Feolyn married an elf named Gwendolyn; her parents were Oblivyn and Ellyn; but Oblivyn never learned of his heritage. However, his parents were Garethyn and Ulienne; Garethyn was the youngest son and heir of Ei'denai Faerndryn and Ei'terel Ithendryl Lorenthien—the Exalted Aryl of Krysenthiel."

"Remarkable," said Therril, more to himself then any one present. "Absolutely remarkable. I always liked Gwendolyn, but I never imaged she was a Lorenthien. Just imagine, me speaking to Faerndryn and Ithendryl's great granddaughter without even knowing it! I should have picked up on it at their wedding—Gwendolyn looked every bit a Lorenthien."

Ellendren's glare hardened, making Devlyn feel worse with every word he spoke.

He tried to muster every remorseful muscle his face was capable of for not telling her earlier. It had simply never occurred to him. To make matters worse, it seemed that she was the only one in the room who had been unaware of his lineage. He knew he should have informed her after that meeting in the Eldin Wood where Boriel, one of the enthiel, appeared and announced to the Eldinari aryls his identity, and everyone else present. Ellendren had angrily left the room a short while before, and missed the pronouncement.

"It appears we have gotten quite sidetracked," said Viren following a strained moment of silence. "Are the griffins our only option?" Everyone seemed to shake themselves out of their thoughts, and then Ellendren spoke.

"What about the Jahronese Seafarers? I'm sure they could secret us into Lankor without anyone there learning of it." She looked at everyone but Devlyn. Her crisp tone was devoid of any emotion.

"Now that's what I call a suggestion!" Therril beamed at Ellendren.

"Yanil will not have forgotten that they attacked Josque. Do you expect the Yanilean navy to allow known hostiles anywhere near their capital, let alone in Lankor Bay, without attacking?" asked Alethea, rekindling the animosity between Therril and herself, and making Devlyn incredibly grateful since it shifted the focus away from his lineage.

Wyn smiled and wielded a globe of water to pass the time. The water spun in sinuous shapes through his hands as he listened to the two older elves bicker again.

"You're just picking at anything I think is a good idea because you're upset that I've always supported the institutionalization of wielding," Therril fired back. "How many times do I have to tell you, that it is simply not supportable for Septyl to divide her resources to such an extent that every ei'ana coddles individual student wielders before they are stable enough to either profess the Counsels or live out their lives beyond Septyl's protection. And besides, as far as anyone knows, the Jahronese Seafarers are nothing but independent pirates, willing to sell to the highest bidder!"

"Don't you start that with me again. It's undeniable, it is absolutely necessary that every young wielder, especially those who intend to become ei'ana, serve in some form of apprenticeship with someone more experienced," retaliated Alethea. "The Seven Masters were rather adamant about it."

"Not even you were alive when they walked in this realm."

Velaria had an odd concentrated look, as if something finally made perfect sense. "That's it! You've both answered it," said Velaria, confusing everyone else. What was she referring to? "We'll have to continue this discussion at a later point. I have to speak with Aaron immediately, because between the two of you, you've come up with the solution to our problem." Velaria turned to leave the room just as the Arenthylean Bells began to toll, and the meeting adjourned. Ellendren was quick to follow behind her, not wanting to give Devlyn an opportunity to apologize or even say goodbye.

Devlyn's apartment emptied, even Viren excusing himself to go attend to something, promising to return quickly but leaving Devlyn and Aliel alone. Instead of moving to a chair or a couch to relax after the lengthy and chaotic meeting, Devlyn returned to the study and planted himself in front of the lierathnil map and stare some more at the ruins of Lankor in their watery grave.

"Where are you?" Devlyn asked aloud to no one in particular.

Aliel remained upon his perch and stared quizzically at Devlyn and the map. He did not convey anything; there was nothing to convey.

As he stared at the tapestry, fixated on the enlarged view of the former city of Lankor, it began to grow hazy and a layer of what seemed to be water washed over it. Huge waves collapsed against buildings and torrential rain fell from the sky. Thunderous lighting crashed through the ominous clouds and Devlyn easily recognized the tenebrys lightning the shadow elves used, only it did not come from wielders, but from the sky. Hundreds of thousands of people panicked in the flooding streets, screaming and running in every direction. Some searched for loved ones, while others sought safety. One woman, dressed in robes with layers of white and purple, ran through the unstable crowds toward a tholos in the center of the city about to founder. She ran through the rising water, through the abandoned tholos to its center where a sculpture of a blind-folded woman stood on a low plinth. The water rose faster and faster, already above the woman's knees.

Devlyn watched as she tried to wrench something from the statue's hands. Her arm muscles strained as she pulled with all her might, yet she could not budge the object resting there. "Help me, if we don't take it from here, it'll be lost forever."

"It's not worth losing your life over," pleaded Devlyn, trying to convince her to flee the doomed city.

"Do you have any idea what this is? An elf should know! Lives such as my own are short without this. I could serve no better than to sacrifice myself if it meant safeguarding this gift."

"What good would retrieving it do if you die in the process?" asked Devlyn, growing desperate to convince the woman to flee.

She looked at him steadily even as she shifted between the statue and him before saying, "Only if you promise with your Life that we will come back to retrieve it."

"Sure, I promise, anything, now let's get out of here," said Devlyn. No sooner did he speak than the vision and the woman in the flooding city disappeared.

Devlyn found himself lying on the floor of the study, his head aching badly. The flooding waters had vanished.

Aliel brushed his warm beak gently across his face. *Where did you go?* asked Aliel, more concerned than Devlyn had ever felt from the phoenix. *You were gone. Your body was here, but not you. It was as though you died.* Panic laced Aliel's communication.

I…I don't know what happened. It felt like a vision, except I truly interacted with someone, Devlyn conveyed. *Whatever happened, I'm happy it did. I know where the lucilliae is. I saw a tholos, and in the center of it was a statue holding the lucilliae.*

FORGOTTEN PRACTICES

How did you not realize what you were doing?" exploded Eagan right after Devlyn described his vision of Lankor. The Druid of Kweil Aitch's face had grown redder by the second as Devlyn had described the woman and the tholos and by the time Devlyn finished, Eagan's face nearly matched his hair color.

Devlyn had never seen the mild-mannered druid so angry, an anger that strongly tempted Devlyn to withdraw from Somnaeniel and wake up in his own bedchamber in Gwilnor Academy, warm and comfortable beneath his blankets rather than suffer the admonishment for having experienced something that Devlyn considered as a good thing. He now knew precisely where the lucilliae lay undisturbed in the sunken ruins of Lankor.

"Did you not realize that you'd left your body entirely? That if you had been killed during Nauto's Wrath—which destroyed Lankor entirely and killed most of its citizens—you would not, *could* not, have returned to your body? That you would have died and passed on to the World-Beyond?"

"What are you talking about? I had a vision, nothing more." Devlyn interrupted the unexpected outburst, trying to recall what Aliel had said when he'd awoken from the vision. It was an odd situation where, as in every other vision he'd had in Somnaeniel, he had visited and explored a place beyond his physical body, although Aliel had never been concerned about any past visions. "Besides, what else could it have possibly been?"

"He really doesn't know, Eagan; you'd better explain it to him," said Abbie. Unlike Eagan, she didn't seem angry, just concerned. Eagan's anger was something Devlyn would have expected from Abbie, whose red hair often rivaled her fiery disposition. Eagan had always been more even-tempered than Abbie.

Devlyn wondered whether she would have had the same reaction as her brother if she'd been the first one to hear of it. More likely than not, she would have.

"What you did should not have been possible. Not even a Phaedryn, not even the strongest Phaedryn who ever lived could manage what you did, and you are nowhere near that caliber!" Eagan slapped his forehead, fury mixing with concern over what Devlyn had done.

Eagan never worried. This was the first time he had ever expressed any sort of emotion while in Somnaeniel. And once Devlyn thought about that, he understood that a dormant and deep-set fear lay encased in Eagan's anger.

Eagan wasn't just angry, he was terrified.

"What's your point?" asked Devlyn. Eagan's ambiguous word choice, better yet, shortage of words only contributed to Devlyn's own and growing ire, a response to being scolded at like a toddler.

"My point is that you should not have been able to do what you did!"

"Which is?" Devlyn asked again, clueless about exactly what he'd done and should not have been able to do in the first place. Neither Eagan nor Abbie had ever spoken of any restrictions before, whatever it was he had done.

Eagan paced back and forth, clearly trying to calm himself before speaking again. Devlyn had never seen Eagan so riled up; he doubted that even Abbie had ever seen her brother so agitated.

"That was no vision," Eagan said taking one last deep breath, and coming to a halt. "You went back in time. You went to the exact moment when Erynor unleashed Nauto's Wrath upon the original city of Lankor, resulting in its flooding and eventual sinking beneath Lankor Bay. Not only did you travel back in time, which you should not have been able to do, but you did what has been forbidden in every codex and law of your people; you interacted with someone from the past! Do you have any idea of the implications, the ramifications, of your actions, what you most likely caused?

"There is a reason that ability was confined to a single object, one possessed by the Keeper, leader of the Time Wardens. For you to have been able to accomplish such a thing does not speak of your own abilities, but rather, of something wrong. It's no secret that Erynor has taken a minum as a prisoner. I can't imagine what kind of cruelty and torture he's going through. For a minum to create a seguian into the Temple of Ceur for servants of Shadow would require unimaginable torture." Eagan glared daggers into Devlyn's eyes.

The more Eagan explained, the more Devlyn's anger cooled. But it was the eye contact that made Devlyn feel ashamed. After all the lecturing and scolding, it was the fierce eye contact that finally impressed the severity of his actions. The connection also stirred in Devlyn the same fear that Eagan felt. His heart beat faster, and his stomach knotted.

Eagan began to pace rapidly again, muttering unintelligibly to himself. Devlyn dared a glance at Abbie, who now looked deeply concerned and oddly, perhaps because he was desperate to change the subject to something positive and away from his grievous error, he thought of asking her about Alex.

Devlyn missed his cousin—even if Alex was not actually his cousin. He wondered whether Alex was still gathering an army with the intent of sieging Gneal. Devlyn remembered the letter he had sent with instructions to do just that as soon as he'd learned that Alex was forming a defensive force for Parendior. The letter had been written under Velaria's careful eye and not-so-occasional dictation. Queen Myranda of Sorenthil had also contributed to the letter's contents. With Perrien as an active foe, the Lucillian Alliance—what remained of it—had to fight the Erynien Empire on two fronts. Dividing their forces between the north and the south would exhaust their resources all too quickly.

"It just doesn't make sense!" said Eagan, unsatisfied with his internal pondering and averting Devlyn's inquiry about Alex. "Causing harm to a time warden could not unravel the wield which binds the use of traversing space and time to the Time Key. And such harm, regardless of how powerful Erynor has become, is still beyond him." He resumed mumbling to himself again, his pace increasing with every inaudible sentence.

"Perhaps not Erynor." Abbie's voice quavered, missing its usual bravado. She sounded too frightened to continue. She kept her gaze focused on the ground, where pits of darkness grew larger by the day. There was still plenty of space to navigate between the pits as most of the landscape remained as it ought to. But it was impossible to look in any one direction and not see the dark pits, and it grew increasingly difficult to avoid looking into them. "But perhaps Rami…"

"DO NOT SPEAK THAT NAME!" Eagan rushed to cover her mouth, then scanned the landscape swiftly and carefully.

Devlyn sensed Eagan searching their surroundings, not just looking and listening, but Eagan was also feeling, allowing their surroundings to press on his awareness.

"You know better than to draw such attention to yourself. Here of all places. He grows more powerful with every passing day. Look at the sky; look at those pools of darkness. The signs are everywhere. His prison weakens, and the more it does, the more influence will he have in this place," he said. "Again."

Devlyn looked up at the sky. It was an ominous mixture of dark and heavy clouds with sinister wisps of grey etched through.

"Why can't you say the name?" Devlyn assumed they were talking about the Evil One. He'd heard others speak the name and he had even overheard Alethea and Therril speak it on occasion.

"Do not even think his name, Devlyn. You know how thoughts are not limited to the mind here," said Eagan. "His name serves as a calling. Servants of Shadow use it to draw attention to themselves. When others unknowingly use it, they can come to most unfortunate ends. Those attuned to him are aware when his name is used, especially here. Even in the World-Below where our bodies dream, his awareness is piqued at the use of his name. Fortunately, he currently has no power there, but do not expect that to endure." The severity laced in Eagan's words increased the fear already bubbling inside Devlyn.

If Devlyn had not grown to know and trust Eagan over the past two years, he would not have taken him seriously.

"Am I right?" asked Abbie, unfazed by her brother's outburst and determined to discover whether he agreed with her, not for the sake of argument, but for the resulting implications of her theory.

Eagan's now shallow gaze looked back to his sister. "I hope not, but I see no other explanation. To unravel so powerful a wield is beyond Erynor's capabilities. I know of few others who would dare attempt such a thing, and none who are capable of accomplishing it."

"Hold on," Devlyn said, brushing his hands through his hair, "are you suggesting that it's possible to wield seguians again? People who aren't time wardens, that is." His mood improved at the possibility of wielding the ability that had been restricted to the time wardens for thousands of years.

"I can't say, it might be. After all, time and space are intricately bound. If you can traverse time—arguably the more difficult task—I can't imagine you not being able to perform the other," said Eagan. "Don't get too excited; you'll be lucky if you find someone who remembers how to do that. The minums do not know the mechanics behind the wield. The Time Key unleashed the ability within them, allowing them to perform what they ordinarily would never have come close to achieving. And for them, as the ei'ceuril recently encountered to their detriment, it does not require the erendinth. The same is not true for you—you have no connection to the Time Key."

Devlyn had never heard of a minum becoming an ei'ana, let alone a wielder. But then, neither had he ever heard mention of them managing anything beyond a seguian, making him curious whether they even had the ability to wield. Was being a mixed race an impediment to wielding?

"Don't be an idiot," remarked Abbie. "Your own brother is half-elf, half-human, and he can wield just fine."

Devlyn had again forgotten that thoughts were not private in Somnaeniel.

"Minums simply never cultivated their ability to wield. Everyone can learn to wield and interact with the erendinth. It has nothing to do with them being incapable of wielding; rather, they just never attended Gwilnor to learn how. After all, very few people learn to wield properly on their own. You're among the minority, as is your sister, Leilyn. Aside from you two, we don't know of any other living elya. Even in the past, when they were born more frequently, it seemed limited to the elves as our records show."

Devlyn regretted the thought but wanted to get back to learning how to wield a seguian.

"What about Alethea?" asked Devlyn. "She's ancient."

"You might have a better chance with her," said Eagan, his calm demeanor returning. "But the ability was largely limited to the Luminari, as they were the ones who uncovered the wield, and they were not keen on sharing a wield they considered dangerous, even among allies. Once they realized its potential harm, they limited its application to the Time Key, lest anyone discover and abuse that power. It is not a common wield, nor is it simple. It's uncertain how the Luminari realized its harm, whether by trial and error or if they reached that understanding by their own means."

"Why did they give the Time Key to the minums?" asked Devlyn; he had nothing against the minums but found them an odd choice to ensure the protection of something so powerful.

"When the Luminari left their Skyland, they found the minums enslaved by humans, sold by the goblins on the Kinzdol Islands, which was once the minims' home. The Luminari banished slavery in Eklean and dedicated a portion of land to them. Seeing their humility and dedication to justice, the Luminari entrusted them with the Time Key, removing themselves from the use of their own discovery, and placing it in the hands of the least among all the anacordel, lest another abuse its power."

Devlyn's thoughts drifted to a potential visit to the Freiton Wood to arrange a meeting with the minums. Even if they didn't know how to wield a seguian with the erendinth, they certainly understood them better than anyone else still alive. Just as Erynor had forced a minum to open a seguian in the Temple of Ceur, Devlyn might be able to open a seguian himself in Lankor. The thought of uncovering a way into the Yanilean capital without anyone discovering his arrival left him grinning.

Eagan and Abbie began to fade from the World-in-Between. Relieved that his scolding had ended, Devlyn too allowed himself to fade.

He opened his eyes in a dark bedchamber to rub the sleep from them. Typically, whenever he woke in the morning, he required a good half hour before he could accomplish anything, yet with all the possibilities unraveling before him, he was too excited to allow even a quarter hour to pass. He quickly hopped out of bed, splashed cold water from the basin on his face, then pulled his grey school robe over his head before hurriedly rushing out the room with Aliel on his heels.

He still felt bitter toward Yvonne and Hannah for forbidding him to wear his lierathnil. There was such an uncertainty about the castle that Devlyn never knew if he would need to bond fully with Aliel, resulting in the embarrassing disintegration of his clothing. However, it took considerably less time to don his school robe than the multifaceted lierathnil outfit.

Aliel also shared Devlyn's enthusiasm, but the phoenix maintained a few reservations about Devlyn's travel back in time. Even though Devlyn had no idea how he had managed to visit Lankor as it was being destroyed by Nauto's Wrath, he had no intention of repeating it. And if he had known he had gone back in time, he would have been more cautious about interacting with people in the past. He had only spoken to one person—what harm could that have done? Yet Aliel was adamant that Devlyn never repeat that form of travel.

Walking through the solar toward the exit and into the corridor, Devlyn found a small note resting on the table in front of the sofa.

Dear Devlyn,

> *As an experienced kien wielder, you have been selected to accompany Kevn Weyvien, an ei'ceuril student, as he begins his formal studies in the art of wielding kien. Your influence will be similar to that of a fellow,*

*however, it will not be reciprocal considering his current lack of training.
You will serve more as a guide, preventing him from causing harm to
himself and others as he begins to learn to wield.*

Your cooperation is appreciated,
Hannah Torin
Chancellor of Gwilnor Academy

Reading through the note a second time, Devlyn scanned the meaning of the message. "So that's how they intend to keep kien wielders from destroying the castle," Devlyn thought aloud.

"That came after you went to bed last night," said Viren. Devlyn had not realized that Viren had come into the solar. "Kevn accompanied the note; he's still sleeping in the spare bed chamber. He was informed that he is not to leave your presence while outside the temple. The other kien wielders who have been admitted to Gwilnor are in the male dormitories, sharing rooms with the few experienced kien wielders already enrolled. Many of the kien wielders among the Eldinari who recently arrived were also asked to take up residence in the male dormitories, to safeguard the inexperienced wielders. When I heard that, I expected that you would also be asked to move, but no such request came."

"How long is this supposed to go on?" asked Devlyn just as one of the other bedchamber doors opened, revealing that it was no longer vacant.

"Sorry to be an inconvenience." Kevn yawned as he entered the solar, his light brown hair sticking out in every direction, and still wearing the white and now rather wrinkled robe of the ei'ceuril. "I was told that I would stay here until I can safely control the erendinth. But I'll only be here three nights a week, and never on weekends. Those of us that are ei'ceuril still have our own studies at the temple."

"I didn't mean any offense," Devlyn said, pleased that it was Kevn who had moved into his apartment, rather than someone he did not know. "Have you had any instruction on wielding yet?"

"Not yet; they wanted to make sure we were all in a secure environment before they started our training," Kevn replied with a hint of resentment. "I'm not sure why they're insisting that I learn how to wield. All I wanted to do was spend the rest of my days buried in books and scrolls, researching what was lost and forgotten. None of which requires wielding. Wielding won't preserve ancient histories in living minds."

"It might not bother you so much after you try it. I can't imagine not wielding anymore; I don't even light candles without ignys."

Kevn maintained a doubtful expression.

Without providing any sort of warning, Devlyn pressed into aerys and swept the air in the room in a gentle swirl. Small pieces of parchment scattered across a table were caught up in the twirling wind. Viren moved to the side of the room, allowing the gust of wind to ruffle his hair and clothing.

"I want you to calm it," said Devlyn.

"How am I supposed to do that?"

"You have to feel it, and not just on your skin, but really feel it—on the inside. And when you do, you have to press into it."

"What do you mean *press* into it? I can't force myself into the air."

"It's not the air you're pressing into, but *aerys*. And you'll know when you feel it."

Kevn's brow creased in concentration as he focused on the unnatural wind in the room. It was odd for Devlyn to observe someone trying to wield for the first time. He remembered how his first time had been a complete accident that had resulted in the destruction of Queen Lara's sitting room. *Better to learn before he does the same here*, thought Devlyn, glancing at the unbroken furniture.

"What was that?" Kevn asked, a bead of sweat dripping down his forehead.

"What was what? I didn't say anything."

"Yes, you did, something about hoping I don't destroy your furniture like you did to a queen's. And what were you doing in a queen's sitting room?"

The wind calmed as Devlyn withdrew from aerys, allowing the air to settle in a more static state. "Tell me exactly what you did, when you were trying to wield that is."

Somewhat surprised by the lack of explanation and the sudden change in topic, Kevn recalled what he did. "I quieted my mind and tried focusing on everything in the room. A book I read mentioned that that's what you're supposed to do. Kind of like how I read, except it was everything around me and not written down. I didn't really do anything, I just listened, but not with my ears. You can't listen to books that way. But you're still listening, it's a kind of awareness I guess."

Like reading a book, Devlyn thought before his thoughts were interrupted.

"No, you're listening to the book; letting the author read to you through the pages."

"You did it again!"

"Did what?"

Look at my lips, he thought.

"Why aren't they moving?" demanded Kevn.

Because you're hearing my thoughts.

"That's not possible," Kevn said, backing away from Devlyn and bumping into a table.

"Well, it is. It's just like how Alex and I thought that all the elves were dead, and that the only race still living were humans. All the other races were either extinct or myths," Devlyn said, confessing his childhood beliefs. "Here, let me try, think something."

"What do you think I've been doing this entire time? Do you honestly think I can just stop thinking at will?"

Devlyn focused his attention on Kevn, reminding himself that all he had to do was listen. Well, not just listen, but as Alethea would say, be attuned to his surroundings; to feel them. Although Devlyn had been able to receive another's thoughts in the past, it had only been when they were intentionally projected on his mind.

"Don't forget to listen."

"Stop talking," said Devlyn, imagining what it was like to read a book, or as Kevn said, listen to the writing inside the book. Thinking of last night, Devlyn recalled what he felt as he read. It was kind of like an interior grasp of something beyond himself, something immaterial, yet incredibly distinct.

Whenever he and Aliel communicated in their unique form, he exerted himself outward to interact with the phoenix, just as Aliel interacted with him.

Quieting his mind, Devlyn felt his surroundings press in on him; most were familiar and lively, while others, like the stone walls, were cold and dead. Aliel's presence was so familiar as to almost not be noticeable, and it was odd because he was not joining with the phoenix, instead searching for whoever else he might sense. He first felt a quiet mind, one that was observing the interaction between the two younger elves, and that had to be Viren, then shifted his attention away from Viren when words of an unknown tongue filled his inner ear. They formed complex sentences, while fluidly joining as though spoken by a poet.

"What's that you're thinking?" Devlyn found himself saying aloud. Whatever it was, it wasn't in the Common Tongue.

"Sorry, it's High Aelish, the dialect commonly used by elven scholars during the height of Krysenthiel. It was the elven language, before they left the Skylands that is, and before their fluid language was simplified as our ancestors interacted more with the mortal races. It's the closest remembered descendant of the Elder Tongue, root of all languages," said Kevn. "I've been studying High Aelish since I was a child. You wouldn't believe the number of scrolls left untranslated."

"Impressive," said Viren. "It went out of common use well before my birth, but it was still used in academic settings. That's incredibly complex philosophy and theory you're dabbling in. Your proficiency with the language is impressive."

"Thank you," said Kevn. "Therril has helped me a great deal. I know he's old and all, but he speaks it as though it's his first language."

Devlyn looked to Viren, daring not speak or think it, lest Kevn discover not just how old Therril was, but his actual identity. "That's good of him. Viren, speaking to another's mind, how close are we?" asked Devlyn, steering the conversation away from Therril.

"Whenever you think, you express your thoughts. Whether or not anyone is listening is a different story. However, you can focus your thoughts on a particular individual, for only them to hear. It's the same principles that you're already applying, you simply need to reverse it."

Kevn remained thoughtful and introspective, scratching his head in some hope of clarification, before finally saying, "It all makes sense now. All of it."

"What's that?" Devlyn asked, not entirely sure whether they were still on the same topic.

"For several years now, I would ask someone to clarify what they were saying." Kevn spoke quickly so that his mouth could maintain the pace of his mind. Everyone at Gwilnor Academy knew of Kevn's intellect. He learned new theories and languages easily, often mastering them in only a few months, depending on their complexities. Devlyn was only just beginning to discover the dizzying speed at which Kevn's mind raced, not staying on one topic long. Not even the languages buzzing around in his head remained a constant. *I always assumed they were speaking under their breath. And they never explained, not once. Instead, they looked at me funny and walked away. And every time, I thought I heard them say something about me being weird. I can't believe that this has been happening for so long now, and I never caught on!* Devlyn heard Kevn without trying to listen with his inner ear.

Months had come and gone since Devlyn had first attempted to use his thoughts to speak to another person without success, other than with Aliel. It was incredible that Kevn not only mastered attuning himself to the thoughts of others, but that on the same day, he had learned how to communicate in that form as well. Granted, Kevn had been sensitive to other people's thoughts for some time now, only just coming to understand that that was what was happening.

FALLEN

Hunched over a desk in the library, Devlyn's eyes glazed over the pages before him. Yvonne's reading assignment that week derived from a purely theoretical tome, one which Alethea had already written off. She had spent a significant amount of time the previous day explaining in fine detail how Yvonne's teaching methods were stunting her students' capacities for learning how to wield. Devlyn wished that Hannah could have heard a fraction of what Alethea had to say about Gwilnor's art of wielding magister.

Even though some students and ei'ana had already learned to wield a transcendental erendinth, Yvonne pointedly avoided instructing any such wields. Instead, she relied on her century-old text, claiming its methodology was approved by the Chancellor of Gwilnor and had served many past students in learning how to wield.

Devlyn had spent the better part of his free afternoon reading Yvonne's assigned chapters, but he still had no idea what wield he was supposed to be learning. He couldn't even tell what type of wield the chapters described. After thirty pages, Devlyn noted a mention of a single erendinth in the text, but that was in relation to a previous and unrelated chapter. Out of all the books filling the library's shelves around him, Yvonne had selected the most impractical text. And worse, removing this selected tome from the library was forbidden.

Only five pages remained of the chapter when Wyn strode around a free-standing bookshelf. He peered over Devlyn's shoulder, looking between the book and Devlyn's parchment, set aside for notes where only a single word was scribbled.

"What's aquaeys have to do with spreading a fire?" asked Wyn, hovering over Devlyn's shoulder.

"Is that what this whole chapter was about? Spreading a fire?" Devlyn couldn't tell whether he was more frustrated over his hours of reading or that Wyn had managed to glean the chapter's intent from a single glance. "It doesn't matter, I have to meet up with Alethea soon anyway." He wanted to share with her what he had learned from his accidental visit to Lankor. Even though Eagan had clearly stated the severity of the situation concerning the potential deterioration of the Time Key, Devlyn remained exuberant at the possibilities, especially if Alethea knew how to wield a seguian.

The excitement of discovering an undetectable way into Lankor had left him almost giddy.

The Arenthylean Bells tolled, leaving Devlyn wondering where Alethea was. She had said she would meet him here in the library.

"Oh, right, I nearly forgot to mention that Alethea wants you to meet her at the city gates for something. That book you're reading is terribly distracting. I can't believe it's not tucked away in a restricted section for how awful it is. Better yet, tucked under a rock."

"What's she doing at the city gates?"

"She didn't say, but she's with the young Ceurtriarch and suggested you change into your lierathnil. Well, unless you want the entire city to see your rosy cheeks again," chided Wyn.

"Let's try to avoid that." Devlyn closed the useless book with a resounding thud, garnering stares from other students nearby. "I wonder what sort of session she has in mind that requires Aliel and me to bond?"

"I'll meet you over there when you're ready," said Wyn, waving goodbye as he left.

Devlyn wasn't two steps out of the library when he crossed paths with Trethien, surrounded by his wealthy friends, all belonging to powerful families. Trethien regularly took opportunities to harass Devlyn when they happened to cross paths. "Danielle, do you think they'll let non-wielders sit in Yvonne's class any time soon?" Trethien asked the girl next to him.

"Interested in learning to wield, Trethien? I thought that was be-low you," said Devlyn.

"What, and bring the world to ruin like you're destined to? Far from it. Actually, I've heard Magister Yvonne treats the almighty Phaedryn as the low-born he truly is."

Devlyn pushed through the gathered group of students.

"I've also heard you're flirting with awful marks in her class too. I have to confess, I'm rather proud of you."

Even though he should have known better, Devlyn turned around. He regretted it when he saw Trethien's sneer, and turned away again to continue down the hall, determined to ignore the mocking group.

"You've finally learned to flirt within your own station," Trethien spoke to Devlyn's back, not done with the ridicule.

"You're not even a full Luminari—who'd your family have to inter-marry with to give you that ridiculous hair?" one of the others taunted.

"HA! Nice one, Naerith." Trethien and all the elves surrounding him had the golden brown Luminari hair color.

Devlyn turned at the first intersecting corridor he came across and trekked through the castle to his bedchamber. Inside the wardrobe hung all four of his lierathnil outfits along with his spare school robe. He quickly exchanged the grey robe he currently wore for the blue and grey lierathnil, then slammed the wardrobe shut. He knew he shouldn't have let Trethien and his friends get to him, but they were right. He wasn't a full Luminari and he was in danger of failing Yvonne's class.

The silky fabric fell against his body, conforming perfectly as though it had been tailored specifically for him. Even the pants were the perfect fit. He buckled the golden clasp and headed through the solar for the door to the corridor, but as he crossed the space, the balcony door caught his attention and Aliel kindly reminded him how much time he could save.

Flying there would certainly improve your mood and we won't risk passing Trethien again.

A second thought wasn't necessary. Devlyn walked straight for the balcony instead of the door and toward the stone balustrade. He gazed over the city of Ceurenyl where it was still snowing. His hair was soon covered, but the snow slid across the lierathnil, the cold particles not sticking to it nor penetrating through to his skin.

Quieting his mind and heart, Devlyn felt that tranquil light within and delved into it, allowing it to fill his entire being. He felt Aliel experience the same movement within as they became a single physical presence.

The snow interacted with his body very differently after he and Aliel bonded fully. There was a fleeting moment when each snowflake waited for Devlyn to wield it, as though it had a desire to interact with him.

The gloom of the cold day vanished; the greyness which had clouded his vision moments earlier altered as the sight of the phoenix mingled with his own. The difference between his own vision and Aliel's diminished every day, however that did not mean that he saw the world constantly alight as did Aliel.

With a single step, Devlyn placed his foot onto the top of the balustrade and with the second, he lunged over and plunged down the side of the stone tower, rushing toward the rocky terrain below.

Halfway down the South Tower, Devlyn extended his golden translucent wings and was suddenly caught by a drift of air that desired more than anything to keep Devlyn from crashing into the ground below. It felt as though the air's sacred duty was to prevent anyone from crashing into the ground.

Soaring down the shaft of the tower, Devlyn wished he could do this more often. It took him an eternity to get anywhere inside the castle. He had to make sure he was awake and moving half an hour before almost every other student to compensate for his spacious apartment's location in the South Tower.

Regaining altitude with every flap of his wings, Devlyn returned to a reasonable height, low enough so people could see him, but high enough that he could identify in advance anything that could harm him from below. Viren would surely be furious enough since Devlyn had not told him that he was leaving the castle. Viren often excused himself to train with the Septyl knights whenever Devlyn had lessons with Alethea. She was more than capable of keeping Devlyn safe. The least Devlyn could do was take proper precautions in getting to Alethea.

Devlyn felt his irritation with Trethien diminish with every flap of his wings. The entire city sprawled out below him, the few people outside in the streets hurrying through the snow to find shelter. No one risked their warm hoods falling off to look up into the sky. Flying toward the ruined gate, Devlyn looked down on the massive piles of rubble. Snow-covered scaffolding lined the broken wall, left there after an unsuccessful attempt to repair the gate. Not a single worker could move one of the gargantuan stone blocks; not even a team of workers could manage clearing the rubble.

When it became evident that the laborers were making no strides in repairing the gate, several ei'ana were brought to the scene to see whether they might wield the repair, but even they were unable to shift the stones, leaving Devlyn wondering what Alethea and Aaron intended, and how they thought he and Aliel might help. The extent of the devastation was so great that it was utterly impossible to imagine how the mounds of debris had once formed the majestic gate of Ceurenyl.

When he arrived at the gate, Devlyn was surprised to see not just Aaron, Alethea, and Wyn, but Therril, Velaria, Ellendren, Kevn, Kaeyth, Taen, and even Clara also waiting nearby.

"Good, you've arrived," said Alethea.

He remained bonded to Aliel, assuming he was needed as a Phaedryn; otherwise, what was the point of wearing lierathnil? He also hoped that his transformed appearance might soften Ellendren's feelings toward him. They had barely spoken and when they did, the exchanges were brief and crisp. Other than Ellendren, everyone gathered looked pleased to see him. She was still angry with him, and although she hadn't said why, he was sure it was because he had not told her about his lineage.

"What's going on?" Devlyn asked, secretly hoping that they did not want his help to fix the gate, apprehensive about what that might entail.

"We're repairing the gate and wall," said Aaron with a slight frown, alerting Devlyn that he had been ogling the Ceurtriarch's sister since he'd landed. "I've been researching, with the invaluable help of Kevn and Clara, the walls and gate of Ceurenyl. They're very old, even older than Gwilnor. When the Temple of Ceur was constructed, there was no need for a wall, since there wasn't even a city here at that point. When people began to make pilgrimages to the temple, some decided that they did not want to leave the area, but neither did they want to live their lives as ei'ceuril inside the temple. And so, a village soon emerged around the temple, growing with every generation.

"Before the foundation of Thellion, wars were common across the entirety of Eklean. Thousands were killed in pointless skirmishes for land and wealth. In that hostility, some of the more aggressive leaders set their eyes on Ceurenyl, which had grown into a prosperous city by then. The city also had natural strategic advantages.

"The ei'ceuril knew that they would have to defend themselves and the people in the growing town against the over-confident kings and warlords who were placing their attention on Ceurenyl. Before any army managed to scale the mountain passes, the ei'ceuril crafted a protective wall with a single bridge spanning the river." Aaron turned to the ruined gate before continuing. "There is no record of compensation to laborers. If Kevn and I are correct in our assumptions, there *were* no laborers to be paid."

"Are you saying that the wall and gate were wielded?" Devlyn couldn't imagine the ei'ceuril using forced labor or slaves to construct the wall.

"I can't say with certainty," Aaron answered. "It would make the most sense. But, no one has been able to wield the stone to its proper place since the devastation, leading me to believe that something additional was done."

Throughout the entire conversation, Therril remained uncharacteristically silent. He appeared focused, his eyes not moving away from the piles of rubble. Devlyn noticed Therril move closer to the debris, then place his hand on a single stone to feel the roughness of its cuts.

Some of the pieces of rubble retained their original shapes that identified the pieces as parts of the wall and gate, though most of the stone blocks had deep fissures or missing bits. Robust carved moldings and cracked statue reliefs remained recognizable.

"Have you discovered something?" Velaria asked, glancing in Therril's direction, noticing that he was trying to puzzle something out; something that he was not sharing.

"What?" Therril scratched his chin, just now tuning into the conversation. "Something is very peculiar about this stone here. At first, I thought, hoped even, that it might be stone from one of the Skylands, and in my desperation, I hoped perhaps Aldinare, given that the great majority of ei'ceuril back then were in fact Aldinari. Alas, this stone is from this very mountain, and not some faraway place."

"So, why can't anyone wield it?" Devlyn asked, thinking that Therril had not told them anything useful.

A throaty laugh escaped Therril and his eyes beamed. "Why indeed? Our ancestors were quite clever in their ways. They were no fools when they were seeing to the defense of their temple and city. Velaria, my dear, come here and try to wield this stone right here," said Therril, gesturing toward a large, roughly cut stone block with missing parts due to the explosion.

Devlyn watched terys wrap itself into and around Velaria as she embraced it. He saw the world as Aliel did, and what typically was invisible to everyone was not hidden from him. A verdant ephemeral mist swooped about Velaria, summoned to her desire, then stretched into the ground, happy to manipulate anything that it contacted. Yet as it approached the rubble, it reached a point where it could not pass. The rubble stayed in place, and terys could not draw closer.

"She can't interact with it," said Devlyn, uncertain whether the others were aware of what he could see. "There's some kind of barrier preventing her."

"Exactly," said Therril, his voice rising in excitement. "Clara, please correct me if I'm mistaken. But is my hypothesis close?"

Clara smiled. "I rarely resided inside the temple. My abbey has always been outside these walls. But, Theseryn knew that wielding would become more common with the passing years, so with his foreknowledge, the ei'ceuril of those days placed a wield upon every stone they used in construction, preventing anyone but themselves from wielding it, lest an enemy wielder bypass their protection just as easily as they moved the blocks. It was a trick they'd learned from Aldarch Lerathel, who with Theseryn designed and wove the Temple of Ceur into existence."

"So, I was right! In that case, Aaron, I want you to try the same wield as Velaria. Move that block," said Therril, his enthusiasm palpable.

Aaron drew near the closest block and again, Devlyn could see the Ceurtriarch press himself into terys. It was fascinating to watch since the emerald erendinth interacted differently with a kien wielder. Where Velaria took it in, Devlyn watched Aaron do the opposite and press himself into the erendinth, just as Devlyn was accustomed to doing himself.

As the erendinth neared the stone block, Devlyn waited with anticipation for it to move, but once again, terys could not touch or influence the rubble. Aaron was clearly frustrated and embarrassed. "I've already tried to wield the stone," Aaron admitted, his shoulders slumping as he withdrew from terys.

"Don't give up just yet. You must reveal yourself. I believe that you must let the stone know that you are who you are. Your identity as Ceurtriarch must flow into your wielding!" Therril said.

The odd remarks typical of Therril never ceased to amaze Devlyn. If his statements had not proven consistently accurate, regardless of how odd, Devlyn would take less than half of them seriously. Yet without fail, the old ei'ceuril continued to surprise everyone with his seemingly illogical deductions.

Devlyn noticed a different air about Aaron when he began to wield again and, as ridiculous as it sounded, imagined that he had taken Therril's advice about making his identity known to the stone blocks strewn about the ground.

Everyone held their breaths as though breathing might negatively alter Aaron's wielding of terys, which Devlyn could see and feel as it approached the stone block. It interacted in an atypical manner with the stone and as Aaron pressed past the ward and further into the rubble, Devlyn felt him overexert himself.

Aaron was becoming an accomplished wielder who showed incredible promise, but as he continued to wield, Devlyn realized that Aaron did not have anywhere near the necessary strength or control required for the gargantuan wall and gate before him.

With his heightened awareness, Devlyn felt his friend's energy wane as he shifted beyond himself.

Not entirely certain what was happening to Aaron, a small worrisome knot grew in Devlyn's stomach, heightened by his intimate connection with Aliel who also conveyed a sense of concern. Opening his awareness to Aaron, Devlyn gently pressed against his consciousness to make sure that his friend was not in any trouble.

No thoughts passed from the brief connection, only an overwhelming sense of panic. Aaron's entire being felt strained to a point beyond exhaustion mixed with a piercing pain in his head, as though he was trying to lift a boulder a hundredfold beyond his capacity.

Devlyn immediately pressed himself fully into the erendinth and joined his strength to Aaron's. Relieving some of Aaron's strain, Devlyn felt his own strength pushed to his limits. Following Devlyn's lead, the others contributed their own strength to the young Ceurtriarch. They did not try to wield but allowed Aaron to direct the erendinth required.

A slow heavy sound rumbled as the ground began to quake from the incredible weight of the stones shifting, pulling timidly together, as though the very movement rebelled against their nature.

Until he leant his strength to Aaron, who possessed a more penetrating connection with the stone blocks, Devlyn had not been aware of a painful scar that seethed through every stone. They screamed of an agony beyond the worst of betrayals; the scars bore a taint which reminded Devlyn of a shadow elf, but there was something distinctly different about it. Not even a shadow elf had this taint of corruption.

Concentrating on discovering the source of the taint in the wall, Devlyn was almost stunned when he felt Aaron withdraw from the erendinth, severing Devlyn's connection to the stones. To his shock, after nearly two years, the once ruined gate and surrounding portion of wall stood whole once more, stretching proudly toward the sky. Two turrets rose on either side of the gate with the iron portcullis situated inside the gate and wrought anew. The stone of the wall melded seamlessly into the portions of the wall that had been left undamaged from the attack.

It was impossible to tell that anything had happened to the wall and gate at all. If Devlyn had not seen the rubble with his own eyes, he would not believe that there had ever been any destruction.

Although the reconstruction was impressive, Devlyn's mind was still troubled by what he had felt in the stone. There was something sinister about the taint, wholly different from the typical residue left by shadow elves, but somehow similar.

Aaron's haunted expression spoke volumes. There was no need to try to listen to his thoughts—he too had felt the taint.

Turning from Devlyn to Alethea, Therril, and Clara, Aaron asked, "Tell me, is there a concealed faction in the Ei'ceuril similar to the Tenebrae School among the Ei'ana?"

Devlyn did not dare consider such a possibility, however as he heard Aaron's words, he knew the answer before Clara cleared her throat to speak.

"As terrible as the Tenebrae ei'ana are, even they pale in comparison to the treacheries committed by those you speak of. They were once ei'ceuril, like ourselves, however, they were swayed from the Creating Light. They forsook Anaweh for Ramiel, willingly serving the Evil One in whatever way they could. To make matters worse, there is no way of distinguishing them from amongst those loyal to the Creating Light, unless they enter the Chamber of Light, which they never will, since they know full well its effects on them. Their betrayal cannot remain cloaked there. Their cruel intentions would weigh them down to the floor, preventing them from moving."

"Deserters!" spat Therril. "Stewards of the Shadow. They hide beneath their moss-covered rocks, misleading those faithful to the Light. They spread tales that Anaweh and Ramiel are equals; neither good nor bad. They profess the existence of two polarized gods, ignoring

Anaweh's creative role and Ramiel's created nature. Their followers choose which god to follow based on their own desires. Why does such filth enter your thoughts?"

"They did this," said Aaron, somber. "I could feel their mark. As you said, only an ei'ceuril can influence these stones. They were the ones who wielded tenebrys, exploding the gate and wall, killing hundreds."

The pronouncement fell on everyone's ears, filling their hearts with a dreaded stillness. Devlyn did not want to speak any further about the stewards of Shadow; if he had not been fully bonded to Aliel, he knew depression would have weighed him down.

ABSENT

The end of class was but minutes away, yet the passing seconds crawled at a deadening pace. Devlyn felt as though he would never leave Yvonne's cramped, overheated classroom. Attendance had more than doubled overnight. Where twenty students had attended Yvonne's class, the influx of kien wielders—and other than Kevn, once lay votaries in the temple—had swelled the number well into the forties and the long rows of orderly desks were packed tight with students.

Most of these new kien wielders had been taken from their families and homes and brought to the Temple of Ceur as lay votaries at a very young age and then restricted to living in the lowest reaches of the temple. It was not necessarily a bad life for them, but it was a life severed from the rest of society. In the temple, the lay votaries were segregated from the ei'ceuril, living a prison-like and near-idle existence other than some schooling so that all could read and write. It wasn't all that surprising that so many of them had chosen to escape through a seguian when the opportunity arose. Life outside the temple promised greater excitement than just reading or chatting quietly all day. Ceurtriarch Aaron's proclamation had allowed the remaining ones to walk outside for the first time in decades, and to move into Gwilnor Academy as student wielders. Their lives now had focus.

Devlyn, under the impression that the influx of new student wielders would enliven Yvonne's class, had looked forward to engaging with the newly admitted kien wielders. Yet, despite their eagerness to learn to wield, the magister's teaching methods dulled any enthusiasm. She had not bothered to test their wielding, and thereby adjust the lessons, and she did not even explain to any of them *how* kien wielders wielded, or that it was different from kiara wielders. So, none of them understood the basic principal that to wield the elemental erendinth, a kien wielder had to *press* into the erendinth while kiara wielders *embraced* them.

Instead, she had every student open a book to a specific page and then starting at the head of one row of desks, required each student, both the newer ones and the ones who already had been in the class, take turns reading aloud, as though they were children, not old enough to be entrusted with reading on their own yet.

Most of the new students were well versed, having experienced lectures and instruction on the holy tomes while in the temple, and instantly saw through Yvonne's tactics, yet there were enough who also gave no thought to the dull lessons, thinking the manner in which Yvonne taught was standard practice at Gwilnor Academy. On the first day, Kevn had glared at Devlyn appalled at the wretched level of Yvonne's teaching.

Because there were so many new students, Yvonne had been asked to increase the number of classes she offered—something she had yet to implement. She chose to simply cram more desks and more students into her current classes. Rumors still abounded that at first, she had outright refused to take on more students, but Chancellor Hannah had managed to coerce her into agreeing. But teaching a lesson with forty to fifty students simply was not feasible and more classes were needed.

The additional sections would include not only the former lay votaries, but also ei'ceuril, both young and old, including the ones who had not yet experienced their novitiate.

Aaron intended to see Gwilnor Academy returned to its former glory where everyone who had the ability would learn how to wield, particularly the ei'ceuril, and had mandated that every kien wielder in the temple had to learn how to control his wielding. Aaron had told Devlyn in private that he intended to send all the Temple of Ceur's ei'ceuril back into the world. Wielding was a requisite to becoming a steward, and because of that, every steward, with the exception a minority who did not pose any harm to themselves or others because of their limited abilities for wielding, had lived inside the temple. Aaron's plan was to send the archstewards back to their own cathedrals, which were scattered across Eklean in every metropolis. But first, they had to be able to control the erendinth.

More rumors than just those related to the conflict between Hannah and Yvonne floated about. Some were about an even larger conflict between the chancellor and the Seven Chairs over the addition to the faculty. No one had managed to extract all the details of that disagreement, almost a first for Gwilnor. Most secrets, especially those involving a conflict, were only kept for a few days before the details began spreading throughout the entire castle. Naturally, since none of the details were known in this case, fictitious ones were woven into the rumors. According to the most recent fabrication, the Seven Chairs had actually threatened to remove Hannah from her post. Such an action was incredibly rare, and although the authority to carry out such a dismissal was available, the rumors surrounding that specific action were unfounded.

Hannah was well-loved as chancellor and respected by a majority of the students, leading most of them to dismiss the rumors. However, the discussions were left without resolution, despite the arrival of two Eldinari ei'ana, the twins, Myrah and Fyreh Glaeda, and Fyreh's constantly growing family.

Both Myrah and Fyreh had been present for Yvonne's lesson today, yet the magister had limited their participation to introductions. They had taken seats at the front of the room, facing the students.

Finally, the Arenthylean bells tolled, and the sound of chairs scraping against the stone floor nearly overwhelmed the congested classroom. Walking out the door with Kevn, Devlyn scanned the crowded corridor for Ellendren who, until recently, would occasionally meet him after his classes, Yvonne's in particular. Ellendren knew all too well how he felt about Yvonne and her teaching methods. There was no sight of her today, and Devlyn's optimistic enthusiasm for the end of the class quickly plummeted.

More than two weeks had passed since she had discovered that Devlyn was a Lorenthien and she had not said a single word to him. He occasionally saw her in the dining hall or passing in the corridors, but she resolutely ignored him and went on with her business. He told himself that her advanced classes with the Vyoletryns and Erendinth Game practice were keeping her too busy. The Vyoletryn team was favored to win the School Cup.

"I have to head back to the temple, I'll see you next week."

"Bye, Kevn."

As if Yvonne's class hadn't put Devlyn in bad enough of a mood, he saw Trethien striding toward him from the far end of the corridor, just as Kevn turned to go. Devlyn's stomach turned sour. Devlyn could not imagine how the day could get any darker than it already promised. The full moon of Borenth was tonight, as was the winter solstice, celebrated by the Eldinari as the high feast of Borephaen, honoring the enthiel who guided their people, Boriel.

Trethien was gloating as he strutted directly toward Devlyn. His eyes narrowed to snakelike slits as he approached, but then his destination seemed to change and he passed Devlyn without slowing.

"Are you looking for someone?" Devlyn did not readily recognize the voice behind him, but hearing it lifted his confusion over Trethien's sudden changed intent.

So many new people had moved into the castle that Devlyn was not surprised that he did not recognize the voice. He turned and saw Fyreh.

"Sorry, Magister," he said. "I was, but I don't see her."

"Ah," said Fyreh. "My sympathies. Young love is a dangerous thing, and matured love, even more so. Careful, young Phaedryn, before you know it, one day you will blink and find yourself wed with children hanging on every limb and you will never know how you once lived without them."

Devlyn, unsure whether the comment was meant as encouragement, looked on blankly. Marriage was the furthest thing from his mind; he was only fifteen after all and the only person he had any romantic feelings for had, at the moment, no desire to so much as look in his direction.

"Can I help you find something, Magister?" asked Devlyn, mentally wincing at the nervous laugh that escaped his lips.

"You'll find I know this castle better than most. I might even rival Therril's knowledge although, I would not wager any number of stellendae seeds on it," said Fyreh with a smile. "No, I was hoping, if you wouldn't mind, to speak in private with you. Well, as private as my accommodations can be. You'll find them quite over-occupied, but not nearly as full as I would prefer them. Some of my children are no longer youths and no longer need to live under the constant care and guidance of their parents; at least that's what they tell me. In my opinion, some of their actions speak otherwise."

"Um, sure," Devlyn replied, "when would you like to meet?"

"Well, if you don't have any prior commitments, I was hoping now. You'll find Suella, my wife, prepares the most wonderful fruit tarts and pies for Borephaen."

Devlyn's stomach rumbled at the mention of food, followed by an apologetic expression.

"If that doesn't sound like a yes, I don't know what does," said Fyreh, chuckling. "Come, let's make our way to my family's quarters. We're lodged in the Azurelle wing."

Devlyn's curiosity about the Eldinari grew as they walked along. "Can you tell me, if it's not too intrusive that is, how is it that you managed, as an ei'ana, to marry and raise a family? I know some of the ei'ana here have done so, but they're so few that I've actually never met one before."

"Believe it or not, there was a time when it was the norm," said Fyreh, not slowing his pace. "There were always a few who never married, my sister among them, and why they tried to live like the ei'ceuril, I'll never know. Some say, as Myrah does, that they're too dedicated to their work to have a family. But I think they just didn't want to get married. No fault of theirs, just who they are. But it was never the standard. Do you know how long this trend of remaining unwed has been going on?"

"Can't say; I only started interacting with ei'ana three years ago," said Devlyn. "I lived in Cor'lera, one of those villages where servants of Shadow managed to convince the locals that wielding was evil and only led to destruction. Before I was born, not a single ei'ana still lived there. Every last one was chased off—at least all the known ones."

"Despicable. Don't they know that every single person has the capacity to wield and that it's a gift? That it's an invitation to interact with the world in a completely different manner?"

Devlyn followed Fyreh up the Dragon Tower's monumental marble staircase, up and up until his legs trembled from climbing. Fyreh finally paused at a landing and turned down a corridor lined in blue tapestries before slowing in front of a door, not stopping before pushing it open and entering.

Loud sounds spilled through the opened door, shocking Devlyn. He had never heard the sounds of a family in Gwilnor, since even the younger students here tended to be awed by their surroundings and didn't make much noise. The more rambunctious ones acting out was the closest comparison.

"Welcome to my humble abode. Just as we left it!" said Fyreh, gesturing toward the congested apartment. Three children ran through an open doorway into the entryway before rushing out a second doorway; they were obviously greatly enjoying their game of chasing each other.

"Suella, we have company," Fyreh called out, then pointed Devlyn into the solar. "Please, have a seat. The rambunctious one in the middle is our second youngest child, Ostol. The other two are our friends' children."

Happy to rest after climbing the many flights of stairs, Devlyn sat on one of the sofas in the room. The apartment offered reminders of Stellantis. The walls were all stone, yet the softness of the wooden furniture provided warmth to the room. "Did you bring this furniture here yourself?" he asked.

"A very long time ago, when Suella and I were still young and freshly married. We had been ei'ana for several hundred years at that point, but I had not yet begun to teach. At that time, Gwilnor was devoted only to studies, while the greater population of ei'ana lived at Septyl."

Fyreh frowned slightly at recalling Septyl.

"You're lucky no one moved in while you were gone."

"Luck had nothing to do it." Fyreh produced a glasslike object from his pocket and held it at eye level. "Before leaving, I crafted a lock and key of eldaryl to seal the place up tight. I knew Suella and I would return at one point or another, it was just a matter of when." As Fyreh finished speaking a young woman entered the room. She was clearly an Eldinari with silver eyes, chestnut skin, and midnight black hair.

"Mother is bathing Teryll for Borephaen and won't be able to greet our guest."

"My daughter, Jivien, is near your age, well, closer to Wyn's age. But she is not yet an ei'ana, still too young for that."

"Nearly every ei'ana in this castle is younger than I am."

"Too right! And some of them even act that way too." Fyreh smirked at his daughter just as she stuck her tongue out at him. "Before you return to your studies, did mother finish her fruit tarts?"

"She said they're for tonight and gave me strict instructions to guard them against you."

"Surely she'd change her mind with our guest here."

"When has mother ever changed her mind on anything? Besides they're still cooling," replied Jivien, walking out the room.

Fyreh watched his daughter leave as two fruit tarts floated in through the doorway. "I've always found that aerys brings them to the perfect temperature."

Devlyn happily took a bite out of the fruit tart, its juice spilling down his chin. "This is delicious!" His mood instantly improved, erasing the memory of spending the past hour in Yvonne's overcrowded and overheated classroom.

"They do tend to have that effect," smiled Fyreh, noticing Devlyn's elated mood. "It's a shame that Suella cannot join us, she would appreciate hearing your words. I wanted to speak with you because I would like to hear your perspective on Gwilnor. Many things seem odd to me, and I would like my suspicions confirmed, if you would not mind."

"Um, sure, what kind of questions?"

"To begin, and without being coy about it, I don't like Yvonne; something about her unnerves me. I'm not one to criticize a fellow magister's teaching style, but it is peculiar—and that's the kindest way to put it. Since you've attended her lessons this term and last, have you acquired any sort of skill in wielding?"

Emotions flooded Devlyn; every grudge he held toward Yvonne rushed to the front of his mind, consuming his thoughts, all of which were plainly visible to Fyreh.

"I feared that was the case. Forgive me, I did not intend to hear your thoughts, but they are very loud and impossible to ignore. You should learn to temper them. If you have secrets that ought to remain so, your thoughts will betray you, and someone unfriendly—and even friendly sorts—will know what they ought not to."

Fyreh's bluntness gave Devlyn the impression that he tended to speak the first thing that came to his mind. And if that wasn't the case, then his mind moved very fast. It had been difficult to discern Fyreh's vast intellect when he'd introduced himself at the start of the lesson, but it was evident now, and it certainly spoke of Fyreh's capacity as a magister.

Devlyn knew he had to work on quieting his thoughts. At first, he had believed that he had to stop thinking while around others, but Alethea had swiftly corrected him. She had explained that suppressing his thoughts would only make them louder because he wouldn't be able to stifle them for long.

"Alethea is trying to teach me; she says it typically requires hundreds of years, but because of my connection with Aliel, it shouldn't take anywhere near as long, because of our form of communication."

"Sounds logical, but you should make it a priority. Information is a powerful weapon." Fyreh scratched his chin as if a beard should be there, reminding Devlyn very much of Therril. "When Yvonne and I met, she described her teaching method to me. How she divides her classes and, in her opinion, best trains young wielders to hone their abilities. First, how long have you attended her lessons, and secondly, do you notice any improvement?"

"Truthfully, I haven't seen any improvement in myself or the other students. She focuses on complex wields that are beyond our understanding, and when we practice them in class, she has us stand alone at the front of the classroom to perform the required wield, yet all the while she wields against us, preventing us from forming the wield. The only time I was able to successfully accomplish a wield was with Aliel's assistance, and consequently, Aliel was banned from her classroom. Since then, he's also been banned from every other classroom."

"Interesting. Do you have any sense that her students will accomplish the wields in the future?"

"That would be nice, but we spend one full week researching the wield on our own, and one week practicing the wield, one at a time, at the front of the classroom. At no time does she explain what we are meant to be doing—the specific actions needed—to accomplish the wield. I would be shocked if a single student learned anything from her." Devlyn couldn't read Fyreh's reaction, and whether he applauded Yvonne's method or not.

"Thank you, Devlyn. Myrah and I will have a discussion with the chancellor regarding our concerns. If you were not already meeting regularly with Alethea, I would have recommended that I provide you with private lessons, but you are in very qualified hands." Fyreh stood and led Devlyn to the door, thanking him for his time and willingness to provide a perspective on the class, and then wishing him a happy Borephaen.

As he walked away from Fyreh's apartment, the blue furnishings in the corridor reminded Devlyn that he was in the Azurelle wing of the Dragon Tower, where Velaria also had an apartment. He fondly recalled his first time on the tower's open balcony on the uppermost level, and when he reached the staircase, he decided to go up rather than down to the main level just to return to his own apartment.

As he climbed, an image of Ellendren floated to the front of his mind. Her continuing absence in his daily routine grew more and more difficult to bear with every passing day. He wanted to find her, to talk with her, and to apologize to her. But, whenever he sought her, he could never find her, not even in the library. The effects of the uplifting fruit tart had long worn off and his brooding found him reaching the top level of the tower quicker than he had anticipated. He didn't realize that he had taken the steps two at a time all the way up.

The bright sun made him squint when he pushed the door open and walked out onto the tiled balcony. It was impossible to see the entire panorama at once because of the central seven-sided drum supporting the roof, which spiraled high over the tower.

Near the tower's base lay the vast circular field where the Erendinth Games were played. It was just as Ellendren had described—colored alcoves, hoops, rings and all. He had been looking forward to learning how to play the game from her, but those hopes had been dashed.

From his current view up high looking down on the field, Devlyn was surprised that he had never recognized it before. Granted, he had never looked directly down the Dragon Tower's shaft—the river swerving around the mountain Ceurenyl was perched on had always caught his attention, especially where the smaller mountain streams from the city joined the larger in crisp waterfalls.

Devlyn walked around the tower's balcony to a different pointed arched opening, halting at the western side. From here his view was limited even further because of the Shroud. The entire city sprawled below, but that's not what he wanted to see. He wanted to see Krysenthiel. He wanted to gaze upon the vast valleys of the golden lotus flowers, the kryseniels, the namesake for the lost elven kingdom. He wanted to see the fabled golden spires of Arenthyl with his own eyes.

Hidden in the Shroud was Lake Saeryndol, filled with water so pure that it was said that you could look straight down to the bottom of its depths and see the exposed roots of the Tree of Life. The Laudien Mountains cradled the lake in a crescent, and the largest mountain in the world was fabled to protrude from the lake's center. And on its southern slopes, the Luminari had erected their crowned city, modeled in the native architecture of Luminare. Devlyn had heard that not even the abandoned cities of that Skyland could compare with the splendor which flowed from Arenthyl, standing beyond his grasp. But as he looked at the Shroud, he knew exactly where it was; he felt the city inside him.

Devlyn desperately wanted to reclaim that lost city, along with all the other cities of Krysenthiel claimed by the Shroud. All he had to do was replicate the piercing wield he and Aliel had managed two years ago. Unfortunately, he still did not know how to wield lumenys and every day that passed made him more doubtful that he ever would. It was simply beyond his ability, and that was something he had no control over.

Abbess Clara had mentioned that somehow the Temple of Ceur was connected with lumenys. But like Phendien, she had neglected to mention how. Devlyn wondered if there was a connection to providing clear explanations and an elf's age. Still, visiting Clara would have to happen sooner rather than later. While he had managed to spend some time in the Chamber of Light since he'd come back to Ceurenyl, trying to obtain the ability to wield that long forgotten transcendental erendinth, he knew it wasn't enough. But the thought that continued to nag at the back of his mind was, how was he supposed to gain that ability, when not even the ei'ceuril who had spent their entire lives in the temple were any closer to wielding lumenys? *Was that why Clara had returned to Ceurenyl as well?*

A familiar and very welcome presence filled Devlyn's being. It had become so natural, so necessary, that he did not feel himself when it was absent. As the sensation within his heart grew, Aliel swooped from above to circle the Dragon Tower.

That quiet inner light within his heart mixed with the other and Aliel's spirit melded with his own, filling them both. On the verge of transforming into a Phaedryn, Devlyn pulled away from Aliel, reminded that he was not wearing his indestructible clothing. A great sense of loss filled his being as the quiet lights were drawn away from each other.

Sorry, if we do that today I'll have to walk through the entire castle with only my hands covering what I don't want others to see, Devlyn conveyed to Aliel as he gestured to his simple grey robes. *And I don't think Hannah will appreciate me requesting another school robe if we destroy this one.*

Being on the verge of the ecstatic joy that was the melding of their two beings and then having to deny it depressed him. Devlyn knew he was making excuses to avoid bonding fully with Aliel. Tapping that innermost place required opening himself to his emotions, and that was something he very much wanted to avoid.

LOOPHOLES

For the past two days, snow had piled against the windowpanes. No one in the warmth of Gwilnor's interior had any inclination to walk outside on the slick cobbled streets layered in snow and ice. The stream flowing through Ceurenyl had frozen over and Jaerol, distracted by the dreary weather, rubbed his arms for some added warmth. He had never liked the snow, a singular trait he did not mind sharing with every other Cyndinari. When he was first told that he would be an Erynien emissary to Gneal, he had groaned about it for a month. But he hadn't been in a position to choose for himself. He had had to be careful that none of the shadow elves discovered that he had never become a shadow elf himself—he had never become an abomination.

His life had changed since Velaria had freed Liam from Gneal's dungeons. Everything had changed because of Liam.

Liam sat next to Jaerol, and he looked as though he was having just as much difficulty paying attention to the lesson. Jaerol wished he could blame his lack of attention on Yvonne who happened to be his—and surely everyone else's—least favorite magister. Once again, Yvonne had made the entire class read through their previous assignment. She tested her students to determine if they had accomplished their reading, and if she had the tiniest indication that one student had not, she demanded that the entire class read their assignment aloud together or, in Jaerol's case, re-read it.

Myrah, one of the two newly arrived Eldinari who were also teaching this class, sat placidly at the front of the classroom. Yvonne did not allow them to teach, but she wasn't able to throw them out of her classroom either. After having several lessons with the two Eldinari in the classroom, Jaerol couldn't believe how a pair of twins could be so different.

Jaerol had never known what it was like to have a sibling. His parents were still young when he had received his assignment and left for Gneal. They could have had another child for all Jaerol knew. It was not only possible, but expected. The death rate among Cyndinari teenagers was exceptionally high, to better ensure that only the strongest among them survived. Supporting a population that encouraged half its children attending the Imperium to murder the other half required all those who could, to produce as many children as possible.

The Grand Tourney that followed the conclusion of every Cyndinari's formal education at the Imperium meant that half of Jaerol's schoolmates had been killed in Broid's colosseum. It was a magnificent structure, but its red sand pits were stained with the sin of his people. A long-held custom of the Cyndinari was to crush and refine cyndaryl and then scatter it as sand on the tourney floor. The colosseum in Broid was not the only barbaric tourney field on the island of Cynethol, just the largest.

According to his magisters in Broid, all of whom were shadow elves, competing on the refined cyndaryl was an ancient custom, practiced in the days when they still lived in the clouds on their Skyland of Cyndinare.

Jaerol hated his people. The Grand Tourney had forced him to kill Kiron. He had not—could not—take Kiron's soul. Though, after his ruse, everyone had been convinced that he had done just that. Jaerol had known from that moment that his time as a trusted subject of the Erynien Empire was limited. People would eventually notice that his skin maintained its natural bronze color, his cinnamon hair did not fade nor lose its luster unlike what happened to every shadow elf.

But Jaerol had not left for self-preservation. He had deserted because of the Grand Tourney. The Cyndinari policy to murder and claim the soul of the fallen was barbaric. Nightmares related to occurrences in his youth still haunted his dreams, waking him in a cold fright. Kiron visited his tormented sleep. Nothing was ever said between them; they just stared at one another. Jaerol missed Kiron terribly, and found that his eyes would water whenever he thought of him. It was only because of Liam that Jaerol could smile again, and Liam knew it. He hoped that Kiron would have accepted that.

Returning his eyes to the book lying before him, Jaerol read the same line that he had read twenty minutes ago when Yvonne first required the class to read the assignment in her presence. It was a re-markably dull book with a title that made the reader think it was an instruction manual for wielding. However, not once did it cover anything remotely useful for wielders. Jaerol was convinced that his ability to wield had diminished since he'd first begun reading it.

The class would soon end, but it could very well have just started; it was near impossible to tell the time during Yvonne's classes. All the students were dependent on the Arenthylean Bells, expectantly awaiting their chiming to end the class.

Yvonne's classes had become more bearable since the Glaeda twins began assisting her, but even with their addition, the lessons continued to drag on and little knowledge was ever gained. And Yvonne had been in a particularly foul mood over the past several weeks due to Fyreh's initia-tive tied to the Erendinth Games.

It was impossible for any kien wielder to compete in the upcom-ing games, although the entire castle was abuzz as the first match ap-proached. The student wielders who had chosen their Schools, all kiara wielders, were practicing constantly. Since there was not enough time for the kien wielders to accomplish their preliminary studies and complete their novitiate, none were eligible to participate in the games. Only stu-dents belonging to one of the seven Schools could compete.

The Erendinth Games went against everything Yvonne taught in her class. It was no secret that Fyreh and Myrah disapproved of her method, but the Chancellor forbade them from providing additional lessons. With the influx of new students and Eldinari ei'ana, Chancellor Hannah had suspended all private lessons between students and their tutors. She had claimed that more time was required to see to the logistics to equally disperse the students. She had a small army of aides helping her catalogue the returned ei'ana and what they were most suited to. Fyreh found the entire process a waste of time and had insisted on knowing when he could begin private lessons with his students. Since Hannah had refused to give him a precise date, he had searched for other ways to provide an education to the student wielders.

While researching the school records, Fyreh had discovered a loophole. Although only the students who had chosen a School could compete for the School Cup, there was no prohibition against a secondary league of students. Nor was there a prohibition against magisters coaching in that secondary league. Before Fyreh's intervention, students not belonging to official teams had participated in informal matches—none were coached or met regularly.

However, over the past weeks parchment flyers and gossip galore spread across the castle as teams and rosters were created for a secondary league. Most notably, they were open to anyone, including kien wielders with minimal training.

Even though Fyreh could not give additional lessons, there was nothing to prevent him, or any other ei'ana, from coaching as many students as possible, thereby also providing coaching in wielding the erendinth.

While Fyreh had an extra bounce to his step, Yvonne scowled whenever she looked in his direction.

Trying his best to focus on the text before him and not the Erendinth Games, Jaerol was relieved to be distracted by an unexpected knock at the door. Yvonne grimaced when the door opened without her acknowledging the knock. A young elf with black hair entered. His hair and darker skin identified him as an Eldinari, yet Jaerol could swear that he knew him from somewhere else.

There was something familiar about his face that he could not place.

"In the future, you will not interrupt my lessons, under any circumstances. Is that clear, Danyol?"

"Perfectly," Danyol replied with a smirk. Jaerol knew that sly grin from somewhere. He could not place it, but he recognized it. "I am here at your pleasure, Magister Yvonne."

Whichever memory Danyol was stirring, Jaerol's reaction was of distrust and great unease in the pit of his stomach. There was something wrong, terribly, terribly wrong about this Eldinari.

The Arenthylean Bells finally tolled ten wondrous bongs and the sounds of ruffling parchment and books and chairs scraping against the floor filled the classroom.

Jaerol pushed through the crowded door and into the corridor, chancing a glance over his shoulder at the newly arrived Danyol who was staring directly at Jaerol. *Who is he?* Jaerol followed the stream of students as they all hurried away from Yvonne's classroom, each one terrified she might call them back in. Bouncing along among the elated students was Fyreh.

Today was the first day of Fyreh's new Erendinth Game league and by the volume of students heading toward the erendinth field, every student wielder who did not yet belong to a School or who could not qualify for their School's team intended to start a team of their own. Each team required seven students, but since anyone could compete, there were far more than the customary seven teams associated with the Schools of Septyl. Most extraordinary about the secondary league, was that the teams were a combination of kien and kiara wielders, something the Erendinth Games had not witnessed since before the fall of Krysen-thiel.

With the influx of kien wielders, Jaerol and Liam no longer stood out as the oldest students at Gwilnor. And with that boon, neither would it appear odd for them to compete against their younger classmates. Jaerol had no idea how Fyreh intended to coach what seemed to be the entirety of Gwilnor Academy, let alone how he would organize the schedule for their games. It was going to be a logistical nightmare. He was going to need his own army of secretaries although it was unlikely that Hannah would provide those resources.

The throng of students pulled their winter cloaks up close as they crossed the bridge to the Dragon Tower. But instead of going into the castle's southern wing, they walked in a long column abreast of the tower, its lofty heights appearing to pierce the sky—Jaerol swore at times that only magic could keep that tower standing.

Following the terrace wrapped about the tower's base, Jaerol finally saw the seven wide vertical hoops suspended in the air and glimmering in the chilly afternoon sun. As far as he could tell, someone long ago had wielded the erendinth to make each hoop float. None were the same color, but each was a color associated with an erendinth.

Jaerol walked close to Liam, crammed into a narrow stone stair that led from the terrace to the erendinth field. They crossed under the spectator seating and spilled out onto the round field. Two rings were positioned in the center of the field, one inside the other. Four shimmering hoops of red, blue, green, and white lined the outer ring, each representing one of the elemental erendinth. The inner ring had only three hoops of grey, yellow, and purple, for the transcendental erendinth. Along the outer perimeter lay seven equally spaced alcoves of a different color, associated with the inner hoops. Inside each alcove, a pedestal supported a colored ball. Jaerol noted the great distance between the outer perimeter and the inner two rings, and already felt out of breath.

Jaerol had never played this game in Broid, nor had he heard of anyone from Cynethol playing such a game. Since it was unlikely that it ended with someone's untimely death, it had probably been deemed inappropriate for the Cyndinari youth. A broken nose was perhaps the most serious injury a student would suffer here.

As the students filed into the field, Fyreh pushed his way through the crowd and toward the center rings. He stopped below the glinting green hoop and cleared his throat.

"Welcome," he called out. "Since returning to Gwilnor Academy, it has come to my attention that this academic sport has been called the Erendinth Games. Is that right?"

The throng of students murmured, inaudible confused whispers spreading across the field. *How was he going to start a new league if he didn't even know what the game was called?* Jaerol sighed. He felt his excitement wane.

"Anyone? I hear you all saying something. Clearly, someone must know." Fyreh waited.

A single hand hesitantly rose.

"Ah, yes, Trefan." Fyreh acknowledged a teenage boy, one of the younger kien wilders who had only lived in the temple for a year before kien wielders were welcomed back to Gwilnor.

"Yes, sir, the Erendinth Games." Trefan looked relieved that it wasn't a trick question as Fyreh smiled genuinely.

"Thank you for your considerable bravery. You will be one of the new captains of your team." A communal groan rose around Fyreh. "But, I'm sorry to inform you, Trefan, that what you've called this sport is incorrect. Honestly, did you think the student wielders, Kien and Kiara's heirs, who played on this field were so unimaginative that they would not have given it a new name?"

Not a single student understood what Fyreh was talking about.

"Do none of you know any of your history?" asked Fyreh, concerned. He scanned across the field of faces, all indicating uncertainty. "I'll have to have a chat with Ethyl then. But that is quite beside the point. Welcome, dare I say, to the grand and academic sport of elthion!"

A rush of wind blew across the elthion field, and with it, all seven balls flew out of their colored alcoves. Fyreh was wielding every erendinth at once. The clamor of the students, Jaerol included, wanting to learn how to do that was almost deafening.

TOUCHED

Cold and tired, Evellyn stood still behind Erynor. Speaking was not permitted and fidgeting was never acceptable. Her legs ached and her lower back was increasingly tender from standing still all day. Nothing was expected of Evellyn, only her submissive presence. She was not expected to bring his meals or contribute to conversation. He only wanted her presence, knowing that was the most demeaning thing he could have requested. But she knew what she was to him—a slave. She had done nothing but stand behind him for what was almost thirteen years now.

She dreamt of lying down in her bed, but not the one she had been given when she'd been brought to Broid, but her bed, the soft, yet firm mattress at the Cor Inn. It came to her mind frequently, and in her dreams. She dreamt of sleeping beside her Dolan. Of her children piling on top of them both in the early hours of the morning.

It was silly to still dream about the Cor Inn. Her precious Dolan was no more; passed into the nether regions of the World-Beyond, never to return to her. She had watched his own brother strike him down with his sword. Nightmares of the event still haunted her. She should have become desensitized from seeing it so often, but she still could not keep her eyes dry.

Her Dolan was gone—stolen from her.

She knew nothing of her children Devlyn and Leilyn, or of Dolan's first born, Liam, who she considered her child as well. She loved them all the same. For all she knew, Liam was still in that wretched dungeon beneath Gneal's castle. If he still lived. She knew that nearly all who had been abducted on that wretched night would never experience freedom again. Did any of her siblings and extended family still live? Only Arlyn had been away from Cor'lera and had not been among those abducted.

She had watched poor, sweet Leilyn run into the Illumined Wood. Never would she gaze upon the world again or have use of her honeyed voice. Evellyn hoped with all her heart that she was still alive. There was nothing dangerous about the Illumined Wood, but neither was it a haven for children. Evellyn secretly hoped that her father was still alive and well and had found Leilyn somewhere safe in the woods.

She did not know why Erynor wanted her Devlyn. Although Erynor did know that Devlyn belonged to Lucillia's line, there was no way of him knowing of the prophecy in full. All those years ago, she had prayed that Devlyn was not the one meant. Just as her father had prayed for her. She had sung the prophecy to her sweet son every night when she was putting him to bed. If she had not been so cruelly taken from him, she would have explained it to him one day. From Feolyn himself on down through the generations, she was the first of that line that had failed to pass down the prophecy from parent to child.

She had failed.

If she died while enslaved to Erynor, the oral tradition would end. Devlyn would never know what to tell his youngest child. Not a day had passed when she did not consider running away. If there had been any way to escape Erynor's prison, she would have. His minions would kill her if she tried. And if she died, the meaning of the prophecy would die with her. She trembled at the thought of how it could be misinterpreted.

Erynor slouched before her, his eyes closed, his fingers tapping the arm of his throne. Even he was dreary of the cold refusing to lessen its hold over Broid despite the approaching spring.

"Your son has his mind set on Lankor."

Erynor spoke with a disinterest that infuriated Evellyn. There was always something he did not say in his ongoing manipulation of her. The fool still believed there was an actual weapon hidden in Cor'lera. In that regard, she had spoken honestly.

"I know what he seeks," said Erynor.

Evellyn's lips remained pursed. Why was her Devlyn going to Lankor? That was the last place she wanted him to go to. The closer he came to her, the more danger awaited him.

Because she had never seen him grow from a toddler, in her mind, he was still only two years old. He had obviously grown, but she had missed all of it. The very thought made her heart ache. *What if he thinks I abandoned him?* She questioned herself yet again.

"You don't know, do you?"

Evellyn kept silent. She truly didn't know why Devlyn would want to go to Lankor.

Erynor rose from his cyndaryl throne and rounded on Evellyn, now face-to-face with her. She felt his breath on her skin. There was nothing vile about his breath, but it repulsed her. His features did not decay as did those of his Deurghol and shadow elves that lived an empty deathless life. Not even their dying flesh retained a sense of touch.

"In order to win Yanil's allegiance, I sacrificed Lankor, unleashing Nauto's Wrath upon that pathetic people who had rejected me. Lost in the tides was a lucilliae." His tone remained steady, and his silver eyes held her own as his lips curled in a mocking smile.

Over the years, she had learned to bury her emotions so that her eyes would not convey what she was feeling.

"One of the seven."

Despite all her hard-earned control, she grimaced. Evellyn knew of the seven lucilliae which formed Ceurendol, the Jewel of Life. Her father had told her stories of the Luminari's sacrifice. He'd spoken of how they had risked their Life immortal so that all might share that benefit and how Erynor's pride and jealousy had deprived everyone of that gift which might have ended all war and famine.

Erynor knew her thoughts. She did not think he could enter her mind, but her deep fear for Devlyn meant that her eyes shouted everything she thought. Erynor's eyes confessed his crimes, the sneer on his face adding further injury.

"You think me an abomination—you cannot hide it."

Evellyn tried to turn her head away, but his willpower kept her looking toward him.

"With the exception of my birth, I'm not so different from the aldarchs, you know. What they managed and kept secret, I alone have uncovered. But my bond is with one stronger still. Haven't you ever wondered why the Phaedryn fell so easily to me?" Erynor's sneer turned to a gloating smile as he turned his back on Evellyn.

Devlyn stood in the Chamber of Light and gazed into the brightness emanating from its center. The shaft of light cascading from the dome pierced the voluminous space, making it impossible to see the opposite wall, as though a dense fog filled the room. He thought back to what Clara had said about this room unlocking the potential to wield lumenys. Something about an Empyrean Sphere.

Whatever that was.

Something very similar to anger lashed from Aliel. A righteous sort of anger. *Do not speak of that holy place in such a way—you know nothing of it.*

What is it? Devlyn asked, taken aback by the rare show of emotion. Aliel had been basking in the warmth provided by the shaft of light, and now hovered just beside Devlyn.

It is not for me to describe.

Irritated, but wanting to switch the topic, Devlyn asked, *How does a phoenix enjoy such warmth?* He wasn't entirely certain whether it was a stupid question.

Do you think only purely physical bodies can experience sensations? A sense of amusement replaced Aliel's prior anger. *Do you not relish in that which you are made of? Your physical body is of Teraeniel. Do you not enjoy walking upon Teraeniel's crust, feeling her soft and firm features against your feet? And likewise, do you not relish in swimming, allowing the water to encompass your entire body, almost embracing you. Pay attention to that inner light you discovered. The more you realize your true nature, the more will you relish in its origin.*

Devlyn shrugged, not sure whether he should thank Aliel or ask for another explanation that would just as likely be as indecipherable. Devlyn could never tell how much time passed while he was in the Chamber of Light, and today was no exception. He had initially come to the temple to speak with Aaron but now, he couldn't remember why he had wanted to see Aaron. Instead, his attention drifted to the brilliant light, his consciousness fading with every passing moment.

A slow drifting sensation overcame him. It felt like falling asleep, only he was not drowsy in the slightest. Part of him wanted the bells to toll. Anything to alert him to the time. How much time had passed since he'd arrived at the temple? Hours? Or was it only a fraction of that time?

Deciding he had spent long enough in the Chamber of Light, he was surprised when his legs moved far too easily, despite standing in the same spot for what had to be an hour. They should be stiff and aching after all that time standing, not budging. Instead, it was only when he tried to move them that he realized that there wasn't any weight pressing down on them. Gravity had completely ignored his legs' burden. Glancing down, Devlyn jolted to find that the floor had completely disappeared in the impenetrable light. No wonder his legs weren't sore from standing the entire time—he hadn't been standing at all. The combination of the light and the white tiled floor made it impossible to discern how close to the floor he was.

Devlyn turned his head to get a better idea of where in the Chamber of Light he had drifted. Every direction he looked held the same cloudy brightness. Pin pricks speckled across his skin. He couldn't see any of the surrounding walls since he had unintentionally glided so far inside the column of light that he couldn't see anything but that cloudy brightness. Trying to determine when he had drifted toward the center of the space, Devlyn attempted to swim through the light and toward the outer rim. He had no idea how far from the edge he was floating and could very easily be directing himself closer to the center.

He searched for Aliel, hoping the phoenix would know a way to return to the floor and outer perimeter, but he couldn't see Aliel nor connect with him mentally.

Wherever Aliel was, it was far from here.

Devlyn began to twist and contort his body, his arms and legs flailing in an attempt to gain some momentum to return to the tiles below. The more he fought, the less he moved. He had no way of knowing the direction he had to go, let alone what he was moving toward.

Suddenly, he felt someone pulling him, startling him so that his heartbeat quickened and his palms started to sweat. The lack of control stirred a deep-set nervous panic, leading him to struggle all the more.

A voice and an image vaguely appeared, but Devlyn's lack of control and trepidation prevented him from concentrating, and neither the voice nor the image took form. Devlyn felt his body descend—well, he *thought* he was descending.

His feet eventually touched against solid ground and his feet and legs once again felt the load of his body. He could feel his heart thumping loudly, and even seemed to be hearing its rapid beating. He was still somewhere in the shaft of light but had no idea how far in it he was. If he chose the wrong direction, he could easily walk deeper into the all-encompassing light.

Focusing, he took hesitant steps, carefully examining his surroundings, noting that the light did not grow brighter. Pleased, he continued in that direction. It felt as though he was walking much further than the actual temple's dimensions warranted, as if the shaft of light inside the temple expanded the further within one ventured. *That wasn't possible. Was it?*

Solidity finally returned as the chamber's walls took shape once more. Devlyn exhaled a sigh of relief.

"Everything all right, Lord Phaedryn?" inquired a voice that Devlyn did not instantly recognize.

Startled, Devlyn turned to find a temple knight standing guard in front of the Ceurtriarch's quarters. "I'm fine," Devlyn said, trying to recall whether he knew this temple knight or not. The knight wore the standard spotless white tunic with yellow stitching embroidering the unmistakable crest of the temple on the breast.

"That's a queer thing you just walked through. I've only stepped in briefly, and even that felt too long," said the temple knight. "Better left to the ei'ceuril, if you ask me."

"Is the Ceurtriarch in his quarters?" asked Devlyn, not wanting to discuss his interactions within the Light.

"He is, my Lord Phaedryn. I'll announce you at once."

Devlyn waited alone, wondering where Aliel had disappeared to. *Perhaps surveying the city?*

Several moments passed before the temple knight returned, holding one of the large double doors open for Devlyn to pass through. As he entered, Ellendren brushed past him out into the Chamber of Light, avoiding eye contact entirely. She was undoubtedly heading to the Erendinth Game field—no, elthion field. Everyone was still adjusting to the new name, or rather, old, correct name.

Devlyn turned to follow her, but he heard Aaron say, "She's still upset with you. Trying to force her to talk won't do you any good."

"How can she still be upset?" asked Devlyn, not really wanting an answer. *Did I offend her that badly?* he thought.

"You know she's not pleased that you withheld your identity from her," said Aaron, sitting in his high-backed chair, his right elbow resting on the desk piled with parchment. "In any other circumstance, the revelation that the Lorenthien line still lives would be one of celebration. But for Elle—for her entire life—her authority to reign as the future aryl of the Luminari belonged to her alone, it was her birthright, only to be thwarted by your sudden declaration of a stronger claim to a throne more noble than Roendryn's."

"What does that matter!" he said, frustrated over the stupidity of their fight. "If we get married, she'll reign as aryl just as well. How does that change anything! I thought that ei'denai and ei'terel reigned as equals as aryl?"

"We'll have to grow accustomed using the proper elven titles again—unavoidable now, with the Eldinari's return." Aaron looked over Devlyn carefully, as though he was determining whether Devlyn's intentions were true. "You love her, don't you?"

Caught off guard, Devlyn found himself unable to respond intelligibly. He had not intended to confess his feelings for her. There were suddenly no words to explain. "I don't know. I thought I was falling in love for her. Granted, I've thought that since we first met, as though some invisible force has been pulling us together. But she's been angry with me for over a month now, probably closer to two. I doubt she'll talk to me at all, let alone permit space for continuing any form of relationship." Devlyn plopped down on the sofa. "As long as she doesn't wind up with Trethien again."

"Who's to say?" Aaron no longer looked at Devlyn, lost in his own ponderings. Or perhaps one of the parchments on his desk held his attention.

"So, I gather she told you everything?"

"Everything? I highly doubt that. But as the news of the Lorenthien line living and breathing has a direct outcome on our family, she had no misgivings about sharing that. To say nothing of me also being the Ceurtriarch. You really should try to speak with her when she's ready, though. She feels as though you broke her trust beyond repair."

"It's not like I intentionally concealed it from her," Devlyn said, his voice rising as he grew more frustrated with the situation. His heart quickened.

"All I'm saying, is that if you care for her, as you admit you do, speak with her and make sure you listen to what she says. *When* she's willing to speak." Aaron now looked directly into Devlyn's eyes before asking, "Out of curiosity, what brought you to the temple in the first place? We didn't have an appointment scheduled."

Appreciative of the change in topic, Devlyn answered, "Honestly, I'm concerned about the taint left in the city gate by the stewards of Shadow. I felt drawn here, as if something was pulling me toward the Chamber of Light. Before I knew it, I found myself floating uncontrollably in the Light toward the center."

"Careful, my friend. There're stories about ei'ceuril disappearing and never returning from that Light." He crossed his arms and leaned back in his chair.

"Since I'm here, what do you know of the Empyrean Sphere?"

A quizzical Aaron looked back. "Do I even dare ask how you came to know of such a thing?"

Aaron was never one for riddles or answering questions with questions, so his reply left Devlyn guarded, choosing his next words carefully. "I was told that in order to wield lumenys, I would have to enter this Empyrean Sphere thing and be found worthy by a six-winged anadel."

"I'm not sure who told you this, but that is not something that you should know about—the Empyrean Sphere."

"Why hasn't anyone tried?"

"What makes you think no one has?"

"Did they succeed?"

"As I said, there are stories of ei'ceuril never returning from the shaft of light in the Chamber of Light," Aaron said in a depressed tone, reclining more in his chair, the rigidity leaking from his body. "There is only a single scroll in the temple's library mentioning the Empyrean Sphere, and as you can imagine, it's ancient. To enter the Empyrean Sphere is to enter Lumaeniel—the World-Beyond. It does not state how to enter and return to the World-Below. Since the Fall of Krysenthiel, anyone who attempted it has passed to the World-Beyond, never to return. Only the old and the young dare. The young believe they can't die, while the old have grown indifferent to the possibility of death."

Devlyn's mind drifted to Clara and wondered if she could teach him how to enter. "There has to be a way."

"I wouldn't risk it. Imagine if you were lost to the World-Beyond. I'm sorry to say this, but you cannot take such reckless risks. Speaking of which, I'm particularly troubled about your desire to go to Lankor. Can you imagine what would happen if you were captured?"

Irritated with Aaron's caution and the change of subject, Devlyn's mind shifted to the Shroud. He knew only lumenys could disperse it. The memory of the wield that had passed through him and Aliel was still vibrant. He knew that if he could only tap that forgotten ability, he could recreate that wield and make the Shroud nothing but a memory.

The possibility of returning to Arenthyl weighed heavily on him; a hopefulness was present, even seeming to promise it.

Thoughts of a bright future in Arenthyl shifted to doubt as the events of the past days ventured to the front of his mind. Everyone in the entire city was relieved that the gate and wall stood whole once more, yet the reminder of the taint left by stewards of Shadow crept into his being. It was a foul thing that reminded him of a disease; he felt a chill in his bones and the urge to retch floated up, wanting to purge whatever stirred inside him. Lethargy fell over him like a blanket, followed by an unrecognizable apathy.

Attempting to shake the irksome thoughts and reminder of the taint, Devlyn finally said, "Have you felt…odd since repairing the city gate?"

Aaron looked at him curiously, as though Devlyn had no right in knowing how he felt. A bitter fatigue flashed across Aaron's face. "My sleep has been disturbed, if that's what you're referring to."

"I didn't mean anything by it, only that I haven't felt myself since delving into the stone of the gate and wall with you."

Before either had an opportunity to say anything else, a knock came at the door followed by the entrance of the same temple knight that let Devlyn in. "Forgive my intrusion, Ceurtriarch, but your meeting with the archstewards will begin shortly."

"Thank you, Renaud. Devlyn and I were just finishing," Aaron said as he stood and began to make his way around the desk toward the door.

"Anything important?" asked Devlyn, his curiosity rising.

"I intend to establish a requirement for every ei'ceuril who has the ability to wield to learn to control the erendinth. It is currently optional for them, but I intend to remove the option and make it mandatory."

"Kevn didn't give me the sense that it was optional."

"No, not for him and a select number of ei'ceuril that I've asked personally, nor for all the kien wielders we'd detained over the years. We cannot preserve our way of life if we cannot safeguard Ceurenyl and the Temple of Ceur. And I don't believe we've dealt with the last act of aggression against this city. I intend to discover how the ei'ceuril prevented Erynor from seizing control of Ceurenyl during and after the Ceurendol War. We cannot remain behind our walls any longer. And the archstewards need to return to their proper sees. Their cities and territories need them to return. There's no saying what havoc these stewards of Shadow have wrought upon Eklean in our absence."

"You know my thoughts on the matter," Devlyn said, alluding to their earlier conversation regarding lumenys.

"And I agree with you." Aaron rubbed his eyes—he really wasn't sleeping well. "I said it was too risky for you to make the attempt; I said nothing about myself. Eklean needs you; you're the only one powerful enough to come anywhere near holding Erynor at bay. If I die, I can be replaced with a new Ceurtriarch in a matter of days, depending on the election process. The same can't be said for a Phaedryn."

Devlyn wanted to argue with Aaron regarding his sense of worthlessness, but didn't get the opportunity as Aaron quickly walked toward the temple knight awaiting him at the door, his elaborate robes billowing behind him.

Devlyn followed them out of the Ceurtriarch's quarters and was left alone as they continued through the Chamber of Light toward the doors leading to the larger part of the temple. Finding himself once again lost in the overabundant light, Devlyn blinked several times to refocus. He walked along the perimeter of the domed chamber until he neared the exit. The temple knights standing guard opened the doors, flooding the corridor with an incredible brightness, which quickly vanished when the doors closed behind him.

The darkened entryway had always baffled Devlyn, and made him squint from the contrast every time he went into or left the chamber. Now, the darkness pressed against him, making him more cognizant of the loss of the wondrous light he had just experienced. Why anyone would willingly leave the temple to walk through this dark corridor devoid of that wondrous brilliance which filled the Chamber of Light was a mystery, even though Devlyn was frequently among those who did.

"Perhaps, you should devote more time to that thought," came a feminine voice whose owner Devlyn could not see, nor did he recognize.

He tried to press into the erendinth but was quickly reminded that he was still inside the Temple of Ceur and hence cut off from wielding.

"That's really not necessary, my dear."

"Who are you?"

"Don't you recognize my voice?" purred the woman before gently caressing the side of Devlyn's face with the back of her hand, her nails adding extra pressure to his skin, making him jerk slightly at her unexpected proximity.

"No."

"Isn't that a pity. I thought we had such an intimate connection in Myrium, before you started killing my soldiers, of course."

Devlyn's heart raced once again and he felt his palms begin to perspire. "Who are you?"

"I don't blame you, of course, how could you possibly know who I am? My generals kept me far behind the front lines. Granted, I was certain victory was ours. Otherwise, I would never have made the journey so far north. I so desired to parade through the Jewel of the River as its conqueror."

"Why are you here?" asked Devlyn, irritated that he had no idea who this woman was.

"To make your acquaintance, of course. I was informed that the silly girl you had affections for no longer desires your companionship. True signs of an immature child, if you ask me. Believe me, Phaedryn, you could do much better. Even if you are still a boy yourself, I believe manhood will fit you well. Already, you have the appearance of a man." Her eyes suggestively scanned over Devlyn's physique, and she drew a line on his chest with one finger then turned to leave. Devlyn's eyes were finally beginning to adjust but he still could not see her walk away from him.

"What's your name?" he called faintly, then blinked again as the doors opened, allowing the exterior light to wash across the woman. She had a handsome beauty. She wore a loose-fitting silk dress with a heavy fur shawl, and more gold jewelry than Devlyn had ever seen on a single person. Long black hair, braided in thin strands intertwined with thin golden lacelike chains, wrapped about her head in an intricate coiffure.

"Alesei," she answered and turned for Devlyn to catch a partial glimpse of her face before the doors closed to fill the corridor with darkness once more.

Devlyn repeated the name in his head. He knew he had heard it somewhere before, but wherever he had heard it now escaped him. Her face remained in his mind's eye, and he could still feel her lingering touch against his chest.

It was difficult to guess her age. She did not look old, but neither was she young. Not a single wrinkle lined her face, but her eyes were old and unattractive. They hid something. *Perhaps Elle would know who she is,* he thought, even though she still would not speak to him.

Ellendren's face floated to the front of his mind, and as it did, he felt his heart ache. The longer the image lingered, the more painful it grew.

TURNING POINTS

The first of spring had come and gone and the wintry snows still claimed Ceurenyl. It would be another month before they could enjoy the warming weather, considering the city's altitude in the Laudien Mountains. The sun was sluggish in warming the city.

Devlyn cared little about the promised change of weather presently though. He turned away from the window and back to Therril.

"I can't stay here twiddling my thumbs any longer," Devlyn said, growing more agitated by the moment.

"Do you really think that you're ready to leave Gwilnor again?" asked Therril. He had asked Devlyn to visit his office—the one in the Dragon Tower at Gwilnor, not the one in the temple with the window that was not a window—at the end of class the other day.

"I'm not learning anything new here, and to make matters worse, I think that Yvonne is actively trying to stunt our wielding. I can't even compete in Fyreh's elthion league. If I don't get away soon, I'll forget everything I've learned. I bet if Yvonne could, she would try to reverse my connection with Aliel, which I'm not entirely convinced she's not trying."

"Settle down, settle down. You're blowing things out of proportion," said Therril. "Have you mentioned your plans to those willing to travel with you to Lankor?"

"Not yet," Devlyn admitted after taking a long, deep breath, not entirely thrilled to think about everyone included in that number. "The longer I stay here, the longer a lucilliae remains within Erynor's grasp. Could you imagine what would happen if he discovered its location?

Without it, we might as well forget about ever reforming the Jewel of Life."

Just thinking of Erynor clutching a lucilliae incited Devlyn to act. Even if he could find every other lucilliae, if a single one wasn't located, he might as well give up now. And if the Erynien Emperor did seize the jewel buried under the waves in Lankor Bay, the only possibility of retrieving it was stealing it from a secure location in the imperial capital of Broid, where Erynor was certain to take it.

Tired of standing after pacing the breadth of the office, Devlyn plopped into one of the spare chairs across from Therril, his head instantly fell into his open palms.

"Are you sure you're ready to leave Gwilnor?" Therril asked yet again as he cocked his head. "You know the dip in your grades isn't encouraging. I understand your desire to find the lucilliae before Erynor, but you're making me think there's another reason you want to leave in haste. Hmmm?"

Devlyn knew what Therril was hinting at, but he had no intention of admitting it. As much as he wanted to mend his relationship with Ellendren, it was so much easier to simply be done with it and move on with his life by focusing on things that mattered. And he could actually do something about finding the lucilliae. All that mattered was getting it back and finding a way to defeat Erynor.

It wouldn't matter if he and Ellendren mended their relationship if Erynor won. Erynor would either enslave or kill them, regardless of the state of their relationship.

Nothing else mattered.

Devlyn had even skipped the first elthion match yesterday. It was the first week of Marenth and both he and Ellendren had shared a birthday earlier in the week, but he could not bring himself to walk out to the elthion field and support the Vyoletryn team against Azurelle and Arantiulyn. He felt rotten over it; he truly had wanted to see how the game was played. *So much for the maturity of a now sixteen-year-old*, he thought.

Therril must have recognized the pain in his eyes before Devlyn buried them in his palms again. "I have no intention of telling you what to do. But I will tell you, that you are running away from something, not to something," Therril said, careful not to mention that that something was a someone.

The Arenthylean Bells tolled ten times, which meant there were still another two hours until dinner. The great bronze-like and silver-like bells echoed across the city and into Therril's tower office. They were too far off to make the stone walls reverberate, but just the sound of them made Devlyn think of their enormity.

"I should get going." Devlyn wiped his eyes, hoping Therril didn't notice.

"Our choices have consequences, Devlyn. Do not do anything that you will later regret," Therril said as Devlyn stalked out the door, his shoulders slumped under the weight of his worries.

Alone in the empty corridor outside Therril's office, Devlyn mindlessly turned left without any destination in mind. Despite his relationship issues, it felt good to walk unaccompanied for once; Viren had stayed back in their apartment in the South Tower. While his sense of urgency hadn't completely disintegrated, he had become laxer with the repaired city gate. Devlyn's stomach rumbled, but he wasn't hungry enough to grab a late lunch or an early dinner and sit in the dining hall with other students. He had had enough of advice for one day, which seemed like the only thing people wanted to talk to him about. His lessons only intensified those feelings.

He did want to talk to Ellendren about what he was feeling, but that wasn't an option. *She's probably spending time with Trethien again*, he thought bitterly. Trethien had probably made it to Ellendren's first elthion match and celebrated her birthday with her too.

Wyn, Liam, and Jaerol were all busy helping the new kien wielders in the castle. Even though Wyn was supposed to also be training with Devlyn, they barely saw each other since Wyn had moved into the boy's dormitory in the North Tower. All three were paired with kien wielders recently let out of the lower levels of the temple. Thinking about that brought Kevn to mind—Devlyn was supposed to be helping him learn to control the erendinth.

Devlyn had nothing against Kevn, but he felt his time was being wasted whenever he had to instruct Kevn in wielding the erendinth. Not only did Kevn resist learning, but when they did spend time practicing, Kevn was always distracted by something else. Too often, Kevn would stop wielding altogether to jot down a thought before returning his divided attention to the task at hand.

Whenever Devlyn wasn't practicing or when Kevn's focus lay elsewhere, they would talk about Kevn's decision to return to the ei'ceuril. Kevn never had anything positive to say on the topic whenever they discussed it. Devlyn still could not understand why he'd returned in the first place, and the more they talked about it, the more he doubted that Kevn knew why as well.

Kevn's schedule, like the other ei'ceuril student wielders', mostly took place in the Temple of Ceur; they were only at Gwilnor for Yvonne's art of wielding class. Their classes at the temple still went on as usual. Devlyn was fortunate though, since Kevn only spent three nights a week in the castle. The other new kien wielders were full-fledged student wielders and residents at Gwilnor and required considerably more time and attention.

While Devlyn enjoyed Kevn's company, he was relieved that it was Karaen and classes would not resume until the following day. Granted, every time Kevn returned to the temple, Devlyn half-expected him to tell whoever oversaw formation that he was leaving. Even though Kevn never actively sought a romantic relationship, that was one of his biggest issues against becoming an ei'ceuril, which was what he had told Devlyn when they first met in Magister Kai's politics class three years ago.

The weekends at Gwilnor tended to have a more leisurely quality about them, not that the students or ei'ana ever truly relaxed from their studies or work, but other than the excitement about the elthion match the previous day, a mellow atmosphere had taken over the castle. As Devlyn walked mindlessly through the castle, he grew tired of spending so much time inside and decided to go for a stroll around the castle grounds.

Gwilnor's walkways had been cleared of snow and the promise

of a warming sun would melt what was left on the rest of the grounds. Devlyn followed several others seeking fresh air out the open entrance and into the quad.

The Septyl knights asked every student or castle resident, not only their name and station, but their intended business outside the castle and when they intended to return. A line had formed, and Devlyn found himself waiting just so he could tell a Septyl knight that he was only going to walk around the castle grounds. The Septyl knight eyed him suspiciously but lowered his gaze in deference when Aliel appeared next to him.

Devlyn felt very aware of his diminished personal guard—Viren shouldn't be too upset if he remained inside the castle grounds. He'd told the Guardian knight that he was only meeting with Therril this afternoon. Security had relaxed slightly after the gate and city walls had been reformed, despite the recent assassination and breakout in the temple. The main entrance to the castle remained barred—as did every other entrance except the one in the quad.

By the time Devlyn made it out of the castle and into the courtyard, he watched several groups of students stream toward the giant archway, while another group of students remained in the quad's confines. Since all the other castle exits were sealed, the archway spanning two levels was currently the only passage to the castle grounds. Following the stream of students, Devlyn had the unfortunate realization that he was the only one walking by himself. Well, not completely alone—Aliel did fly beside him.

Devlyn always wondered what others thought. They had to have noticed that he spent most of his time in the company of a phoenix, and other than Viren, only a phoenix. And since ruining everything with Ellendren, his group of friends had severely shrunk. Did they see Aliel as a simple animal or did they know what he truly was? Surely some book in the castle's library covered that—Kevn or Ellendren would know. Suddenly, the thought of others seeing him walking alone without a group of friends pressed against him.

He felt all their eyes staring at him—judging him.

The longer he walked outside, the more difficult it became, especially when he noticed that most walked in groups of two, and often, holding hands. His fingers remembered the familiar feeling of entwining with Ellendren's. Their hands fitted so perfectly together. It was as though they were meant to hold one another.

Avoiding the path where most of the couples walked down toward the stream to look over the rooflines of Ceurenyl, Devlyn went in the opposite direction and toward the erendinth—no, the elthion field. Aliel remained quiet, but whenever they did not converse in their unique form of communication, a tune of sorts hummed in Aliel's mind. Or, was Aliel present to the melody? Devlyn could never understand the relationship, but, because of his connection to Aliel, simply accepted the always-present harmony.

Devlyn walked with his head down, staring at the cobbled path just a few paces in front of his feet. There was nothing particularly interesting about the individual stones, even if he did have a higher respect for all forms of creation since Alethea had begun instructing him. Still, he didn't see how stones and dirt had once been alive. He simply did not feel like holding his head up. It felt as though he had a chain of weights draped around his neck, pulling him down.

The sounds of happy chatter, flirting, and laughing finally faded as Devlyn drew closer to the elthion field. There was no gate to prevent anyone from going into the arena so he walked through an opening between the benches and onto the vacant field. There was nothing spectacular about the arena; it had a large circumference and raised benches enclosed its entirety. Devlyn knew the benches would have been packed the day before. He had heard cheering fans all the way from his balcony on the South Tower but hadn't mustered the will to leave his apartment to join the spectators.

The results of the match had made their way quickly through the castle. No one remembered the last time an elthion match had ended with such a high score—likely the last time it was called elthion. Naturally, Ellendren had ensured the Vyoletryn's victory. She was the only player capable of wielding animys and umbrys. She knew the game better than most and had capitalized on wielding the different erendinth together to reach the incredible score of 295 points. Apparently, she had even managed to score the coveted seventeen-pointer. And he hadn't even been there to see it. Knowing Ellendren, Devlyn assumed that she was probably disappointed that she hadn't scored the twenty-pointer or the highest achievable single goal of twenty-four points.

Devlyn walked onto the field next to a purple alcove. A ball of the same color rested on an elevated pillar twice his height in the center of the alcove. As he approached the alcove, Devlyn was suddenly drenched from head to toe by a ball of water. Humiliation and anger swept through him as he searched for whoever was responsible for the cruel and wet wield.

He looked over his shoulder, but saw no one. There weren't any large groups of students nearby to mock him and he didn't hear anyone laughing at him either. Looking every which way for the wielder responsible, Devlyn simply could not determine where the callous wield had come from.

"Perhaps if you weren't moping, you would have seen the wield before it came anywhere near you," said a familiar voice. Devlyn hadn't thought to look at the benches to see if anyone sat there.

"Very funny, Elle." Devlyn pressed into aquaeys and pulled the water from his grey robe and drenched skin. "How long have you been up there?"

"Over an hour," she said, settled on one of the benches with her legs crossed and a book in her hands. "It's too nice of a day to read in the library."

"Too nice of a day to read at all," Devlyn said. Ellendren responded with a snort of disapproval. "I'm sorry."

"You think I care that you don't like to read on nice days?"

"I'm not talking about that." Devlyn's nerves were racing and he was afraid he was about to say something that would make matters worse. "I'm sorry for not telling you as soon as I found out that I'm a Lorenthien."

"How could you forget to mention something like that?" snapped

Ellendren, refusing to look away from her book.

"I don't know; I'm an idiot. I didn't know what a Lorenthien was until last year." Devlyn tried to think of the right words. "I didn't think it was important. It's not like knowing who my ancestors are changes anything about who I am. It's not like I'm a different person. I'm still Devlyn—nothing has changed. So what if I have a different last name?"

"Everything has changed and it matters a great deal." Ellendren slapped her book shut with a crisp snap. "Do you have any idea of the implications of the Lorenthien line being still whole and intact? Of course, you don't! Since learning that you were a Lorenthien, have you done any research on them? Have you read that they were the first Phaedryns? That because of them, the Luminari learned to wield the erendinth? That because of them, the Luminari departed their Skyland safely and established Krysenthiel? That because of them, the Guardian Senate was founded, and for a brief time, all Teraeniel convened in peace? That only a descendant of that House can rightfully claim any authority over the Luminari as a whole and by extension, call the Guardian Senate back into existence? My family has served our people for thirteen hundred years, wrongly naming ourselves as their rightful liege, believing the Lorenthiens were wiped out by Erynor. When in fact, it turns out that Feolyn's descendants have been the rightful heirs to the throne all this time. And even if we ever did manage to return to Arenthyl, never could we sit upon the Crystal Throne as the Exalted Aryl of Krysenthiel; never could the Roendryns serve as High Kings and High Queens of Eklean."

"What does any of that matter? And who knows if we ever will return to Arenthyl since, as you can see, the Shroud still covers all Krysenthiel." Devlyn gestured behind the castle and toward Krysenthiel's territory. "And even if we did manage to reclaim that realm, do you think I would want any person to sit on the Crystal Throne as high queen other than you? What part of 'I love you' don't you understand? I've never been so miserable in my life as these past months; not even when I was treated no better than a ward at Cor'lera. Of course, I haven't done any research concerning the Lorenthiens, that's your thing, you actually enjoy reading. And even if I tried to research them, how far do you think I would have gotten without your help? How much do you think I would have missed or read over thinking it unimportant? Do you honestly think I would have learned anything of value without you pointing out every important detail and thread?"

Ellendren didn't say anything. She no longer looked into her book, but toward the hoops in the center of the field, still avoiding eye contact with Devlyn.

"I miss you," he said, more of a plea than anything else. He could hear the desperation in his voice and didn't care if she heard it too. He wished he could hear her thoughts. He was getting better at doing so, but he dared not attempt it with her. He doubted she would ever forgive him if he did. He was on enough thin ice.

"You promise you've been miserable?" she asked, arms crossed, now looking directly into his eyes, daring him to try to lie.

"What kind of a question is…" started Devlyn before cutting himself off. Aliel nudged his consciousness, unable to hide his relief at the mending relationship. "Of course, I've been miserable." He wanted to say more, to go into more detail about how lonely he had been and how little he had accomplished since she had stormed off and refused to speak with him. How his grades had plummeted and he was now receiving common marks in most of his classes.

"Good," Ellendren said, not allowing him to say more. "I've been angry with you. You know that, right?"

Devlyn only nodded, unable to admit it again.

"All right, if this is going to work, no more secrets. Agreed?"

"Of course!" Devlyn felt like a scolded puppy and if he had had a tail, it would be between his legs.

"Good," said Ellendren, as she abandoned the bench for the field. "Come here," she said and pressed her fingers against Devlyn's temples.

Visions from the previous months surfaced, thoughts and past temptations. He felt exposed since Ellendren could see everything inside him. Everything.

This is worse than being naked, he thought, quickly remembering that

Ellendren was connected to his mind, making them both blush as the thought brought with it an image of himself without clothing.

Ellendren's cheeks turned a bright crimson. "You're lucky that you feel guilty for not coming to the first elthion match. And don't even think of missing the second," she said, removing her fingers and her connection from Devlyn's thoughts. "You really have been having an awful time."

"Did you expect anything else? Elle, not being able to talk with you was worse than all my days at the abbey school in Cor'lera," Devlyn said, only just remembering all his present difficulties, the lucilliae in Lankor most pressing. "Out of curiosity, when did you learn to listen to someone's thoughts?"

"Do you think you're the only elf here training with the Eldinari?" she asked. Devlyn admittedly felt stupid for asking.

"Also, we'll need to talk about your grades. I won't be courting someone who can barely manage common marks while flirting with bad and awful marks."

With the lucilliae coming to his mind once more, and his relationship mending, he found himself saying, "I think it's time we leave for Lankor."

"I've honestly been thinking the same for a while now. I just can't fathom what would happen if Erynor found out about the lucilliae and retrieved it before we did. However, if you ever speak to that Alesei woman again, you'll find out exactly what I'm capable of!"

"Who is she?" Devlyn asked as innocently as he could muster.

A single eyebrow rose. "You really are useless without me, aren't you?" Not for the first time since they started talking again, he simply nodded in agreement without saying anything else. "She's the Tieli queen and a wretched woman to boot!"

"Why is she in Ceurenyl? Better yet, how'd she get into the city?"

"I'm afraid to ask," said Ellendren, more to herself than to Devlyn. "But we'll have to worry about that later. We should schedule a meeting with the others tomorrow. Hopefully they're all available. I doubt Velaria will be able to leave Ceurenyl again though. Who knows what would happen to the kien wielders without her support. They could just as easily be sent back to the Temple of Ceur."

Devlyn stole a glance toward the violet ball atop the pillar.

With a quick smile, Ellendren wielded the ball from its place. "This ball represents the transcendental erendinth, animys. You want to get it into its proper goal in the central purple goal. But, to get the most points with it, you'll want to get it through one of the outer goals and a different inner goal," said Ellendren. "To get it through any of the goals, you have to wield the erendinth proper to the goal you get it through. Otherwise, the ball won't go through and you won't score any points."

Devlyn watched as she burst into a sprint, daring Devlyn to chase her across the field, wielding animys all the while.

Careful not to enter the central rings, which was against the rules, Devlyn ran after her, noticing that she started to wield terys with animys. Pressing himself into terys, Devlyn tried to block her as the ball raced through the air and toward the green goal.

The ball pierced through his wield and into the green goal and then the purple goal.

"Why didn't it stop?" he asked, out of breath from sprinting and wielding at the same time.

"Because you're clearly not as good at this game as I am. I'm not sure if you've heard, but my performance was rather stellar yesterday. Also, you have to wield both erendinth. It also helps if you can wield another ball to block it." A competitive grin replaced her casual smile. "We should start heading back to the castle; the sun won't be out for much longer and I want to look at your current assignments." She quickly retrieved her books and moved toward the exit.

Devlyn wanted to keep playing. He did not think it was fair that he only had one chance at defending the goal without knowing how to do so properly.

Trailing after her, Devlyn called out, "Did you have a nice birthday?"

"It could have been better. I remember receiving a particularly good gift last year."

They headed back to the quad, not seeing any other students until they had walked around the Dragon Tower's girth. It was mostly couples lounging on the snow, huddled together. He chuckled, recalling his frustration at seeing them not too long before.

"What are you laughing about?" asked Ellendren.

"I hated every one of those couples as I walked past them earlier," Devlyn admitted, still laughing to himself. "But now, I couldn't be happier for them."

"I felt the same. I actually thought about melting the snow under their blankets," she said and Devlyn felt her hand touching his.

It was exactly as he remembered it. He no longer cared about the other couples enjoying the snowy spring afternoon, all that mattered was his hand in hers.

Aliel continued to soar to his side and Devlyn felt a hint of accomplishment flow through their bond.

Without putting any thought into the phoenix's emotion, he said aloud, "You've been communicating with Aliel, haven't you?"

"Actually, Aliel reached out to me," Ellendren said, without a single trace of guilt in her voice. "You weren't the only one miserable."

You set this up? Devlyn conveyed to Aliel.

Absolutely. Your mood was getting annoying and now you can properly focus on training and retrieving the lucilliae. If Andrew's mind was open to me, I would have also sent you to the knight's courtyard to get a proper beating from a practice sword.

Devlyn passed a reassuring sense of gratitude to the phoenix before conveying, *So, that's where you disappeared to when I was with Aaron.*

Devlyn walked through the castle with Ellendren and toward his apartment in the nearly abandoned tower to continue their much-delayed planning. The South Tower, compared to the other towers, was relatively close to the unbarred entrance.

When they reached his apartment, Devlyn was stunned to find his door ajar.

He never left his door open and it was never unlocked, let alone unguarded. He shared a quick worried glance with Ellendren, and they each began to wield the erendinth, Devlyn pressing into them and Ellendren embracing them. Even in his concern over what took place in his apartment, the reminder of how different kiara and kien wielders were never ceased to impress him.

He bonded with Aliel to increase his ability but not fully since he was wearing his school robes and didn't want them to turn to ash in front of Ellendren. The mental picture he had accidentally shared was embarrassing enough. Still, Devlyn and Aliel bonded near the verge of transforming. Devlyn fully pressed into the erendinth, as he opened the door, quickly scanning the rooms to search for others.

It was as though a tornado had passed through the antechamber. Loose parchment was scattered everywhere, drawers were left open, and furniture was upturned. Quieting his mind, Devlyn searched the area for another presence, for whoever had forced their way into the room. Pressing his hand to his chest pocket, he felt the only two things in his possession that he truly worried about another stealing. The lumols that rattled against the lucilliae in the pouch were also valuable, but it was feeling the lucilliae that provided a measure of relief, although it did nothing to remove the concern about what had happened in his apartment.

He again used his interior sense to scan the room and felt Viren unconscious in the solar. Not sensing anyone else in the apartment, he rushed to Viren and pressed into aerys to push off the debris that was piled on top of the bloodied Guardian knight.

Rushing past Devlyn, Ellendren quickly began a healing wield.

Devlyn watched as the erendinth encompassed Viren, entering his body through his various wounds.

Coming to himself, his breath quickened and his eyes sprung open. He quickly pushed himself to his feet in a panic, his eyes searching the room. "So, they've gone," he said.

"What happened?" asked Devlyn.

"The Septyl knights that were guarding your apartment, and six others forced the door open and attacked me. There was a wielder with them. I don't think he was a shadow elf. If he was, he didn't wield tenebrys against me. Look around, see if they've taken anything. I doubt they broke in just to knock me unconscious."

WITHIN THE WALLS

Classes were canceled for an entire week and every student was confined to their dormitories, or in Devlyn's case, his apartment. Meals were served in the closest dining room to avoid having students walk unsupervised through the entire castle. The additional security measures seemed a bit much to Devlyn, but they were enacted by the chancellor herself, and the Seven Chairs did not object.

The ei'ceuril student wielders were asked to remain at the temple until the imposter and traitorous knights were discovered, which meant that Devlyn was deprived of Kevn's company.

Mother Melanie Birkwell, Chair of Arantiulyn, frequently requested Viren's presence to investigate the events that had occurred in Devlyn's apartment since he was the only witness. While his perspective was important for uncovering the intruders, Devlyn noticed him growing increasingly frustrated as the Chair constantly pulled him away from Devlyn when the castle was on high alert. Viren's priority was to keep Devlyn safe. Devlyn respected the Guardian knight's sentiment, but at the same time he found his vigilance unnecessary; Devlyn was a Phaedryn after all.

Having lost confidence with the Septyl knights, Viren began selecting individuals among their ranks personally, and only accepted those who passed his stringent examinations. Currently, six of those he had selected stood outside Devlyn's apartment, each belonging to a different School.

In a cruel twist of fate, the increased security not only postponed the meeting about Lankor he had intended to have earlier in the week, it also kept Ellendren secluded in her own apartment in the Vyoletryn wing of the castle. Devlyn didn't want to count the number of months that had passed where they had not spoken a single word to each other, and once they had finally mended their relationship, they couldn't see each other.

They shared thoughts with one another occasionally, but it was a poor substitute when he sat alone in his apartment. His thoughts were ever unstable, and he much preferred it if Ellendren didn't bob around inside his head too much.

While the chancellor had no authority over ei'ana, she did request that they too remain confined to their rooms until Mother Melanie could make a statement regarding the Septyl knights.

The sky had long ago darkened and although he couldn't hear them from his apartment, the glasslike Arenthylean Bells of the late hours chimed across the city. A particularly boring book about a theorized history of the other continents sat open on Devlyn's lap. He looked from the book to the solar's window, now showing an inky reflection of himself.

Devlyn could not remember a week with such amazing weather as this past one. Unfortunately, not once had he been able to enjoy the weather with a walk across the grounds; no one was allowed outside. He blamed his lack of concentration on not getting adequate exercise or sunlight. Putting the book down on a table, Devlyn walked toward the door leading out to the corridor. He gave the door a firm tug to ensure that it was properly locked before pressing into the erendinth to feel the protective ward that he had placed on it after Viren had gone once again to assist Mother Melanie.

The ward was another security measure Viren had insisted on. Feeling it secured in place, Devlyn didn't think anyone but himself would have the strength to breach it. He had wielded it into place shortly before Aliel had left to survey the city.

Pulling away from the erendinth, Devlyn went into his bedchamber. Even though he was restricted to his apartment, Devlyn readied himself for sleep as he would any other night. First, he removed the pouch with the lucilliae and lumols from one of his hidden pockets. Taking them off his person was always one of the most stressful moments of each day. They should be locked inside a vault and guarded by ei'ana and knights to ensure their safety—not kept in a sixteen-year-old's pocket. Since the break-in, Devlyn had begun hiding the lucilliae in a drawer before going to bed and placing a ward over it to prevent anyone but himself from opening it—the same ward he had used in Myrium. The added precaution helped him sleep better. Just as the ward over his door did the same for Viren.

Quieting his mind, Devlyn reached out to Aliel, who was enjoying an evening flight high above the city, keeping an ever-present and hidden eye on it. After what had happened to Viren, Aliel took his charge from Hannah all the more seriously. "Kyrenth, Vespenth, Orenth…" said Devlyn aloud, counting out the months that had passed since Hannah had offered to exchange his tuition fee for Aliel's nightly services. "… Estlenth, Borenth, Lierenth, Marenth."

Can you believe I've had seven months of lessons with Yvonne? A full two terms and all I have to show are common marks. And she didn't award the foremost mark to anyone! conveyed Devlyn. A sense of shared amusement passed through their bond at the realization. *I'll see you in the morning.*

Withdrawing from their bond, Devlyn finished getting ready for bed and as he pulled the covers over himself, he realized that he had left a candle burning in the sitting room. Pressing into the erendinth, Devlyn felt the source of the flame and snuffed it out, pulling the air from the flame. It was a useful hint that he had learned from Alethea, and it made him thankful that he was learning how to wield from someone.

A warm breeze swept across his body; it was still dark outside, and Devlyn found it odd that he was not asleep. Eyes closed, he waited for sleep to return.

The expected sensation of drifting to sleep returned, yet it was different. Devlyn was acutely aware of his inhibitions lessening, something that usually happened without him realizing it. Trying to move, he found it too difficult. He could neither roll over nor move his head.

"He's trying to move," came a hushed voice. "He's waking up."

Panic pulsed through his veins at the sound of the voice, a panic that intensified as he found himself unable to move no matter how hard he tried to.

"Well, don't just stand there," said a second voice.

A moment passed while Devlyn struggled against whatever was holding him still.

"You're useless."

Devlyn felt the air withdraw from his lungs and whatever nervous energy he previously had was now gone. His eyes grew heavier and he could not fight what was happening.

"There—now let's move him quickly before that bird returns."

"What do you mean no one came out this door?" Viren thundered at the Septyl knights outside Devlyn's apartment. The door had finally been opened after Velaria, Alethea, and Wyn had exhausted themselves to remove the wield that Devlyn had placed over it. *By the Light, that boy's strong.*

Velaria observed the knights carefully as they stood at attention, enduring the Guardian knight's wrath—they had all heard stories of the legendary knights' vigor and bravery.

"When did you learn something was wrong?" asked Velaria, trying to diffuse the anger—level heads were needed right now.

"Not until after Aliel woke me from a deep sleep an hour before dawn," Viren said, pressing his thumb and index finger to his temples. "I was with Mother Melanie well into the early hours of the morning inspecting the Septyl knights. I didn't want to have to wake him to bring down his wield to let me in, so I slept in a vacant room in the North Tower with the other knights. I came here as fast as I could to find these six bleary eyed knights ready for sleep."

The Septyl knights had their arms crossed and received the accusation grudgingly.

"It was only after I couldn't sense Devlyn inside his apartment that I reached out to you three," said Viren.

Velaria always thought that the nearly empty South Tower was an odd choice for Hannah to place Devlyn in the first place.

"Sir, I assure you, no one entered or exited through this door. Nor did we hear any sort of commotion from behind it," said the Septyl knight who wore the green sigil of Emradiel on his breast.

"Then how do you explain the empty apartment!" Viren roared, rounding on the knight.

"Shall we inspect the rooms?" Alethea asked quietly, revealing her disdain for raised voices, even when warranted.

Velaria followed Alethea into the apartment, Wyn and Viren trailing behind her, Viren demanding that the other knights remain where they stood.

The solar looked just as it would if Devlyn was still in his bed chamber. Nothing appeared out of place. Alethea stood next to a table, looking curiously at the book on it.

"Are they actually requiring students to read this?" she asked.

"Shouldn't we be focusing on what happened to Devlyn?" Viren spoke through clenched teeth.

Velaria had never seen the Guardian knight so distressed before. Although she herself was troubled, a completely different character emerged from Viren, one that seemed wholly alien to the typically reserved and controlled knight.

"There's a secret passage in the wall," Alethea said from Devlyn's bedchamber, ignoring Viren's tone. "Just over there."

Velaria pressed her hand against the stone wall that Alethea had indicated. She allowed the erendinth to fill her being; terys coursed through, giving her a heightened awareness of the stone blocks of the castle. Focusing her attention on the stone along the far wall, she felt the cavity inside. Furious, she wielded the stones out, exposing the passageway.

A sickness stirred in her stomach at the evident treachery.

Aliel waited for no one and rushed in, lighting the passageway ahead of them, his light dimming the further he went. Viren and Alethea followed.

"Wyn, stay here, in case someone comes back," Velaria instructed before following the others.

The temperature dropped instantly as she walked through the narrow corridor. The path broke off in several places, leading to different parts of the tower. Delving into terys once again, she quickly discovered that every apartment of the South Tower was connected by a series of passages hidden behind the inner walls.

Dust and cobwebs attested to the disuse of most of the passages. However, there were two where the dust and cobwebs had been disturbed. Aliel followed the one that led up a narrow spiral stairway all the way to the tower's attic.

Velaria quickly followed the others up the winding stairs. The stairway passed several landings, but the levels were clearly vacant. At the uppermost landing, the stairway opened, not into another passage, but into a large attic filled with all sorts of furniture crammed into the space under a severely steep roof.

An assortment of scrolls littered the attic floor and the last embers of a fire still burned in the hearth. Velaria thought it was from the night before. It was all too obvious that the fire had been intended to destroy any evidence that might identify who had taken up residence there.

Knowing that they were wasting precious time, Aliel quickly led the small group out of the attic and down the narrow winding stairs inside the castle wall.

Velaria's legs ached by the time they reached the bottom landing. After descending the spiral stairway for what had to be the entire length of the tower, Velaria had lost all sense of direction and by the time she began walking along a long narrow passage, she had no idea whether they walked through the rest of the castle or toward Ceurenyl.

Aliel had not bothered waiting for the others to keep pace and was soon beyond Velaria's sight. She couldn't even see his light illuminating the secret passageway.

Viren sprinted to keep close to Aliel, while Velaria remained with

Alethea. Neither spoke as they hurried along. There was nothing to say. Velaria was too worried about what had happened to Devlyn, and assumed that Alethea felt the same.

Devlyn was not dead; that much she knew. If he had been, the phoenix would have turned to ash, only to be reborn to find another to bond with. But, the fact that Aliel could not connect in any way with Devlyn was a terrible concern. Velaria didn't know of any wield that could prevent their connection. Alethea had not said that it was impossible, but neither did she share that it might be a possibility.

It must have been an hour since they had found the secret passageway in Devlyn's apartment before they reached the end of the subterranean passage. A small ladder stood propped against the wall with an open trap door above. Aliel and Viren must have already gone through, leaving Velaria and Alethea to climb the ladder and discover what was above.

Velaria went up the ladder, and sticking her head above the trap door, she saw that it opened to a small cellar. Stepping into the space, she waited for Alethea to climb into the cellar before they both walked up another staircase, fortunately only one flight, to find themselves in a small house.

Aliel was gone, but Viren had a young family sitting against a wall.

"They were tied up and gagged the entire night," he said, not taking his eyes off the young family, now free of their bindings. "They said five women came out of their cellar with a young man—unconscious. You can speak to them if you want. But I doubt they know anything useful."

Velaria walked toward the frightened family of four. The children were no older than eight. "Do you know who I am?"

The husband and wife nodded.

"Can you identify the unconscious young man?"

"He had funny looking hair; it was mostly light brown, but it had threads of red, blond, and even black in it," said the wife. She spoke in quick breaths, and her eyes kept darting back toward Viren. "I couldn't see his eyes, but he wore nothing but his small clothes, as though those women had dragged him from bed. He was definitely an elf though—can't mistake those pointy ears."

"Did it look like he was injured at all?"

The husband and wife both shook their heads.

"How could they manage to overcome a Phaedryn?" Velaria asked Alethea. "Surely they couldn't best him in wielding, even if it was five to one."

"It's possible he was never given the chance to wield or reach out to Aliel. They could have done something to keep him from waking. He might not have even realized that anything was happening."

"Is Aliel searching the mountain road?" asked Velaria.

"I believe so," said Viren. "If Aliel doesn't find them along the road, we might have to face the possibility that he is still in the city."

The chance that Devlyn was still inside the city walls was exceedingly thin, even if Aliel was not capable of locating them along the mountain road. Velaria found it difficult to imagine what his abductors would hope to gain by remaining in the city. *Surely it was not to frighten Devlyn.*

As terrible as it was that Devlyn had been abducted, the possibility that there were Tenebrae ei'ana hiding in Gwilnor was now a reality they could no longer ignore. Five of them had managed something that should have been impossible. The only question that kept Velaria from focusing entirely on Devlyn's whereabouts was how many more of her sister ei'ana belonged to that wretched unrecognized School?

Velaria had only known Viren for a short time, but thought of him as a steady, reliable sort. Yet there was now something unpredictable lingering in his eyes. She doubted that he would remain in the city, given the circumstances. She had witnessed firsthand the devotion and loyalty between knights and their lords or ladies, but never had she seen one so protective as Viren. The more she thought about the connection, the more it made sense; after all, he had spent well over a thousand years waiting for Devlyn to be born. To have bided all that time and then to have someone kidnap his charge was beyond imaginable, especially now that they knew Devlyn was a Lorenthien. Viren had lived through the

Ceurendol War and had spent fourteen hundred years believing the Lorenthien line had been snuffed out.

Not bothering to ask when or if he was leaving, Velaria asked, "Where will you go?"

"Toward Lankor," said Viren. "Tiel is currently without a navy and I suspect that his abductors intend to present him as a gift to Erynor. Sudern would be the wisest choice, but I doubt they would find a ship that would openly take them to Broid. Lankor would be their surest choice."

"Do you intend to go alone?"

"I would prefer to. Time is of the essence."

"But you won't," Velaria said, not as a question, but a statement.

Viren nodded, and Velaria felt relief for the first time since she had been woken.

"I understand that you won't be able to join me," Viren said, knowing full well that she could not leave Gwilnor while it was under the threat of Tenebrae ei'ana.

Viren looked toward Alethea, and without even asking, Alethea said, "These old bones would much prefer getting as far away from the institutionalization of wielding as possible. Even if it is to chase a bunch of wayward ei'ana to Broid. Wyn will of course join us; he's still too young to be without proper instruction."

"I assume Ellendren will join you as well," Velaria said, piecing the group together out loud. "I would like to include Liam and Jaerol, but they are nowhere near ready to leave Gwilnor. And besides, they are needed here to help the newer kien wielders. Their role here, as inexperienced as they are, is pivotal if we want our program to have any luck at succeeding."

"Is there anyone else you would recommend?" asked Viren. "I doubt the four of us, only three being wielders, would last long against five Tenebrae ei'ana."

Velaria shuddered. Not only was the castle infested with Tenebrae ei'ana, but a student had been taken—Devlyn had been taken. *We'll get him back, Evellyn, I promise it.*

RUMORS

Classes resumed, yet the castle residents were little comforted, least of all Liam and Jaerol. Not a single ei'ana pretended everything was fine. Everyone at Gwilnor knew that Devlyn had disappeared, and they also knew that he had been abducted by someone inside the castle. Jaerol had to convince Liam on a daily basis that he would better serve Septyl in the castle then searching for his brother. Whoever had abducted Devlyn, could just as easily abduct Liam—again. He never shared that thought with Liam but neither would Jaerol let anything happen to him either. Jaerol refused to lose someone else.

The students had been told that the Seven Chairs were investigating the matter. Jaerol was under the impression that they wanted to compile a list of ei'ana currently residing in the castle and from that list, discover who was missing.

Jaerol didn't believe that their strategy would provide any fruit. Ei'ana were never known for being stationary and rarely remained in the castle long. Most kept busy trying to avert the heightening war, gain allies among lesser known nobles, or strengthen diplomatic relations across the kingdoms. Still, others carried out their projects and research across Eklean, not allowing a silly war to dampen their progress.

Perhaps the Seven Chairs were spreading word of their technique to get others to stop asking them how they intended to go about their investigations. Even if they had another plan, Jaerol didn't think that they would discover the culprit, let alone prove anything of worth. Whoever was responsible for Devlyn's abduction was far away by now.

The ei'ceuril student wielders returned to the castle a week later than intended. Since they had not been allowed to leave the temple, they knew very little of what had happened at Gwilnor, only that the castle was under high alert and that no one could enter or leave.

Despite the pious ei'ceuril claiming they had no taste for gossip, which Jaerol knew firsthand was an outright lie, they garnered just as many speculations as the castle's inhabitants had. Jaerol had never seen so many people gossiping to others they had never met before, just to hear their opinion about Devlyn's disappearance.

The biggest surprise for everyone were the hidden passages inside the South Tower. It was rumored that Chancellor Hannah was the first ei'ana interrogated by the Seven Chairs. Placing Devlyn in such a location was convenient for anyone who might want to remove him from the castle, making her motives for doing just that suspicious.

No facts were publicized about that hearing, if such a hearing even took place. Figuring out the difference between rumor and fact was impossible. Jaerol wished the Seven Chairs would just confirm or deny the rapidly spreading rumors at the end of each day.

Although classes had initially been suspended with students restricted to their dormitory wings and most magisters had suspended their assignments, one did not. Jaerol was not at all surprised when he received a note on the first day of their canceled lessons advising him of a reading assignment. The mandatory readings were three times as long as her normal requirements. When it had been declared that classes were canceled for a second week, Yvonne had a second note delivered to her students with an even longer reading list.

Jaerol had been relieved when classes had resumed, since there would not be a third note. Sitting toward the rear of Yvonne's class, he kept a close eye on Danyol. Ever since Jaerol had become aware of something abnormal having occurred inside the castle, he had immediately linked it to Danyol.

He still couldn't say why, but he had never distrusted anyone so much. There was something about Danyol that demanded an explanation, and perhaps time spent in one of the temple's prison cells. Unfortunately, the ei'ceuril did not just throw random people into their cells at the whim of a student wielder, especially from a student wielder who had spent a day in those cells himself.

When Jaerol and the other students took their seats in Yvonne's class after their extended break, they were shocked to discover that she intended to test them on their readings and demanded that they display the proper wields. While her lectures were never informative when it came to wielding, none of the students were prepared. Jaerol could barely recognize the wields in the required text and he was only confident about one of them.

Half the class had already attempted and, as usual, failed miserably. Jaerol didn't think anyone could have completed the wields, even without Danyol's influence. Since his arrival, he had taken Yvonne's place of interfering with her students' wielding, a role that made Jaerol dislike him even more.

Focusing on his own disdain for Danyol, Jaerol did not hear Yvonne call his name.

"Jaerol," Yvonne called a second time, clearly impatient at having to repeat herself.

His pulse quickened as he made his way to the front of the classroom, preparing himself for the guaranteed embarrassment about to take place.

Yvonne never asked whether her students were ready. If they did not begin to wield as soon as they had the opportunity, they would not stand a chance against Danyol's wield to prevent their own.

Pressing into aerys and ignys, Jaerol felt those exuberant erendinth pulse through the room. The classroom was alive with the erendinth, invisible to the naked eye. Yet, after pressing into them, he felt the residue they had left from the other students' attempts. Jaerol had a certain confidence whenever they were asked to perform a wield that required ignys; as a Cyndinari, he was particularly gifted with it.

Air and fire rushed through the classroom, Jaerol could do anything he wanted with those two elemental erendinth and not just the wield required of him. He was tempted to condense the two together and form a pillar of sorts, directed toward Danyol. He wished he knew why he distrusted him; there was something there but whatever it was, it was beyond his grasp.

Rather, Jaerol wielded the two erendinth to recreate one of the useless wields Yvonne had them research over the last two weeks. The room began to warm. He was the first student who had managed to raise the temperature even a single degree.

Danyol lashed against his wield, nearly crippling it.

Not giving in, Jaerol held firm, intensifying his wield.

Danyol was relentless. When the classroom continued to warm, a hint of pride sprung in Jaerol at succeeding where none of the other students had yet managed. Jaerol stared into Danyol's eyes as he wielded, wanting nothing more than to beat Danyol. Jaerol tried the exercise that Devlyn had mentioned to him, quieting his mind to gain better control. That was something his childhood magisters at the Imperium had never taught—control was for the weak.

A heightened awareness fell over Jaerol as he followed the required steps with careful steady breaths. He closed his eyes to better slow his breathing.

You're not going to best me, flaming deserter, Jaerol heard outside his own thoughts.

His eyes sprung open, and his control gone, Danyol easily overcame him, extinguishing his wield. The room returned to its customary temperature, the useless wield now a distant memory.

Danyol wore a smug look, making Jaerol want to punch the expression right off his face. Everything finally made sense. Despite Danyol overcoming his wield, Jaerol could not help but feel that he had accomplished something important, even if it brought a crushing sense of dread.

"You failed; return to your seat," Danyol said, sneering all the while.

Having no reason to argue, Jaerol turned away, making eye contact with Fyreh as he did.

Fyreh did not appear shocked, but he did grimace.

The rest of the class attempted the wield against Danyol. Between every attempt, Danyol looked to Jaerol, who returned the stare from his seat at the back of the classroom. As satisfied about his accomplishment as Jaerol felt, he had no idea how to prove what he now knew as fact: Danyol was a Cyndinari. Now Jaerol suddenly saw all the identifiable features of his kin in Danyol, disguised behind some sort of wield. His natural red hair had been dyed black. His skin was more bronze than chestnut, and even his facial features were different than those of the Eldinari. *How could I miss it?*

The art of wielding class finally ended, and Jaerol rushed from the classroom with Liam, barely restraining himself from pulling Liam by the hand.

Navigating through the throng of students, Jaerol only made it halfway down the corridor with Liam when a hand firmly clasped Jaerol's shoulder. His stomach lurched at the thought of the hand belonging to Danyol but settled when he turned to find Fyreh behind him.

"There's something we need to talk about," said the Eldinari magister, looking around the crowded corridors before adding, "privately and immediately. My apologies, Liam, but would you excuse us?"

"Of course." Liam looked from Fyreh to Jaerol, curious. "I'll wait for you in the dining hall, when you're finished."

Without waiting for Jaerol to agree, Fyreh turned on his heel and walked in the opposite direction through the crowded corridors with Jaerol trailing behind.

Following Fyreh, Jaerol walked through the base of the White Tower that contained the Albien wing. It was the closest of the seven towers to the library and looked over the main courtyard, holding the northeast corner. An impressive bridge spanned the distance between the White Tower and the Dragon Tower, not just connecting the two seven-sided towers but joining two of the three castle structures.

Fyreh pushed open the door and walked onto the bridge. A surprisingly small number of students crossed the bridge, most probably heading in the opposite direction to the dining hall for lunch. Jaerol's stomach groaned as he thought of food.

Without warning, Fyreh stopped and turned on Jaerol. A harsh wind batted against him as he looked down toward the river that flowed past half the city. "I'm afraid to say that you cannot share what you discovered in class today. Not even with Liam."

Jaerol was suddenly aware of the bridge's height. It was not a tall bridge compared to the castle as a whole, especially with one of Gwilnor's towers piercing the clouds directly in front of him, but it rose well above the rocky crevice below and the narrow mountain stream which fed into the larger river. A fall from this height would break more than just a couple of bones. Jaerol held his breath, afraid to ask why he couldn't speak of Danyol's true origins.

Fyreh did not come off as an intimidating elf; he was quite gentle and had a jovial temperament. To see the shift in character not only confused but also frightened Jaerol, because of where they were now standing. Luckily, he had learned long ago to hide his emotions, else he would surely have been killed years ago.

"I've known for some time that Danyol has never gazed upon the stars in the wonder of twilight. He belongs amongst the Eldinari as much as this castle belongs in the Eldin Wood."

"You've known! Why hasn't anything been done?" Jaerol demanded, no longer worried for his own safety, but furious that appropriate actions had not been taken against Danyol. "Do you have any idea what kind of harm he is capable of? How long do you think it will be until he starts stealing the souls of others here to extend his own life?"

"I understand your anger. But, we lack the support required to expel him from the castle."

"I'm sorry, but what do you mean 'we lack the support?'"

"Are you aware of what happened to Devlyn?"

"Of course, the entire castle knows, probably the entire city. Liam is worried sick."

"Do you think those five ei'ana were the only Tenebrae in the castle?"

A moment of nothing but the quiet wind blowing against their ears passed. "We don't know who's who, do we?" asked Jaerol.

"Our hope is to use this so called Danyol as bait. If he's exposed for what he is, he'll be useless to us, but if we can study his network here in the castle, we might be able to figure out who has betrayed Septyl."

Taking in the gravity of their circumstance, Jaerol was left in shock at how desperate their situation truly was. He had known that it was bad, but he had never imagined that the ei'ana would allow a known shadow elf inside their walls.

"You did well yesterday, by the way," Fyreh said.

"My elthion team didn't win." Jaerol wasn't sure whether he was comfortable with the change of topic—he wasn't done with talking about the threats to Gwilnor.

"True, but you and Liam have had very little training as well. Especially, since you must completely relearn how to wield with control. I can only imagine what bad habits you were taught at Broid. Most of the students you faced in the match have already chosen their Schools and are well ahead in their studies."

If Devlyn's disappearance was not the focus of daily gossip, elthion surely was. Jaerol still felt his heart skipping a beat due to his team's narrow loss. He had managed to wield the umbrys ball through the aquaeys and umbrys goal, yet it still hadn't been enough to win the game. His team came in second of the three competing teams. Jaerol had heard the entire castle groan when his match ended.

The best thing about competing in the unofficial league was that the players had the advantage of learning how to wield from someone other than Yvonne.

"I'm sorry, Jaerol, but this has to stay quiet—for now." Fyreh left Jaerol standing in the middle of the bridge.

Turning away from the Dragon Tower, Jaerol made his way to the dining hall. He had no desire to pass the art of wielding classroom again, so he took the long way around and through the brightly lit library where the colorful stained-glass windows let a mystical light spill across the vaulted room and its many bookshelves.

After spending most of his life in Broid, Jaerol had acquired a skeptical nature toward other people, but ever since he'd been in an environment where he felt relatively safe, his guard had lowered, not much, but enough that he could interact pleasantly with people. He had even begun assuming most people had good intentions, mostly because of Liam. After his discovery and then his talk with Fyreh, his eyes lingered with a heightened sense of distrust on everyone he passed. Some of the students smiled at him, while others completely ignored him.

He brushed past them all.

When he finally reached the dining hall, he saw Liam sitting with a small group of students. Jaerol knew most of them, although there were a few unfamiliar faces. He went to a buffet table to grab a bowl of soup and then joined the others. They were speaking warily amongst themselves; the castle was still trying to gather details regarding Devlyn's disappearance and every student had taken it upon themselves to ferret out the truth.

Jaerol forced a friendly smile, but he couldn't stop thinking about Danyol. *How'd I miss it? How could I miss seeing him for his true nature?* Jaerol's inner thoughts ruminated on the Cyndinari claiming to be an Eldinari named Danyol.

In a Dream

Legs crossed, Ellendren concentrated as best she could on reaching Devlyn by means of the process Therril was guiding her through. She kept her eyes shut as the corners of her lips quivered.

"You're not focusing enough."

She wanted to argue with the elf she had recently discovered was her distant ancestor and not only husband to Lucillia, but father to Roendryn and Feolyn.

It was not the first time she had heard him say those words in this session. She had argued the first time though, and it had led to wasting twenty minutes. Taking a deep breath, she filled her lungs with air. It was one of the rare occasions where the old elf opened the windows of his office, perhaps as a kind gesture. Most of the time, whenever she had cause to enter his office, her nostrils were filled with a mustiness, a scent that reminded her of most elderly men.

She exhaled, allowing the air from her lungs to return to the rhythmic cycle. Her eyes remained closed. Therril had never instructed her to do so, but she found that keeping them open provided too many distractions, even if there was only one other person in the office.

"It's not his face you need to identify, but his actual being—his spirit," said Therril.

Ellendren knew that he was trying to help, but whenever he spoke, she lost her focus and had to restart the entire process. She took another deep breath with hopes of clearing her mind and repeated the ritual.

She knew Devlyn better than anyone other than Aliel. At least, she thought she did. Focusing on who he was should have been a simple task, yet the better part of the afternoon had already passed. Thoughts of when they first met sprang to her memory; he had been so embarrassed when she caught him wielding outside the castle. It was incredibly foolish of him to do so, especially as an untrained kien wielder. *He should have known better.*

Looking back on that encounter, she only just realized how awkward that meeting must have been for Devlyn—his introduction to Trethien. Devlyn had confessed to her much later that she had mesmerized him from that very moment. She hadn't admitted that he had done the same to her.

"Perhaps it is necessary for you to enter Somnaeniel, the World-in-Between, first," muttered Therril.

"I just need more time—I'll get it."

"Oh, that you will! I have no doubt of it," chuckled Therril. "But, I'm afraid to admit that Alethea was right. I was hoping that we could bypass that minor step. I've never trusted that place. Even less so now."

"Devlyn mentions it with mixed feelings. I still can't believe that Abbie Wintyr had actually managed to keep her identity hidden from the ei'ana at the time of her admission to Gwilnor."

"The Druids of Kweil Aitch are a remarkable people," said Therril, seeming to look back on a memory from a different age.

Ellendren could not help but worry whenever Devlyn mentioned that he had been drawn into Somnaeniel by Abbie or Eagan. She trusted Abbie, and to an extent Eagan, even though she had never met him before, but the thought of someone capable of drawing another into a dangerous life-threatening realm that you had little control over made her incredibly tense. She was haunted by the thought of it. If the druids knew this skill, doubtless there were others who did as well.

"When will I try?"

"You are determined," laughed Therril in his throaty chuckle. "Well, despite my experience and Alethea's combined, it will take much longer than it took Abbie and Eagan to teach Devlyn. The druids might not know that place as well as the aldarchs, but they still know it better than most dwarves know their own mountains, although don't mention that to Oma; she'll skin me from ear to toe if she knew I said such a thing!"

Hearing Oma's name made Ellendren smile slightly. She had only met the dwarf briefly, that time in the stables when she had introduced Devlyn to Laureniel, but Oma had left a remarkable impression on her. Especially how she had been able to make Devlyn squirm.

"How could I not be determined?" Ellendren asked, her smile fading and with it the memory of Oma. "Devlyn's been gone for over two weeks and we still haven't gone out searching for him."

Ellendren's confidence wavered. By necessity, these exercises went beyond her mental defenses. She guarded herself scrupulously, especially in the presence of others. Any attempt to conceal how she felt about Devlyn's disappearance would not get past Therril. She knew the old magister saw past her weaknesses, but there was nothing she could do to prevent that; he was very talented at reading others, frustratingly so at times.

"We're all worried about him. But the sooner things settle down here, the sooner you and the others can join Aliel. Truth be told, I don't even think Viren will be able to catch up with Aliel, let alone figure out the phoenix's location."

"How long will it take to learn?" Ellendren asked, not wanting to spend any more time than necessary thinking about the reason. The longer it took her to enter Devlyn's dreams, the further away his captors would have taken him by the time Ellendren and the others could leave Ceurenyl with a clear destination. They had already wasted enough time waiting.

"Well, if Alethea has the same skill in Somnaeniel that she used to, she should be able to draw you in after you've fallen asleep. The only disadvantage is that we must wait until you are both tired enough to sleep. The druids, on the other hand, all they need do is touch someone physically or mentally in order to pull them into the World-in-Between. After thousands of years of this academy's existence, not a single ei'ana has uncovered how they manage it. Remarkable, isn't it?"

Ellendren found herself agreeing with a nod. In all honesty, she found it unlikely that Septyl had never managed to uncover Somnaeniel's secrets. They must not have devoted enough of their energies to it, nor thought it important enough to devote their time toward. There was nothing the ei'ana were incapable of—there was nothing *she* was incapable of. And she would accomplish it, even if she was not yet an ei'ana. No matter what it took, she would find Devlyn.

Just the thought brought a mix of emotions. Avoiding them entirely, she allowed her curiosity to consume her attention. "I still don't understand why Aliel can't do this. After all, there's no one more intimately connected to Devlyn than Aliel."

"I'm not going to pretend to know the answer," Therril said, scratching his chin. "But, I'm under the impression that there is a wield or contraption that's suppressing their connection. I haven't the slightest idea of how or what it is. But it's the only reasonable explanation."

"So how will entering Somnaeniel help me reach Devlyn if not even Aliel can contact him?"

"A certain connection has to be present and what Alethea and myself have been theorizing is that it might be possible for you to enter not only Somnaeniel, but into his dreams themselves," Therril said, with a hint of excitement. "Whatever is blocking his connection with Aliel will doubtlessly also prevent anyone from pulling him into Somnaeniel. So, if we can't bring him into the Dream, perhaps you can enter his dreams."

"Forgive me, magister, but how in the Light is that possible?"

"Well, it's quite simple really. He has to already be dreaming about you. I know that young elf quite well, better than yourself most likely. Not to insult, but it comes with age. Anyway, the reason I or Alethea won't be able to manage it, is because we highly doubt that he will be dreaming about us. Now there might be a sporadic dream, sure, but those are impossible to monitor. But you on the other hand, ho-oh! he probably hasn't stopped dreaming about you since you first met! But be warned, you will be entering a teenage boy's dreams."

Ellendren shivered at the thought of what Devlyn dreamt of, especially when she was the subject of them. The whole theory sounded absurd in Ellendren's opinion, but to a certain extent, it made sense. Still, she had no idea how they expected her to bridge the gap into another person's dreams. Even if it was someone that she cared about. Falling into her own thoughts, her mind strayed to her upcoming elthion match. Vyoletryn was matched against Albien and Crimsyn.

Her stomach knotted at the thought of competing against Crimsyn. She still felt connected to the School even though she had opted to join the Vyoletryn School during the Choosing ceremony.

"I'm still uncertain whether I should compete in today's elthion match. After all, I should focus on reaching out to Devlyn," Ellendren admitted, her left hand massaging her upper right arm.

"Don't be ridiculous. There's nothing we can do until it's time for bed, and I'm sure your nerves will keep you from sleeping soundly as it is. You performed very well in the last match. I still can't believe how quickly you scored that seventeen-pointer! I bet your speed made the other contenders freeze in disbelief. Not to mention you wielding a transcendental erendinth."

Ellendren couldn't stop the modest smile from broadening. She had no intention of admonishing herself for her impressive wielding.

The second match was only an hour away. There was still time to grab a quick bite to eat, but she did not want to compete with a full stomach; she had already made that mistake before practice one day and nearly lost her entire meal.

They agreed to a time to attempt entering Somnaeniel later that evening, and Ellendren left Therril's office. Therril would let Alethea know when to be ready.

Whenever she knew they were working together, Ellendren would utter a small prayer that they would not argue the entire time. Considering the gravity of what they wanted to accomplish this evening, she found herself spending more time in prayer than she typically would.

The second elthion match was set to take place at the ninth hour. Fortunately, there was nothing inherently dangerous about it. The excitement from the previous match was still buzzing and spectators had begun heading out of the castle and toward the elthion field. Since it was the weekend, students weren't required to wear school robes. Instead of crowds dressed in grey, the students spilling out of the castle wore hues of reds, purples, and whites to cheer on their favorite team. Ellendren already wore her purple uniform. Its cut reminded her of Devlyn's lier-athnil robe.

As she walked through the crowds, students patted her on the back and cheered for her. Everyone was excited to see the youngest competitor and heir to the Lucillian throne bring another win to Vyoletryn.

Diverting from the rest of the students, Ellendren walked away from the spectator benches and toward three tents. Each tent was assembled and disassembled before and after each match and every School had their own. Ellendren pushed the violet canvas flap aside and entered the Vyoletryn's team tent. She was the last of her team to arrive, and they all stared at her as she walked in. It didn't help that they were all her senior either.

In the center of the six other girls stood a tall, lean woman. Everything about her identified her as a Luminari, from her light brown hair, to her silver eyes with emerald encircling the iris, to her pointy ears.

Wilven Faroh had professed the Counsels as an ei'ana twenty years prior, and before abandoning the elthion field as a competitor, had won more medals for the Vyoletryn team than any other student wielder in fifty years. Almost immediately after becoming an ei'ana, she took on the mantle of coaching the Vyoletryn team—and had done so ever since.

Wilven looked at Ellendren. "Good—you made it."

Ellendren noticed Jenni, another student wielder, who had not made the first string of the Vyoletryn team, because Ellendren had taken the last place. Jenni had then been placed on the substitute team. *They expected me to skip.* The thought pained her, that her own team had anticipated that she would not be playing, even though she fully intended to do just that.

"Ellendren, I need you to focus on the umbrys ball, and if you can, score through both the aquaeys and umbrys goals. I don't expect much of a challenge from the Albiens, but the Crimsyns will not simply give up," said Wilven, keeping her penetrating gaze on Ellendren.

A loud sonorous bell tolled from the center of the field. Seven more chimes and the game would begin. Wilven eyed her team, measuring their readiness.

A second toll.

Wilven turned and walked from their canvased tent to the field. The team followed her out of the tent then separated to go to their respective starting points. Ellendren stood between the white and yellow alcoves, holding the aerys and lumenys balls respectively, the furthest distance from the grey alcove and the umbrys ball inside it.

Two other student wielders stood beside her, both at least three years older. Julia and Nadel were always kind to her when they passed in the corridors, but now they had nothing but fierce competition in their eyes since they played for the Albien and Crimsyn School teams.

The seventh bell tolled and Ellendren darted onto the playable field—crossing through the central rings was an immediate penalty. Julia and Nadel sprinted after her. The field was a frenzy as the three teams raced across the grass, some already in possession of the elthion balls.

Ellendren had the advantage though, as she was the only player on the field capable of wielding a transcendental erendinth. Yvonne should have seen to it that her students had learned how wield the transcendental erendinth, but had not. She never taught anything useful.

Opening herself to the elemental erendinth, Ellendren felt them interact with her very being. Her spirit felt afire whenever she wielded, but to wield the transcendental erendinth, she had to go against her entire training. *Giving to receive—receiving to give.* She repeated the mantra in her mind. How she had once misconstrued it was beyond her imagining. And it wasn't just her, but the entirety of Septyl had mistaken it for over a millennium.

Aware of the transcendental erendinth, she felt umbrys just beyond her grasp. She pressed herself into it as she lunged toward the grey alcove holding the umbrys ball and wielded the ball from its pedestal. She had long reconciled with the shadowy erendinth. Her bias had been misplaced—it was tenebrys that made her stomach lurch—not umbrys. Umbrys was one of the seven erendinth that had created Teraeniel.

Dodging around other players with the umbrys ball in her possession, she made her way back to where she had started.

Both Julia and Nadel were on her heels, working hard as they wielded every elemental erendinth to wrench the ball from her possession, but only the erendinth proper to the ball could do that. They could block the umbrys ball with another elemental ball, but the other players possessed every other ball, trying to score as many points as possible. They had to compensate for the twenty-pointer that Ellendren was about to score, with as many three and seven-pointers they could manage.

Cheers roared from the spectators in the stands as she neared the umbrys goal.

Still filled with the elemental erendinth, Ellendren wielded aquaeys with umbrys and launched the ball at an incredible speed. She watched as it pelted through the aquaeys goal and then sent it through the umbrys goal.

A confident smile crept to her face, knowing that she just scored twenty points for her team. Unlike last time with her seventeen-pointer where she controlled one of the elemental balls and scored it through an elemental and transcendental goal, this time, she had possession of a transcendental ball and scored it through both types of goals, something that required her to wield two erendinth at once.

The game finished as it had started with Vyoletryn overwhelmingly dominating Albien and Crimsyn. Taking first place meant an additional one hundred fifty points for Vyoletryn, bringing their overall score to three hundred in the School Cup ranking. Albien managed to come in second, bringing them an additional one hundred points, while Crimsyn came in last, giving them seventy-five points.

Vyoletryn would not play again until the sixth match. Only three teams would continue to the championship to compete for the School Cup.

Ellendren left the elthion field pleased with her performance, yet not eager to be swept away into the festivities which were sure to follow in the dining hall and later in the Vyoletryn student common room. Several Vyoletryns pulled her arm to keep her from leaving, but she easily wrestled it free and left the crowds behind, hoping that she could fall asleep at the designated hour.

Knowing that she would have to manage falling asleep without much difficulty, she spent her evening studying an extremely complex scroll covering the delicate actions required to unravel a barrier wielded of every elemental erendinth. The barrier was a rather simple wield, yet undoing it required the utmost control and precision. She had never found the wield necessary in the past, since there was always an alternate route to circumvent a shield. She also hoped the scroll might provide a method to improve her unravelling ability.

She had requested the book from Gwilnor's library over two months ago, the longest she had held a book without even opening it to skim through its pages. Like most books written by Albiens, it had the reputation of being incredibly dry and boring. The only other person she knew to have read the book was Velaria, who had recommended it to her in the first place, and even Velaria had admitted to dozing off while reading it.

When the designated hour finally approached, Ellendren lay down on her bed. She had been tired for the past two hours and had been reading while sitting up with her pillows propped behind her against the headboard. She had forced herself to read longer than she wanted, the fear of waking up before Therril and Alethea called her into Somnaeniel keeping her from putting the book down until she was as tired as she could be.

Standing beside a river that did not act as most rivers would, Ellendren took in her surroundings, which were quite foreign to her. The only familiar sight was Therril and Alethea. She did not feel as though she was asleep, but there was no other explanation. After all, it simply was not possible for another to transport you from your own bed without you realizing it.

"We're in what is known as the Qien Dynasty," said Alethea, "and it has remained so since before we left our Skylands. Only the Daer Empire in Daereneth can claim a longer autonomy reigning over an entire continent than the Qien Emperors and Empresses."

"What's wrong with the river?" asked Ellendren, still fixated on how it did not seem to move as it should. She had read a brief history regarding Qien, but there were many gaps and much was left to the imagination.

"Water is an element that belongs to Teraeniel, the World-Below. Since it is not of this place, it is manifested differently," said Alethea. "Nothing in this realm is physical."

"I'm sorry, but why did you bring me here? Couldn't we have done this from the castle?"

"We could have," said Therril, "but, the castle is doubtlessly being watched. Both in Teraeniel and Somnaeniel—and perhaps even in Lumaeniel for all we know. Regardless, we thought this a safer location. After all, none of us have any connections to this vast land, which shockingly, is not the vastest."

Ellendren always found it odd how Therril's thoughts never ended at the expected termination point, but rather rambled on through several deviations.

"My thoughts exactly," replied Alethea. "But if you don't want your thoughts known here, it's better to not think them. Thoughts act in the same way as your voice does here. Granted, the louder they are in the World-Below, the more audible are they there too."

Unable to hide her embarrassment, Ellendren apologized to Therril.

"No need for that! You aren't the first who's had such thoughts, nor will you be the last," said Therril. "Now, let's do what we came here to do and leave!"

Ellendren was about to sit on the ground when she noticed pits of black ooze dotted across the landscape. "We don't have time to explain; stay away from them, and you'll be fine," said Alethea.

Despite her curiosity over the black ooze, Ellendren once again found herself sitting with her legs crossed and her eyes closed. Part of her wanted to explore this place, but a larger part wanted nothing to do with it. The irresponsibility of coming to such a place—with those pits of whatever that black ooze was—was just asking for trouble. She wanted to leave as soon as she could, and resolutely put aside her frustration with Devlyn for visiting this place on a regular basis.

"Under what pretense did you think it was a good idea?" asked Ellendren, not noticing that her surroundings had shifted. She now faced Devlyn and was sitting on his lap of all places. She could feel that they had just been kissing, and not briefly either. This was just a dream, but she tasted his breath in her mouth.

"Um, what?" muttered Devlyn, confused at the interruption. "Did I do something wrong?" He wasn't wearing a shirt.

"Is it really you?" Ellendren asked, unable to prevent herself from embracing him, despite the improper posture.

"Who else would be kissing you, um, like we were," Devlyn said in a playful, yet confident manner.

"That's not important, it wasn't real." Even as she said it, she wanted it to be real. "Where are you?"

"What are you talking about? We're in the abbey school. Don't you remember? Alex is spending the weekend with his family. Ents lets him do whatever he wants."

Ellendren gave him a look that required no words to punch a hole through his feigned reality.

"You've never been to Cor'lera…" Devlyn trailed off, trying to figure out what was happening. "And you've never met Abbot Entiel."

"You're dreaming; this is a dream. You were kidnapped two weeks ago," she said.

Devlyn's form flickered.

"No, you can't go yet. Stay with me."

"It's hot and humid," he said, his form stabilizing.

"Have you heard anything of where they might be taking you?"

"I…I don't know," said Devlyn, his eyes panicked and darted about. "I don't think I've even seen their faces. I can vaguely overhear them at times, but nothing useful. Elle, they've locked me in a box of some kind. There're no holes in it, I have no idea how I'm able to breathe; it's so hot. They're treating me like a caged animal."

"That's awful." The humidity would explain why he wasn't wearing a shirt here. At least, that's what she told herself.

"Whatever it's made of, it's preventing me from wielding and reaching out to Aliel," Devlyn said, growing more concerned with each word he spoke. "Whenever I try to press into the erendinth, I can feel them, they're just on the other side of the box, only I can't touch them."

"So that's how they managed it," Ellendren said, terrified at the thought of being locked in such a box.

"Hold on, how are you here, in my dreams that is?"

"Therril said it was because you would already be dreaming of me that I could, that's why neither he nor Alethea are here. Aliel has left the city, hoping to catch up with you, and Viren is losing his patience at not being able to follow. But we have no idea where you are or where you're going. The rest of us are waiting for me to learn how to contact you before we leave as well."

"You're amazing; you know that, right?" Devlyn said, infuriating Ellendren as he flirted with her, now of all times. "I'm sorry, it's just, I've missed you."

It was impossible to stay mad at him, even if she wanted to.

"You missed the second elthion match." Ellendren smirked. *Two can play that game.*

Devlyn blushed.

"We crushed Albien and Crimsyn," Ellendren said, still excited over the events.

His body started to fade, as did her own. She wanted nothing more than to stay where she was with him. To touch him. Even if it was only a dream, it made no difference.

When the room in Cor'lera's abbey school faded, Ellendren did not return to Somnaeniel, but rather to her own room at Gwilnor in the Vyoletryn wing in the East Tower. She opened her eyes to darkness, making her wonder if it was even past midnight yet. She knew she would not be able to return to sleep. It was impossible to know what time it was and she never had the need to know the time at such an unreasonable hour of the night.

Her heart was beating quickly and she wanted to speak to someone, anyone about her experience. Even though she had now accomplished it, she had never heard of someone entering another person's dreams before Therril had said they would try to do so. If it was not for the circumstances, she didn't think she would have even attempted it. The thought of what could have happened stirred within her. What if he never realized he was still dreaming? The more startling revelation was that a small part of her had wished he didn't realize it. He had never been so forward with her in person before, and she found that she liked it.

Getting up, she walked to her window, which looked east over the river snaking around the city. She could only see so far, not only because of the lack of light, but because of the mountains that also surrounded the city. The river was nestled between the mountain Ceurenyl rested on and the surrounding ones before eventually emptying into Lake Saeryndol, which was allegedly frozen. That was now a fact as Therril had admitted to walking across it when he'd confessed his origins.

She thought of going for a late stroll through the castle, hoping a nice walk would help center herself. It was unlikely that she'd run into anyone that she'd want to tell of her experience. Leaving her bedchamber for the sitting area, she made her way toward the door leading to the corridor. Placing her fingers on the handle to pull the door open, a hushed conversation seeped through from the other side. She was only able to hear every other word at first but managed to understand what they were talking about.

"They know we're in the castle," said the first female voice.

"Of course, they know, don't be absurd," said the second, also a woman.

The voices sounded familiar, yet there was no way of discerning who they belonged to.

"It's about time they figured it out too, and even better, they're terrified of us. It won't be long before they stop trusting their dearest friends."

"Imagine, a single dominant School for all Septyl, just as it should have always been."

"Quiet, you fool!"

The voices trailed off, as did their soft footsteps. If she had had any hope of returning to sleep, there was none now. Her mind raced as she considered who might be the best person to tell about what she'd overheard. Velaria and Paurel, her own Chair, were the obvious choices. Who else?

After creating a mental list of possible ei'ana, she started checking different ones off the list, thinking that they might already belong to the Tenebrae School.

How anyone could desire Septyl to have a single School was beyond her. The richness of Septyl was its diversity. The seven Schools formed a unified Septyl. It was the Tenebrae that divided Septyl.

CHILDREN OF THE STARS

Laureniel held her pearly wings at a steady level, gracefully flying through the early morning sky. The sun had just crested above the eastern horizon, painting the clouds a robust mixture of pinks and golds as the purple dusk faded further west. Ellendren was ecstatic to have finally left Gwilnor. Alethea and Therril had insisted that she make a second attempt to enter Devlyn's dreams and learn as much as she could about his location before leaving the castle, which delayed them by a further week. But even with the additional, successful visit to Devlyn's dreams, she had learned nothing new—only that wherever he was, it was hot. Unlike her first visit to Devlyn's dreams, she did not alert him immediately to her cerebral arrival. Her curiosity had gotten the best of her. *Is this what he wants?* she asked herself, finding that she liked it as well.

As eager as she was to leave the castle, the conscientious student part of her was worried about leaving a month into the spring term. She had never received a grade below an excellent mark, so she attempted to complete as much homework as possible to soften the negative impact her absence would have on her grades.

With the situation being what it was at Gwilnor and the restrictions placed on the movement of students, Ellendren rarely had the opportunity to let Laureniel out of the stables, let alone visit her there, so she was feeling quite joyful as she nestled her legs behind the alicorn's wings and looked past her impressive horn. It was of a material Ellendren was wholly unfamiliar with. For some reason, ever since she had first seen Laureniel in the Illumined Wood at the end of her novitiate, she had thought she should recognize that material. It shimmered white in the sun, yet as dusk fell over the land, it slowly transformed to the most incredible silver-like substance Ellendren had ever seen.

Alethea and Wyn flew on their griffins to either side of Ellendren, while Viren flew in the lead like a bird of prey on a borrowed griffin.

They had left Ceurenyl hours before the sun rose, hoping that no one would take immediate note of their departure. Even so, she was certain the stable hands knew about their departure, and even if they did not know exactly when they'd gone, the absence of an alicorn and three griffins would not remain a secret past the first ten minutes of their shift.

Ellendren worried about who else knew that they'd gone. And more importantly, how much time did they have before others started searching for them? Would they know they had left the castle to search for Devlyn and his abductors? Would the Tenebrae School send someone to hunt them in return?

Before leaving the castle, Viren had wanted to find at least one more ei'ana to join them but agreed that the smaller the group, the better. Ellendren well understood the benefits of a smaller group, but still, that decision made little sense to her, especially since they anticipated confronting at least five Tenebrae ei'ana.

Ellendren had no reason to doubt Alethea's abilities, but neither had she seen the ancient elf demonstrate them. And was Alethea's advanced age a reason for concern? She was fairly certain that Alethea was one of the oldest elves alive. After all, she had once lived on the Skyland of Eldinare! It was entirely possible that Anaweh would call Alethea to Lumaeniel, the World-Beyond, at any moment. Immortality did not mean spending all one's days on Teraeniel.

The wind rushing past and the sound of Laureniel's wings against the invisible air filled Ellendren's ears. She allowed the sounds to distract her, imagining her every worry abandoned to the wind behind her, unable to keep pace with Laureniel.

While abandoning the Vyoletryn elthion team was the least of her concerns, she did feel a tinge of guilt. She had brought the Vyoletryn team to an impressive lead and although they would not play the next three matches, she was not at all sure that their group would return in time for their next match. That regret did little to sway Ellendren from her current path and she would certainly have felt worse if the reason for her absence was anything less than going to rescue Devlyn. Ellendren scoffed, remembering a story she had been told as a child about a handsome prince rescuing a princess in distress.

She still felt his lips on hers from the dream and his hands on her waist. Despite it being a dream, something about the way he held her comforted her. There was nothing real about it, it was a dream, but part of her wanted to relive it as soon as possible. She knew her heart belonged to the fool; after all, she had abandoned the relative safety of Gwilnor to rescue him from Tenebrae ei'ana, some of whom might even be disguised shadow elves.

Ellendren could not believe that she was flying intentionally into enemy territory, not that she lacked the necessary courage, only that it went against all her better judgments. Vast swaths of the continent were under the Erynien Empire's control, yet the further south one traveled, the more open his supporters became. Elves with light brown and blond hair were not likely to be welcomed with open arms. And certainly not a Lucillian princess—heir to Roendryn's throne no less. Ellendren could hear her childhood tutors reprimanding her for her poor judgment.

Stories of Yanil enacting and enforcing a law that required enslavement of anyone wielding had haunted Ellendren since she was a child. It was ludicrous to consider wielding a crime. With a little education, the people who enforced that law would quickly understand that the gift of wielding belonged to every person. Some began wielding without intending to when they reached adolescence, and others learned how to interact with the erendinth from trained wielders. If she had the chance, she would rescue those wielders. Although, as much as she desired it, she didn't think she would ever have the opportunity. She simply had too many other priorities and the diplomatic nightmare that would follow was reason enough to avoid such a daring adventure.

Even though she was willing to travel all the way to Lankor, a large part of her hoped that they would not have to make the entire journey.

She hoped they would catch the Tenebrae ei'ana well before they crossed into Yanil territory.

She knew that Devlyn intended to retrieve the lucilliae from the Drowned City, but perhaps—considering the circumstances—he would postpone it. The thought of rescuing him just to go further into enemy territory seemed absurd.

She understood perfectly well his desire to retrieve the lucilliae, but surely, they would find a better opportunity. After all, it had remained undiscovered for well over a thousand years, and the likelihood of its discovery now was incredibly slim.

Ellendren opened her eyes after another failed attempt to enter Devlyn's dreams and made her way to the small stream to join Wyn and Alethea who sat silently gazing at the stars above.

"Ah, Ei'lythel Ellendren, were you able to contact him?" asked Alethea.

"Not this time."

"We'll find him," Wyn said, refusing to accept another option.

Ellendren observed that in the brief time that Wyn and Devlyn had known each other, they had developed a fierce friendship. They were cousins after all, and Wyn's additional three hundred years of age didn't seem to affect their appreciation of each other.

"Do you know how long it will take to catch up to Aliel?" Ellendren asked, hoping that the sooner they reached the phoenix, the sooner they would find Devlyn.

"I doubt we'll see the phoenix again until Devlyn is found. His mind is still open to me, but he never remains in one location long. Phoenix do not have the same physical restrictions that we do," said Alethea.

"Do you think Aliel will be able to find him?"

"I can't say; whatever that box they locked him in is, it's blocking their connection, and his ability to wield. Devlyn is invisible to Aliel."

Their conversation faded into silence, Wyn and Alethea still gazing into the sky above, and Ellendren noting the sound of the stream.

The alicorn and griffins rested almost silently and Viren lay asleep nearby. Ellendren was happy to see Viren finally sleeping. He had been pushing himself to his limits, and often insisted that he take the nightly watch. The idea of returning to sleep herself was tempting, but she knew her anxiety would prevent it.

As the stream continued to trickle past, Ellendren allowed its melody to fill her ears. It was a simple, dignified tune. Without intending to, Ellendren felt the stream in her being as a warm healing embrace. Her first inclination was to remove herself from aquaeys, but in the comfort of wielding kiara, she found herself unwilling to.

The water began to churn gently, as though someone ran a hand in the opposite direction of the current.

Neither Alethea nor Wyn looked at the stream, focusing instead on the stars above. The sound of the water certainly reached their ears, but when Ellendren saw their concentration on things above, she removed herself from aquaeys.

"May I ask what you're focusing on?"

"The heavens," Alethea replied.

The brief response made Ellendren look toward Wyn, hoping for something more thorough. She knew as well as the next elf that Lumaeniel was a different realm entirely, a place completely other than the world they dwelt in. Viewing it from Teraeniel wasn't possible.

"The night sky, populated with nothing but stars, is one of the best representations we have here of Lumaeniel's likeness. The stars, if you know how to commune with them, provide counsel to those who seek it," said Wyn.

"How can a star give advice?"

"Don't you know?" asked Wyn taken aback, looking at Ellendren as though she had two heads.

"Much has been forgotten," offered Alethea. "Do not hold it against them."

"I'm sorry, but how can *that* be forgotten?"

"How can *what* be forgotten?" Annoyance bubbled in Ellendren's tone. She felt like she was being left out of some sort of joke; a joke that everyone else understood.

"The stars, of course," said Wyn, waving his arms as if trying to make his point stronger. "They're anadel. There's a reason we call ourselves Children of the Stars. The anadel that guide the elves are the stars. Each speckle of light above falls under Uriel's dominion. Lord of the stars! The irythil who brought lumenys during the creation of Teraeniel."

Ellendren took a second look skyward, watching the multitude of lights above glimmer in the dark. From the time Ellendren had been small, she had been told and believed that the anadel were all around her, that Teraeniel was filled with more anadel than anacordel. She believed it was true, that they were spirit-like creatures, invisible to the naked eye, not bright lights in the night sky looking down on her. There was nothing invisible about the stars. And even if what Wyn said was true, why was he the first to ever mention it? Before she'd gone to Gwilnor, she had spent time around and been tutored by both ei'ana and ei'ceuril. Wouldn't they have mentioned it at some point? Did they know?

Culture and refinement oozed at the seams of Lucillia's palace. Metaphysical discourse and debate occurred sporadically throughout its halls. All she had to do was walk through the palace corridors and keep an open ear to stumble across some sort of philosophical discussion. Healthy debate about the plausibility of anadel and elves was a common occurrence—whether the inhabitants of Lucillia were in fact elves, or simply the remnant of the elves. She had attended every official debate and symposium, but no one had ever argued that the stars themselves were anadel. She knew of the anadel hierarchy, of the four types involved in Teraeniel, how the irythil brought the erendinth from Lumaeniel and created Teraeniel through Anaweh's guidance, how, to this day, the enthiel guided and safeguarded the various kingdoms, how the lorendil, more commonly known as guardian anadel, served as protectors of individual anacordel, and how the naril or nymphs dwelt throughout every land and manifested the erendinth they were associated with. Ellendren also knew about the theory that there were three more, found only in Lumaeniel. There had to be seven types of anadel in their hierarchy—all things were done in seven.

How could the stars be anadel? How could that be possible? Ellendren yearned to return to Lucillia and find her mother—she felt it in her stomach. After every intellectual debate she had attended, she would validate her conclusions with her mother. Was her mother even alive anymore? Ellendren's eyes watered at the thought. Either her mother or father had given their life for the Protection of the Wood to shield Lucillia against Erynor. Deep down, Ellendren knew that it had been her mother. Her mother was a direct descendent of Roendryn, and through him, Lucillia. She would not be able to validate this metaphysical phenomenon with her.

"Why does this startle you?" asked Alethea, intrigued. The stars above no longer held her gaze. Instead, Ellendren had her full attention now.

"I can't say," she replied. "I honestly can't."

"Do you see that star there?" Alethea pointed west at a star brighter than most at the center of fading constellation. It was not the brightest star, but it was certainly distinct; familiar even.

Ellendren nodded.

"I want you to tell me who that star is."

Looking at the star, Ellendren wondered how it could be anything but a star.

"You'll never discover her by questioning. You have to recognize her within yourself."

So, it's a she. Do anadel even have genders? Ellendren thought. Devlyn always referred to Aliel as though the phoenix was masculine, but Aliel seemed to transcend gender. Accepting Alethea's advice, she stopped inquiring on the nature of anadel and quieted her mind. Her placement in the world rushed before her: *where* she was and even *when* she was. She felt the world around her, the ground beneath her, the stream she sat next to, and the air encompassing everything. Extending her concentration upward, she held that particular star in her focus. An insurmountable distance stood between them.

It shimmered like the others, perhaps not as frequently. She was vaguely aware that time passed but remained unconcerned with its passing as the star held her attention. The infrequent shimmers made Ellendren aware of an overwhelming gloom, a heavy, even unbearable burden of sorts.

The star continued to hold her gaze. A distant stillness filled her being.

Someone spoke, but she did not hear what was said, as though it was spoken in an unfamiliar language, or perhaps the person speaking was miles away trying to get her attention.

"Ellendren," she heard the same distant voice say, "who is she?"

"Vespiel—the evening star," gasped Ellendren, realizing that it was Alethea who had spoken. Coming out of the trance, it was only then that she noticed that the stars were not shining as brightly. A splendid light now emerged from the east. It had not yet claimed the transitioning purple sky. "She's depressed."

"Aldinare was the largest and most populated of all the Skylands. She weeps for her children lost to a fate we can only imagine. Only a small number of the Aldinari managed to escape that fate; she mourns for those lost to her. Her aldarchs were precious to her."

Even as Alethea spoke, Wyn peered at Ellendren with a demanding curiosity. He did not address Ellendren but said to Alethea, "She communed with her."

"I'm sorry?" Ellendren replied, not understanding what Wyn meant.

"You were not aware of the time passing, were you?" Alethea asked. "Nor were you aware of many other things happening around your physical body. Such a phenomenon happens when one interacts with the anadel, especially with the enthiel."

"No one has managed what you just did since Aldinare was lost. It's said that not even the other enthiel could reach Vespiel; not even the irythil, Uriel!" said Wyn, barely containing himself.

Not realizing the significance, Ellendren said, "I don't understand why you're getting excited; nothing happened."

"Time will tell otherwise," said Alethea.

Pricne Sanjin

The last of the winter snows had finally melted and the grassy hill-tops offered refuge from the muddy valleys. Aurenth, the second month of spring, had claimed Alexandria, which, to Alex's disgust, had transformed into a distinguished city—a damned metropolis. When they had first arrived at Aewen Bridge, his company had included mostly men and women training for battle. None were soldiers by trade, but according to Sir Oliver, no one was and the Parendians would fight just as well as anyone else who held a sword or bow.

Alex opened the windows of the command room to allow a pleasant breeze access, bringing the sounds of the city into the five-month old castle and sweeping out the musty smell of inhabited rooms.

Standing inside his own castle was overwhelming. It had been constructed in a single hour thanks to the ei'ana, yet he still expected it to disappear just as quickly as it had formed. Unnatural things could never endure.

Oliver, Arlyn, Reia, Sara, and several other advisors selected as generals by Oliver stood around the table with Alex staring at maps of Perrien and Gneal.

Alex had kept them in Alexandria long enough. If they did not begin to march toward Gneal, he feared they never would, and this blasted city would continue to expand.

Gneal was practically defenseless just now with the majority of Perrien's forces currently occupied with their siege of Everin and blockading the Cyrillean Pass. Everyone staring at the map knew that if they did not act soon, they would lose their chance. There would not be a second. Alex held his breath, unwilling to admit that they intended to siege one of the great cities of Eklean, a city that predated Perrien and once flew the flag of Thellion over her battlements. With only the sounds of callers and merchants alike outside the opened windows filling the command room, the others had nothing else to say on the matter. It was time to start marching toward Gneal.

Tieli and Torsillian armies had sieged Myrium, another former Thellion city, for nearly a year before a battle finally broke out, which thankfully the Sorenth had won. The siege of Everin had begun well before Sorenthil even heard of a threat and the mountain city was still under siege.

It was obvious to the group gathered around the map that if they did not devise a swift and effective plan of attack, Perrien's army would desert the Cyrillean Pass and find them still outside Gneal's walls, vulnerable, and easy prey for both fronts to hammer them.

"Tell me again, why can't you use your wielding as weapons?" Alex asked, his voice noticeably frustrated with how the day was proceeding.

"Our Counsels forbid it," said Sara.

"Inconvenient. Believe me, I know," said Reia, just as frustrated as Alex. "The only way we are permitted to wield against the city is if our lives are in immediate danger. And even that has its own set of restrictions. However, our Counsels place no restrictions against fighting shadow elves."

Oliver parted his lips to speak, but was interrupted by a soft knock at the door, immediately opened by Aen who was startled to find every pair of eyes turning to him. The boy had an apologetic expression as he walked fully into the command room.

"Yes, Aen?" Alex asked, trying to hide his frustration with the situation because he was in fact quite relieved by the interruption.

"There's someone here to see you."

"Who?" Alex kept his tone in check. It had already been a long and tiring day. And this meeting was not helping.

"He says he is Prince Sanjin of Charren," Aen said, twiddling his fingers nervously. "I've never heard of it before. I think he's making it up, but he has some sort of eagle-horse thing. I think they actually flew here on them."

"They?" questioned Oliver.

"At least fifty, could be more."

Oliver glanced quickly at Alex before asking Aen, "Are they armed? Did they enter the city?"

"No, they're still outside. But Prince Sanjin is here inside the castle. He's waiting in the parlor."

"I guess we're taking a break," said Alex as he followed Aen out of the room, with Reia trailing close behind. Would they ever trust his leadership enough to allow him to have a private audience with someone?

Two soldiers stood guard outside the parlor Aen led them to. One of them opened the door, revealing a teenager with caramel skin and jet-black hair pacing the room. He was only a few years older than Alex, and whoever he was, he was certainly dressed like a prince, but not a prince born in Eklean. That much Alex could definitely say as he stared at the vibrant, colorful silks that clad the young man's body. His sleeveless shirt left the gold bands inset with colorful gems around his well-defined biceps on view. Whoever this Sanjin was, he was incredibly wealthy.

Sanjin made a formal bow and an odd, flourishing hand gesture that ended with his palm raised upward. "I am Sanjin al'Sanhir, Crown Prince of Charren of the Royal House Irithru. Are you Alexander, ruler of this city?" asked the teenage boy with an unfamiliar, almost musical accent.

Alex extended his hand in greeting.

The gesture received an odd glare from Sanjin, as though the thought of touching another's hand was absurd.

"Yeah," said Alex informally, withdrawing his hand, "but please, just Alex."

"You are young to rule a city, are you not? Did you inherit this magnificent place? It must be so, for you are so young. I hope it was not through ill terms."

"Actually, it's barely five months old yet. Only the bridge predates our arrival."

Sanjin's eyes widened in disbelief, then insult. "You shame me! How ignorant do you believe me to be?" asked Sanjin.

"No, really," Alex said, startled by Sanjin's response. Granted, Alex would have taken what he had just said as a lie as well if he had not seen it with his own eyes. "I speak truly, the ei'ana wielded it from the very stone."

"There are ei'ana still in this land? That is good. Charren was deserted by their kind. But, the Charrenese, we learned to breach the arcane gems. Long have we studied the gems. Some of our greatest mages no longer require them to perform their wonders. But none have managed to create a city, if you speak honestly."

"What are these arcane gems you speak of? And who are these mages?" asked Reia.

"Your people do not know of the arcane gems?" Sanjin asked in disbelief, taking on an air of authority. "Well, it's magic, of course, much like your ei'ana wielding. I have not had the luxury to study the arcane gems. I do know that it is different from what the ei'ana do. You will have to speak to Roshal an'Durran, he has studied the gems his entire life—he is a mage of the Kilnae Del."

"We're getting off topic, Sanjin; why are you here and not wherever Charren is?" interrupted Alex. If Reia wanted to find out more about these arcane gems and mages she would have to do so on her own time. Alex wanted to quickly end this meeting and begin their departure for Gneal as soon as possible.

"We wish to strike an alliance," Sanjin replied, not fond of Alex's tone. "Charren has been overrun by the ogres to the north, and the senators of the Daer Empire refuse to offer aid, undoubtedly hoping that their northern neighbor perishes, allowing them to claim what has fallen from the sky for themselves. I was sent by my father in Karithel, King Sanhir al'Gahnir, to venture to these lands north and south that have undoubtedly forgotten us in Ogren and Daereneth."

"Ogren? Daereneth?" asked Alex. "I thought you said you were from Charren."

"They are the continents Charren resides on, of course," said Sanjin, looking at Alex as if he knew nothing. Sanjin turned to Reia, as though he questioned the possibility that she might know something of the broader world.

"Do not presume to look at me in such a way," said Reia, visibly insulted by the young prince. "The Ei'ana of Septyl have not forgotten the lands you speak of. Neither have we forgotten Qien nor Ja'Horan."

Sanjin's prideful expression remained, turning somewhat challenging.

Diverting the conversation away from geography, Alex said, "Even if we knew you well enough to strike an alliance, Eklean is deeply involved in its own war. It's simply not possible for us to leave for Charren."

"I don't understand," stammered Sanjin, "the ei'ceuril giant at the northern pole—he told us an alliance would be struck in Alexandria."

First talk of ogres and now giants. If Alex had not already heard of giants, he would have dismissed it altogether. And now ogres were to be added to the list of races that, for him, had not previously existed, but truly did. And they were on a different continent. Alex wanted to argue their existence away but knew from past experience that it was fruitless. Grappling with the concept of another unknown race, Alex remembered that Aen had mentioned the visitors were accompanied by eagle-horse creatures. "How did you get here?"

"As I said, we flew north from Karithel to Glacien until we reached the ei'ceuril giant at the northern pole. From there, we flew south, not back to Ogren, but the other south, toward Eklean," said Sanjin, annoyed with the question.

"And how exactly did you *fly* here?" Alex asked, excited and intrigued at the same time.

"On our hippogriffs, of course," said Sanjin. "Do you not have hippogriffs here?" Sanjin's disbelief at the lack of Eklean's merit rose with every passing moment.

"It would be wise of you to not question what wonders Eklean holds within her borders," said Reia, practically growling through gritted teeth at Sanjin, only contributing to her earlier frustration. "Assist us in this war we're confronted with, and you will discover exactly what Eklean has to offer."

Sanjin paced with an air of disinterest, considering Reia's proposal. Alex was on the edge of insisting that he decide; it was impossible to gauge the foreigner. Reia kept her steady gaze on Sanjin with her arms crossed, daring him to refuse.

"Here is my proposal," said Sanjin. "I will stay with my retinue and assist Eklean in this war. However, you also must pledge your aid to Charren. The moment this war no longer requires our attention, you will come to Charren with a sizable force to push the ogres out of Charren. I will also require briefing on this war of yours."

Reia gave Alex a look that said if he did not agree, he was an idiot. It was a look he had grown far too accustomed to from Reia, but unlike the other occasions, Alex found himself agreeing with her. Alex stuck his hand out in agreement. He still didn't fully understand why he was the one forming this alliance. On what ground—on what authority—could he uphold his end of the bargain? How quickly would this army dissipate after the Council of Perrien was dealt with and Parendior gained their independence?

"What are you doing?" asked Sanjin, appalled. "First you shove your hand at me in greeting and now you want it to serve as a contract? I would prefer a written contract, in both our scripts. I do not think I will ever fully comprehend you Ekleanese and your poorly named Common Tongue."

"It is customary in Eklean to shake hands upon meeting someone, and when coming to an agreement. But if you prefer, we can draw up a contract," Alex said, never having needed a contract before. "I'm sure we can find someone capable of drafting it."

"Don't bother," interrupted Reia, "I'll take care of it."

"I will have to read it before it is signed," said Sanjin, not acknowledging Reia.

Reia stared daggers at the foreign prince. There was no way of knowing whether her look did not affect him or whether he chose to ignore it.

"Let's take a look at this retinue that accompanied you," said Alex, trying to divert a potential rift between the ei'ana and the prince.

"First, I would like to be shown to my chambers," said Sanjin, offering no room for debate. "It has been a long journey and I would have a bath before returning to my entourage."

Alex wanted to slap his forehead, but after spending an extended period of time with ei'ana he had learned how inappropriate that was, especially in front of a royal dignitary. "Aen, please escort Prince Sanjin to the guest quarters."

Sanjin looked expectantly at the young boy, waiting for him to lead the way through the expanding castle. There were only four empty rooms in the castle for guests. When the castle had been wielded into existence, Alex had thought the inclusion of guest quarters absurd. And now that Sanjin was his first official guest, part of him wished they had never been wielded. That space could have better served as storage rooms.

A couple of hours later, Aen found Alex waiting impatiently. Alex had spent the entire time staring at the maps of Perrien and Gneal, hoping to devise a plan for sieging the city. In the back of his mind, all he could think about was how useful these hippogriffs might prove. What he would not give to have a fleet of dragons at his command. The stories of the battle of Myrium that had reached them were impossible to believe. Hippogriffs might get them over the city walls and into the city, but dragons would have done that and taken the city in turn! Not even the stoutest of warriors could withstand a dragon. A wielder might. And a shadow elf might even prove the better of the two. *There better not be any of those still in Gneal.* Unfortunate that Jaerol wasn't still a resident in Gneal's castle.

Alex followed Aen through the small but expanding castle until they reached Sanjin at the modest entrance where a large group waited. Both ei'ana were present, along with Arlyn, Oliver, his generals, and even Abbie. Alex thought better of asking her how she'd heard of Sanjin's arrival.

"Shall we be on our way?" asked the Charrenese prince.

A chorus of agreements sounded and Alex followed the prince into the warm, spring afternoon.

They passed through Alexandria at a steady pace, although not nearly quickly enough in Alex's opinion. The pace at which this foreign prince moved was starting to bother him. If the hippogriffs proved as useful as he imagined, he hoped Sanjin and his people would not delay their attack on Gneal due to their sluggish movements.

Beyond the open gate, Alex could see a sea of odd onion-shaped tents in vibrant colors each one flying a flag displaying a crest he had never seen before. The flags were just as colorful as Sanjin's robes and the tents they flew proudly over. Unlike the crests of Eklean kingdoms, this one had no animal depicting its people. The crest was a complex design of geometric patterns.

In the tented area, Alex was overwhelmed at the sight of what they called a hippogriff. It was an incredibly fierce looking beast with a dark, almost black beak that looked as though it could remove his arm cleanly from his body. Its talons matched the color of the beak, but were the largest he had ever seen, except Yelaris', yet even these looked like they might do some damage to a dragon. The hippogriff's body transitioned at its midsection from that of an oversized eagle to a horse. The feathers were predominantly brown, with a mix of various hues of black, grey, and white.

It was difficult to say which part of the beast was the most terrifying.

Even more terrifying than the singular hippogriff was the fact that every which direction Alex looked, he saw more. The camp was full of armed soldiers and hippogriffs. Alex could not disguise his pleasure. He could easily imagine a force of hippogriffs flying over Gneal's stout walls and the soldiers riding them opening the gates for the rest of his army to enter the city.

The image was perfect. His grin stretched from ear to ear. "Sanjin, my new friend, tell your soldiers not to get too comfortable here in Alexandria." Alex's grin shifted to a devious smile. "We leave for Gneal at sunrise."

"Then tonight, we feast to new friends!" Sanjin replied.

A Servant's Judgment

Devlyn banged hard on the side of the box, hoping to get the attention of anyone—if there was anyone—nearby aside from his captors. From listening each time he'd been let out, he'd learned some of their names, but quickly discovered that his abductors did not act alone. There had been four or five who had taken him, but the number of people traveling in the group was at least triple that. Only Devlyn was locked in a black box all day, preventing him from connecting to Aliel and from wielding. He did know that his box was concealed inside a covered wagon. To anyone who might look at the group, nothing would have appeared out of the ordinary.

He was allowed out of his box twice a day, once in the morning before they resumed their journey, and once in the evening when they started to set up camp for the night. It was impossible to tell the time inside the box. It permitted no light, and he could barely hear any sounds from outside. The jostling of the wagon across the uneven road was the only thing he was aware of, and that jostling had stopped quite some time ago. Were they done traveling for the day? Was it evening already?

A crack of light formed at the edge of the box, forcing him to squint momentarily as his eyes adjusted to the widening brightness.

"You know what we will do to you if you even so much as think of contacting that bird," said Indryl, one of the Tenebrae ei'ana. She was a Luminari, and Devlyn was under the impression that until recently, she had belonged to the Vyoletryn School. At least, that's what the brooch she'd worn at Gwilnor indicated.

Devlyn refused to dignify the woman with an acknowledgement. He stared at her, unblinking. As desperately as Devlyn wanted to reach out to Aliel, who was no mere bird, he couldn't. These ei'ana took no chances with him and they would know if he tried again. They had wielded some sort of link to him when he was outside of the box. That wield not only prevented him from wielding and reaching out to Aliel, but it also alerted the ei'ana whenever he tried to do either.

She moved out of the way and followed Devlyn to the edge of their camp where a few servants were busy fetching water from a near-by stream. Devlyn wondered why the ei'ana didn't just wield the water themselves and save their servants the energy.

"Because," said Indryl. She was aware of everything he thought. He'd found that out the hard way when they first opened the box to allow him to relieve himself. "They're our slaves. Their job is to serve us, not us make their life easier, fool boy."

When he turned to walk back to the camp and his box, after a very public breach of privacy where anyone who wanted to could see him empty his bladder, a hooded figure stopped Devlyn in his tracks.

Indryl did not seem concerned, so whoever it was belonged to their group.

"I do hope your accommodations are meeting your every desire." Devlyn recognized the voice. "I would have provided you with something more comfortable, but there's simply no trusting you. Especially after you returned to that child."

"You did this?" Devlyn asked.

Queen Alesei of Tiel lowered her hood, showing her delighted smile. She wore just as much jewelry now as she had when he first met her in the temple, none of it the same. "Absolutely. I found myself thinking about offering an engagement present to my soon-to-be betrothed. The more I thought on the perfect gift, the more obvious the choice became. Granted, I was willing to settle for another lover, but you declined that opportunity," Alesei said, running a fingernail across Devlyn's dirty cheek. "What a shame, I think we could have done well together. Perhaps he'll permit me to borrow his new pet, from time to time."

"You're making an engagement gift out of me?" Devlyn asked, incredulous at the very idea.

"Of course, child. He might finally take my hand after I bring him an addition for his trophy room. Living and breathing trophies are his favorite. Especially those with golden hair. But yours is something entirely different." She brushed her fingers through his hair, hair that showed traits of every elven line.

There was no doubting who Alesei referenced. Devlyn felt his stomach turn over at the thought of someone dragging him locked up in a box to Broid, only to be presented as a shiny bauble for the emperor.

"Who knows, Erynor might even accept my hand as his bride this time. He's used that excuse of me not being an elf long enough. Our similarities far surpass silly racial discriminations such as those; our constitutions share a connection nobler than mere elven blood." Not understanding what Alesei meant by similarities and connection, Devlyn noted the glance Indryl gave Alesei.

She might have mentally said something to the Tieli queen but there was no way for Devlyn to know. All three of them started to walk back to his black box where he would know nothing but darkness until he was let out again in the morning. They had not gone far to begin with, and although Devlyn dragged his feet trying to determine a solution without thinking about it, in a matter of less than a minute, he would be standing before the box concealed inside the wagon.

He really needed to work on shielding his mind since Indryl knew every thought coursing through. Unexpectedly, one of the servants bumped into Devlyn, causing her to spill her pail of water, some of it almost on Alesei.

Furious at the servant's clumsiness, Alesei struck the woman hard across the face, making the servant fall to the ground, the pail of water emptying completely. "Get up, you useless slave!"

Without hesitation, the woman stood, but did not look up until instructed to do so. Slowly shifting her gaze upward, she chanced a glance at Devlyn. Their eyes met for only an instant, but he saw the recognition in them. She knew who he was. Devlyn had never seen her before, but she knew him, and not because he was her masters' prisoner.

The occurrence was odd, and before Devlyn could even try not to think what it might mean in case he was heard, he found himself in front of the box, about to be cut off from any source of light once again. He never saw how the hinges on the box worked, nor did he ever see the handle to open it. The ei'ana who brought him out never permitted him to learn anything about his cage.

There was no use in attempting to find out either since they always knew what he was thinking when he was outside the box and the moment he even considered making an attempt, the ei'ana would punish him, refusing to let him out of the box for two days. It had already happened once and he had no intention of repeating that smelly occurrence.

He shuffled into the box, Indryl sealed the door behind him, and the wield she held over him disappeared. At least his thoughts were his own again. Indryl couldn't wield her link through the box's material.

Ange returned to the camp with another large pail of water. Whatever Alesei thought, Ange was not clumsy. After a year of forced service, that was the first time she had ever spilled anything, and it was not due to clumsiness.

She knew the prisoner. Everyone in her order knew who he was.

Ange had always believed that it was only a myth passed down through the generations to give hope to a people in servitude. She thought it was just a story—a story to help her and others like her, who had willingly gone into bondage for the sake of their order, the Judges of Yanil, to sleep better at night.

But she had seen him. His face was the same as the one in the portrait, as was his uniquely colored hair; even the eyes had that impossible golden sheen she remembered seeing. She had thought it was only for the sake of artistic expression. No one had gold eyes; no one. But she had seen them for herself. He was real and he was alive.

They said he would come back. They said those were his own words to the former Supreme Judge, Ramira Bir Ginthol, long dead. It was her conviction that he had existed that let her continue her order's work, even after their purpose had been lost. Even after the Yanilean stripped them of their status following Nauto's Wrath.

Ange had never believed the stories. She believed in their purpose, but never the stories about the elf-boy.

Her superiors said they became servants for the purpose of finding him. That if they were servants, they could be everywhere and not draw attention to themselves.

They had been servants for sixteen hundred years, searching for a single person, ever since Nauto's Wrath took Lankor from them and with the Drowned City, their right to rule in their lawful places as the Judges of Yanil.

They were never the sole authority in Yanil, that privilege was shared with the Yanilean. But in the time of the Judges of Yanil, there was a balance to his rule. Now, there was nothing to keep the Yanilean in check.

Ange spent the rest of the evening carrying out her chores. Her training demanded discipline. But her training also demanded that she get word of the elf with the golden eyes to the other judges, to the ones who did not spend their days serving filth.

The night was half spent before Ange dared sneak out of the servants' tent. It was small and everyone slept too close for comfort. It was a common occurrence for someone to wake in the middle of the night and leave the cramped tent for fresh air or to relieve themselves, a small dignity they retained.

Ange walked carefully on her tiptoes not to wake the other servants, the ones who were not judges, just servants. They had no education and no options. Their families were impoverished and so would they remain. Ange was a member of one of Lankor's wealthy merchant families, educated by the best tutors in the floating city, and later found herself involved with an organization that claimed they had a stake in Yanil's authority—the Judges of Yanil.

Her tutors spoke of the ancient judges and how they had been unworthy to rule, responsible for allowing wielders inside their kingdom, and eventually inviting Nauto's Wrath, thereby destroying their prized city. If she had not fled Lankor in anguish over a broken engagement, she never would have involved herself with the Judges. But she had needed to get away from Lankor and quickly disappear. She simply could not have gone forward with her betrothal.

When she had joined the Judges of Yanil, she had been shocked to learn that she was going to be a servant. Most of the group, known as judges, posed as servants because it was easy to infiltrate suspect organizations as menial labor; only a handful did not. But the menial labor had finally paid off.

Ange found herself outside the servants' tent with no one around, right after she had removed her bracelet and placed it beside Leah's bedroll. Leah was another servant, one who had cast countless glances at the bracelet on Ange's wrist, coveting the simple piece of jewelry, although Leah had no way of knowing that that bracelet would lead the Judges of Yanil directly to this treacherous caravan. She waited momentarily to make sure that she really was alone; all she heard were soft sounds from the various tents. She dared a glance toward the wagon that held the elf the judges had been searching for. All she had to do was get a message to the other judges, but the thought of how quickly she would rise through the ranks if she showed up with the elf herself was tempting. They would praise her; not even Supreme Judge Ramira Bir Ginthol, who had recorded the elf's image, would be remembered as well as herself.

The idea was terribly tempting, yet if something went amiss, history would remember her in a very different light. With one last look at the wagon, Ange turned and left the camp. She remembered the town they had passed earlier that same day. With any luck she could reach it and get back to the camp before anyone noticed she was missing. She ran as fast as her legs would carry her to the village, trying to preserve some energy for the return trip.

She assumed they were either in Sorenthil or Torsil. Their location was never spoken aloud. The ei'ana were taking every precaution necessary to maintain an air of secrecy, even among themselves, as though they didn't trust each other.

By the time she reached the village, not a single light remained lit in the residences. She was fortunate that the village was not large enough to have a wall and gate protecting it. If it had, she likely would not have gotten inside. No guard would open a gate in the middle of the night for someone dressed like a servant.

Looking around at the quiet buildings, Ange looked for signs that would indicate where the messenger bird handler lived or worked. It was common for villagers to have multiple occupations. For all Ange knew, the person she searched for could also be the baker.

The inn, as in most villages, was easily identified, always larger than any other building in the village, unless the village had a lord and manor house, and the only building with light showing through the windows. A painted wooden sign with an orange carriage on it hung by the inn's door.

Trying the handle, Ange sighed in relief that it wasn't locked, and pushed the door open. She saw two hooded men talking in hushed tones, and not too far away from them was a woman who was wiping a table. The woman noticed Ange immediately, and came to her.

"A bit late to be strolling into town, wouldn't you say?"

"Oh yes," Ange said, trying to concoct a story. "My master requested a message to be sent immediately." She might as well go along with her role as a servant.

"It can't wait 'til morning?" the woman asked, giving Ange a suspicious look.

"I'm afraid not. My master threatened me with the lash if I didn't get it out tonight. Do you know where the messenger bird carrier resides?"

"Well, you're in luck, my husband takes care of the birds," the woman answered. "Can't imagine he'll be happy to be woken up at this hour though. How about you leave your message with me and I'll be certain it gets out first thing in the morning."

"I have strict instructions to see the message off myself," Ange said, leaving the woman no room to argue. "I'd rather not face my master's wrath, if it's all the same to you."

"Very well, you wait here and I'll wake Henry. It'll cost you a silver jent, mind you."

Ange grimaced at the price. Messenger birds had cost a fraction of that price in Lankor, but she wasn't in a position to argue the cost and pulled her coin purse from a hidden pocket in her dress and took out a jent. The woman took it and went to find her husband.

Taking a seat at one of the empty tables, Ange waited for Henry to arrive. She thought over the message she would send. How to say it in such a way that if it fell into the wrong hands, no one would have the slightest idea what it meant.

The woman returned with a groggy Henry. He carried the small slips of paper used for messenger birds, as well as a quill and ink. He blearily looked around the common room, first at the two hooded figures and secondly at Ange. "Well, what's so important that it can't wait until morning?"

"Could you tell me what town and kingdom this is?"

Henry looked at his wife, as though saying *you woke me for this?* before replying, "Torsil and this is the village of Norton. Now please, dear, it's very late; what's your message?"

"Right, my apologies." Ange couldn't believe they were in Torsil already, let alone in southern Torsil. "The old golden-eyed portrait is in southern Torsil looking toward Lankor."

"Is that all?" Henry asked, showing Ange the slip of parchment he had written on, doubting whether a servant could actually read it. "How would you sign?"

"J. Ange."

Henry rolled up the slip of parchment and Ange followed him through a simple wooden door on the side of the common room and into a tiny room. The room was filled with soft cooing sounds and a dozen or so pigeons. "Where is this going?"

"Auten, addressed to S. J. Catalina Turlan."

After scribbling the information on the front of the parchment, Henry attached it to a particular bird before throwing it out the side window.

Ange thanked Henry and walked out the door. There were still a few hours until dawn, and with any luck she might return to the camp without anyone noticing her nocturnal disappearance.

She walked out of the village just as she had entered, and for the first time since she had received her assignment as a judge, she felt she was actually making a difference.

She began to jog and the village was soon concealed behind trees. Before she made it halfway to the camp, she was suddenly grabbed by the shoulders from behind. She almost screamed as she fought against the firm hands holding her, but a second person appeared and pressed his hand over her mouth. *How did I not hear them sneak up on me?* she thought, rebuking herself for not paying closer attention.

Both were hooded. Suddenly it struck her that they were the two figures who had been at the other table at the inn. How could she have been so stupid—openly delivering her message for anyone to hear? Either they knew the elf she referred to or they knew what gold meant and wanted her to lead them to the master she spoke of.

"Tell us the name of the one with the golden eyes," said the hooded man holding her by the shoulders.

Her training with the Judges of Yanil came back to her. Squirming would accomplish nothing and there were two of them and only one of her. She didn't even have a weapon to defend herself.

The figure who was covering her mouth slowly removed his hand and pulled down his hood, revealing a chestnut face and pointed ears sticking past the darkest hair she had ever seen. No wonder she hadn't heard them. She remembered hearing stories that elves could sprint without making the slightest sound.

Some of the ei'ana she traveled with also had pointed ears and angled features, but there was something different about this one. None of the elves she traveled with had black hair and darker skin. She wished she could see the other man's face.

"Who is it that you spoke of in that message?" asked the elf standing in front of her. "Are his eyes actually golden, or was it merely a trick of the light?"

She began to stammer, too afraid to utter a single word.

"Time is of the essence; we know your master is not an art collector," said the hooded figure behind her. "Do you or do you not know where Devlyn is?"

Ange heard the desperate ferocity in his voice; it was impossible to miss. He cared for him.

"Are you friends?"

"Yes," replied the elf standing before her. "We've been searching for him. Take us to him."

The grip on her shoulders loosened, and she turned to see a second elf, this one with light brown hair and lighter skin. "Who are you?"

"My name is Viren Dekenurel, and I am a Guardian knight," said the elf who had been holding her by the shoulders.

Great, another myth. She was tired of hearing of things that no longer existed. Everyone knew that the Guardian knights and the Guardian Senate had all died when Krysenthiel had fallen.

"And I'm Wyn Lierafen. Now please, will you take us to Devlyn?"

25

DISTRUST

The first sun rays peaked over the horizon and no one cared to speak; they did not even stand near each other. The alicorn and griffins rested by the stream at the edge of the clearing. Even though they were intelligent creatures, they seemed indifferent to what was going on around them. They lapped up water from the small stream, most likely a tributary of the River Eindol, and just waited for the elves to decide where to go next.

Wyn had contacted Alethea and Ellendren two hours ago, telling them to hurry and the women had rushed to the clearing by a stream where Ange had led Viren and Wyn. Ellendren, like Viren and Wyn, was currently occupying herself by pacing the area, hoping to discover something—anything that might give them a clue. Alethea rested a hand against a tree and it was unclear whether she was using it as support or something more. The woman who claimed to be one of the Judges of Yanil kept her distance from both Ellendren and the creatures.

Ellendren glanced at the woman, not sure whether they should trust her. She wanted to hear Ange's story and that of the Judges before passing any verdict of her own. As far as she or anyone else knew, the Judges of Yanil had lost their status when Nauto's Wrath fell upon the original city, raising the water level of Lankor Bay, claiming much of what was once dry land and washing away the Judges' authority.

One of the first things Ellendren had discovered about this girl was her name. Ellendren tried to remember everything she knew about the Yanilean's court and whether an Ange belonged to it. Linking any woman to that misogynist court was not an easy task, as they had no official role there. Ellendren glanced yet again at Ange, convinced that the self-defined judge was lying about the Judges of Yanil. Every form of government, whether official or not, was known to the Lucillian aryl. Not even the covert tax-dodging Goblin Guild was unknown—she would have to do something about that when she took the throne.

Despite her distrust of the woman, she was slightly impressed that Ange knew about the Judges. It was only Ellendren's extensive tutoring as a child that gave her knowledge of the Judges of Yanil herself. Gwilnor Academy certainly didn't teach about the Judges and their role and diminishment in Yanil. Admittedly, Ellendren did not have a full grasp of Yanil's current education system, but gauging from their attitude toward ei'ana, she doubted it was anything illuminating.

Wherever Ange had uncovered this bit of forgotten history, she was undoubtedly using it to her advantage. Perhaps it made her feel better; she was little better than a slave for wicked women. And since she was lying about that, how could they trust anything she said about Devlyn?

Glancing out of the corner of her eye yet again at the obvious liar, Ellendren felt a jolt of panic when they locked eyes. She tried to look away but found it impossible.

"What?" asked Ange.

"Nothing."

"You've done nothing but stare at me since you arrived. Why?"

"Fine," Ellendren said, more calmly than she expected. "I don't trust you. I think you're fabricating this story about the Judges of Yanil. How do you even know of them? I doubt any institution in Lankor passes on that knowledge. And your claim of being undercover? Do you really expect us to believe that? You were among servants of Shadow, Tenebrae ei'ana among them. For all we know, they could have sent you to find out whether they were being followed."

"I snuck out at my own peril to send a message to my superiors about finding the elf we have been searching for since the sea claimed Lankor." She pursed her lips as her eyes bled into Ellendren's.

"Did you discover something?" she heard Wyn ask, breaking the tension between Ange and herself, which was thick enough to cut with a knife.

Alethea's hand still rested against the tree. The ancient elf's eyes were closed—perhaps she was tired. One thing that Ellendren had learned over the months they had been traveling together was that her appearance was always misleading, and she had never seen Alethea, or Wyn for that matter, drowsy.

"The trees here are very tired. This one has never communicated with an anacordel before, and it's older than everyone here except Viren and me," said Alethea, not looking toward the others, but focused on the tree.

We're wasting our time here. We should've left once we realized no one was around. Either Ange was lying or the Tenebrae ei'ana knew of her identity. Ellendren tried to quiet her thoughts.

"Do they remember anything?" Wyn asked, trying to get a straightforward answer from Alethea.

"They might be sleepy, but they remember well enough," said Alethea, catching Ellendren's attention. "Devlyn was here, and not all that long ago. We missed him by a day."

"Why are we still here if he no longer is?" Ellendren asked, her patience waning.

"Even if we did come across the group with Devlyn, we have no way of knowing whether they have him, because we have no way of knowing precisely who took him," said Alethea. "However, unlike the long dead stone of Gwilnor, the slumbering trees were able to see those in that group."

Alethea extended a hand to Ellendren's temple. Faces flashed across her mind, some familiar, others not.

"If we came across those women, before you saw them just now, would you have questioned them?"

The faces of the ei'ana she knew flashed before her. She had trusted them all. Never in a million years would she have doubted their loyalty to Septyl. Indryl belonged to Vyoletryn. Their apartments were only several doors apart. The reality of what that meant crashed around her.

There was no way of knowing which of them belonged to the Tenebrae School; anyone could have joined. She was just as likely a member as anyone else.

A hooded woman wearing more jewels than any woman with dignity would came into her mind. The woman looked familiar, but she had never seen her at Gwilnor and the hood made it even more difficult to identify her. She did not look like an ei'ana; something about her was off. Keeping the face in her mind, she suddenly recalled meeting a similar-looking woman when she was much younger. The woman had worn just as much jewelry then as she did now, but she also had worn clothing that was much more revealing at the time. It was just before her brother, Aaron, left for the Temple of Ceur. And she remembered that even his reverent tongue stuttered around Queen Alesei on her diplomatic mission to Lucillia.

"The Tieli queen is behind this," said Ellendren.

"There was no queen with us."

Just hearing Ange speak infuriated Ellendren. It did not matter that she disagreed with her; she could have said the sun would rise soon and Ellendren would still have snapped at her.

"That woman with all the jewels, *that* is Queen Alesei of Tiel," Ellendren said, almost daring Ange to disagree with her. "How many women do you imagine can afford such a caliber and quantity of jewelry?"

"If she's a queen, then where were her knights? She may be rich, but that doesn't make a woman like that royalty."

"Forgive me," interrupted Alethea, preventing the argument from escalating to something larger. "That woman is indeed Alesei of Tiel. From what I have learned, only the ei'ana knew her identity, and none were permitted to speak of it."

"So, what do we do now?" asked Ellendren, feeling vindicated at Alethea's support. "How are we supposed find *Queen* Alesei and the Tenebrae ei'ana with her?"

"Not by sight alone," said Alethea.

"Pardon?" Viren's comment revealed more disbelief than Ellendren felt herself.

"They're using some kind of wield that makes them invisible to the naked eye, and also conveniently removes whatever tracks they leave behind."

"So how do you propose finding them?" asked Viren.

"They're only invisible to that which is outside their wield," said Alethea. "Fortunately, everything they pass goes through their wield. I've always thought it a shame that everyone east of the Vespien Mountains forgot how to use their inner sense to commune with that which surrounds them, but that ignorance will now work to our advantage."

Relieved that they finally had a legitimate trail to follow, Ellendren was ready to act. Part of her wanted to take a moment to study what Alethea was doing so that she might replicate it, but her desire for haste dictated otherwise.

Alethea had been kind enough to share many aspects of her vast experience when she had come to Gwilnor, and Ellendren was learning how to better access the interior sense Alethea often spoke of. But she had no intention of sitting on the ground with her legs crossed to commune with the natural world around her at the moment, despite how useful the trees had been for Alethea. What the oldest living Eldinari, and by extension possibly the oldest anacordel in the world, could manage in a few seconds would undoubtedly require at least an hour for Ellendren.

Looking at Viren to gauge his readiness to move, Ellendren was invigorated by seeing the same amount of determination in his eyes as she knew he saw in her own. Wyn also appeared eager to get moving.

Alethea, however, gave no physical nor emotional indications that she was prepared to move on. She remained as she was, peering through her silver eyes, but it was impossible to discern whether she looked at anything in particular.

Ellendren had grown accustomed to her apparent lack of interest. After spending time with her and other Eldinari, especially the older ones, she had understood that they rarely displayed their emotions.

Deciding not to ask whether she was ready, Ellendren made her way to the alicorn and the griffins. She had no intention of providing any choices for the elf; they were leaving. Viren and Wyn seemed to be in agreement as both mounted their griffins. When Alethea's griffin came to her, she smiled and gratefully mounted the creature.

Ange stayed on the ground. They had not brought an additional griffin; there was no need to. When they freed Devlyn, he would simply bond with Aliel and the two would fly on their own, back to Ceurenyl.

"You can fly with me." Wyn offered his hand to Ange, who looked between the ground and the griffin hesitantly.

Ellendren wanted to leave her behind. Something about the self-proclaimed Judge of Yanil did not sit well in the pit of her stomach, however, as far as she could tell, she was the only one who felt that way.

The woman had seen Devlyn. Jealousy pumped through Ellendren's veins, but her anger was far greater than her envy. Ange had not just seen Devlyn, she had left him with those traitorous ei'ana. All she had done to *help* was leave a bracelet behind for her superiors to track. *Small chance of that helping*, Ellendren thought.

BOXED IN

Sitting in the box in the dark, Devlyn stared at the nothingness before his eyes. To a certain degree, he thought he was staring at the compartment's door, but there was no way of truly knowing until someone outside opened it, which would not happen until morning. He hoped that morning might be soon.

His grasp of time and reality was currently non-existent. He wasn't sure, but he thought that it was sometime between evening and morning. A quarter hour could have elapsed since they last allowed him out of the box or well over five hours. He could have fallen asleep and woken up without realizing. He just didn't know.

He hugged his legs to chest and thought of the ei'ana who allowed him out of the box. He wanted to please her. She was not a bad woman; after all, she did let him out.

There were times when he was surprised that it was morning when the latch opened, expecting to see only torchlight and the moon hanging somewhere in the sky. The time of day and the number of days that had endlessly started and ended since his abduction no longer mattered to him. He simply woke in the same small black box wanting the day to end. Wanting it all to end.

He spent most days in a semiconscious sleep, since there was nothing he could do but sleep. Whenever the same ei'ana let him out of the box and he could move, he could tell that his body was growing weak. The little identifiable muscle he'd had before his capture had deteriorated over what had to be months by now. His legs were unsteady, and he didn't think he could carry anything heavier than one of Yvonne's tomes. He felt his mind falling deeper into a drowsy sleep every day. Even when he was awake, his mind slept. He was shutting down. A small part deep inside nagged at him to do something to stop the process, but he couldn't summon the energy to care. He only wanted to please the ei'ana who opened the latch.

If she likes me, she might open the door more often.

The pain in his stomach constantly screamed for more food. They fed him only enough to make sure he did not die—only a mouthful of stale bread once a day. At least, he thought it was once a day. Days could have easily passed without him eating anything. Ellendren would be ashamed of him if she were to see him like this.

She'll probably return to Trethien.

Trethien's face surfaced in Devlyn's mind, and the small pleasure he felt at seeing an identifiable face made him realize just how lonely and desperate he had become. He could not feel the phoenix, but the need to bond pounded inside him. Part of him was gone and his heart wanted to forget that connection rather than accept the phoenix's absence. There was no way of bonding while inside his box; when he was let out to relieve himself, the ei'ana did something to block him from not only wielding, but from exerting his being outward. That wield did what his box did, but it was much worse. It was constricting, as though someone was squeezing his heart, like it was going to crush his heart inside his chest. He still had access to his interior sense, but it did little good to simply be aware of his surroundings.

He closed his eyes again, hoping to fall into another half slumber. Even with his eyes closed, nothing changed. Eyes open or closed, there was nothing to see but black emptiness inside his box. The one thing to look forward to while he slept were the dreams where Ellendren visited him. But even those were diminishing. At first, he'd believed she was entering, joining him in his dreams, but the longer he spent in the box, the more he believed they were just dreams and the less he dreamt about her.

He hoped she was safe at Gwilnor with Trethien. There was no way of discovering it on his own. He felt useless and without purpose.

Hopefully Trethien will take good care of her.

Suddenly, something was happening that would only happen in a dream. The muffled sound of women yelling came to his ears and he could feel some movement outside.

It did not matter; this dream would end just as every other rescue attempt he'd imagined would end: him waking and that same ei'ana opening the door to allow him to relieve himself.

The faint sounds and movement continued. Devlyn found himself critiquing the people outside his box. They were too loud to succeed in his rescue since the louder they were, the more likely they would wake his captors. And the moment that happened, the ei'ana would dispatch these figments of his imagination.

The sounds outside his small cramped box dissipated and the welcome silence returned. "There was no chance of them succeeding. They were too loud," he said, surprised at his raspy voice but relieved that he could return to his interrupted half-sleep.

Devlyn felt a tug then a pull on the wagon that concealed his box, the same kind of tug and pull that he felt once every single day. They were supposed to let him out to relieve himself before they started traveling for the day. They would not stop until they reached their destination that evening.

Infuriated that they had started moving without letting him out, he wanted to pound on the side of his box, but couldn't muster the energy, and he did not want to displease the ei'ana who normally opened the door. She might keep him locked in the box twice as long if he upset her.

He felt the wagon quicken its pace, and on the rough path, he was thrown about inside the box. In his weakened state, he couldn't brace himself against the sides of the box.

His head hit the roof of his cramped box several times, and his irritation grew with each occurrence so that by the time the wagon finally slowed, then stopped, he was furious. Was it evening? He breathed heavily, outraged that he'd not been permitted to relieve himself before their morning journey. With the anger, the adrenaline rushing through him brought a sense of his old self.

He waited for the door to open. They had to open it. It was evening. And when they did, he would waste no time in attempting to wield no matter what they would do to him for trying to wield. If he had not been so upset, he might not have been so determined, but he was enraged.

The door creaked open, yet this time, he did not immediately sense the constricting wield that cut him off from the world.

The ei'ana had made a mistake, the wield was not there. There was no constriction; no limitations. He reached out to Aliel, who with a rush of anticipation, bonded fully with Devlyn as he leapt out of the box.

The long-unused link between them erupted in an explosion. His eyes streamed with tears from the light flooding into them as they bonded. The door to his box had barely opened, yet that was all he had needed to connect with Aliel and he flew out of the wagon in a fury, bent on wrathful vengeance.

Devlyn pressed fully into all four of the elemental erendinth and embraced the transcendental erendinth, umbrys and animys. He looked around for those who had bound him in his sleep and spirited him away from the castle. He searched for the ei'ana he had wanted to please but moments before.

But none of the ei'ana holding him captive or any of the rest of the caravan that had become familiar to him during his brief excursions out of his box were on the dirt path below him. Of that caravan, there was only the covered wagon that concealed his box. Even the horses pulling the wagon were not the same. None of the men and women staring at him, even as they shielded their eyes against his exuberant light, were part of the caravan he had grown accustomed to.

He knew the ratty clothes the ei'ana had given him had disintegrated instantly when he had bonded with Aliel but he did not care. The incredible light prevented anyone from seeing his emaciated nakedness. He wanted explanations.

The people below started whispering among themselves but they did not look menacing or dangerous. Despite this, Devlyn's blood boiled.

"Who are you?" He spoke harshly, aware that he could not trust them, nor could he trust his weak body which would undoubtedly fall in a heap the instant he withdrew from Aliel.

"You never said that he was a Phaedryn," said one of the men standing next to a proud looking woman.

"We have searched for you for one thousand six hundred forty-eight years," said the woman. "We have done so with no more than an image of your face, depicted by Supreme Judge Ramira Bir Ginthol who saw you when Lankor was lost to the sea."

Devlyn's heart rate slowed and he lowered himself to the ground as the pounding inside his chest lessened. He felt Aliel pull himself away and as the two became separate physical entities once more, his weakness returned and his famished body nearly collapsed.

One of the men quickly wrapped an arm around Devlyn's gaunt torso for support. Someone he did not see brought a cloak to cover his feeble nakedness.

In a much weaker voice, Devlyn again asked, "Who are you?" It sounded more like a scratchy whisper than anything else. The man supporting him helped him sit down on a fallen log and another handed him a canteen.

"We are the remnant of the Judges of Lankor. Since Lankor was lost to Nauto's Wrath, we have lost any claim to authority, but we have endured with singular purpose," said the same woman. "My name is Catalina Turlan, Supreme Judge of Yanil. You met my predecessor, a champion of justice, Ramira Bir Ginthol, one thousand six hundred forty-eight years ago. She was the last Supreme Judge to exercise any power in Yanil, and she would have died in the city if it were not for your interference."

"I told her I would come back for the lucilliae," said Devlyn, now understanding what he had done and why it had so upset Eagan. He had not had a vision of Lankor's demise—he had truly been there when Nauto's Wrath devastated the city. He took a long draught from the canteen. Had he changed the course of history? Was this Ramira supposed to have died all those years ago?

"She died waiting for you," said Catalina. "Why didn't you return to her?"

"I was born only sixteen years ago, not sixteen hundred." Devlyn could feel everyone looking at him in bewilderment. What he suggested was impossible. The immortality of elves was an accepted phenomenon, even if most were now mortal.

"I won't pretend to know what elves are capable of, especially one who is a Phaedryn, but you will have to explain yourself," said Catalina.

"I'm not sure how it happened either. One moment I was in my quarters at Gwilnor, only several months ago, and the next I was amidst Nauto's Wrath in Lankor where I saw a woman desperately trying to remove a lucilliae from a statue of a blindfolded woman. She would have died if I had not insisted that she flee the city."

Everyone was quiet for a time. Devlyn wanted to know how they had come to take him away from his captors. "How did you manage to get me away? How did you know how to find me? Are the ei'ana still nearby?"

"About a week ago, we received a message from one of our judges who was with them disguised as a servant. She informed us you were in the area. You can imagine our disappointment at not finding her with the caravan. Fortunately, she left her bracelet among the company. It has a wield embedded in the silver that allows us to track it. All of our judges posing as servants have one like it," said Catalina. "We didn't know that those women were ei'ana. It mattered little though. Yanil is home to a variety of fungi, some are beneficial, while others have poisonous qualities. The one we used on those women rendered them unconscious. They will have no idea what happened when they wake up."

The mention of a knock-out fungi made Devlyn wonder if that was what they had used on him to spirit him away from Gwilnor and into that box. Just thinking about Gwilnor brought Ellendren to his mind, and he realized that he had not yet made any attempt to contact her or the others.

He tried to calm his mind enough to reach out to her, but couldn't. Reaching Aliel had become second nature; it required neither thought nor preparation. All he had to do was will it and it happened. But to reach Ellendren, he had to achieve a concentrated meditative state, and that was impossible just now.

Without explaining himself, Aliel reached out to Ellendren. Devlyn's thoughts were ever present to the phoenix, and to a lesser degree, Aliel's thoughts mingled with his own. Ciphering his thoughts required a subtlety beyond Devlyn's grasp.

They're on their way; they should be here soon. Alethea became aware of your presence the same moment I did, conveyed Aliel.

The news comforted Devlyn more than expected and he found it impossible to suppress a burgeoning grin. He conveyed his thanks to Aliel.

"My friends will be here shortly."

Barely finishing his sentence, a sound of ruffling wings and leaves filled their ears.

The alicorn soaring above was impossible to miss. Unlike the griffins who easily disappeared in the night sky, the alicorn's brilliant features demanded recognition. As wondrous as the winged unicorn was, Devlyn was convinced that the rider exceeded her mount's beauty.

The grin he was unable to hide stretched into a full-blown smile. He saw her worried expression, that like his own, was mixed with relief. She looked exhausted, as though she had not slept in days, but to him, she was still beautiful.

Ellendren was joined by Viren, Alethea, Wyn, and a woman he did not know but who had her arms wrapped around Wyn, holding on for her dear life. When Wyn's griffin landed, Devlyn recognized her as the servant who had bumped into him, spilling water and being punished for it by Alesei. The strangers smiled at her, and then drew her into the group where Catalina began to question the woman.

Wanting to run to Ellendren, he found himself barely capable of standing at all. His legs were shaky and sore, and he had no energy. He tried to force himself to stand, pushing his weight against his even weaker arms. It was useless; he slumped back on the log.

His feebleness did not faze Ellendren. She came to him. He wanted to embrace her as she sat on the log beside him, but he couldn't even move his arms, needing them to support his weight and keep himself from toppling backward and off the log. It mattered little to Ellendren, her arms wrapped around him and her face nuzzled his neck. He felt her tears on his skin as her body convulsed slightly.

"I missed you," he said, wanting desperately to wrap his own arms around her in a mutual exchange, exuberant that Trethien remained firmly in his imagination and that the foolish doubts he'd had only hours ago had no foundation.

Her arms still held him tight, and he didn't think she'd be letting go any time soon.

Warmth spread through his body as though it flowed from her own. He could not remember the last time he'd felt so content, despite his current fragility. She sobbed quietly, holding tight, refusing to even loosen her arms. When she finally did release her hold, which was admittedly becoming painful on his wasted body, she pulled back and said, "You look…"

"Emaciated," interrupted Wyn. "Did they forget to feed you?"

"I think they did some days, but the rest wasn't anything to write home about," Devlyn said, trying to lighten the atmosphere and relieved to see Wyn smile.

Viren rooted through his pack and tossed a bundle of blue and grey fabric at him.

Barely able to move quickly enough, Devlyn reached for the lierathnil that landed on his lap. He dressed as quickly as possible, managing to do so while not disturbing the cloak currently covering himself. He found it surprisingly difficult, especially with everyone, including the judges, surrounding him. They had the courtesy of looking away, but he was still careful to not lose the cloak and Wyn was gracious enough to help.

"I hope you don't intend to maintain the diet they had you on. It looks like you'll slip right out of those pants if you're not careful," Wyn chided with a wry grin, digging through his bag and tossing Devlyn an apple. "Here, eat. We'll get you a proper meal once we set up camp."

The hefty bite he took out the apple was possibly one of the best things he had ever tasted. It was almost as good as the purple vaer in the Illumined Wood. The apple's sweetness filled his parched mouth and he finished it in five large bites.

"You have our sincerest gratitude," Alethea said to Catalina. A round of introductions followed.

Still hungry, but with his mind functioning more clearly, he asked, "Does anyone know why Alesei was with Tenebrae ei'ana?"

"Servants of Shadow, the lot of them," said Alethea. "Their hearts hold no Light."

"So, what's the plan?" asked Devlyn, looking from one vacant expression to the next. The natural sugars in the apple had brought an unexpected, but welcomed alertness.

"We should get as far from here as possible," Ellendren said, glancing at Catalina with a frown, then turning back to Devlyn. "We need to get you back to Gwilnor where you can get proper medical attention while you recover."

"We can't do that," said Devlyn. "We're so close to Lankor, we can't just turn around now." The Judges of Yanil listened without interrupting.

"True, but you're not exactly in the best condition to do anything of use," admitted Wyn.

"I'll get my strength back quick enough," said Devlyn, not wanting to admit how weak he truly was.

"Even if you do recover in a timely manner, we have no way of getting into Lankor," said Ellendren, reminding everyone of the harsh reality. "The instant we draw near the gate, they'll know that we can wield."

"Why do you assume that the gates are the only way into Lankor? It is a port city after all," Catalina said, breaking into the conversation. "However, why enter Lankor in the first place? That which you promised to return for lies at the bottom of Lankor Bay, not in the peninsular city floating atop the water."

She was right.

"What are you suggesting?" asked Viren.

The small gathering remained still as everyone looked to Catalina.

"There are alternatives. For instance, Auten is our best chance to hire an inconspicuous ship."

"I'm sorry, but where are we now?" Devlyn asked. Not only was he curious about where they were, but knowing that might also answer the question of when and how long he had been locked in that wretched box.

"A day's ride east of Freiton Wood," said Viren, looking west toward what Devlyn assumed was the home of the minums. "Less than that with wings if you are you still interested in seeking their guidance."

That consideration required no thought; the possibility of learning how to create a seguian and travel from one part of the world to the next in the blink of an eye was more tempting than he could handle. "Very interested," he said, careful to not explain his desire for travel to Freiton Wood in front of Catalina and the other judges. Even though they had rescued him from Alesei and the Tenebrae ei'ana, they were still products of Yanil and prone to suspicion toward anything that involved wielding.

"What of this?" Catalina asked, eyeing the black box.

"It should be sent to Gwilnor," said Ellendren, as if there was no other obvious option. "Septyl needs to study it. Especially in days such as these."

"You would support the study of such a foul contraption?" Alethea asked, her voice noticeably hurt. "Have you so quickly forgotten its capabilities?"

"There are servants of Shadow inside Gwilnor, Tenebrae ei'ana among them, and possibly shadow elves who can undoubtedly wield tenebrys. What defenses do we have against that?" asked Ellendren.

"You would stoop to their level if you placed anyone, even Erynor, in this box."

"I thought we wanted Erynor incapacitated?" asked Devlyn, stunned by Alethea's ethical view.

"But at what cost?"

WITHDRAWAL

A shiver trickled through Jaerol's spine as he walked alone through an empty corridor adjacent to the main courtyard headed to the Dragon Tower where he hoped to find Velaria. The only sound he could hear were his own two feet patting against the stone floor. There was a tangible fear within Gwilnor that no one could ignore. Jaerol felt that the ei'ana were pretending that there was nothing to be afraid of. Every time he came across one, they conveyed a sense of ease, yet even they refrained from walking through the corridors alone.

Sporadic ambushes were occurring on a regular basis, increasing by the day. They'd been described as unexplained accidents that had students, castle servants, and ei'ana flooding the infirmary.

No one believed they were accidents though, especially with the rising number of incidents. At first, it had looked like the accidents were concentrated on students, since they were the only ones with unexplained bruises appearing. After a month, the accidents included castle servants and just recently even the ei'ana had started showing the inexplicable bruising.

Not a single victim spoke of their attackers, or of having been attacked, as though speaking of them would lead to something even worse.

The story was always the same. Someone had run into a doorframe or they had fallen down the stairs or a similar tale of an unfortunate event, which had never occurred in the castle before. The tales did become more inventive when the ei'ana began showing bruises similar to the ones the others had sported. Jaerol overheard one very embarrassed ei'ana say, quite unbelievably, that she had been wielding terys and inadvertently brought down a portion of her ceiling on top of herself.

Despite the accidents extending to the ei'ana, there was still no formal investigation under way. Many were starting to think that the Seven Chairs were locked away in their apartments, oblivious to anything peculiar occurring in the castle.

Finally reaching the Dragon Tower, home to the Azurelle wing, and the very place he hoped to call home one day, Jaerol found his way to the grand central stair. Broad enough for ten people to walk abreast without feeling claustrophobic, it was an impressive structure that switched back from the bottommost depths of the tower to the highest reaches of the attic, all of it made of the same grey marble.

The stair, like every corridor Jaerol had just walked through, was empty. It wasn't until he had gone up almost four flights of the staircase that he heard footsteps. *It's about time I came across someone else*, he thought to himself as he continued to ascend.

At first, he'd thought the sound came from ahead of him, but now the sound resonated from somewhere below. Thinking that it was just an echo in the vast space, he continued at his usual pace. Velaria and the Azurelles occupied the upper floors of the tower, although not the highest, but still a decent climb up the grand marble stair.

The sounds he'd heard just moments before returned, only this time, he noticed that there was more than one pair of footsteps. *Two other brave—or foolish—souls.* He didn't put any more thought into it.

Jaerol was nearly halfway to Velaria's floor when he finally reached the person he'd heard from the lower levels. His back was toward Jaerol and he was looking over the edge of the railing. Having no intention of stopping to ask his business, Jaerol continued on up, passing behind the other elf.

"It's a long way down," said the elf, his voice easily recognizable.

Not wanting to engage, Jaerol agreed without stopping, pretending he did not know the elf.

"I never took you for rude," Danyol spoke into the void below, not turning to look at Jaerol. "A coward and deserter, certainly. But managing to fool some of the best, that takes a subtlety that I could never muster."

A lump formed in Jaerol's throat. He had not turned nor stopped, but rather quickened his pace then noticed another person stepping onto the landing above. Deciding it best to not remain on the staircase, Jaerol turned onto the landing just behind the other person and went down another empty corridor. He'd never needed to go down this corridor before and was taken in by its obvious disuse. Long ago, when Gwilnor had taught student wielders from across all Teraeniel, not only those born in Eklean, the school had admitted many more students and this part of the tower had most likely been used for either residences or classrooms. Clearly, it hadn't been used in many years.

Footsteps trailed behind him and he knew they were following him. Crossing an intersecting corridor, also empty, he tried opening a door. The first four doors were locked and the lump in his throat only grew.

The next door was unlocked and he rushed in and locked it behind him. A quick look around showed him that it had once been a classroom, since there were assorted, very dusty, desks and chairs in the room, but he couldn't move any of it quickly enough to form a barricade against the door.

Instead, pressing into the erendinth, Jaerol felt the wood of the door, and strengthened it and the walls surrounding him, making a fortress for himself. He knew Danyol was strong in the erendinth, but hoped he wouldn't try wielding against him inside the castle—others would notice. His anxiety escalated and he could feel cold sweat dripping from his brow. Part of him wished that Liam was with him—the two of them together might have a better chance. A simple knock came at the door.

"I just want to talk," said Danyol. A second knock followed. "I am curious about how you managed to fool us into believing that you were actually one of us."

There was no third knock. Instead, Jaerol felt an incredibly strong force slam against his barrier. Teeth clenched, he pressed further into terys, knowing that he could not stop Danyol from coming in. Dividing his wield, he pressed into ignys, and with a sudden flash, he lifted the wield that held the door and launched fire toward it just as it exploded inward. He heard Danyol's derisive laugh beyond the door.

Jaerol had put all his strength into that wield, and it had only made Danyol laugh. Danyol was capable of much stronger wields than Jaerol could manage, and even as he desperately tried to form another one, he was knocked to the ground, hitting his head hard against the floor.

Stunned, he tried to regain his bearings, and touched the back of his head. He felt a warm wetness in his hair and knew it was blood.

"What do you want?" he called out.

Danyol walked past the rubble that had been the door and the walls to either side and casually took a seat with his legs crossed before addressing Jaerol. "I was there that day, at the Grand Tourney. You remember it, don't you? I remember it quite well; it still sickens me. You truly fooled us. I think the only reason you got away with it is because the thought of any Cyndinari doing what you did was so unthinkable—disgraceful and cowardly. Surely, no one with Cyndinari blood pumping through their veins would perform such a stunt. I was actually betting on that useless sack of flesh to win and steal your soul for himself. I did hear some intriguing rumors regarding the both of you."

"His name is Kiron." Jaerol's fear quickly turned into anger at Danyol's mention of Kiron.

"Whatever—he was weak and deserved to die. That bit with umbrys was clever, I'll give you that. I never thought you'd be strong enough to wield a transcendental. Oh, and I hear that you're experiencing similar *sentiments*, but toward a flaming half-elf, half-human this time. Really Jaerol, a lethien of all people? Are you that desperate?"

Jaerol growled, despite himself, relieved that Liam wasn't here.

"Pathetic! I should claim your soul for my own and rid Teraeniel of you for good."

Staring into his eyes, Jaerol tried to determine who this elf was, who claimed to know him from before.

"You still don't remember me, do you? Weak and stupid! Perhaps this will jog your memory." The air rippled around Danyol, undulating then shifting to a shadowy presence, one that had been cloaked not a moment earlier. His skin sickened and turned ashen, his hair lost its lustrous black tone, replaced by lank, fading orange locks. His eyes were empty, a harsh deadened grey replacing the silver irises which moments ago had been bursting with life.

Jaerol couldn't breathe when he recognized the shadow elf before him. The last time Jaerol had seen him, Razcul had been a handsome Cyndinari student at the Imperium.

"A clever name, don't you think? Danyol? It reeks of Eldinare, but it served its purpose," said Razcul, lifting his hand slightly so that black lightning crackled above his palm.

"How…" Jaerol trailed off, fear seizing his entire body as Razcul stood and closed the distance between them, grabbed Jaerol by his robe to pull him half off the floor, and struck him full across the face.

"Pathetic."

The light in the room was sucked away and the crackling sound of the black lightning filled his ears before pain beyond anything he had ever felt slammed into his body. It felt as though every single bone was being smashed into bits. He did not hear himself scream in agony.

Everything went blank.

For a blissful moment, the pain was gone and with it, the memory of what had happened. Then it returned at an excruciating speed and level. Trying to open his eyes to look for Razcul, he found that he was alone in a bed in a room he did not recognize. Only the pain told him that he was not dead.

The room was bright and white curtains trimmed in red surrounded the bed he lay in. Had someone found him and brought him here? Liam was the obvious answer, but he had no idea that Jaerol had gone to the Dragon Tower. There was a chair next to the bed, and it looked as though it had recently held someone. Again, Liam came to his mind. How long had he sat there waiting for Jaerol to wake? Bits of memory returned. The Dragon Tower and the vacant room. Danyol was there; no, not Danyol. Razcul, the shadow elf who had once been his peer at the Imperium in Broid and the champion at the Grand Tourney. *What was he doing here? How did he get into the castle?* His weak thoughts strayed uneasily from the memories.

Then the blankness returned and the pain disappeared once again.

Every now and then, Jaerol opened his eyes and saw people in the bright room. He did not recognize any of them, but once, he thought that someone—Liam?—had been holding his hand while sitting in the chair beside the bed. The pain was so intense that he could only keep his eyes open for a moment before passing out again.

This time, when his eyes popped open again, Velaria sat on the edge of his bed in the bright room with the white curtains completely drawn open. She looked at him and gestured when he tried to speak.

"Don't talk yet," she said. Her ever present small smile was missing today, but her voice was gentle and comforting. "The Crimsyn ei'ana say you will recover. You'll have to let your body heal of course; some things can't be done instantly, even with wielding. We're not sure what you did to yourself, but whatever you did, it brought down half of the sixth floor of the Dragon Tower. The noise drew dozens who worked hard to pull you out of the rubble."

Jaerol tried to lift a hand to protest that account, but he felt the incredible pain return and the familiar feeling of losing consciousness. Fighting the sensation, he lay still with his eyes closed and tried not to clench his teeth, fighting to maintain consciousness. *They believed I did it to myself,* he thought, furious at the very mention that he would do such a thing and opened his eyes to look hard at Velaria.

He tried to speak, but Velaria gestured that he shouldn't and he eased back against the pillows. Through tear-soaked eyes, he watched her pull a slip of parchment from the rich blue robe that covered her leafy dress, a single leaf dangling from her sleeve. The robe resembled a dress more than a cloak, but served the same purpose. She held the parchment so he could read it.

I know you are not responsible for harming yourself or the castle.

The Seven Chairs are currently investigating the situation, but there is no evidence to suggest otherwise and any that you provide will be discarded as it will come from someone mentally unsound. <u>Trust no one.</u> Gwilnor is no longer in the hands of Septyl and our only chance for survival is to flee.

When Jaerol looked up at Velaria, surprised by the dejected tone of the note, he realized that Velaria's expression matched the note. She no longer looked at Jaerol, but out the open window into a courtyard bathed in a summer sun. "You should know," she said, "that since your accident, and others similar to it, the chancellor has forbidden students from wielding outside of lessons." The parchment she held caught fire, and she allowed the flames to engulf it before she tossed it out the window. "The unofficial elthion league has also been suspended."

"When?" Jaerol managed to say. Not being able to compete in another elthion match was a blow. What was truly upsetting was that being part of the unofficial league was the only way students were learning how to wield since Yvonne's class had no real instruction.

"The Crimsyns say you should heal in a week or two. It will be difficult to move your entire body without pain, but we believe it manageable. Liam has rarely left your side, only for classes and meals—the Crimsyns won't let him eat here. He's fallen asleep in that chair every night this week." Velaria placed a comforting hand on his shoulder before standing to leave. The news was overwhelming. The idea of the ei'ana abandoning Gwilnor was simply unheard of. Gwilnor was a beacon of hope, one of the only remaining places of power capable of standing against the Erynien Empire.

The moment Velaria left the infirmary, he thought of questions he should have posed. Where did she expect they could move nearly a thousand ei'ana and their students without drawing the attention of the Tenebrae School? Even if they managed to get everyone away from the infested castle, where could they hope to go that was safe?

Jaerol's mind raced as he tried to think of where the Seven Chairs intended to hide the entirety of those Gwilnor residents still loyal to the Light. The castle had originally been constructed to not only house and educate a vast number of wielders, but to protect them. Where else could they go that would serve the same purpose?

With his growing concern, the pain intensified and the blankness he had managed to fight off while Velaria was present returned, and with it, he again lost consciousness.

Aaron sat at his desk, thumb and forefinger pressed against the bridge of his nose. The meeting had finally ended and his decision was final. He had spoken with the finality of the Ceurtriarch, High Archsteward and Arbiter of the Light. There was no other alternative and the inexperienced kien wielders of the ei'ceuril were now his responsibility—again.

He had spent months configuring a plan and fighting for their reentrance into Gwilnor Academy. Countless debates had taken place among the wise ones; he had heard more opinions on the matter than he cared for, both publicly and privately. Some opinions had been reserved to sharp criticisms in the form of anonymous notes delivered while the temple slept.

His original opponents would, undoubtedly, be relieved at his decision. *At least, they'll support one of my actions as Ceurtriarch, even if they're not aware of my intentions with the kien wielders.*

It was Gwynthaen, the start of a new week, and every kien wielder among the ei'ceuril, both those vowed and those still too young to profess, would soon discover that they were now prohibited from attending lessons at Gwilnor.

The ei'ceuril wielders were, once again, cut off from life outside the Temple of Ceur. The Seven Chairs had been informed, and he had written a personal apology to Gwilnor's chancellor. He had never cared for Hannah, despite her all too kind charisma and his sister's opinion of her. Elle loved the woman, but there was something about her that he simply did not trust. He had only met Hannah on official business as Ceurtriarch and could tell that the aging woman despised him for his rise to power at such a young age. He thought that it was something she had likely spent her entire life and career trying to achieve.

Her envy mattered little to him. After today, a formal break would take place between the castle and the temple again. He hoped that none of the ei'ceuril student wielders had remained at Gwilnor over the weekend. They were, of course, forbidden from doing so, but a common phrase among the ei'ceuril raced through his mind, *better to seek forgiveness than ask permission*. He deplored the saying and had always discouraged its use even as a young ei'ceuril, although he found himself particularly fit for it.

Tired of sitting, he stood and walked toward his balcony. The Ceurtriarch had access to several luxuries that few others in the temple could enjoy. Not only were his quarters extensive and he had access to the temple's largest private balcony, but his office and apartment were right next to the Chamber of Light.

The closer one was to the Chamber of Light, the greater his or her rank and authority. There was no way around the ei'ceuril hierarchy. He dreamt of addressing it at some point, but knew, as a young Ceurtriarch, he would only be met with strict criticism. He had to bide his time and save that fight for another day.

He moved to the balcony and walked along it, enjoying the warmth before leaning against the balustrade. Looking over, he followed the stone of the temple downward, seeing it plummet into the depths of the canyon below. A canyon that very few were aware of.

Moving his gaze from the canyon to the mountain on his left, he thought about how the mountain was the only thing in Ceurenyl that rose above the temple. Not even the highest towers of Gwilnor rose above the Temple of Ceur, but that was due to its altitude on the mountainside. If the castle and temple had been built on the same level plane, the castle's towers would soar above the temple.

Another little-known fact was that a valley lay between the mountains, hidden from anyone in the city. Various tunnels connected it to the temple and the city, but no one, save himself and a select few knew about that valley. It had largely been forgotten.

On his elevation to Ceurtriarch, certain secrets of the temple had been revealed to him by the temple itself. While he had known of the hidden valley because he and a few others had spent time there practicing wielding with Devlyn, he had not then been aware of the numerous tunnels and passageways. Now, he was privy to not just knowing that they existed, but also exactly where they were and where they led. That was only one of many secrets that were not recorded in the temple's archives, but which had been revealed to the new Ceurtriarch by the temple.

Looking in the direction of the hidden valley, hidden even from his current vantage point, he considered how to inform the wise ones of his decision to continue teaching the kien wielders. They had already begun their training—it would be criminal to discontinue it now—and he refused to be remembered as the Ceurtriarch who had impeded kien wielders. Every archsteward had hoped for that though, some secretly and some not so secretly.

The main issue with continuing their lessons, was that it could only take place beyond the temple's wards. The hidden valley was the most obvious choice, but having them learn to wield there meant it would no longer be secret. The ei'ceuril were already a talkative bunch, and they would hardly restrain themselves to maintain that secret for the sake of gossip.

Before his decision had been announced to the wise ones, Phendien, Chair of Emradiel, had sent some of the recently arrived Eldinari to the Temple of Ceur with an offer to instruct the kien wielders in Gwilnor's stead. Aaron had been surprised, yet elated to discover that there were still some ei'ceuril wielders among the secluded elves of the Eldin Wood, and delighted to accept the offer. While he did not wish to cut ties with Gwilnor Academy, there was no alternative; Gwilnor no longer belonged to the Seven Schools of Septyl. Evidence overwhelmingly indicated that it now belonged to the Tenebrae School, with Erynor as its sole, self-appointed Chair.

The greatest asset at Aaron's disposal was Abbess Clara—the Poor Lady. A female steward. The female stewards were believed to have been exterminated shortly after the Ceurendol War, when Erynor reigned supreme in Eklean. But Clara had maintained her hidden monastery in the

Ashton Wood all that time. If anyone could return Balance to the Order of Ei'ceuril, it was Clara.

To Freiton

Jax deplored pity and didn't want it from any of his fellow minums. He knew that they were aware of the torture he was subject to at the hands of the shadow elves and the Deathless that Erynor Meriden, Emperor of the Erynien Empire, had tasked to unlock the secrets of the Time Wardens. Despite his torturers' most grueling efforts, the minums were left unscathed in the Freiton Wood, and the Time Key remained beyond Erynor's knowledge. Surely if he had known its location, he would have burnt down their entire forest and killed every minum before finding the artifact and righting his past defeats.

Jax knew Erynor's desperation. The emperor only visited him on occasion. For the most part, his torture was entrusted to one who Jax had learned was one of Erynor's true children. Not just any child, but his first born. And if Erynor would do everyone the courtesy of dying, his heir.

Unlike his other countless children who clawed for their father's attention, leaching off his power and influence, this son was much more than any other shadow elf.

His crime had defined him. That crime had cursed him and the others responsible for placing the Shroud over Ceurendol and by extension the entirety of Krysenthiel, even if the latter had been unintentional.

The Luminari had been severed from their Life, and the Cyndinari cursed for the crime. But none suffered from the curse as extensively as those directly responsible: the Deathless—the Deurghol.

It was rumored that six had been involved with forming the

Shroud. None besides Erynor and the other Deurghol knew for certain how many they numbered. Legend favored six, but Jax knew very well that there could easily be nine or sixty-six or a hundred or more even. It mattered little exactly how many there had been. Although the thought of a hundred Deurghol was terrifying.

He was locked away somewhere in Broid, most likely below Erynor's lush imperial palace. While the spaces on the upper levels welcomed the warm winds of the southern seas, ruffling silken curtains, the lower levels had no windows or balconies to speak of, carved from the very bedrock of Cynethol—one of the Kinzdol Islands. Jax had no idea how far beneath the island's surface he was. The smell of salt and fish filled his nostrils, and not even the depth of his cell could thwart Cynethol's humidity.

For all Jax knew, he was the first minum in five thousand years to have succumbed to slavery and torture, on the island where his race began. The central island of the Kinzdol Islands had once been their home, long before the Cyndinari arrived and named it Cynethol. It was the place of their birth where two races, humans and goblins, lived in mutual disinterest. Over time, in the usual way of things, they had interbred, unintentionally giving birth to a new race, a different race that was named minum. They did not choose the name; it was given to them. And as the centuries passed, that central island became inhabited solely by minums. The minums belonged to neither goblin nor human race and neither race wanted them. The minums knew that, without the Luminari, they would still be enslaved to the southern human kingdoms, where they had been sold into bondage by the goblins following the fall of the Kingdom of Thellion—sold from one progenitor race to the other. To this day, Jax still felt discriminating glares from goblins and humans alike, especially from Tieli or Yanilean humans, their original slaveowners.

If not for the Exalted Aryl of Krysenthiel, and their mandate to end all forms of slavery in Eklean, his kin would still know the lash and poverty at the hands of another race. Before the Luminari left their Skyland of Luminare to come to Teraeniel, they had uncovered a type of wielding with incredible power. It allowed them to open portals and travel to any place and any time. Whether or not those ancient elves truly understood what they had discovered is a mystery, but what is not a mystery is that Ei'denai Desmyn and Ei'terel Valeriel Lorenthien, Aryl of Arenthyl, the Exalted Aryl of Krysenthiel, and High King and High Queen of Eklean, contained it in the Time Key, and then gifted the key to the least of Eklean's races, believing that the minums would not abuse the tremendous power it provided. Only those born from the mixture of humans and goblins were entitled to this gift.

The Time Key and the creation of the Time Wardens allowed the minums to survive the sad fall of Krysenthiel and the rise of the Erynien Empire during the Ceurendol War. In his quest for world domination, Erynor had no way of harming the minums in the Freiton Wood. Jax desperately wanted to return home to the free town of Freiton in the Freiton Woods. But to go home meant also bringing the ire of the Deurghol.

Daily, the Deurghol visited Jax. After all his time in captivity, he had yet to learn his name. And he imagined it would remain that way. He had yet to hear anyone give a name to any of the Deathless.

The complications arising from that astounded Jax; perhaps 'deathless' was more a description of who they were. No longer alive but too wretched for death. Perhaps they vied for release. Were they mere instruments stripped of both name and will? Were there souls left in their corrupted husks?

Jax had no idea, and he accepted that he was not likely to uncover the reality. All he cared about was that his family remain safe. The thought of this Deurghol going into the Freiton Wood to destroy the minums was too much to bear.

The Deurghol did not threaten to enslave his family. The only slaves that Erynor valued were those with elven blood—the Luminari among all others. Instead, he threatened to destroy every minum and wipe them from living memory.

Jax knew that was not possible; to erase something entirely was impossible. To make something nothing was beyond even Erynor's ability. But, he did not doubt the destructive force the Deurghol were capable of, especially if they boasted about it. A shimmer coursed through Jax's blood as he thought of another capable of it. Just thinking of Ramiel and all his corrupted creatures of Darkness locked away in their dungeons beneath Teraeniel's crust was enough to keep Jax from sleeping at night. Not even the Deurghol could stir those types of nightmares.

To safeguard his family, Jax remained compliant to his new masters. He committed the crimes obediently. He had felt the death of a great elf ripple through time when Ealyndol exhaled his last breath and transitioned to the World-Beyond.

He had opened the seguian that let Dwonian warriors and one assassin enter the temple and then allowed hundreds of kien wielders to go from Ceurenyl into Broid, bypassing hundreds of leagues in a single step. None of them knew how to control the erendinth. They had never been instructed on how to do so, nor was there any intent to, just as with Erynor's shadow elves. Erynor kept his new forces in reserve, secluded along Cynethol's coast, far enough from Broid that they could not damage the city, biding his time before unleashing them on Eklean to wreak havoc beyond imagining across the continent. Occasionally, Jax felt the ground tremble, the cause of the tremors obvious. The island was likely to sink with their meddling in powers beyond their control.

Jax felt these sins in his bones. They were not personally his own, but without him, they would have never been committed. Without him, Ealyndol would still live, continuing as Ceurtriarch, and the hazardous kien wielders would have remained locked inside the Temple of Ceur, keeping the world safer.

These crimes weighed him down—burdened his heart. A stronger weight was the knowledge that the crimes would continue. Erynor was not finished with Jax. There were other heinous offenses waiting to be committed against Eklean.

Footsteps came from beyond the cell door, and tears spilled from Jax's eyes. The memory of pain returned; his body felt the agony he would soon endure. It was but moments away. If he made even a slight hint of resistance, the minums would be destroyed; his entire family would be wiped from Teraeniel as if they were an infestation.

The door opened and what little light was present in the cell fled to the corners when the Deurghol entered, unable to touch what had once been an elf. The room had been dark before, but not even the lightless room could compare to the presence of a Deurghol.

Jax felt himself shake uncontrollably as the Deurghol neared. The little warmth left to his body vanished, the humidity in the room a distant memory as sweat frosted over his skin.

They were going to ask him to do something bad again. He knew it; his heart was heavy, but there was nothing he could do. The sickening dead voice spoke in near-silent whispers, crawling across his skin and seeping into his ears. There was no mouth to be seen in the darkness of the Deathless, no eyes, let alone any identifiable feature of what had once been an elf.

"The Phaedryn searches for a lucilliae," said the chilling voice. Ice shot down Jax's spine at the words. "His mind is bent on Lankor. He travels for that which lies beneath the currents."

"I…I…" Jax stammered.

"You will," said the Deurghol, "take me to him."

"Please," squeaked Jax. His voice was barely audible, but he regretted even that.

The Deurghol smiled.

Jax could not see it, but he felt the lifeless form smile at him from the darkness.

"Their fate is sealed then."

The Deurghol left, yet the icy darkness he brought remained. Jax's bones felt frozen, too cold to even shiver. Or was it his fear that crippled him? He had just doomed his family—his entire race—the Deurghol would burn every minum in the free town of Freiton.

He had to warn them. The only thing that had kept him from creating a seguian before was knowing that the minums would not come to harm—that the Freiton Wood would not be destroyed by fire. Waiting several minutes to pass after the Deathless had left, he formed the familiar silver globe of light that was not a light between his palms. His cell disappeared and the space in the globe appeared around him, a place he knew well.

Not a single cloud hung in the clear blue sky in southern Torsil. Devlyn would have been overjoyed on any other day, yet Viren cautioned against taking to the sky, explaining that anyone traveling would easily identify them and their destination if they flew too high above the ground. Having to walk meant doubling their travel time, but they finally reached the edge of Freiton Wood.

Devlyn knew he had been kept in that box for a good amount of time, but he had never imagined that he had missed nearly all of spring, locked away until the month of Dynenth. An entire three months gone and he had nothing to show for it except a gaunt body. Not even Yvonne's lessons were that capable of stunting his progress.

Aliel was no stranger to Devlyn's mind, and conveyed a sense of compassion, shifting Devlyn's focus away from the box only a few paces behind them. It felt like a hug, and if someone tried to say it, he would have taken offense. The words would have sounded empty and possibly clumsy. What could anyone say? *I'm sorry.* What did they have to be sorry about? They were not the ones responsible for his imprisonment. Ellendren had said those very words several times since they'd reunited, and he responded with his best smile, but it felt hollow and she had to see it as well.

Relating with the phoenix was unlike any other communication. It wasn't even conversation. Devlyn recalled when he'd been in the Illumined Wood and first tried to speak with Aliel. He'd stumbled across what seemed beyond mere words, or something prior to words. The thing that words tried to express. What feelings attempted to share—the source of music, the inspiration of paintings and sculptures, the very soul of poetry. What was meant was somehow conveyed to the other.

Whatever *that* was, that was how phoenix communicated; that was how they were meant to communicate. Not just the phoenix, but everyone. He wondered what had happened to sever anacordel from that incredible form of communication. Whatever it was, it must have been terrible. Did everyone simply forget?

Walking in silence through Freiton Wood, Devlyn was left to his thoughts. Did anyone even know where they were going? There were maps showing the location of the Freiton Wood, but he had never seen any map display the layout of the forest or where the minums dwelled therein. No roads or villages were penciled in.

Even the minums' architecture remained a mystery. Would it resemble human homes above the ground? What if they were more like the dwarves, and dug beneath Teraeniel, forming vast halls invisible to every eye searching above? There was even a chance that the Eldinari had influenced their architecture, creating dwellings in the tree tops high above the ground.

Devlyn had no way of knowing for sure and he had never read or overheard anything concerning the minums' home. Ellendren might know something since there was little that she was unfamiliar with. And both Alethea and Viren had lived in a time when the world was open. One of them might have visited here before and knew exactly where they were walking to.

Aliel soared somewhere ahead of them, and the alicorn and griffins followed him through the canopy. The judges watched the mythical creatures in awe. The trees in the Eldin Wood and in the Wooded Hills of Thellion stretched twice as high as these trees, and they were only half the height and girth of those in the Illumined Wood. It crossed Devlyn's mind as they walked through the shorter trees that these might be the normal height of trees. At least, the normal sort of tree which did not come from the Skylands or belong to whatever genus made up the Illumined Wood. These trees did still tower high above everyone's head.

Alethea guided the group, even though she was not at the front. They had traveled a fair distance into the forest when she called for a stop to strike up camp. Judging by the sun filtering through the trees, the day was far from ending and they could cover quite a bit more distance. But no one objected and Devlyn did not feel like inquiring about the reason for their early halt. Alethea always had her reasons, even though they seldom made any rational sense when she did share them.

Before Devlyn had the chance to do more than sit and rest his legs, Viren offered him a thick slice of bread, and then watched to ensure Devlyn ate every last crumb. Then, he handed Devlyn a second slice and an apple. Devlyn's stomach lurched at the thought of more food.

Viren had made it his mission to see that Devlyn ate frequently since he had gotten out of that wretched box. Not that Devlyn was ungrateful for the food, but his stomach began to hurt when he stuffed more food into it. His strength was only just beginning to return, but surprisingly, walking the last leg of the journey had done him wonders.

Everyone had offered Devlyn a ride, either on their mount or on the wagon with the box. But he wanted to be as far from that box as possible, so he refused the wagon. Even though the exercise drained him, the walking was enjoyable as his weak legs rediscovered their long-unused muscles. It was a good sort of hurt that stung his thighs and calves, the sort of sting that was followed by promised muscle growth and he seemed to have muscles that he had not been aware of before.

The bustling activity in the small camp slowed as everyone finished their assigned tasks. Devlyn was the only one to not contribute to setting up camp. Part of him wanted to help; he felt useless sitting there and eating while everyone else kept busy. But he knew his sluggish body would only get in the way and slow the entire process.

It was the judges' turn to prepare the meal, and while they were getting it organized, Catalina made her way toward Devlyn, sitting under a tree at the edge of the clearing where they'd stopped.

"It must drive you crazy to watch everyone do something and not help," she said, taking a seat beside him.

Devlyn kept quiet, not wanting to admit his own failings, concentrating instead on Catalina's face. It was hardened by her past. Devlyn had no idea what had caused it, whether war or internal strife, but her years had left a visible mark. He had never seen her smile and wondered if she remembered how to.

"We should speak of how we intend to retrieve what was lost, and exactly what it's capable of. My order held power in Yanil for four thousand years, and it was only when the object referenced by Ramira was buried beneath the water that we lost it."

"It's not a weapon, if that's what you're hoping for. And it likely wasn't entrusted to your order for more than a century. Erynor started his war against Krysenthiel shortly after my ancestors created Ceurendol."

Devlyn couldn't tell if that disappointed her. It might not have, but he doubted that he would have known if it did.

"What is it then?"

"It's called a lucilliae, a jewel of sorts. The Luminari of Krysenthiel fashioned seven unique lucilliae. Most jewels inspire their onlookers with wonder at their beauty, wealth, and the splendor they contain. These have a different effect; they were indeed a source of incredible inspiration, but they were infused with attributes that their creators held most dear."

"Can the Erynien Empire use it against us?"

"As far as I understand, only by keeping it from us."

"But what does it do? Why did Ramira nearly die trying to retrieve it? Surely they must do something to harm the enemy."

"They fill the onlooker with virtues prized by the Luminari. Together, they formed Ceurendol, the Jewel of Life, and granted Life immortal to the onlooker, banishing disease and suffering. The Luminari of Krysenthiel wanted to share their blessed lives with the rest of Eklean. That's why Erynor did what he did. He refused the idea that the Life of the elves be shared with what he calls the lesser races."

"Do I understand you correctly—your ancestors actually succeeded in crafting this Jewel of Life? That if anyone looked upon it, they would live forever?"

"Yeah. Well, at least as long as Anaweh willed before calling them to Lumaeniel."

"If that's the case, then how did they die? How is it that the Luminari live only slightly longer than humans now?"

"Because they created Ceurendol. They infused their Life into it; in order to partake of that Life, they too would have to look upon the jewel, just as everyone else, including their children."

Catalina remained quiet for a time, seeming to consider Devlyn's account, weighing it in her mind. Devlyn couldn't tell whether she believed him or not. He didn't care if she did. His responsibility was in retrieving the lucilliae and reforming Ceurendol; it mattered little if others believed him. And currently, a lucilliae lay in the ruins of the Drowned City, hidden among Erynor's strongest ally.

"Auten is our best choice," Catalina said at last, giving no indication how she felt about what Devlyn said. "I'll send two of my judges ahead of us tomorrow. You cannot walk through Lankor's gates, but neither can you simply go to the shore and jump into the bay and swim to the bottom. I have no idea how you intend to manage that, but what I can do, is get you a boat that will take you above the Drowned City. How long do you intend to remain in Freiton?"

"No more than a week."

OPEN GATES

A dense fog blanketed the hills, the hazy moisture clinging to Alex's skin and clothing as he sat on his grey courser peering in the direction where Gneal supposedly sprawled. He had ridden ahead with a small scouting party, the bulk of the Perrien resistance only a thirty-minute march behind. If he had not visited the city before, he would have questioned whether this was the right location. He was sure though that they were close to Perrien's capital. He nudged the patient courser forward even as he shivered in the chill of the predawn fog and despite its tactical advantage in hiding the size of the force behind him, Alex could not decide whether the presence of the fog troubled him.

There was certainly nothing unnatural about fog this time of year, but it did make it hard for him to see the others in the scouting party, and it made him nervous—it just felt wrong. He had no intention of sharing his nervousness with anyone. He had to appear strong before the soldiers. Neither a general nor a monarch, he somehow had been placed in a leadership position. Despite Aen's conviction that Aewen spoke truly in saying Alex was descended from Dennion, that ancestry did not automatically make him any king or lord. He still didn't understand how the ei'ana had managed to place him in his current predicament. He wasn't even a knight yet.

Alex assumed that his recent elevation in standing was most likely due to his kinship with Devlyn, but even that made little sense. His cousin might be a Phaedryn, but that didn't make Alex a king, let alone fit to lead a rebellion against the Perrien Council. While Devlyn had the advantage of having provided help to Myrium and fighting shadow elves, Alex had never seen a battlefield before. All he had was his education as a student knight at Gwilnor Academy.

When they had left Aewen Bridge behind, Alex had been relieved to also leave behind Alexandria. Having a city named after him was the most ludicrous thing he had ever heard of, and he shuddered at what Devlyn would say about it, let alone his mother. If she sided with her brothers, there was no way she'd think he merited such recognition. It's not like he had done anything extraordinary. All he had done was ride across Perrien and Parendior, gathering troops to form a resistance army. Going from town to town and one farm to the next, citing their need for independence from the Perrien Council did not make one a lord or king. Even if the response had been amazing. Young men and women, even some older folk had decided to join. Everyone in Parendior was tired of the council's influence over their lives.

What Alex still didn't understand was why they had decided that he should be their leader. It was Oliver, Arlyn, Reia, and Sara who gave the speeches. He barely said anything. It was only after the speeches were all done, when they relaxed at inns and taverns with the local folk that he talked to anyone. In his opinion, it was a terrible reason to elevate a boy of seventeen to leadership.

A vague outline against the fog came into view and he slowed his horse to a halt, the rest of the scouting party coming closer so they could confer as they tried to make out useful details.

In the distance, the city looked like an indistinct blot crowning a hill. While the hills rose and fell naturally, the straight lines of the stout city marked it for what it was. And Gneal currently stood defenseless; her army was preoccupied terrorizing the Cyrillean Pass even as a rebellious siege neared her walls.

Alex and his advisors had spent every evening over the past two months devising a plan to take the city. The Council of Perrien had to be aware of their march toward Gneal. Even for a city with lowered defenses, an army marching directly toward you was the sort of news that spread rather quickly.

Hiding an army was impossible. Alex half expected to find Perrien's army returned from their siege of Everin, which was well into its third year by now. The Evellion capital was proving its impenetrable reputation quite well.

As the Perrien resistance marched ever closer to the city, his soldiers met no opposition. Alex and his advisors had considered striking Old Gneal first, but some of the generals feared a force from New Gneal would swoop in from behind as they sieged the castle. It was prudent advice, but that meant fighting through a densely populated area and Alex didn't want to guess what panicked civilians might do while their city was under attack.

The walls of the city became more distinct the closer they drew. The fog was still thick, making it impossible to discern anything useful. Alex couldn't even see if archers lined Gneal's battlements.

Oliver came from behind Alex and stopped beside him. "Our soldiers are in formation and the Charrenese await your signal."

"Give it." Alex looked on toward the foggy city, somewhat puzzled by his instructor in combat arts and strategy at Gwilnor now asking his permission to give the signal. Alex barely heard Oliver's whistle after he had left him, but not a moment later dozens of hippogriffs flew over his head and they too disappeared into the fog.

The rest of the army had caught up and now waited, anticipating what they hoped would be a quick matter of opening the gates. They had agreed that the soldiers would wait no more than half an hour before marching on the gates.

Counting the time off in his head, Alex nudged his horse forward leading the army onward, but before they were within range of the archers who lined the walls around the gate, they heard then saw riders coming from the city. In the fog, the sound of the hooves reached their ears before their features were distinguishable. It was not a large group, only six, but they were on grey coursers and Alex had no intention of taking any chances. For all anyone knew, they could be shadow elves. Arlyn, Reia, and Sara rode up to surround him as the riders, wearing the colors of Perrien, approached and stopped before their small group.

"We've heard that an army was coming to topple Gneal's corrupt council and return Perrien to what it once was." Alex had heard that voice before but couldn't immediately place it.

"That is our intent," Reia responded on behalf of the resistance, "for we know the true heir to the monarchy and can present him." Alex didn't see her expression, but assumed she held the retinue from Gneal firmly in her glare with her orange brooch proudly and prominently pinned on her lapel. Everything about Reia screamed Arantiulyn.

"As it happens, the true sons and daughters of Gneal desire our monarchy returned and that detestable council ousted. New Gneal awaits you with open arms. Not a single knight loyal to the council remains; the council's puppets have barred themselves in Old Gneal and the castle," said the same man who had first spoken.

I know I've heard someone say the sons of Gneal before, Alex thought. Pushing his horse forward so that he was at the front of their group, he faced the speaker and smiled at him.

"So, I take it you weren't entirely useless," said Karl with a derisive snort. Alex had not seen Karl since the man had helped Devlyn and himself flee from Gneal three years ago, before Devlyn learned that he could wield. "I see you have a sword now; did they teach you how to use it?"

"Sure have," said Alex. "By Sir Oliver Penault himself."

"Is that good-for-nothing here? Where is he?" Karl said, searching the ranks of soldiers.

"Reunions can wait," said Reia, "there are pressing matters at hand. What would happen if the army entered the city?"

Karl took a moment as if considering the next move for Gneal and the greater kingdom of Perrien. He was, if anything, a son of Gneal and would do nothing to bring harm to her. "Depends. We're done with that wretched council. They can take their loyalty to the Erynien Empire all the way back to Broid for all we care. You said you know the identity of the heir. Where is he?"

Arlyn nudged his horse forward slightly so that he was next to Alex.

Alex half hoped he would ride into the ranks of soldiers behind them and pull out a random general disguised as a common soldier, but he felt Arlyn's gaze linger on him, and knew Reia and Sara also turned to him.

"You must be joking! He's not even old enough to be a man. And I know for a fact that he has older siblings and parents still living. Not to mention his uncles!" Karl said, making Alex hot with anger.

At first, he agreed with Karl; Arlyn and the ei'ana had to be out of their minds. He wanted to see the council gone just as badly as anyone, but that didn't mean he wanted to be the heir. He *did* have older siblings, and parents.

"It has long been known that when the monarchy of Perrien lost its power, they were exiled to Cor'lera. Arlyn is quite the expert on the village, and it only took a few weeks of asking the right questions to uncover the truth of the matter, which Lady Aewen herself has verified," said Reia.

"His father is the great-great-grandson of the last king and queen of Perrien," said Arlyn, his horse still beside Alex's.

"My family tried to return the monarchy to its rightful place when I was studying at Gwilnor. They answered the council with their lives, as did other supporters. Fortunately for our cause, the council is not well loved by New Gneal and a whole new generation of support has risen, eager to uproot the corruption seeping from the castle." Karl now frowned in concentration, trying to decide one way or the other.

"Do you think Gneal would accept him?" asked Sara.

"They might," Karl replied, "but, they won't be all too eager to allow a boy to take control of Perrien. Especially when there are older relatives in the line. That being said, they aren't here with an army, are they?"

Alex felt his ears redden with every word that came out of Karl's mouth. He still was not accustomed to the ei'ana trying to pass him off as a king, despite what Aewen had said. And he did not dare allow himself to consider what they were hoping to accomplish by doing so. But whenever Karl opened his mouth, Alex's response was to tell Karl the many reasons why Karl was wrong, and perhaps plant a strong fist in the man's dour face with the next insult.

"Well, I suppose there's only one way to find out," said Karl before Alex could do something he already knew he would regret. "We'll have to go back into the city first, followed by Alex, you three, and Oliver as well—he's from a good Perrien family and well respected here. New Gneal can't fit your entire army—it's overcrowded as it is—but you should bring a squadron or two to show New Gneal what you came with. The rest of the army should start setting up camp. We won't be sieging Old Gneal today. Those foreigners with those flying beasts can wait in the city. If you brought any other foreigner to your cause, we probably would have rejected you, but we were too impressed to get angry. Don't get me wrong, we'll most likely resent you for it later. Shall we get moving?"

Reia gave a flick of her hand, which was passed through the channels of command. The army behind them stirred and prepared to reorganize itself. Karl and his small group led the way through the fog and back to the city.

Alex rode his grey courser and followed at a short distance behind with Arlyn, Reia, and Sara just behind him. As pleased as he was with the outcome, a tinge of disappointment at wasting their element of surprise nagged at him.

Gneal's large gate rose before them, the features growing more distinct the closer they drew to the monolithic structure. The walls and gates were the only structures of New Gneal that mirrored the original city. The rest was nothing but overcrowded shacks and shoddy buildings waiting to fall over. The gates were open and they rode beneath them and into the city.

Just past the gateway, two lines of Charrenese on their hippogriffs formed a laneway into the city. When Alex passed through, Prince Sanjin brought his hippogriff out of formation to ride beside Alex.

"Tell me, my friend, why did you keep this truth from me? When we arrived, they greeted us as allies awaiting their king's return. Friends do not keep such facts from one another. I might have had the need to barter for a stronger alliance had I known you were a king."

"I'm not a king," grumbled Alex. "At least, not yet."

Sanjin clearly wanted to press for more details but wisely decided this was not the moment. Past the Charrenese lines, the inhabitants of New Gneal filled the streets, eyeing the group suspiciously as they passed by, while Alex considered whether he would be any better than the councilors. Some of the people they passed looked tired and dejected, others were visibly injured, and all appeared rather thin, as though it had been a long while since there had been enough food for everyone. *What happened here?* thought Alex. They continued rather slowly down the broad street, passing side streets with worn cobblestones making Alex wonder where Karl was taking them.

Karl showed no signs of stopping as he guided his horse through the crowded street, parting the many inhabitants of New Gneal. The slow, parade-like pace along the slight incline of the city forced on them by the crowds meant it was nearly an hour before Alex finally saw their destination. His heart fell to his stomach and he tried to take a deep breath but found it too difficult. Ahead was one of the gates separating Gneal's two districts—old from new, or more aptly put, rich from poor.

The closer they drew to the inner gate, the more the city resembled a battlefield. Broken furniture, carts, and wagons barricaded the streets framed by charred buildings, with a motley assortment of residents armed with inferior weapons of rusted swords and pikes hid behind them, hoping to prevent the supporters of the council from entering their reclaimed portion of the city. New Gneal would not give their district back to the council willingly.

Perrien soldiers still loyal to the council stood on the top of the old walls, standing proud and strong, their grey cloaks pulled back to show that each held a bow. The gate was barred and in the middle of the archers stood a thin old man who had no place in a battle but still managed to stand even prouder than the soldiers. His cloak was of a finer fabric and a different cut, but the same color. A ceremonial sword hung at his waist; Alex doubted he knew how to hold it, let alone use it.

"Is it peace?" inquired the Councilor of Perrien. His voice was firm and commanded authority.

"What have you to do with peace?" asked Alex, surprising himself. "Under your council's command, Perrien's army sieges Evellion unprovoked. You crossed the River Arvil claiming the vast lands of Parendior for Perrien, putting any who refused to the sword. You abducted a Cor'leran family and fed them to Erynor's shadow elves in your own dungeons. This council's treachery is not unknown." Alex spoke loudly opposite the gate of Old Gneal, supported by two squadrons of a large army filled with righteous zeal, an army that came from the lands east and west of the Arvil, a ten-thousand strong army that was larger than the council could ever have anticipated.

Because not a single battle had transpired when Perrien's forces had crossed the Arvil a century ago, the council had taken and still took Parendians as a weak and timid people, who had allowed a nobler people to claim them and their land for their own. Then, the farmers had owned no weapons to defend their borders from their mighty neighbors.

The Perrien archers kept their bows taut, awaiting the command to release their arrows on the rebels. Alex's group was one of the few in range.

None of the inhabitants of Gneal, save Karl, stood within two blocks of the wall separating them from Old Gneal. They had allowed the shoddy buildings to form their own barrier between the archers and themselves.

"And who is this boy who dares speak to the council? A poor farmer's offspring who plays with a stick he thinks a sword?"

"This is the true King of Perrien. Your days of selling Perrien to the Shadow are over, wretch! You speak to Alexander of House Vaerin; descendent of King Harold and Queen Kristine, the true king and queen that your predecessors stripped of their titles before banishing them to Cor'lera," roared Karl, his voice venomous. It was clear to anyone looking on that there was much history between Karl and that particular councilor.

The councilor's eyes met Alex's, holding them in his own before he turned and disappeared from the top of the wall. Indistinct commands came from the other side of the wall.

Turning to Karl, Alex asked, "They're not going to open the gate, are they?"

"They'll die behind those walls before they betray the Shadow. They'll receive much worse than death if they betray Erynor." Karl turned his mount. "We're too exposed here."

Alex turned with the others to find a safer location. He had barely managed to turn his horse around in the narrow space when he heard the order: *Release.* Dozens of bowstrings snapped in the air followed by the whooshing sounds of the released arrows. Alex's hands instinctively rose to cover his head as he hunched over in his saddle, trying to shrink his body mass. He heard Oliver shouting orders, but in the noise made by their small group trying to evade the arrows, he could not tell if they were meant for him. But arrows were swift and no matter how fast he reacted, there was no outrunning them. He was a sitting target.

An eternity seemed to pass while he crouched in the saddle, his arms still covering his head as his courser danced on the cobblestones amid whinnying horses and much yelling. Unless he was experiencing shock or was already dead, there was no pain.

Then, he realized that the arrows had missed. Sitting up, he steadied his courser and turned back toward the wall to see dozens of arrows suspended in the air. He must have looked just as puzzled as the archers on the walls as they stared blankly at their arrows dangling in midair.

"I remember reading about an age when those who wore the grey cloak of Perrien were noble men," said Sara, from beside him, her horse steady, her arms raised. Her voice was not fierce, but neither was it gentle. "They once rode their grey coursers, for the sole purpose of protecting their borders and people as true knights. Attacking others when their backs were turned, shooting to kill like cowards, now *that* is a new trait that must be recorded."

She moved her hands and the arrows still floating in the air quivered and spun toward the archers, each directed toward its owner. "By attempting to take my life, my counsels permit me to kill you."

Every archer took a step backward, some even dropping their bows as they scrambled to get off the top of the wall as the arrows drew closer, terrified of what the ei'ana was capable of. Sara did not say another word but lowered her hands, and the arrows fell to the bottom of the wall.

Alex felt the tension loosen among their group, and saw it also ease among the remaining archers. Sara turned her horse away from the wall, made eye contact with Alex, and led the others away from Old Gneal.

The same fog still hung in the air. A light breeze had cleared some of it, but the hills that elevated Gneal were still wreathed in it. The castle stood on a cliff, keeping vigil over the city and surrounding lands; it was nothing more than a blot in the fog.

A Lingering Trace

The world shook, jolting Devlyn awake in a panic, heart thumping wildly. Whatever he had dreamt of was gone and the familiar sound of leaves rustling in the night breeze filled his ears. Devlyn had no idea of the time, only that the sun had yet to rise. The only source of light came from a small fire a short distance away. And beside him, barely illuminated, crouched Wyn. The world was not shaking; Wyn had shaken him awake. A sense of relief passed through him as he came to terms with the reality surrounding him, his heart slowing to a normal rhythm.

"Everything all right?" Devlyn asked.

"Yes, nothing to worry about. But, Alethea would like to speak to you."

"Now?" Devlyn rubbed the sleep from his eyes and forced himself to sit up. With a glance around the small camp, he noticed that Wyn wasn't the only one awake and moving. By the looks of it, Devlyn had been the only one still wrapped in a blanket on the ground. Slow and steady movements filled the camp.

Still unable to form complete thoughts, Devlyn stood and followed Wyn toward the small campfire. A gentle flow of awareness passed from Aliel to Devlyn, letting him know that the phoenix was near. Phoenix did not sleep, they rested, and never experienced drowsiness. Since Devlyn's rescue, Aliel had refused to leave his side. Devlyn still couldn't believe how stupid they all had been, how little care they had really taken for his safety. Granted, they had no way of knowing of the plot to abduct him, nor of the secret passage hidden in his bedchamber's wall. He felt more foolish for not taking the time to check. The castle was known for its hidden passageways.

No matter how much Devlyn tried to remind himself that nothing could have been done to prevent his abduction, if they had not agreed to Hannah's proposal to a nightly surveillance of the city, Aliel would have been in the room when the Tenebrae ei'ana abducted Devlyn. Those rats in the walls would have been unmasked and revealed to the Seven Chairs and Devlyn would not have spent three months caged in that forsaken box.

By the campfire, Alethea sat on a fallen log, the others on the bare ground or makeshift seats on packs in a loose circle around the small source of light and heat. Her eyes were closed and Devlyn couldn't tell whether she was meditating or sleeping. When Devlyn and Wyn approached, Alethea's silver eyes opened, and she held Devlyn's golden eyes in her own. It wasn't necessary for her to speak; Devlyn knew she had something important to tell him, especially if she had asked Wyn to wake everyone in the camp while it was still dark.

"You should know that you will not find what you seek in this place," she said.

"What are you saying?" Devlyn asked, almost reflexively. "I thought you had agreed with this plan? Surely learning how to wield a seguian is a good idea."

"Coming here was a mistake." She spoke simply. Based on the tone of her voice, she could have been speaking of the weather. "This forest belongs to the minums, and only the minums, but they are gone and I cannot say to where. There is no trace of them; they have simply vanished."

"Do you think the Time Wardens took them somewhere safe?" asked Ellendren.

"I believe so." Alethea looked past the smoke climbing toward the leafy canopy. "However, what concerns me is why they left. Doubtless they deserted this place for their own safety. They might still inhabit this forest, but in a different time."

"That means whatever they were afraid of is either here or on its way," Devlyn said, immediately grasping the significance of their situation. "We have to leave."

"We can't leave until we get a response from Auten. We're expecting our messengers' return and if they don't find us, they'll search the forest. I'll not allow two judges walk into Freiton Wood unknowing that Erynor has his sight set on it," said Catalina.

The muted whispers and shuffling around the fire stopped. No one knew what to say. Devlyn racked his mind for ideas, searching for an easy answer, but the harder he thought, the more desperate their situation appeared. Splitting up seemed the best solution, but there was a very real possibility that one or both groups would run into a shadow elf.

Catalina stared into the flames, considering her options. The judges were her responsibility and she had no intention of abandoning two of them to a fate worse than death at the hands of a shadow elf.

Wyn shared a quick look with Alethea, then Devlyn before addressing Catalina. "What if I wait for them while everyone else goes to Auten?"

"Don't be absurd," said Ellendren. "Imagine what would happen if they found you here. At the very least they would rip vital information from your mind, revealing our intentions. Do you have any idea how disastrous that would be?"

"I would only engage them if the judges were under any threat. These trees will keep me hidden and Eolwn will keep me company," said Wyn as he glanced in the direction of his griffin.

"If it is settled, we should leave now," Viren said, uneasy about their safety.

"Is it settled?" asked Ellendren, her voice rising. "I'm sorry, but I don't find this acceptable. In case you have forgotten, there are several Tenebrae ei'ana tracking us down, along with that wretched Alesei. Who knows what they are capable of? And if Erynor has set his eyes on the Freiton Wood, Wyn will be caught between them."

"He understands the danger he is putting himself in," Alethea said, her voice noticeably calmer than Ellendren's. "Despite the risk Wyn is accepting, we cannot remain here. We are terribly exposed and to remain here any longer only wastes precious time."

Again, the small camp quieted with everyone weighing their options. Wyn looked determined; he had no intention of altering his decision.

Without warning, Alethea's expression turned grim and Devlyn felt her embrace the erendinth. Viren, noticing Alethea's concern, quickly unsheathed his crystalline sword, scanning the area past the firelight. Ellendren embraced the erendinth as well, while Devlyn and Wyn pressed into them.

With little thought, Devlyn sought that quiet place within his heart. He felt Aliel there, that wondrous creature native to a realm other than Teraeniel. Their beings melded. His vision lit with a golden brilliance, and once again, he saw the world differently through the phoenix's gifted sight. Brilliant wings burst from his shoulder blades, extending outward to their full span. Even in the middle of the unfolding events, he was glad that he wore lierathnil, relieved to find himself still clothed.

Despite his increased sight, he couldn't see what had alarmed Alethea, but he had no intention of waiting to find out. His pointed ears perked at the sound of soft footfalls drawing near. Devlyn's stomach twisted in knots when he could not see who it was.

"You should not be here," said a squeaky voice below his eye level.

"Identify yourself." demanded Viren.

"My name is Jax, and I'm a Time Warden. I escaped Erynor's prison to warn you."

"Warn us about what?" asked Viren.

"He knows you seek the lucilliae and that you travel to Lankor. Aren and the Deurghol await your arrival."

"How can he possibly know that?" asked Devlyn.

"Does it matter? I don't think he knows where the lucilliae is, but make no mistake, you will not sneak into the city without him knowing. Even more important, you need to leave Freiton, for if they so much as detect any intelligent life here, they will not hesitate to burn this forest to the ground—or worse, do what they did to the Briel Wood. You know it as the Dead Wood now, and for a good reason. Wraiths now haunt those corrupted trees."

No one spoke and the tension rose in the small camp.

The thought of Erynor knowing what they sought left Devlyn disheartened, his eyes fixed on the ground as he struggled with the temptation of returning to the safety of Ceurenyl.

"We can't simply abandon our search for the lucilliae and leave it within Erynor's grasp," Ellendren said with more determination than Devlyn expected to hear, given that she had been opposed to the operation since Devlyn's rescue. "The longer we wait to retrieve it, the stronger he'll become. If we abandon our mission now and try again later, it might very well be impossible to cross Yanil's borders by then."

"Ah, the golden fire of the Luminari burns brightly as ever," Viren said quietly, the Guardian knight remembering a time long past.

"If he knows we're coming, and staying here is impossible, we had better leave," said Wyn, acknowledging that not even he could remain behind.

With their growing enthusiasm and determination, the chill that suddenly entered their bones was shocking. The surrounding shadows grew darker, Devlyn quieted his mind and searched the area, trying to locate the cause.

The darkness creeping around them was no barrier to Devlyn's lighted vision. He saw every muscle in Jax's face slacken, his bottom lip quivered uncontrollably. It looked like he wanted to flee or hide. As he rapidly searched through the trees, he felt the presence above him before he heard or saw it.

It felt as though death itself flew above their heads, demanding that the living submit to their ultimate fate. A great emptiness filled with dread enveloped Devlyn, intensifying when whatever it was above them gave a horrible screech, a sound he had heard before, when Erynor attacked Ceurenyl, just before Devlyn had left on Yelaris, headed for the Illumined Wood.

Devlyn shared a quick look with Viren, sword already in hand, then pressed as fiercely as he could into the erendinth, feeling the others do the same. Above, outlined against a threatening cloud of shadow flew a serpentine beast with dreadful wings devoid of any color. The massiveness of the dragon's belly hid whoever it carried, but by the look on Jax's face, he knew exactly who rode that beast.

With little opportunity to consider their options, Devlyn had a split second to respond to a bolt of tenebrys, streaking uncontrollably through the night sky toward their small camp. Pressing more deeply into the elemental erendinth, Devlyn tried to manipulate what remained of the elements in the tenebrys wield. In the same way he had done with the shadow elves at Myrium, he intermingled his wield with the black lightning but he quickly discovered that this wield was magnitudes more powerful. The shadow elves who had attacked Myrium were children compared to whoever rode that dragon.

With a last burst of energy, Devlyn barely managed to divert the devastating wield so that it exploded beyond their camp. A second bolt fell from the sky followed by an ear-piercing screech from the dragon. Too weak to circumvent this second attack so soon, he felt Alethea and Wyn direct the black lightning away as it too exploded nearby.

When Devlyn prepared to leap into the sky, Jax cried, "You cannot beat him, he is Deathless—one of the Deurghol!"

Devlyn had of course heard of the Deurghol, but he had always imagined that they were just a group of shadow elves, not something other—a single something stronger and more sinister.

Ellendren and Wyn seemed to know more about the Deurghol than Devlyn did, since they shared a look of terror, but they lacked the consuming fear which came from experience that was evident in the two older elves' expressions. Whatever the Deurghol were, knowing they were fighting one made the blood vanish from Viren and Alethea's faces.

Devlyn glanced at Viren, whose attention was on the minum. "Get us away from here," said Viren, his sword still raised. Jax lifted a questioning eyebrow.

"Auten," said Viren.

Jax raised his trembling hands just as a third bolt of black lighting formed in the sky above. Luckily, Devlyn had recovered enough energy to divert it away, not as far as the first, but still a safe distance. The explosion that followed made Jax's hands quiver more. He took a moment to calm himself, then the familiar small translucent sphere formed between his palms. It was hard to see what was on the other end where it was still night.

Wyn had had the presence of mind to gather their mounts, the horses appearing more startled than the elven mounts. The alicorn and griffins were not much calmer, but they did move more obediently toward the seguian. Viren quickly ushered everyone through, while Devlyn and Alethea redirected the black lightning as it crashed toward them, then followed the rest through the seguian.

When it closed and the ground ceased shaking from the explosions, Devlyn slumped to the dew-slick grass, exhausted but alert. He and Aliel were still bound and neither had any intention of separating until they were certain the group was out of harm's way. Alethea sat beside him, eyes closed, trying to regather her strength.

Wyn now attempted to calm the mounts while Ellendren paced and the judges huddled together. The covered wagon with the black box had been left behind. *At least one good thing had come out of this*, Devlyn conveyed to Aliel.

It was only as he looked around to take account of the others that he took in their surroundings and noticed that hills enclosed them on every side. They were not the gentle rolling sort of hills he had grown up around in Cor'lera; these were the steep kind that undoubtedly often ended with cliffs.

Jax stood alone off to the side, trembling, his arms hugging his chest.

After several long moments of tense anticipation, Viren finally sheathed his sword and muttered, almost to himself, "How did he know where we were?"

Whimpering to himself, Jax hugged his chest even harder, rocking back and forth on his toes. Concerned for the minum, Alethea went over and placed a hand gently on top of Jax's head. Devlyn didn't pay close attention to what Alethea did, but was surprised when Jax burst into tears.

"I'm s…sorry," said Jax, having difficulty forming words. "I di…didn't know."

Viren's fierce look was not directed at Jax, but at Alethea. "What is it?" he asked.

"The Deurghol placed a shadow over his heart. There is not a place that Jax goes that is unknown to that abomination that was once an elf."

"Can't you remove it?" asked Devlyn. "The ei'ceuril removed a shadow from Liam's heart."

"All our wielding together is not powerful enough; not without the Temple of Ceur. And even then, I fear it will not be enough to remove a shadow impressed by one of the Deurghol."

"How is he that strong?" asked Devlyn, grappling with this Deurghol's unimaginable strength.

Jax took a deep breath, trying to settle his emotions. "You can't stay here—none of us can. I need to go where he can't follow me, and you need to get as far away from this valley as possible and the sooner you get away from Yanil, the better!"

As he spoke, a second seguian formed between Jax's palms. The silvery sphere remained between the minum's hands as he addressed Devlyn. "Your mother, she's alive—Erynor has her in Broid," and the seguian carried him away, leaving empty space where Jax had stood seconds ago.

Dismayed by the implications of the Deurghol knowing exactly where they were, or at least knowing where Jax was and where he had been, no one knew what they should do next.

Devlyn stood frozen, his mouth hanging open. *She's alive.* While no one had ever suggested that she had perished, Jax had seen her. Jax had confirmed that she lived.

Viren gestured at Catalina, who had not spoken since Jax appeared in the Freiton Wood. She stood hollow-eyed amid the stunned, silent judges, as though she could not see the world rightly anymore. She blinked a few times, and intelligence slowly returned to them.

Viren held her gaze steadily. "Catalina."

She blinked again, coming back to herself.

"Where can we go for shelter? Can you get us into Auten or will it be best to remain outside the city?"

"No," Catalina started, her voice distant, "we cannot go into the city. We cannot disguise your mounts and you yourselves would stick out like a sore thumb. There is a cave just outside the city, maybe half a league from the road to Lankor. It's where Ramira secretly reorganized our order after Lankor was lost to the sea. At the time, it was an independent city-state, but Yanil retook it after they joined the Erynien Empire. Another promise from their new emperor."

"You're certain we will be safe there?" Viren asked. He was not trying for rudeness; he only cared for their safety.

"Yes," said Catalina, the strength of her voice returning with every syllable. "It's close enough to Auten that some of us can travel to and from the city to arrange a boat to Lankor."

"Right, then let's start moving." Viren turned to Devlyn, still sprawled on the ground and illuminating the area around them.

Understanding his meaning, Devlyn reluctantly withdrew from Aliel. As always, dimness fell over everything he could see as the night returned to its usual dullness.

Dawn was still hours away, yet the excitement had driven off any sense of weariness for now; it would return within the hour.

Viren had everyone mounted and moving in minutes. Devlyn rode obediently on a grey mare as she carried him through the valley, his thoughts spinning.

She's alive.

ANOTHER CAPTIVE

Jax had no way of knowing where the Judges' cave was hidden in the steep hills surrounding Auten, and when he had brought them here, had not intended that they would need to walk a full day in the oppressive summer heat of Dynenth. Fortunately, his seguian had brought them on the west side of the River Dun, saving them from having to cross it. Flying was not an option and not simply because they had too few flying mounts—Auten was a Yanilean city and their all too recognizable mounts would have invited unfriendly attention.

Under Catalina's lead, the group had reached the secret cave shortly after the sun started to rise, the day following their run-in with a Deurghol. The air was thick with humidity, and it intensified when the sun peeked above the hills. Even in the early morning dawn, sweat trickled down the center of Devlyn's back. In a few hours, his damp shirt would undoubtedly cling to his skin as it had the previous days since they'd been inside the cave. The one benefit of the cave was that the sun could no longer beat its strong rays upon them. The humidity was one thing, but the rising temperatures had made the journey difficult.

The judge's cave was damp, but larger than Devlyn had allowed himself to hope for. He imagined caves as tiny burrows dug into cliffs, barely providing enough space to stretch without bumping into someone. The dwarven halls were the sole exception, but he didn't think those halls could ever be classified as simple caves without offending a dwarf. And Devlyn would rather hide in a cramped burrow than insult a dwarf.

Catalina was speaking privately to her fellow judges near the cave's mouth. Ange and three other judges had returned after visiting Auten to gather information. The number of judges in this cave seemed to fluctuate hourly. There was still no sign of the judges Catalina had sent in advance. Their disappearance had to bother her, but if it did, she didn't show it.

Devlyn hoped they would have easy access to a craft of some kind—even a fishing vessel would do. As long as it could make the voyage from Auten to Lankor, Devlyn didn't care what type of vessel they took. An inconspicuous fishing boat might even be preferred. Who would expect that a handful of people fishing would dive into Lankor Bay in search of a lucilliae in the Drowned City? And it was unlikely that Yanil would welcome back a Jahronese ship into Lankor Bay any time soon, not after the supposed pirates' unified assault on Josque.

Despite wanting to leave Yanil as soon as possible, Devlyn didn't think recovering the lucilliae would be as simple as he had imagined, especially since Erynor already knew what they wanted to do. Devlyn had only just managed to survive his previous confrontation with Aren, something that became possible only because he had finally bonded fully with Aliel as a Phaedryn. But now, the Deurghol had entered the fray—very much real and not just a myth used to scare children. Devlyn was still shocked at how strong the one they'd met was. If not for the collective strength of everyone resisting him, and Viren's quick thinking to have Jax open a seguian, they would not have escaped.

Aside from Catalina, no one else in the cave felt much like speaking. Tension didn't necessarily grow between them, but the heat and humidity had taken its toll. None of those who had traveled from Ceurenyl were accustomed to Eklean's southern climate, yet among all the elves, Ellendren and Devlyn were having the most difficulty adjusting. He kept a careful eye on Alethea, Wyn, and Viren. They didn't seem to be doing anything different, at least nothing that Devlyn noticed, but they appeared rather comfortable. Quiet, but comfortable and not sweating.

Devlyn sat with the others, resting while he could. Viren still pressed Devlyn to eat double portions, which now solely consisted of fish, being this close to the sea. Ellendren devoted her attention to devising a plan to retrieve the lucilliae and insisted on practicing the first wield Devlyn had learned in Yvonne's class during the autumn term. It felt as though that lesson had happened ages ago. Ellendren admitted feeling embarrassed that she had not thought of it sooner. She remembered how ill-prepared Devlyn had been for Yvonne's test, and how he had only, and with Aliel's help, just managed to succeed, which unfortunately had resulted in the phoenix's ban from the Art of Wielding classroom.

When Ellendren rose to make her way to Devlyn, he knew exactly what she was about to suggest. His eyelids weighed heavily and he desperately wanted to sleep. He was exhausted enough that he would only need to close them for a moment before drifting off to sleep, where he hoped that he could dream soundly without any interruptions from Abbie and Eagan. They had probably given up on pulling him into Somnaeniel after the months he had spent in that box. Devlyn had simply become inaccessible to the druids without any explanation and he knew he would get an earful the next time he saw Abbie.

The temptation to sleep passed when Ellendren caught his eyes in her own. Even though he knew what she was going to say, he wanted to hear her speak.

"Would you mind a session of wielding? We need to master that water breathing wield if we're to have any chance of recovering the lucilliae."

"I suppose, but in all honesty, I don't think it's necessary," said Devlyn. Ellendren's eyes narrowed and he knew he'd said the wrong thing. "We've both successfully managed the wield, after all."

"Remember how difficult it was when Yvonne prevented you from completing it?" Ellendren asked, not giving him the chance to respond. "Do you think it will be easier if Aren or one of the Deathless try the same? If you can honestly tell me that you can ward either of them off, then we won't practice."

Devlyn remained seated, wanting to argue the point, but he also knew better than that. He stood without further debate and followed Ellendren to an unoccupied part of the cave. Having overheard the brief conversation, Wyn joined them.

They all knew how to perform the wield but doing so with interference was a different matter. Performing a wield and preventing someone else from wielding were technically the same, both required wielding. However, someone trying to prevent someone else from wielding was at the disadvantage. Pressing into the erendinth, Devlyn began to form a sphere of aerys and aquaeys around his mouth and nose while Ellendren and Wyn performed their own wield of aquaeys. Having two close friends try to drown you was an extremely odd sensation.

The water pressure continued to grow and a ringing sound started in Devlyn's ears. Their combined strength was more than he'd anticipated, and he was forced to focus more intently. The ringing did not cease, but the water pressure started to subside and soon there was no need for his wield.

The water was gone from around his head, returned to wherever Ellendren and Wyn had drawn it from. Devlyn sighed in relief, and found himself unable to suppress a triumphant smirk.

"Could you join us here?" Viren called, gesturing them over. Catalina's conversation with the other judges was done and she had something to report.

An image of a boat flashed through Devlyn's mind. The sooner they were aboard a vessel of some kind, the sooner they could return to Ceurenyl, if it was even safe to return there now. The castle was undeniably infested with Tenebrae ei'ana.

Devlyn knew that Ellendren wanted nothing more than to go back to Gwilnor. If he had not been rescued in southern Torsil, he imagined that she might have insisted on returning to Ceurenyl sooner. Lucilliae or not, they were far from friendly borders, and if they were discovered as wielders by Yanilean authorities, there was no telling what would happen. Devlyn feared what they might have to do to escape the southern kingdom with their lives.

Catalina, several other judges, Viren, and Alethea formed a semi-circle, waiting for Devlyn, Ellendren, and Wyn to complete it so Catalina could deliver her report. She took a moment after everyone had gathered, presumably collecting her thoughts or figuring out how to phrase what she wanted to tell them. The silence irritated Devlyn—he just wanted to know if she had arranged passage on a boat or not.

The question had nearly reached his lips when she directed her attention to Ellendren, "There's no easy was to say this, so I'll say it as straightforwardly as possible. Your sister is being held captive in Lankor."

Any thoughts of a boat instantly left Devlyn's mind as everyone looked at Ellendren.

"It's unclear how long she has been their prisoner, but we understand that she was delivered to the city in a public display as a guest of the Yanilean. To be honest, I'm surprised it took this information so long to reach Auten. Our order observes nearly everything in Lankor. It worries me that I was not informed sooner."

Ellendren's lips were pursed and her eyes tightly closed as though she wanted to stop her tears, but Devlyn knew she did not want the others to see into her.

Devlyn wanted nothing more than to pull her into a hug; to let her know that he was here for her, that whatever kind of support she might need he would give it. Subconsciously, he began to calculate how their plans were about to change. They had hoped to avoid going directly into Lankor, but that was now impossible. Leaving Princess Kaela Roendryn a captive of Yanil was not an option.

"Do we know where she's being held?" asked Viren, his thoughts mimicking Devlyn's, and presumably everyone else's.

"I'm afraid we do, and there could not be a worse location." Catalina paused a moment, looked down, then taking a deep breath, looked at all of them to speak. "The Yanilean's Keep. It sits on one of the floating islands, between the two sections of the city where the River Eindol meets the bay. No bridge joins it to the rest of the city. The only way to enter is by ferry to its private dock."

No one spoke, the silence in the cave intensified by its emptiness. The fear of having to choose one option over the other filled Devlyn with dread. They could not abandon the lucilliae, but neither could they pretend Ellendren's sister was not a prisoner. If they managed to rescue Kaela first, retrieving the lucilliae would be near impossible.

"We have to do both at the same time," said Devlyn. Everyone shifted their gazes to him, a hint of confusion as they tried to figure out what he meant. "Rescue Kaela and retrieve the lucilliae, that is."

"You want us to divide our efforts?" Catalina asked, giving Ellendren a nervous glance. "Should not the princess receive our full attention?"

"We cannot leave the lucilliae within Erynor's grasp. He knows it's there. He might not know where, but if we leave without it, he will find it, and we'll never get it back," said Ellendren.

"But your sister," said Catalina.

Ellendren blinked away the tears forming in her eyes and turned to look into Devlyn's. "He's right, we have to do both simultaneously."

"No elves can enter the city, let alone the keep without them knowing us for who we are," said Alethea, speaking for the first time. She looked to Catalina and the other judges. "The Judges have a substantial history among Yanil. Even though you no longer possess any political authority, it might be possible for you to be received on some sort of official business. As far as Yanil is concerned, the last judges died out over a thousand years ago. Imagine what the people there would think if they learned differently."

"We have survived this long by remaining a secret society. We assist our people from the shadows. If our existence was discovered, it would be impossible for us to act discreetly again." Catalina breathed heavily and spoke quickly. "Besides, even if we did reveal ourselves, what are the chances of a formal invitation into the keep? They would more likely place us in the cells before publicly acknowledging our presence."

"I don't believe that would be the case; their curiosity might get the better of them," said Alethea, her hands clasped.

The other judges remained silent, allowing their leader to speak on their behalf, but there was a suppressed excitement about them as they glanced at each other. Devlyn wondered how long they had been cut off from civilization; what families had they left behind to enter their order?

"What would you suggest? Go in beneath Lankor's gates and make our identity known to anyone who would listen?" asked Catalina. But, as she listened to her own words and saw her fellow judges' expressions, her sarcasm faded and her shoulders slumped, knowing that that was exactly what she was about to do. "If we're invited to the keep, how long would you suggest we stay there before getting the Lucillian princess out? How can we even attempt to coordinate this if we can't communicate?"

Another moment of silence passed, then Catalina's eyes widened in horror. "How did you manage that?" Catalina demanded, as everyone looked around questioningly. "Stop that!"

Wyn smirked and Devlyn understood that the ancient elf was speaking to Catalina inside her head.

"Now that our communication dilemma is resolved, we should prepare for our departure." Alethea didn't smirk as her younger relative did, nor did her voice carry any sense of amusement.

Catalina looked at the elves skeptically, fearing that they all might have the ability to get into her mind, which to some extent they did. She turned to leave and the other judges followed her to gather their belongings, Ange among them.

Devlyn saw Ellendren give Ange an odd glare as she turned. "Are you all right?" Devlyn whispered, glancing between Ellendren and Ange. He still could not understand what had happened between them, only that Ellendren did not trust her.

She stared blankly at him, almost daring him to ask again. He could have been asking what she thought of the weather and he didn't think he would have received a better reaction.

"We'll have to contact the merpeople if we want any luck uncovering the lucilliae's location swiftly," said Viren.

Alethea nodded, letting the others know she would reach out to them.

32

Unbroken Line

Is it peace?" called a Councilor of Perrien looking down at them. It was impossible to miss the councilor in his bright jacket and pantaloons, magenta with hints of Perrien's grey and white colors woven in but not dulling the primary color of the outfit. The wind had ruffled the councilor's hair, which seemed to annoy him a great deal, as he kept patting his head to straighten it so it would cover the spots that were thinning.

"Interesting choice of clothing," commented Sara from just behind Alex as their small group stood far enough back from one of Gneal's original battlements along the walls of Old Gneal to take cover should an archer attempt to shoot them down.

"He's dressed like he's late for his afternoon tea and we're nothing more than bothersome uninvited guests at the door," Karl spat.

Alex pointedly ignored his two advisors. They were right, of course; the councilor looked ridiculous in his attire. It was a different councilor than before and this one didn't bother to wear a decorative sword. "What do you know of peace? The blood of Evellion's king is still wet upon your swords. Your butchery is well known," Alex shouted.

The news of King Amry's death had come to the ei'ana that very morning. Although Everin had barred every entrance and exit through the city's tunnels, the message had said that the assassin had not only lived in Everin for a decade but belonged to the Royal Guard. The king had been killed while under the assassin's protection. No one knew when the presumed loyal knight had become a servant of Shadow, but his allegiance was no longer a secret. Following the assassination, Everin's knights had taken the assassin prisoner, and the ei'ana who remained in Everin were taking part in the interrogation.

No one knew just how deeply the servants of Shadow were entrenched in Eklean. The councilor standing on the battlements could very well be a servant of Shadow himself, and if not, an accomplice at the very least. He had to know of the foul creatures he had permitted into the castle and the deeds they had committed against Devlyn's relatives. This councilor could simply be a wealthy pawn of Erynor, who could turn his puppets in whichever fashion he pleased. Alex wasn't aware of any way to identify a servant of Shadow, and from everything he had heard from Reia and Sara, neither did the Ei'ana of Septyl.

The thought of servants of Shadow hiding in his own camp sent a chill through his spine. It was possible after all. But how could he circumvent an assassin if they were also trusted inhabitants of the camp? Alex cringed at the discord and panic that would arise if he and the others in charge tried to filter out servants of Shadow among their ranks.

"The Council of Perrien does not recognize your juvenile aggression," spat the councilor. "We do, however, hold you accountable for stirring rebellion in Parendior and bringing your madness across the Arvil and to our city. It is the council's unanimous decision that you are all to be executed for high treason against Perrien. If you refuse to bring peace, so too will it be refused unto you." Without saying another word, the councilor turned away and descended from the battlement. Alex's anger at the man flared.

"I have a few words of my own for that pompous…" Oliver said before trailing off, cursing under his breath.

"Do we know how many Perrien soldiers are in Old Gneal and guarding her walls?" Alex shook off his disgust at the councilor's words—his animosity toward the Council of Perrien would have to wait.

"More than we initially expected. Although the numbers are severely diminished, it turns out that they didn't completely deplete their reserve forces," said Oliver. "Our meager force of once weak and timid farmers east of the Arvil still outnumbers them six to one." The knight's lips curled as he spoke the last, now looking toward the walls, as if appraising the best way to bypass them, yet also how to defend them in the near future. "And as we've learned, the entirety of New Gneal is rising against their oppressors."

"Are Sanjin and his hippogriff riders ready?"

Oliver lifted his hand in signal and in minutes, hippogriffs soared over their heads. The rhythmic twang of archers on the battlements releasing their arrows came, but to Alex's amazement, though the arrows soared toward the foreign soldiers and their curious mounts, not a single one struck.

Sanjin had spoken of a type of magic his people employed, something called the arcane, and at the back of his mind, Alex hoped that this had the makings of a long-standing alliance. Perrien and Parendior might have the best horses—all Eklean envied their grey coursers—but they did not have the advantage of the sky. With all the magical beasts returning to Eklean, Alex wondered if Thellion's sigil was less of an artist's imagination and more of an accurate depiction. If so, where had the winged horses of Thellion disappeared to?

The flying force landed inside the old walls and the sounds of swords clashing soon sung from the opposite side of the gate. They couldn't see the fighting in Old Gneal but heard the oddly curved Charren blades meeting the Eklean straight-edged swords. Alex had no way of telling how the events opposite the gate were unfolding but surely, the Charrenese would not fight the entire battle for them. A dozen Charrenese had landed on the battlements and saw to clearing away the troublesome archers, allowing Alex and the soldiers to approach the gate. The soldiers gathered around Alex in the plaza beneath the looming gate and lined in ranks along the broad boulevard behind him and waited impatiently for the gate to open. Only a portion of the Perrien resistance had entered the city to take Old Gneal and oust the council, the rest waited in reserve, camped outside the city. They had been wronged their entire lives by the Council of Perrien which had declared Parendior their own and were eager to join in the fight.

Spilling into the much narrower side streets off the main boulevard were the inhabitants of New Gneal who outnumbered the residents of

Old Gneal four to one. The two city districts were roughly the same size, but the inhabitants of New Gneal had been forced into cramped inhumane living quarters, practically living on top of one another in shoddily constructed housing. It was questionable who despised the Council of Perrien more: Parendior or New Gneal.

Blades continued to clang, but a different noise came; the sounds of gears and pulleys moving had Alex watching expectantly. Oliver shouted something to the soldiers as the gate creaked inward and the portcullis lifted. The conflict beyond was finally visible.

Alex stood in amazement as he observed the Charrenese fight. They did not fight so much as dance, their curved blades an extension of their arms, moving rapidly from one soldier to the next. The hippogriffs they had ridden into battle stood by their riders and clawed at the Perrien enemy. They did not attack offensively, only to defend their masters. Alex was lost for words at the spectacle. The only time he had seen someone move so artistically with a sword before was when it was held by Viren.

Not wanting the Charrenese to receive the entirety of the credit for conquering Gneal, a few squadrons of Parendian soldiers rushed past Alex and into the confrontation. Their movements were boisterous and clumsy, compared to the fluid motion and trained technique of the Charrenese.

A Charrenese alliance would have to stand. Watching Prince Sanjin's warriors fight as they did, made Alex want to learn from them, even as the idea of going against them in battle terrified him. *Much better as allies than enemies.* As Alex watched in awe, Prince Sanjin sauntered toward him, his own hippogriff at his side.

"You have the look of one who has not seen a Charrenese dance before," Sanjin spoke as though they were observing a sport of some kind, not as though he had just fought in the battle himself.

"Does all Charren fight as they do?" Alex heard himself ask, still astounded.

"A technique gifted to us long ago. Charren has not forgotten our pointy-eared friends from the sky. Come, let us join our blades to place this council in the cells where they belong. And perhaps recommend a new tailor. Their raiment is appalling."

The fighting ended as quickly as it had begun. The residents of Old Gneal had kept their doors locked tight and their windows shuttered, not even permitting shelter to any of the retreating soldiers. The buildings of Old Gneal were soundly built; kicking in any door would be quite foolish. Whoever did so was more likely to break a toe than fracture the solid door.

Alex wondered how they would respond to the invasion. Would it be seen as liberation? Did they have the same sentiments about the council as those in New Gneal? Would they welcome foreigners to their city, or would they keep their doors locked while they schemed to overthrow the invaders?

Alex and Sanjin walked side by side along the broad boulevards of Old Gneal, bypassing many Perrien soldiers lying on the ground, eyes staring at nothing. The sight was difficult to look at. Alex caught a mutter from Arlyn as he passed one Perrien soldier propped up in a doorway, his right leg nearly chopped off. The elves looked at death differently than humans, but Alex was sure that even they would not look favorably on so many wasted lives. The reality of war was a dreadful thing. The stories he had heard growing up about knights in shining armor never spoke of people dying, men and women with families lost forever. There was nothing glorious about it.

Soldiers of Parendior and Charren returned to their formations, lining the streets in apparent victory. There were few casualties among them, thanks to the superior fighting of the Charrenese. Prince Sanjin had come with a retinue of only fifty, but they had proven themselves the better fighters with their hippogriffs and arcane gems.

Gneal's castle was visible from every point in Old Gneal. The original city had been planned in such a way that the castle had a vantage point over its entirety. That original urban plan had not been extended to New Gneal, which aside from the main thoroughfares and gated walls, likely had not been planned at all.

The fortified castle loomed ahead as they drew nearer. The impressive stronghold itself was much older than the city; Alex vaguely recalled his father mentioning that the castle had been constructed during the time of Thellion. Whether or not it was true mattered little. So long as the castle remained untaken, the rebel forces remained vulnerable.

Alex did not have the slightest idea of what might occur after they seized the castle and who had the right to decide the fate of the council. So long as the council was disbanded and met proper justice, he cared little for what came next for the individual members.

Alex's thoughts revolved on what was about to happen. He was still uneasy about the ei'ana and ei'ceuril's intention to place him on Perrien's throne, his supposed bloodline notwithstanding. It also seemed that the rebel army agreed with them. Did that mean the council's fate rested with him? Or did the ei'ana and ei'ceuril intend him to become a puppet monarch?

Would that massive stone structure become his? Would he spend the remainder of his days inside its cold granite walls? The thought of his family returning to Gneal, especially the relatives from his mother's side, worried him greatly. After all, Lex still commanded Perrien's military and led the siege of Everin. He had probably orchestrated King Amry's death too.

Alex's musings found him standing in front of the castle gates before he knew it. Sanjin still stood at his side, while Arlyn, Reia, Sara, Oliver, and Karl followed steps behind. And behind them, soldiers gathered from Parendior's villages and farms were reforming for another attack. Oliver had mentioned that many of the lower class restricted to New Gneal now marched proudly through the streets they had spent their entire lives envying, barred from going into Old Gneal because of their social and monetary status. Visitors could pass between Old and New Gneal, but not the inhabitants of New Gneal.

The gates to the castle were just as formidable as those of the city. Alex looked over at Reia, remembering that she had mentioned that she would wield something to amplify his voice. Her raised arms moved rhythmically, and then she looked to him expectantly as she lowered them to her side.

"Speak, the castle and the entire city await to hear you." But, now that it was time to speak to everyone, he worried what was about to come out of his mouth, especially if the entire city could hear him. He also wasn't completely comfortable with having a wield placed over him.

"Council of Perrien," he began, barely recognizing his voice as it boomed against the stone wall. "The atrocities committed by you and your predecessors are at an end. As the rightful heir to Perrien's throne, I order you to vacate the castle and restore Perrien and Parendior to the will of their people who have endured the poverty your tyranny brought about long enough."

Alex heard the last of his words echo before they faded. There was no indication that anyone in the castle was going to respond. Those gathered outside remained still; it felt as though the entire city held its breath, as though everyone in Perrien and Parendior held their breath together, waiting for whatever was about to transpire. His heart pounded, beating loud enough that it seemed as though it would break free from his chest. He imagined everyone else's was doing the same.

There was no sign of movement inside the castle gates.

Alex took in a deep breath, preparing to speak again; he didn't know what he would say, but they had waited long enough. His lips parted but as they did, the sun grew dark, hidden by a massive storm cloud that covered the entire city in its shadow. Alex chanced a nervous look over his shoulder at Arlyn and saw that the ei'ceuril was deeply concerned.

Finally, there was movement behind the castle gates. Alex had never seen past them but knew there was some sort of bailey or courtyard between the castle proper and the walls and stout towers that surrounded the castle.

Looking up, Alex's heart sank as he watched a dragon wreathed in smoke and shadow rise past the outer wall from the castle bailey. It was impossible to tell the color and shade of the dragon which seemed to have black scales, but the smoke and shadow made it hard to tell. Alex remembered all too well the attack on Ceurenyl, when Erynor himself had ridden on the most fearsome creature he had ever seen or heard of. This beast was much smaller in comparison, but even so, it shamed Velaria's blue dragon. Yelaris was a domesticated dog next to this wild wolf. On the dragon's back sat a figure, wreathed in the same shadowy cloud.

"Did you think Erynor would allow a boy to wrench Perrien from his grasp? Did you think he would leave the city completely defenseless?" called the sinister shadowy figure.

Goose bumps raced across Alex's skin, and he felt the others around him shifting nervously.

"The Council of Perrien has served our emperor well. He does not desire their death, least of all at the hands of a petty boy."

Alex heard the whooshing sound of soldiers drawing their swords, metal against leather crisp in the still air at ground level. The Charrenese stood beside their hippogriffs, their curved swords unsheathed.

The ominous sky continued to darken and the clouds churned ever more violently above. The darkness surrounding the shadow elf was devoid of any color and Alex saw that her hands were moving. He remembered the destruction caused by the shadow elves at Ceurenyl; he remembered their black lightning and the havoc it wrought on the city. He also remembered them cackling and screeching in pleasure as they murdered their way through the city streets.

Before he could voice a warning, the air crackled and a bolt pierced the sky, aimed toward those gathered below. Springing in front of Alex, Arlyn extended his arms and a bright light that made Alex squint and hold a hand in front of his eyes exploded from the ei'ceuril's palms.

"So, the little ei'ceuril have learned to play with the light again."

The darkness was still there and the lightning without light grew stronger, thrashing with power, but Arlyn stood strong. The stark difference between the two wields was terrifying. How a world could exist with two entities so polarized was unimaginable.

Then the Perrien soldiers who had been in the bailey behind the now opened castle gates rushed through to attack. With the shadow elf's help, their victory was certain, even with Arlyn somehow holding back the thrashing lightning. The area erupted into fresh battle, this time with Alex in the thick of it. The clashing of swords filled the plaza in front of the castle gate and screams of agony indicated that arrows had been unleashed from atop the walls and battlements.

Arlyn seemed to be gaining momentum against the shadow elf, but quickly lost it when the tenebrys wield intensified.

Time lost its hold over Old Gneal and its castle. Sinister flames licked at the buildings, and residents rushed screaming out into the fighting to escape the unnatural fire. Unarmed and terrified, they dodged the fighting soldiers as they rushed for the apparent safety of New Gneal, a place these now desperate residents of Old Gneal had always looked down on.

Amid the fighting, a second figure arrived in the sky. An exhausted Alex feared that a second dragon and shadow elf had joined the first. Yet through the smoke and shadow covering the battlefield, he saw an incredible light banish the darkness that until moments before had blanketed the sky. The dark clouds and smoke began to lose their hold as the sun shone through once again and something bright restricted the darkness to the shadow elf and her dragon.

Alex looked to Arlyn, but he was still fighting the unrelenting wield, cast by the shadow elf. Looking up, Alex saw a creature of a brilliant silver light high above the city. It was not as bright as Devlyn's phoenix, but it was incredible to look upon. Focusing his eyes, he wondered if it was one of the fabled anadel, come to save Gneal from the shadow elf. Perhaps the enthiel Gneal was entrusted to?

"You have no power here, slave of Ramiel," the owner of the voice seemed to sing. Her voice felt like rainfall on the hottest of days. "Begone, ere you are destroyed."

"You are the slave!" spat the shadow elf. "Ignorant of the true power granted by our Master."

"The only power granted unto you is Death and slavery."

"You will return to the filth you call sisters and brothers of Aldinare; then you will learn the true meaning of slavery!"

Whoever was the source of the brightness in the sky sent a beam of pure light at the shadow elf. It easily penetrated the shadowy cloak wrapped around the shadow elf as though it was nothing more than water. The darkness faded and both the shadow elf and dragon screeched piercingly, a sound more awful than anything anyone watching below had ever heard. Alex was convinced that not even the multitude of shrieks that had been heard during the attack on Ceurenyl had been so dreadful. The screech ended abruptly, and the shadowy beast dropped to the city below, crashing against the castle's granite gate. The strongly built structure crumbled beneath the dragon's weight, its scales melting the stones the gate was made of.

The woman aloft glided down toward the city street below, riding on the back of a winged unicorn. Its coat was a brilliant white, its incredible silver horn gleaming luminously. The horn was not reflecting the light of the sun, but was a source of light. Alex recognized Aewen as the wondrous creature's rider, looking every bit an elven queen in the beautiful silver gown she'd worn when she'd first met Alex. Today, her silver hair and skin glowed from within, as if her spirit emanated so brightly that not even her body could contain her inner light.

"The generations that lie between us are many, perhaps as many as the hairs on your head. Since Thellion's death, much has changed. We built a vast kingdom together, a realm stretching from these northern hills and beyond to the most southern points of Eklean. Everything between the Vespien Mountains and the Unarian Sea were under our domain, and after us, our children's. Those lands eventually divided. Some are still held by Thellion's and my descendants.

"For a hundred years, that was not so. What happened in the southern kingdoms long ago occurred here. Erynor corrupted Perrien's children, and Thellion's descendants were exiled as criminals. As the mother of Thellion's children, and your ancestor, I ask you, Alexander, will you return to Thellion's halls and sit upon his throne in Elothkar? Will you defend humanity as your forebears once did?"

Alex's heart raced uncontrollably.

Arlyn, Reia, and Sara had only alluded to him becoming king of Perrien; they had never said anything about reclaiming the ancient kingdom of Thellion to reign as its king.

His mouth was dry and all he wanted was a glass of water, or perhaps something a bit stronger, but what he didn't want was to become a Thellion king—anything but that. Had this been Velaria's intention all along? The corpses of the shadow elf and dragon still burned in the crumbled mess of what had been the castle gate. Dust and smoke of destruction rose all around him. Bodies littered the broad streets, both living and deceased. Taking a sharper look, Alex was relieved to note that more were standing than crumpled on the ground. He took a deep breath, cast a quick look around at his companions among the soldiers, all of them awaiting his reply in expectant silence. With a direct look at Aewen, he answered her.

"I will."

The words fell heavily from his mouth. He heard himself speak, but it felt as if someone else had spoken from a faraway place leaving him to listen from an even further distance.

SALTY MERMAID

The boat rolled with the sea, rising only to fall with another wave. It was not a large boat, but it couldn't be called small either. Captain Terrance of the Salty Mermaid, a fisherman from Sudern, was a thin man with wild black hair and a beard to match. Devlyn had never seen skin look so much like leather before; too much time exposed to the sea and sun probably. Devlyn had taken him for a weak and aging old man, but that was before he'd watched the captain pull his fishing nets in from the water. Earlier that day, Devlyn had helped toss the nets over the starboard side, a word he had only just learned, and they had been heavy then, mostly dry and empty of fish.

Deciding not to underestimate the fisherman again, Devlyn kept his thoughts from further misguided judgments based on Terrance's physique. Catalina had arranged their passage in Auten and the moment everyone came aboard Terrance's boat, he had quickly identified their elven features. He even knew that they were not all the same kind of elves, which was very impressive for someone not entrenched in personal affairs with elves. Keeping secrets from the fisherman was not an option.

Even if they had wanted to keep their identity a secret, that would have been impossible once Catalina described how his new patrons intended to board his vessel—after he left the dock. Leaving the griffins and alicorn behind had also been out of the question. But, neither could they simply stroll through Auten to the docks with them. The people of Auten might not notice their hooded elven features, but they most certainly would notice their mounts. Instead of joining the others on the

Salty Mermaid, Aliel flew high above their heads. They had all agreed that keeping Aliel a secret from the sailors was a necessary precaution and Devlyn had instead flown with Wyn on Eolwn to reach the boat.

The Salty Mermaid rose and fell endlessly with the sea. Devlyn had heard countless stories of people getting sick on boats and that was all he could think of as his stomach sank once again with the waves. Fortunately, the Erynien Bay had once been known as Calm Water Bay and Devlyn never had the need to use the sick bucket or lean overboard.

Captain Terrance was equally impressed with the elves' sea legs; he confessed after their third day aboard his boat that he had expected them all to have gotten sick, despite the relatively gentle waters. City folk rarely fared well on the open sea.

Devlyn caught a glimpse of Ellendren by the stern, looking over and into the disturbed water created by the boat's forward passage. Slipping away from the captain, Devlyn joined her there. Before he could even mutter a greeting, she said hotly, "I don't approve of the name for his boat."

"I think it's kind of funny."

"You would; boys laugh at the dumbest things. It doesn't even make sense! The ocean is salty, not merpeople."

"Um, right. Are you comfortable with the judges rescuing your sister?" asked Devlyn, trying to steer the topic to something different. It was only after the words were out that he realized he should have said anything but that.

"Comfortable? No." Ellendren's gaze returned to the sea. "I want to trust them. And considering that they are our only option, I do not have much of a choice."

"They should have reached Lankor by now," said Devlyn.

"I suppose they should have." Ellendren refused to look away from the water. "And, to make matters worse, I haven't been able to contact Kaela."

"What? Are you saying that she doesn't dream about you as much as someone else does?" Devlyn smiled. "If you don't mind my asking, what's Kaela like? I've met everyone else in your family except for her."

Ellendren waited to answer, debating whether to comment on his suspect dreams. Devlyn was about to repeat the question when she responded.

"Well, not all my family. The royal family of Lucillia is quite extensive. You wouldn't imagine the number of royal relatives living in either the palace or the royal district. Even those who can only trace their lineage to the crown by counting back ten generations still consider themselves a royal cousin. They like to remind everyone that they're just as closely related to Roendryn as is the Aryl of Lucillia." Ellendren turned from the sea to face Devlyn. "But Kaela is very kind and more confident than I'll ever be. Aaron and she have similar personalities."

"That's funny, I thought you and your brother were already terribly alike."

"Don't let his new position fool you. Those two have quite the history. I think my parents were relieved when I did not take on their less favorable habits. Before Aaron was sent to the temple because of his disposition for wielding, they both had snuck away from a formal ball to watch a traveling troupe, while wearing their finest clothing," said Ellendren, still visibly disturbed by their actions.

"That's what upsets you, Elle?" Devlyn laughed. "Anaweh forbid you ever catch me sneaking away from a ball!"

Ellendren stared daggers at him for his choice of language. He also took a mental note to never abandon her at a banquet to watch a traveling troupe. "Under what pretense would I be the one chaperoning you on such an occasion?" Ellendren asked, implying something Devlyn desired, but not for years to come. "You might be a Lorenthien—something we still need to discuss in detail, mind you—but don't think for one moment that I'm going to fawn over you like the countless other Luminari ei'lythels will because of your name and future position in the Luminari court," whispered Ellendren.

"Um…" Devlyn couldn't think of how to respond. All he could think of was them at a ball together and him stumbling over his feet again, and most likely his words as well.

Ellendren's eyes softened and the daggers receded. He had no idea how she did it. She could have him walking on glass in one instant and make him feel like he was the happiest and luckiest boy in the world the next.

"I suppose that conversation can wait a few years. We are still young." Ellendren smiled, allowing a nervous energy to pass from Devlyn's body. Ellendren looked back to the sea. "To return your prior question, both of my siblings have their faults, but I love them dearly. I wonder if anyone has told Kaela about the Protection of the Wood." She trailed off, the memory of her mother's likely fate returning to the front of her mind.

Devlyn placed a comforting arm around her. He knew she was sad but holding her was the best feeling in the world. Part of him hoped that she felt the same about it and that it was in fact consoling—hopefully it was, because he had no idea what else he was supposed to do.

"Mother once caught all three of us in the palace kitchens, our hands coated with chocolate. We intended to bake something for our father's birthday, even though none of us knew anything about baking. After pulling all the ingredients out, at least the ones we thought were necessary, we just started eating the chocolate. The chefs were far from pleased the following morning when they saw the mess we had made. Mother was furious; she gave us a firm talking to about overindulging in sweets and sneaking around the palace. The three of us still laugh about that when we're together. But that hasn't happened since I first started my studies at Gwilnor. Kaela has become a talented diplomat, traveling from one kingdom to the next. She would never have gone to Lankor willingly though—she knows to avoid the southern kingdoms, despite the need to strengthen relations with them."

Devlyn wanted to change the topic to something else—anything else. The harder he tried to think of what to say, the more questions revolving around her family arose. It was becoming one of those awkward silences, the kind where both were thinking the same thing, but neither wanted to dwell on it any longer.

"I think that was the first time I've heard you address yourself as an ei'lythel, instead of as a princess," he said, thinking back on something—anything he could comment on to steer the conversation away from her family.

"Was it? It's all Alethea addresses me by. Even I can't argue against adopting our elven titles. As inconspicuous as she appears, there is nothing subtle about that elf."

"She really isn't," he laughed back. "So, is there anything I should know about Lankor?"

"Haven't you studied Yanil before? I specifically remember lending you a book on its history."

"Well, yes, but that was also a while ago and I did intend to review my notes before I was abducted. But I do remember that it was once part of Thellion."

"Everyone knows that." Ellendren now turned from the sea, a determined glint in her eyes. She and Kevn were very similar in this; the quickest and surest way to get them out of their funk was to ask them a question about something related to history or politics. "Well, before our ancestors left their Skylands, the first Yanilean had tried to claim the entirety of the Eindol as the property of the kingdom he took his title from."

"I'm sure Evellion responded kindly to that."

"Actually, Evellion wasn't a century old yet and they were still recovering from their exodus from Thellion's capital city, Elothkar—Everin was only partially constructed at that point. The entire continent was in upheaval and Yanil was first to do away with any connection to Thellion after its collapse, which meant usurping the Thellion nobility. But no, Evellion did not take it well, and both Evellion and Mindale rejected the Yanilean's meritless claim; Evellion pointed out that the Eindol's waters began in her mountains."

"How was the conflict settled?" Devlyn asked.

"Who's to say it ever was? Mindale doubled the size of her military and restored the forgotten Thellion keep at the fork of the Eindol and Krasi Rivers, just north of the Houlk Wood. There's some dispute as to who now controls that castle." Ellendren paused and Devlyn could practically see her tactical mind churning behind her façade. "Despite the age-old quarrels between Yanil and her northern neighbors, Yanil controlled the Eindol's sole access to and from the sea, ensuring Lankor's prosperity."

Unlike most cities, Lankor's defensive walls were unique. Ange thought nothing of them—born and raised in Lankor, they were as all walls should be. Why other cities insisted on surrounding themselves with stone and mortar was beyond her. Just imagining the stench that would cause in a humid climate was enough to banish the thought. This wasn't Josque after all—Lankor had no need for Tieli perfumes and oils. Besides, the sea was a better barrier than any wall and for Lankor, the sea did not limit its growth either. Her people refused to live on top of each other as in other cities. Instead of growing vertically, Lankor grew boundlessly into Lankor Bay when it needed to.

Lankor sat at the mouth of three rivers emptying into Lankor Bay. The River Reifen's waters came from Briel and Freiton, the River Enellio flowed from the Shadow Mountains and through the Dynthol Mirk, with the River Eindol as a great artery joining the south and north. Lankor's people defined themselves as a sea people, and if the elves were right, Nauto, an enthiel devoted to the irythil, Theniel, Lady of the Seas, still watched over and guided them. But, Nauto had lost the people's trust when he unleashed his wrath upon them, destroying their original city.

The Lankor that Ange had always known had the distinct strategic advantage of floating in Lankor Bay, a declaration that not even the sea would claim her once again. The city was not far from its marshy surroundings; in fact, it took a mere fifteen minutes to cross the well-kept floating bridges connecting the capital of Yanil to the land. But, to get halfway across one of those bridges, travelers were scrutinized at one of the gates. Lankor's only protective walls housed those gates at the four floating bridges leading into Yanil's capital. Each gate stretched high over the road but fell like a wave into the marsh. Ange had always thought the gates were unnecessary. Not only would no one dare siege their city, but the floating bridges could be retracted from the mainland if needed. She had never seen the bridges retracted, but it was possible and the gates were most likely for show.

The floating city, while not built on land, looked like two distinct peninsulas jutting out into the bay. All three rivers appeared to extend further than they did through the marsh and into the bay, given the layout of the city. Reluctant to thwart Lankor's greatest assets, the architects of the nascent city planned to allow each river to carve its way through the cityscape, permitting any vessel to pass for a modest fee.

At the heart of the city rose the exclusive exception. Forming its own island between the two floating peninsulas was the sole obstruction in the Eindol: the Yanilean's Keep.

One of the first projects following Nauto's Wrath, the Yanilean's Keep had been designed strictly for naval warfare. It was not a tall keep, but it was encompassed by thick and strong fortifications. Like the rest of the city, there was no need for an external wall to prevent an enemy from forcing their way into the floating structure. The buoyant keep was the entire makeshift floating island, with no space between wall and water, not even for gardens, for the rivers and bay were the gardens of Lankor.

Ange had heard rumors that the keep rose directly above the Drowned City, as a reminder that not even Nauto could destroy the Yanilean, but it was never proven. No one had ever attempted to search the waters beneath the keep. Not only was it impossible to see further than ten paces into the murky waters, but tales of vicious merpeople waiting to drag any unsuspecting swimmer into the depths of the bay were rampant. There wasn't a single fisherman who did not warn anyone willing to listen about the devious water breathing beasts.

Merpeople stories, in Ange's opinion, made Yanileans appear ignorant. People breathing and living normal lives under water was simply ridiculous. She assiduously disregarded any reference to merpeople. At first, she had refused to read any history mentioning them, but was forced early on to abandon that ideal when her list of credible sources was reduced to a mere five books in a library boasting volumes well into the thousands.

Ange wondered how many of the people walking along the canal around her believed that merpeople truly existed, let alone shared the classification of personhood. If she ever learned which scholar first wrote of fish-people living beneath the water, she would do everything in her power to strike his name and opinions from history.

Thankfully, the times were changing and she knew for a fact that not every person in Lankor believed that merpeople existed. Yet people were just as sensitive about the topic as they were over the existence of Anaweh, a debate she found just as discouraging. Debate was expected in a city as diverse as Lankor.

Traders from all over Eklean came to live in Yanil because nowhere else could they find treasures from every corner of Teraeniel. Before Eklean's isolation, Yanil had attracted merchant ships from every continent and while those trade routes had long been abandoned, Ange had grown familiar with the foreign extravagances still available in the city. Not all those foreign merchants had returned to their native countries after the collapse of the Guardian Senate—that had disbanded following the Fall of Krysenthiel.

Returning to Lankor felt odd; she had not come back to her home city since joining the Judges of Yanil. Her parents were both merchants; her mother, like hundreds of others, claimed to descend from the original Yanilean. Most women did so to attract the noblemen into taking them as wives. According to Yanil law, only full blooded male Yanileans could be nobles. Even those women who were daughters of Yanil's greatest Yanilean had no official standing in court.

Ange despised every part of Yanil's government. She accepted that the new Yanilean had to descend from the first Yanilean, not necessarily born of the current one, but the fact that only men could be the Yanilean infuriated her more than the merpeople myth. Perhaps if one of the Yanilean's daughters had assumed the title after Nauto's Wrath, her people would have never aligned themselves with Erynor. The history of Yanil could have been written entirely differently. Old alliances would not have been deserted, and merchants from every corner of the world would still dock their ships in Lankor's harbors, declaring it the epicenter of all trade.

Her mother had never missed a chance to remind Ange that she descended from the first Yanilean and that Ange's father, proven through scrupulous investigation, was a full blooded Yanilean. He did not descend from the first Yanilean as her mother did, but his blood was exclusively of Yanil. That combination meant that Ange, with her intelligence and beauty, was the perfect candidate for a noble betrothal. Granted, as the daughter of a lord, her mother had had even better chances of marrying a nobleman and not just a Yanilean merchant.

During her studies, Ange had been among countless other girls who had swooned over Yanil's aristocracy. They all wore their heritage proudly, making certain it was known they also descended from the first Yanilean and that they too were full blooded Yanileans.

To her mother's great relief, Ange had been one of the lucky few. A young nobleman with a direct paternal bloodline to the first Yanilean had found her amusing. Her teenage eyes saw him, with his dark hair and skin bronzed by the ocean sun, as the spitting image of that first Yanilean. She could not count the number of times she had lost herself in his deep brown eyes.

In her youthful innocence—more like stupidity—she had heard the rumors that the Yanilean nobility were accustomed to infidelity. Increasing the number of true Yanilean descendants was all that mattered to the men of that bloodline. Not once did she allow herself to believe that her beloved Enrico would succumb to such base practices.

Her bliss had lasted a full year and then Enrico declared his intent, and her younger, foolish, eighteen-year-old self was betrothed. Before their first month as a betrothed couple had ended, she had learned that Enrico was already a father.

Her mother tried to calm her fury but found herself unable to dissuade her daughter from, not only breaking off the engagement, but leaving Lankor entirely.

Neither of her parents knew of Ange's decision to join the Judges of Yanil. People knew the judges had once ruled beside the Yanilean, but no one knew the order still existed. The judges had guarded their order's survival for over a thousand years. Standing as servants of justice under Erynor's leash would have meant betraying that which was just, or ending up executed. Going underground was the only alternative. Given their circumstances, they served as admirably as permissible, but as of today, that they had survived was no longer a secret.

The moment they had walked through Lankor's easternmost gate, Catalina Turlan, Supreme Judge of Yanil, had declared their identities as Judges of Yanil. The guards escorting them along the canals had not heard of the Judges of Yanil, angering Ange at the lack of historical education, if any, they had received.

She regretted glaring at them now, mostly because Catalina had reprimanded her for her actions. Neither guard looked like full blooded Yanileans. Ange had the ability to identify, always correctly, whether someone was a full blooded Yanilean, an unfortunate trait passed on from her mother.

These men were definitely Yanilean, but their heritage was not limited to Yanil's borders. The one's skin had a hint of red, making Ange think that part of his heritage might belong with the Dwonians. That hunch faded quickly. The Dwonians were more concerned about their tribal bloodlines than even the most prejudiced Yanilean. While a Yanilean might father a child in a fit of unplanned passion with some woman not of their own heritage, no such rumors revolved around the Dwonians doing the same. Besides, Dwonians rarely came into the city anyway. They preferred to preserve their traditions by living out on the open plains.

The guard most likely suffered from over exposure to the sun. *Fool probably didn't dress properly. Why men believe they can walk around in the sun all day without a shirt or hat is beyond me,* she thought. Not that her opinions ever remained private or quiet long. Every person she had ever lived with knew exactly how she thought about certain things.

Their modest entourage included five judges, and within an hour of crossing the bridge into the city, the guards led them onto a gilded ferry intended only for respected dignitaries. The guards had intended to escort them onto one of the less ornate vessels until a message from inside the Yanilean's Keep directed that the Supreme Judge of Yanil, along with *his* retinue should cross aboard the Yanilean's personal ferry. The guards both glanced in embarrassment at Catalina; apparently, her gender was not known to those inside the keep. That a woman could hold power was unheard of for those inside the keep, a perspective that contributed to Ange's distaste for her homeland.

The gilded ferry crossed the water smoothly, and to Ange's relief, she did not feel seasick. She detested boats of any kind, despite having been born on a floating city. The thought of capsizing into the murky waters of Lankor Bay was appalling and sailing in open waters without any sight of land was simply unbearable.

As they neared the keep's private docks, Ange looked up the familiar stout walls of the keep, rising four stories above the water. The black stone was a rare mineral in the Shadow Mountains. Their records claimed it had been a generous gift bestowed upon the Yanileans in the hour of their greatest need by their eternal friend and neighbor, the Erynien Emperor.

The story made her sick, but it explained their swift alliance with Erynor after Lankor had been lost to Nauto's Wrath. The floating stone had been mined by the dwarves of Zorik Schtam and tossed into the River Enellio, a name that was supposedly attributed to the first Yanilean before taking his title. The entire city had then been built on top of that black stone, but only a handful of buildings, including the Yanilean's Keep, employed it for the actual construction material seen above the water's surface. The stone was too precious to waste on an entire city, and the dwarves demanded a hefty price for every ounce, making the stone's value outweigh gold.

Ange glanced over the gilded ferry's side and gasped at a rare moment of movement in the water. It was far too murky to see very deep, and few fish swam through the waters in and around the city limits, smart enough to avoid that filth.

"Don't let him pull one so beautiful as you into the depths," said the ferryman. His words ran together as fluidly as the water. Although Ange did her best to disguise her own, his accent was unmistakably Lankoran. There was no doubting his blood line. Not a noble himself, he was driving a ferry after all, but there was no doubting the stock he was bred from. Perhaps his family was only one or two generations removed from nobility. His mother's father was most likely of the Yanilean's own blood, just as Ange's mother was, but unlike her mother, had not properly scrutinized her husband's ancestry and married poorly.

"Don't tell me you believe such tales." Ange scoffed at the ferryman.

"On my very own did one plant her salty lips," said the ferryman. "If it were not for my father's warning, I would have torn off my shirt and shoes to dive in after her. It also helped that my brother wrapped his arms around my chest to keep me planted in our ferry. Truly, I would have been hers."

Ange turned and rolled her eyes just as the gilded ferry docked. There were two other gilded ferries docked, amid twenty others without any ornamentation or gilding. Moored at the center of the dock was the Yanilean's Pride, flagship of the Yanilean navy.

She followed the others off the ferry and into the keep. It felt like an age since she had last walked into the Yanilean's Keep.

The guards who had accompanied their group across the Eindol boarded one of the standard ferries to return to their post, replaced by full-blooded Yanileans. Their polished armor shone in the sunlight, a stark contrast to the black stone surrounding them. The Yanilean's Keep had its own order of knights, the Sons of Yanil, dedicated to protecting the Yanilean and his keep. It was a strict order, and only men who could prove their pure bloodline were accepted, so men with the first Yanilean's blood who were not nobles filled most of the order's ranks. If Ange had been born a boy, she would have likely joined those knights.

The judges crossed through the grand corridors of the keep and to Ange's worst fear, the last person she wanted to bump into called out her name.

"Angennia!" Enrico sung it out and she felt her knees quiver despite her best intentions. "You have come back to me after all these long years." If Ange thought the ferryman had spoken fluidly, it was nothing compared to Enrico's speech—there were no pauses between any of his words. She had forgotten how lovely his voice sounded. "Tell me, my love, why have you not returned until now? Console my despairing heart, for it has not been whole since you left."

34

BETRAYED

Jax's palms sweated and his entire body screamed in pain. He had tried running as far away from Eklean as possible after warning the other minums still in the Freiton Wood, jumping from one continent to the next as soon as he'd regrouped in each location, not waiting for another living being to come across him. If he had the slightest hint of the presence of any other being, he would immediately create another seguian and disappear. He knew the only safe place was inside the Temple of Ceur, but he could not bring himself to open another seguian inside that holy site. Not after the last time—not after what he had allowed to happen, even if it had been under extreme duress.

The pain coursing through his body had not abated since the Deurghol had launched a bolt of tenebrys directly at his chest, just after he'd closed a seguian. He hadn't been able to move his hands quickly enough to open a new one.

He did not know how long he had been unconscious after that, only that it was no longer night when he awoke. He remembered seeing his surroundings moving in a rhythmic motion that was not comforting, constantly falling and rising when he had finally opened his eyes. His stomach had turned; he'd felt wretched and wanted to get as far away as possible. That part he remembered. He remembered the chains too— binding his wrists together. He couldn't open a seguian without parting his hands.

He also remembered the torture. That he could not forget. The Deurghol had tortured him whenever they had not been flying on that horrific dragon. It could easily swallow Jax in a single gulp, which would be better than being torn apart by its razor-sharp teeth. Had the Deurghol brought him back to Broid? Jax didn't recognize the fortress he had been taken to. An eerie light lined the chamber and there was no scent of saltwater in the air. No gulls cried out. There was only an unrecognizable and unpleasant scent.

Jax's body throbbed, the pain interfering with further memories. He remembered that he had run away, but not why or how he'd managed it. It no longer mattered to Jax. His body hurt too much to think and the Deurghol that chased and caught him did not like him thinking.

He opened another seguian, and five more men rushed through. He heard someone scream from the other side; it was a woman, most likely an ei'ana; there were hundreds of them there. Just like during the Ceurendol War, the last time Erynor had warred against Eklean, the Ei'ana of Septyl were his first target.

Gwilnor Academy was eerily quiet. All doors and windows were tightly shut and locked. No one crossed the grounds and no one walked along the cobbled path and bridge connecting Gwilnor to the rest of Ceurenyl. Rumors had reached past the castle walls and into the city. The residents of Ceurenyl actively avoided the road leading to the castle. No one knew for certain whether the rumors were true, but Jaerol hoped that some out there believed them, if only to heed the warnings and stay away from the castle and increase vigilance at the reconstructed city gate. People in Ceurenyl had hailed it as a miracle that it was whole once more, but now, no one was allowed to pass through it to enter or exit the city. The gate was closed. The Ceurtriarch had enacted the current security measures over the city until further notice.

Aaron was well aware of the infiltration of the castle. It was no longer inhabited solely by the Ei'ana of Septyl and their students and knights. The Ceurtriarch's swift and sudden action to prevent ei'ceuril students from returning to the castle for their studies was all too clear. Only those in lofty positions had received an explanation, but no one questioned the Ceurtriarch's reasoning.

Jaerol had been released from the infirmary and the Crimsyns' care, but he was still far too weak to leave his room on his own. Fortunately, Liam was nearby, even though they weren't sharing a room anymore—hopefully that wouldn't last too much longer. When he had finally been able to walk again, he had insisted that Liam take him to see the damage Razcul had caused. It had taken quite a bit of convincing, but Liam eventually gave in. He had a habit of doing that with Jaerol. They would spend half of their conversations at odds with each other before coming to mutual terms for the second half.

When he'd seen the wreckage, Jaerol had been amazed that he still breathed. Even more remarkable was that Razcul hadn't fled. Jaerol refused to call the imposter anything but his real name now. It didn't seem to matter that others would learn of his true identity, even though Jaerol's credibility was damaged from his apparent *accident*, one of many around the castle.

Reports of mysterious injuries flooded into the Crimsyn wing, students and ei'ana alike appearing with broken noses, large discolored bruises, and even dislocated shoulders. Not a single person was in doubt as to the reason for the multitude of injuries, but no one dared say it aloud. Those who had spoken openly were next to arrive in the infirmary, seeking healing from the Crimsyns.

Awake in his narrow bed, thoughts roiling, Jaerol's ears perked at the sound of footsteps outside his bedroom. No one walked about the castle at night anymore. His current paranoia and subsequent wakefulness had heightened his senses and he knew he wasn't imagining the footsteps. His current roommate, a new student wielder named Talen who still hadn't quite mastered controlling his wielding, was fortunately a quiet and surprisingly immobile sleeper. But after the attack, Liam had refused to leave Jaerol alone with anyone and he was also sound asleep, curled in his blankets on the floor.

He should roll over in his narrow bed and return to sleep.

A second set of steps passed their door. Jaerol had locked it securely with a wield the previous night, barring the wooden frame as well.

Theoretically, the extra precaution helped him sleep better. Lying in the open infirmary had driven his anxiety to an all-time high, with expectations of Razcul appearing to finish what he had started.

A third set. A fourth. A fifth.

The movement was too regular, too evenly spaced, too well executed. A group of five was sneaking through the male dormitories, intending to go unnoticed. Jaerol slipped from his bed, careful to step over Liam, then stooping to wake him as well.

"What's wrong?" Liam whispered, careful to not wake Talen. Jaerol pressed a finger to his lips then walked over to the door as Liam rolled over and pushed himself up from his bundle of blankets to look out the window to see how late it was. The south facing window provided a mesmerizing view of the castle stretching out below from the male dormitory in the North Tower, the other towers rising to their level or soaring above them to dizzying heights.

In the dim moonlight, Jaerol saw Liam hurriedly gesture him to join him at the window. There, Jaerol's jaw dropped when he saw that several of the windows of the East Tower, home to the Vyoletryns, were ablaze. Smoke and flame billowed skyward, disappearing into the night. Jaerol shared a distraught look with Liam, both appalled at what it might mean. As their common terror escalated, it struck Jaerol that most in the castle still slept. They had to do something to wake the sleeping residents.

With a final look at Liam, Jaerol pressed into the erendinth, sending ignys and aerys together in an explosion in the central courtyard, a decent distance from where they stood by the window in the North Tower, but loud enough to wake everyone in the castle. Jaerol formed the wield a second time, and sent it bursting across the castle so that even those in the Temple of Ceur would be alerted. Talen shot up out of his cot, wide awake but confused.

Agitated voices came from the corridor, followed by shrieks of pain and further explosions, these not wielded by Jaerol or Liam.

Jaerol removed the wield over the locked door and pushed through the doorway and into the corridor to find kien wielders throwing fire in every direction. Their attacks were unrefined, striking anyone nearby, exploding outward in bright spheres, the heat of the growing flames lashing and setting ablaze anything not made of stone.

Pressing more fully into the erendinth, Jaerol wrestled ignys away from the wielders, minimizing its destructive force before turning it against the ones who had first wielded it. Forced to address the change of tactics, the unskilled kien wielders were put on the defensive as Liam and Jaerol fought to subdue them.

Wrestling a destructive wield from one of the men, Jaerol's eyes widened in recognition—that man was Dunstin, one of the disappeared lay votaries from the temple.

Flames exploded around Velaria.

Yelaris had burst through the stone wall of Velaria's apartment into the corridor, crushing two unsuspecting rogue kien wielders against the opposite wall. Fire poured from the dragon's maw as she incapacitated yet another, leaving Velaria to deal with the remaining two.

The men had appeared in the middle of the night and tried to force their way into her quarters. Fortunately, her protective barriers had prevented exactly that. Before they could push through, she attacked them from behind her ward. Whoever they were, they had no training. They couldn't even identify a ward. All they knew was brute force and throwing fireballs.

Now exposed with the ward down, she fought them head on. Those kien wielders were terribly strong—much stronger than should be possible. There was no mistaking them. They were the kien wielders that had been locked away in the lowest levels of the Temple of Ceur, recently liberated following the assassination of Ealyndol. Their minds were now bent toward vengeance and destruction. What lies had those men been fed to hate Septyl so? Velaria grasped her verathn tightly in her right hand, focusing her wielding to better overcome these craven wielders that attacked a school in the night.

She felt the two men before her weakening. They had no idea how to preserve their strength, only capable of quick spurts of remarkable power.

She hoped these were the only five currently attacking the castle, but she was certain that there were more. This was not a simple attack to heighten the growing fear in Gwilnor, but something much more sinister. With a final swish of air, the two men collapsed before her, just as another attack struck Velaria.

This one did not come from either end of the corridor, but to her horror, from the apartment adjacent her own where Lauren, a Sorenth woman lived. She'd been an Azurelle ei'ana longer than Velaria had been alive. Velaria had known her throughout the entirety of her studies and held a great deal of respect for her.

A second lash of terys came at Velaria and, sickened by the betrayal, she brushed it aside to hurl a burst of ignys at Lauren, throwing her backward. Struggling to stand and renew her attack on Velaria, Lauren was stopped when Yelaris poked her head through the ruined wall to Velaria's apartment, smoke billowing from her snout, daring Lauren to rethink another attack.

As Velaria considered what to do next, her heart fell to her stomach. The castle swarmed with untrained kien wielders and Tenebrae ei'ana, endangering everyone who lived there.

The castle had hundreds of exits, some disguised as tunnels, but most were simple doors to the castle's exterior, yet only one was accessible. Only the chancellor or a Chair had control over the wield which maintained the castle's security, however, it could only be reversed from the chancellor's office. In the deepest part of her heart, she prayed that Hannah would have sense enough to release the wards, allowing students, knights, servants, and ei'ana alike to flee the chaos.

Yelaris was quick to respond to Velaria's thoughts, turning herself around in Velaria's sitting room, which allowed Velaria to mount the dragon with a swift leap to Yelaris' back. They moved toward the balcony then out into the night. Through her connection with Yelaris, Velaria felt the blue dragon's reluctance to abandon Ceurenyl a second time. It was as much her home as it was Velaria's. The memory of Erynor's attack on the city had left a searing impression. Obliged to flee from that monster with Devlyn, even if it had been for a good cause, still tormented the dragon.

Yelaris' powerful wings drew them toward the tower above the main entrance, where Chancellor Hannah was probably still ensconced in her bed, most likely unaware of what was going on in the rest of the castle.

Hannah's attitude had bothered Velaria from the moment she had accepted the nomination to her new position. The students all had a favorable impression of the once magister of the art of wielding, which had greatly influenced the Chairs in selecting her to replace the murdered late chancellor, Oranna. Velaria herself had supported Hannah's elevation to chancellor. They were both Azurelles after all.

The slender Chancellor's Tower had no balcony for Yelaris to land on, only round plated glass windows and stone separating the office from the elements. As Yelaris brought her near the tower, Velaria embraced the erendinth. She felt the glass in the circular frame; it was strong and had withstood thousands of years. Focusing her will on the glass, she threw a lance of aerys at it, sharper than any needle she had ever held.

Her wield struck the glass, and for a moment nothing happened, then it shattered.

Yelaris swept past the round windows, close enough for Velaria to leap into the room. They were large, but nowhere near large enough for Yelaris to fit through.

With all the strength her legs could muster, Velaria launched herself from Yelaris into the room, bruising her knees as she landed hard on the stone floor. Verathn in hand, she scanned the room for Hannah.

"Have you gone mad?" Hannah cried, scrambling through a doorway dressed in a flowery yellow nightgown, drawn by the sound of the shattering glass.

Velaria eyed the woman without responding. She strode to the pedestal to the side of the room, set below one of the circular windows. A translucent ball of a wondrous hue nestled on top, looking like it had been sunken into the pedestal so that only a dome remained. Velaria had never used the device which protected Gwilnor from intruders, but tucking the verathn under one arm, she placed her hands on its glassy surface and the vast strength contained in the castle came to her. She instantly became aware of every part of Gwilnor Academy—every door, window, wall, and tunnel. She sensed every single footstep that walked on the castle's floors.

"You knew," Velaria gasped. *That was how they had taken him under everyone's noses!* "The Tenebrae who abducted Devlyn, you knew they were in the attic. You knew about the tunnel—you told them about it, didn't you! You're supposed to protect Gwilnor; protect your students. How could you?"

Hannah smiled, but not the usual pleasant grin Velaria was accustomed to from the chancellor. "I always considered you an intelligent and gifted ei'ana." With every word, Hannah embraced the erendinth but to Velaria's horror, not the elementals nor the transcendentals, but tenebrys.

The little light from the flickering candles dulled as the shadowy power consumed Hannah's features, transforming her into something other than the kind grandmotherly woman everyone had known.

Grabbing her verathn and embracing the erendinth herself, Velaria felt the sweet scent fill her being, sharpening her vision and intensifying her awareness a hundredfold.

"There's no need to fight, child." Hannah said, just as a tenebrys wield burst from her palms.

Hannah's wield did not come close to the powerful wields formed by the shadow elves Velaria had fought against, but neither was she by any means weak and incapable. She had taught as a magister at Gwilnor Academy for over two decades—she had even taught Velaria as a young girl. Twenty supposedly loyal years to Gwilnor before becoming its chancellor. The Seven Chairs of Septyl would never entrust the responsibility of Gwilnor to the weak.

Bolts of tenebrys flew across the large tower office toward Velaria. Pressing into animys and umbrys, she wielded the two transcendental erendinth against the forbidden one and she felt the erendinth lurch in her grasp. They wanted to scream and fade back into the world rather than interact with tenebrys. Velaria herself wanted to shy away from that foul wield as well, her entire being repulsed at being so near. Yelaris roared outside, frustrated that she could not help Velaria without further destroying the Chancellor's Tower and perhaps Velaria herself.

Because she could only slow the pace of the reckless wield, Velaria employed a trick she had learned as a student many years ago and wielded the stone beneath Hannah. There was nothing honorable about it, but it did unbalance Hannah and her vile wield faltered just enough that Velaria could redirect it out an unbroken window and into the night, shattering a second of the tower's ancient round windows.

Refusing to submit, Hannah wrought the tenebrys lightning again, but Velaria had no intention of allowing the woman before her to damage the castle any further.

Through her verathn, Velaria focused a combined force of every elemental erendinth with the two transcendental erendinth she could wield and with a swift lash of determination, struck the chancellor with it. The blast threw Hannah from her feet before she had formed a second wield of tenebrys throwing her backwards and slamming her head against the stone wall behind her, knocking her unconscious.

Velaria once again placed her hands on the orb set into the pedestal. Again, she felt the entirety of the castle. Gwilnor thrummed with violence. She felt someone die; she could not tell who it was, but one moment the person had been there, and the next, gone. It could have been a student. Her heart ached with the intimacy of the experience. She wanted to stop it, but knew she could not fight hundreds of rogue kien wielders and the Tenebrae ei'ana who had exposed themselves for what they were. Instead, she impressed her authority as the Chair of Azurelle—a Chair of Septyl, over the orb and connected with the various exits out of the castle.

Reversing the lockdown on the castle, she opened the hundreds of latches and locks that had been magically bolted. Then, she flung every exterior door open so that everyone in Gwilnor would know that they could leave. If anyone could escape, she wanted them to run, especially the students. She hoped they would have sense to flee to the safety of the temple. They had been betrayed by the very person they had all trusted. Velaria turned to look at the despicable woman lying in her flowery nightgown on the floor.

Hannah would not remain unconscious long. Soon, she would stir and throw her black lightning again. Thinking quickly, Velaria summoned Yelaris to take the disgraced chancellor to the only place where she would not be able to harm anyone: the Temple of Ceur.

Velaria scribbled a note, declaring Hannah's allegiance to the Tenebrae School and describing the state of Gwilnor Academy, then lifted her body with the erendinth toward Yelaris waiting just outside the shattered window. Velaria watched the blue dragon fly off with Hannah dangling in her claws and felt tempted to do the same. But if she left now, she would never make it back into the castle. Once the Tenebrae School openly took control over Gwilnor, it would belong to them, and they would not relinquish it. She would not, could not leave behind those loyal to Septyl.

Again placing her hands on the orb, she searched the castle for a place none knew of, somewhere that not even she would have known of without the orb. She hoped everyone would manage to flee the castle but understood that that was unrealistically optimistic. The majority of Gwilnor's population would not escape; many would die in the fighting currently taking place, but what she feared most was the aftermath. What would happen to Gwilnor Academy in enemy hands? What would happen to the Ei'ana of Septyl?

Deep below the tower she was standing in and deeper than the Chamber of the Seven Chairs below lay a vacant cavern; it did not appear to have been constructed, rather, it was part of the mountain the castle had been built on. Delving further into the cavernous space, she felt something that did not belong there. Small critters were known to inhabit the lowest reaches of the castle, but this was not a mouse.

"So, that's where she's been hiding." Oma had disappeared before Velaria had returned to the castle ten months ago. She had assumed that the dwarf had gone back to Belin's Watch, or perhaps, back to Oern Schtam to be with her son, Patriarch Forvl VIII. Had Oma been hiding in that cavern all this time?

Before leaving the chancellor's office, she used the orb one last time to seal the room, permitting only the chancellor or one of the Seven Chairs to open it. She prayed that none of the Chairs had betrayed Septyl, that it had been only the chancellor, fearing the further harm such a betrayal would cause.

YANILEAN HOSPITALITY

Ange and the other Judges of Yanil were the personal guests of the Yanilean. The invitation was a great relief at first, since they were given free range of the public sections of the keep. The moment they had arrived, they had been told that the Yanilean would formally greet them and the judges had been led to their guest suites to wait for the summons.

But a week later, the Yanilean still had not summoned them. While all the judges were pleased with their accommodations, Ange wished her suite was further removed from Enrico's quarters. He was still without a wife but had fathered two more children since she'd left. His sons would likely one day join the knights protecting the Yanilean Keep. Ange had to remind herself that Enrico was not her problem. He was free to make his own choices and none of those choices had anything to do with her.

Of course, Catalina knew of Ange's past; she had demanded an accounting when Ange had sought entrance into the supposedly non-existent order. Fully aware that the young Yanilean lord still had feelings for Ange, Catalina, as Supreme Judge, had encouraged Ange to meet and talk with Enrico. In fact, she ordered it.

Ange understood the reasoning well enough, but the past week had been unbearable—undeniably excruciating. Not only did she have to listen to Enrico boast of his place in the Yanilean's Court, his multiple children, and the women he was courting, but, to Ange's worst fear, she had discovered that she still cared for the pompous ass.

During their first secluded walk through the Yanilean's Keep, Ange listened to herself speak with Enrico in dismay. Her fluid Lankoran accent had returned when she talked with him, mirroring his own flowing voice. She had barged into Catalina's room after that first walk interrupting Catalina's discussion with another judge and demanded that the Supreme Judge revoke her command. Catalina had smiled a wicked smile, shooed Ange out, and continued the discussion, the topic of which Ange never discovered.

Today, Enrico held her arm in his as they walked through the keep's polished black stone corridors—again. Despite the color of the stone, the keep was well lit, and not once did she consider the ominous dark stone as overbearing or confining. It was the first time they had walked arm in arm since before she had left Lankor and Enrico behind. Ange was furious with herself that she allowed the familiarity and even more so that she had privately hoped that he would have taken her arm in his during their first private walk together.

They talked as any couple would; the keep's many eavesdroppers took their ears elsewhere rather than listen to the endearments and nonsense spewing from their mouths. A very small part of Ange wanted to do the same herself, but she was finding Enrico's speech and demeanor as enticing as ever.

Crossing another intersection, Ange saw from the corner of her eye a woman who had no place in the Yanilean's Keep. A twinge of jealousy pricked her chest at the immense beauty this woman effortlessly held. Her silver hair hung over a single shoulder and her elven eyes sparkled. She stood taller than any woman, and even some of the men in the keep. She walked alone, her head held aloft and dignified, yet she wore Lankoran clothing. Her beauty made the rich gown she wore look cheap.

Ange knew instantly that she had found Princess Kaela Roendryn, pointed ears and all. Ellendren had an uncanny resemblance to her older sister, but Kaela held herself with a confident ease that her younger sister didn't possess, at least not yet. Enrico noticed her staring and, smiling broadly, led them toward the elven princess.

"Ah, Kaela, how are you? I have not seen you out of your quarters for nearly a month now." Enrico let go of Ange's arm to gently lift Kaela's hand to kiss it. "Might I introduce you to Angennia, the warmth of my heart. And Angennia, this is one of Lucillia's princesses, daughter of the elven king and queen—they prefer their unified title of course, but I will not bore you with the proper name."

"A pleasure," said both women as they inclined their heads in greeting.

"You look as though you've never seen an elf before," said Enrico. A slight flicker crossed Kaela's features, barely noticeable.

Ange wanted to grab Kaela's arm and flee the keep. The longer she remained, the better chance Enrico would charm her into staying in the keep forever. She had left him behind once before and she doubted that she had the strength to manage it a second time, nor would he allow it. As kind and fluid as his words were, he was a terribly dominating person, and if he did not want something to happen, it would not.

The elf seemed unwilling to remain and share idle talk. She did not come off as impatient, but something about how she carried herself seemed to say that she had more important business to see to, even if it was sitting alone in her room for the rest of the day.

Kaela excused herself before continuing her stroll through the keep, neither guarded nor followed. There wasn't need as the Yanilean's Keep was an island. The only way in or out was aboard a ferry, and it was unlikely that she could take one without being noticed. Plunging into the murky bay was an option, but Ange doubted anyone would willingly submerge themselves into that filth, especially an elven princess with hair spun of silver and gold.

"My apologies, I did not anticipate Princess Kaela to be so impersonal," Enrico said as his hand returned to her own, fingers once again intertwined.

The remainder of their afternoon stroll was enjoyable, and by the time Ange returned to her accommodations, she was again frustrated with herself for enjoying Enrico's presence. She sat in her large and well cushioned chair, only intending to remain for a moment before finding Catalina to report that she had seen Kaela. Her thoughts wandered as she sat. Revolving around the princess first and how they might secret her away from the keep, her mind next shifted to Enrico and how infuriating and irresistible he was in a single breath. *Had his shoulders always been that broad? Had his hand always felt so right in her own?*

Ange was ashamed at the amount of time she permitted herself to dwell on Enrico, especially when he walked away from her. She couldn't help but stare after him—admiring his physique. Her mind drifted to past memories when she used to watch him and other young lords in the practice field, how they fought with swords and wrestled without shirts. Glancing toward the window in her chambers, she was appalled to discover that the sun was nearly gone. She couldn't see it set from her south facing window, but she could see the sky transition to dusk as bright yellows, oranges, and reds shifted to subtler hues. It would only be another few moments before deep purples would claim the sky.

Rising and moving to the door, she noticed how stiff she was after sitting for so long. Just before she placed her hand on the doorknob, a soft knock came from the other side.

The knock was so gentle, that if she had been standing on the opposite side of the room she would not have heard it at all. Such knocks were cast by people who did not want others to discover their presence. No one in the corridors would know of anyone visiting Ange's rooms. In the pit of her stomach she feared Enrico on the opposite side of the door. Could she deny him again?

Turning the latch, she opened the door to find Kaela waiting in the corridor and Ange felt a tinge of regret that Enrico had not come to her.

Kaela stood tall and proud, yet she did not look condescending as Ange had expected from an elf, especially one related to Ellendren. Ange took a step back and gestured to Kaela to come in. Kaela looked over her shoulder before quickly entering the room and closing the door quietly behind her.

"I would not have left my room—my prison, really—today, if I had not been informed about you and your purpose," said Kaela, scanning the chamber. "I cannot say how my sister managed such a thing, but she entered one of my dreams. At first, I thought it was just a dream, and as I do miss my sister terribly, it was not at all surprising that she appeared in my dream. Yet, she was not part of the dream, she was truly before me, speaking to me. She showed me what you and the others looked like. So, the moment I saw you in the corridor, I recognized you. I did not anticipate one of Yanil's nobility to side with a Lucillian, particularly one with her arm entwined in the arm of one of the Yanilean's favored."

Is he really one of the favored? Ange thought to herself, making Enrico even more desirable since he might one day wear the Yanilean's Mask. Enrico was not one of the Yanilean's own sons, but rather a nephew—a favored nephew. It was not unheard of for the Yanilean to choose someone over one of his own sons, but such a declaration was exceedingly rare. She suddenly heard her mother in her head, *one of your sons would be the next Yanilean!* Even as she attempted to push the thoughts aside, all she could see was herself and Enrico, both smiling proudly as one of their sons took Enrico's place as Yanilean.

One of Kaela's eyebrows rose with the length of time Ange was taking to respond.

"Sorry—I was not aware that he was favored. So, how exactly did Ellendren enter your dreams?" The thought seemed impossible, but Catalina did mention that they were able to communicate in some fashion. She had refused to discuss what the elves were capable of. But, whatever it was, it wasn't because of wielding—wielding in Lankor was not only illegal, but impossible.

"I cannot say, I wasn't aware of such an ability—I didn't even think it was possible. While I did not become an ei'ana myself, I did study at Gwilnor for a year before returning to Lucillia, where I received most of my education. And not once did I hear of people entering other people's dreams," Kaela said, pausing and then asking, "Is it serious with Enrico?"

"Is it that obvious?" Ange blushed and told Kaela of her history with Enrico and the reason she had left Lankor in the first place. The two women spent the next couple hours chatting easily about many things, and to Ange's surprise, she was beginning to see the elf as a friend. They were much closer in age than she and Ellendren.

"Well, if we're going to get me out of here, you'll have to keep your hands clean. We don't want to ruin your chances with Enrico or tarnish his reputation," Kaela said, beaming a bright smile. Ange couldn't help but return the smile; this woman was by every definition a practiced politician.

"Yes, but how?" asked Ange. "This place is impenetrable from within and without.

––––––––––

Ange sat alone in her chamber, occupying herself with one of the books she had found in her room. It was awfully boring and recounted the deeds of a past Yanilean. There was no name attributed to the Yanilean since the author did not refer to the Yanilean as anything but his title, as was customary. The only way to uncover the actual identity was to search the annals for the years mentioned in the book. She was only slightly tempted to do so, and might very well have made the trip to the keep's archives if a knock had not come at the door.

Opening the door revealed one of the Sons of Yanil. "Judge Angennia Soricci, the Yanilean summons you," he said, without seeming to move his lips. His only movement was to step to the side to allow Ange through the door so that he could escort her through the keep and to the audience hall. Unlike the deep blue uniform of Yanil's military, the Sons of Yanil only wore black. They rarely had the need to wear their black plated armor, typically preferring loose fitting fabric due to Lankor's humidity. But today, this knight had donned his full and very intimidating armor.

With the summons, the massive keep had become quite ominous. No stranger to the Yanilean's Keep, Ange knew precisely where the guard was taking her even though she never had had cause to visit the audience hall before.

Audiences with the Yanilean were the rarest luxury in Lankor, reserved for his immediate family and state business. It was said that all friendships formed prior to one becoming the Yanilean ceased, as the Yanilean was no longer the same man he once was. The Yanilean did not make public appearances. On the rare occasion that he left the keep and went into the city proper, an entourage of guards would surround him and make it all but impossible for the inhabitants to catch a glimpse of their sovereign.

The grand doors to the Yanilean's audience hall finally appeared before her. The other judges were already present, each also accompanied by a knight, an armed knight. Ange suddenly saw the knight escorting her and her fellow judges in a very different light and her eyes darted to his sword. Her heartbeat quickened as she considered how poorly this could go. Was the Yanilean summoning the judges to hear them and recognize their order? He could very well have summoned them to silence the Judges of Yanil once and for all. Each judge understood the risk they had taken in coming to Lankor and thereby exposing their order.

The moment Ange had arrived, the bronze doors creaked open to a poorly lit interior. There was no natural light here, leaving braziers as the only source of rather meager illumination. Ange's eyes followed the dimly lit columns upward, disappointed that she could not see the ceiling.

In the center of the room rose a round dais with a winding stair to somewhere below. The Yanilean had his own entrance to his audience hall, and none but he was permitted to use that stair. None but he knew where that stair led. When she thought about it, Ange highly doubted that no one else knew, since his army of servants had to know, not to mention his guards and wife.

The Yanilean stood proudly in the center of the dais, legs spread, wearing an opened black coat over a tunic and trousers in the dark blue of Yanil. Eight of his knights surrounded the dais, backs to their Yanilean, something permitted to only his personal guard for security reasons. A bronze mask said to have been molded from the first Yanilean's face when he was in his prime, hid this Yanilean's face. The bronze features were stern and forbidding. It could have been an exact mold of Enrico, minus his thick black hair. The mask made one appear bald. Imagining a bald Enrico was intolerable. Ange adored his thick black hair.

There was no throne upon the dais; the first Yanilean had refused anything and everything that could link Yanil to its Thellion overseers. Sitting was viewed as a weakness, and so, the Yanilean stood for all his people.

Despite her fear of the man standing before her, Ange was impressed by him. Her heart raced as they waited for him to speak. His word was law. If he so desired, the judges would not leave this room alive.

"Were you aware," declared the Yanilean in a strong voice behind the bronze mask, "that the Judges of Yanil were once my left hand? Their words held the weight of my own." He had the flowing Lankoran accent, although his speech was not poetic but powerful, as if the words themselves had the same effect as a sharpened sword. He spoke in the immortal tongue, reserved for the Yanilean alone, since the Yanilean did not know death. Men became the Yanilean for a time and passed the mantle to the next man, but the Yanilean never died. "You disappeared after Nauto's Wrath. Why?"

The last stung Ange. It was an accusation, not a question.

"We are not immortal as are you, my Yanilean," said Catalina, Supreme Judge of Yanil and, in that role, the Yanilean's equal. The Judges of Yanil had never been the Yanilean's left hand, they were the left hand of Yanil, and the Yanilean was the right hand. Ange was shocked at how easily Catalina spoke, and grateful that it was not her responsibility to do so. "If I knew the reason for our disappearance, I would share it, but I cannot say why our forebears went underground," confessed Catalina.

"Why have you returned to me?" The Yanilean was noticeably unsatisfied with the Supreme Judge's answer.

"The tides change once again. The Judges are part of Yanil's very fabric," Catalina replied.

The Yanilean remained silent. The mask made it impossible to tell whether he sneered, or squinted, or even smiled. The only hint to his reaction was his silence.

Ange felt her palms grow sweaty, and her heart pound even harder.

The Yanilean's gaze shifted. He was looking at her. Ange's heart stopped mid-beat.

"Angennia," the Yanilean began, in an almost friendly tone, "your mother is Madalena, is she not?"

"Yes, my Yanilean."

"I remember her well. It is a shame she could not wed one deserving of her standing, but fortunate for you that she did marry a full blooded Yanilean. You have the beauty of the Yanilean's own blood."

Silence fell over the audience hall, followed by a quiet shuffling of feet behind her. Taking one's eyes away from the Yanilean was forbidden, yet the temptation to look over her shoulder to see who walked behind them was unbearable. What had she gotten herself into? Was it another knight approaching? An executioner to wipe out the Judges of Yanil?

She fidgeted slightly, but not enough to see who it was. Her mother would never forgive her if she learned that Ange had disrespected the Yanilean.

"You are curious?" mused the Yanilean. Ange felt her heart stop. She was about to apologize when the Yanilean spoke again. "You should be."

She did not have to wait much longer to know who was approaching. Enrico stopped beside her; she could finally see him out of the periphery of her eyes that still looked at the Yanilean. Enrico had changed outfits since their walk; he now wore a similar coat to the Yanilean's.

"Enrico Desillio, son of Philippe, from this day forth, you are wed. Angennia Soricci, daughter of Madalena, from this day forth, you are Angennia Desillio, wife of Enrico Desillio." Ange nearly gasped; the words fell on her ears, the reality lying heavily on her. The word of the Yanilean was final. She and Enrico were married. She was Enrico's wife.

There was a time when she had had a choice in whom she married. She had chosen to leave her prior engagement with Enrico because she could not accept that he had fathered children with other women. Her heart ached, knowing she would have to live with that burden until she died, a burden that would only be heavier if she did not bear him a son. Helplessness clenched her heart. Women of the Yanilean's court had no voice, no rights aside those assigned to them by their husband and the sons they bore. She would live a life of luxury for certain, but it was no longer *her* life, it was her husband's.

Enrico's apologetic expression asked permission from the Yanilean who nodded in response to the unasked question. Enrico planted his lips on hers. Her heart suddenly lifted from its depression as she kissed her husband.

36

DROWNED AND INTACT

Devlyn woke to the Salty Mermaid bobbing in Lankor Bay. The sun would not peek above the watery horizon for another several hours. Sitting up and placing his legs over the edge of his narrow cot, his eyes adjusted to the dark cabin filled with the male crew and passengers. Captain Terrance had been kind enough to forfeit his personal cabin to Ellendren and Alethea, the only women aboard.

Devlyn tiptoed across the cabin, creeping between the cots and hammocks filled with blobs of sleeping bodies that grew more distinct as his vision sharpened. It was far too dark to tell who snored the loudest, but whoever it was, was louder than Alex, which he would have never believed possible. If it were not for all the years that he and his cousin had shared a bedroom, he was sure he would not have been able to get a moment's worth of sleep aboard the Salty Mermaid.

The cabin had no door and considering the number of men sleeping in one space, there probably was not much need for one. Devlyn assumed that privacy was not a luxury given to those on the open sea, other than for the captain.

Passing through the cargo hold toward the stairs to the deck, Devlyn heard the flying mounts make soft deep sounds in their throats. It was impossible to tell whether it was the usual noises made when they slept or whether they took note of him passing by, making him wonder whether they were like Aliel in that they did not truly sleep, they simply rested. He knew they had a certain level of intelligence, but did not know to what degree. Whether or not they slept was another question, but Devlyn was confident that they did. Unlike Aliel, they had physical bodies.

But tonight, Aliel was not resting. Not only had they decided to keep the phoenix a secret from the crew of the Salty Mermaid, but they had realized that the closer they drew to Lankor, the more noticeable the phoenix's light would have been—a clear giveaway to anyone who might glimpse the Salty Mermaid in the distance. And keeping a phoenix below deck was not advisable; the griffins and alicorn barely tolerated it. Instead, Aliel soared high above them, as he had the entire voyage from Auten, appearing as an out-of-place star to anyone who looked at the night sky.

Still scarred by Devlyn's abduction, neither Devlyn nor Aliel were comfortable with the separation, but they had few options. Devlyn felt Aliel's concern through their bond. *We'll be fine*, he conveyed, trying to assure the phoenix.

If anything goes awry, don't hesitate to bond with me.

Devlyn lingered by the flying mounts as a series of floorboards creaked behind him. He glanced over his shoulder to see Wyn approach; he looked as though he had not gone to sleep. His eyes were not bleary, and his black hair was smooth as always. *One of the perks of immortality*, thought Devlyn, self-consciously patting down his thick light brown hair, which he knew stuck out in every direction. Diving into Lankor Bay would at least solve that problem.

Wyn nodded a small greeting then cupped a hand against Eolwn's head. The griffin made a soft cooing sound at the touch and Wyn bent his forehead to the griffin's, holding it there for a moment or two. Stepping away from Eolwn, Wyn nodded toward the stairs to the deck.

Above, they found themselves in the predawn chill. Viren and Captain Terrance stood on the starboard side, sharing a private conversation as they looked west toward Lankor. Devlyn could just make out the silhouette of the city. The two men were not alone on deck; Devlyn saw Alethea sitting at the bow with legs crossed and eyes shut. Devlyn readily recognized that meditative pose.

"Are you ready?" asked Wyn, his voice low, as if he did not want to wake the world before the morning sun rose.

"I can't say that I'm looking forward to diving in." Devlyn glanced toward the dingy water. The water's texture had changed after they crossed into Lankor Bay—the clear blue sea of the Erynien Bay was now behind them. "The closer we sail to the city, the more soiled it turns. I can't imagine what they're throwing into their own water that would make it so tainted."

"Just don't wear your shiny lierathnil when you dive in." Wyn smirked. "Has it been decided when we'll make the dive?"

"The sooner the better. Ellendren is coordinating with her sister and the judges. I was advised to avoid entering Somnaeniel, especially this close to Lankor." Devlyn couldn't disguise the hint of irritation in his voice. Somnaeniel was just as dangerous for Ellendren as it was for him.

Just as Devlyn considered making disgruntled comments about the recommendation to avoid the World-in-Between, the door to the captain's cabin opened, revealing a readied Ellendren. She wore a calm and gentle expression as always, but something about it caught Devlyn's attention. It seemed forced. She crossed the deck of the Salty Mermaid to Devlyn and Wyn.

"Everything all right?" asked Devlyn.

"Ange was married off the other night."

Devlyn could not see his own face, but knew that unlike Wyn's usual expressionless calm, his shock showed. "She's only been there a week," said Devlyn, incredulous, his voice louder than he intended.

"The Yanilean himself officiated the wedding between her and her former fiancé. A noble named Enrico."

"Is that common here?"

"More than you would think," said Ellendren. "The Yanilean's word is irrevocable in Yanil."

"Will this delay us?" asked Wyn.

"No," replied Ellendren with a hint of hesitation. "The judges reaffirmed that they will see to it that Kaela is on the specified parapet at dawn. I wish we knew why Alethea hasn't been able to contact any of the judges in Lankor. Our coordination efforts have been limited to my sister's dreams. Are we certain that we're allotting enough time to search for the lucilliae?"

"The merpeople know its location," said Devlyn. "It's only a matter of swimming there and retrieving it."

"I suggest we don't linger any longer," said Alethea. She had come up to them so quietly that Devlyn hadn't noticed her approach. "The merpeople await us."

They crossed the short distance to the port side of the craft and looked over to see four merpeople swimming below. Only their heads and the top of their shoulders were visible in the moonlight, but even in the darkness, Devlyn could see their bright blue eyes.

"Did Ferinn send you?" Devlyn asked, trying to make polite conversation with the merpeople.

"Ferinn is not a Meridean, and only the Merideans have a voice at the Meridean Conclave," said one of the merpeople. There was a beauty to her, a deep and mysterious sort. "Ferinn is currently under trial for acting against a decision made at a past Meridean Conclave and will answer for that crime."

The severity with which she spoke made Devlyn suck in his breath. Without Ferinn, the battle of Myrium would have been lost, the Sorenth imprisoned or slaughtered on the spot.

"You are very expressive for an elf," commented the same merperson. "But there is nothing to worry yourself over. While Ferinn's crime is serious, the Meridean Conclave will doubtlessly forgive his transgression. Sorenthil is well-loved by our people. Now come into the water, for our time is limited."

Devlyn glanced apprehensively at Wyn, both understanding that it was now or never. They undressed quickly, leaving only their small clothes on. Swimming through Lankor Bay was bound to be difficult enough, their clothing would only hamper them further. While Wyn removed his clothes confidently, Devlyn was self-conscious about his still-emaciated body on view for all to scrutinize. A small thought in the back of his mind wanted Ellendren to turn her head. He smiled weakly to disguise how uncomfortable he was and dove awkwardly and with a loud splash into the tepid water. Wyn dove in as gracefully as any merperson.

Devlyn looked up and saw Ellendren looking over at them nervously. "Be careful," she called out.

The merpeople dropped below the surface, and looked expectantly at them, curious to see how they would manage to breathe under the water.

Pressing into aerys and aquaeys, Devlyn and Wyn each drew the precious oxygen from the water, formed a pocket of air shielded by a wield of aquaeys. Air continuously circulated through the watery barrier. The wield was not particularly difficult, but they would have to maintain their wields the entire time under the water.

Satisfied, the merpeople turned from the submerged hull of the boat and swam westward toward Lankor and the Drowned City below. Their tails had a florescent quality, allowing Devlyn and Wyn to follow them through the waters although with some difficulty because of the murkiness of the water and only moonlight above, waters that darkened further the deeper they submerged.

Devlyn could barely see five feet in front of him, and there was no way of knowing there was anything unfriendly swimming beside, below, or behind their group. He had no reason to distrust the merpeople, but neither did he know what else called these waters home.

It was only because his arms and legs grew sore and heavy that he knew they had been swimming for a long while. They were not far from the ruins of the Drowned City now, and he wished he could float weightlessly in the water for a moment to allow his muscles to revive.

The large city which floated above had to be near, but there was simply no way of knowing. Even as Devlyn glanced up and toward the surface, he couldn't see anything. The polluted water and dark night had made it impossible.

The merpeople knew exactly where they were in relation to both cities, and while he and Wyn could communicate through their minds, Devlyn felt uncomfortable doing so with merpeople he had just met. *How did they communicate with each other under water? Perhaps they used their hands and signs?*

Pushing aside those thoughts, Devlyn focused his mind on keeping pace with the merpeople. His sense of time had left him and the water flowing by as he swam was almost soothing. The water appeared darker in one spot from the corner of his eye, and he allowed himself a quick glance but he saw nothing as he swam past.

The merpeople slowed their pace, shifting direction downward until it felt like his feet were where his head ought to be as they dove deeper. His body rebelled against the descent, fighting to drift back to the surface. It was difficult to wrap his mind around how deep Lankor Bay was. *How had this city once been above water?* Forcing himself to continue the descent, he dug deeply into his energy reserves, his growing fatigue worsened by the increasing iciness of the water temperature. The dark spots he'd noticed before grew larger and occurred more frequently.

Seaweed growing on larger objects floated in the perpetual current, resembling flags along a wall. When the merpeople swam beside one of the dark objects, Devlyn realized that it was a ruined stone wall covered in green algae.

None of the original stone was visible; algae had covered the entirety of the Drowned City. Slowing their pace considerably, the merpeople navigated effortlessly though the city claimed by Nauto's Wrath. The original buildings, now in ruins, had once been high elegant towers with intricate sculptures. Only bits and pieces of what had been the beauty of Lankor lingered. Once tall spires now lay on the watery floor, some largely intact but most nothing more than a pile of stones.

Compared to the current buildings in Lankor, Devlyn was shocked to discover how tall the original city had once soared. Perhaps the architects of the new city saw the original height and weight as a flaw for a city built on marsh and sand. It was only a guess, but it seemed logical enough.

A colonnaded tholos, the only intact building but covered in algae came into view. Devlyn easily recognized it from when he had first glimpsed the lucilliae and interacted with Ramira Bir Ginthol, Supreme Judge of Yanil. A single row of slender vine-like columns twirled upward in sinuous braids to support the dome. Beneath the algae, Devlyn recognized that the tholos—columns, dome, and all—had been crafted from a cloudy semi-opaque stone. The stone shimmered softly—Devlyn knew that muffled golden light emitted from only one substance. He couldn't believe he hadn't recognized it before, but the entire tholos was woven from lumaryl.

The merpeople continued to lead the way to the tholos, but it was no longer necessary as Devlyn knew precisely where the lucilliae had lain undisturbed for over sixteen hundred years. Kicking hard to push ahead of the merpeople, he entered the algae-covered tholos and saw the statue of the blindfolded woman. Resting in her extended hands, unmoved since the Luminari had placed it there countless years before, gleamed one of the lucilliae. Unlike the rest of the Drowned City, the jewel was not covered in algae and glimmered with a soft light of its own, the blue glow glistening gently in the water.

Just above the bay floor, his body at a slight angle, Devlyn swam past the vine-like lumaryl columns and floating in front of the statue holding the lucilliae, Devlyn extended his hand. The warm light embraced his fingers in sharp contrast to the chilled water. Closing his fingers over the jewel, the elven virtue imbued within the lucilliae permeated his being. A combination of justice and mercy rushed through him, and Devlyn understood why it had been entrusted to the Judges of Yanil.

His entire concept of justice shifted dramatically. Doing what was right and deserved was fulfilled in the presence of mercy. Justice involved all civilization. A just kingdom was not identified by its leaders and their execution of what they believed to be just, but by the least of its members living a fulfilling life and showing kindness to all others. Every person had to be their best self for a kingdom to be truly just.

Holding the images in his mind, Devlyn turned from the watery grave and propelled himself with a kick, using the column itself to push off. Legs and arms already sore, he made his way around the domed roof and toward the surface, which was a frightening distance above, followed by Wyn and the merpeople. Thankfully, the upward swim was easier than it had been to descend to the Drowned City. The surface was still far off, and only a soft glimmer overhead indicated their direction.

Suddenly, a biting tear severed his control over his wield, defusing the pocket of air around his mouth. Shocked and unprepared for it, Devlyn panicked, and looked for help. But Wyn no longer had control of his wield either.

Devlyn had no idea exactly how deep they still were but had a gut-wrenching feeling that they would never reach the surface unless each of them could recreate their air pockets.

Lucilliae still clutched in his hand, he pushed upward with every fiber of his body. His buoyant body refused to carry him fast enough to the surface. Arms and legs growing heavier by the moment, Devlyn desperately screamed mentally at the merpeople, hoping that they could hear him. *Help. Help. HELP!* he pleaded, growing sluggish and feeling his body weaken. He grew drowsy—wanting to sleep and never wake again. He was drowning; he was going to drown in Lankor Bay. The thought made him fight all the harder, trying to keep swimming and press into the erendinth. But his connection to the erendinth was gone. The interruption wasn't as severe as during his time in the black box, but he still couldn't wield.

Finally, the merpeople seemed to realize the severity of the situation and they grabbed Devlyn and Wyn under their armpits, two merpeople for each elf, and pulled them upward at a dizzying speed.

Grateful for the help, Devlyn stopped his mental screaming. He continued to kick, but each kick was weaker than before, the already dark waters darkening further, his vision fading.

Time seemed to slow as every second felt like an hour. His mind emptied; it felt as if he was falling asleep.

The fear was gone, he was fading—dying. It did not matter; nothing mattered anymore. Images filled his mind. Erynor would destroy everything Devlyn had fought for over the past few years. Gwilnor Academy would be no more. The Temple of Ceur would be destroyed. The Illumined Wood would burn and Lucillia with it. The Luminari would fade again. His family and friends would be enslaved. But they would not submit, they would die as well. Ellendren would die. His sister, Leilyn, would die. None of it mattered as the emptiness embraced him, enveloping his mind like a blanket.

He sensed the concern of the merpeople carrying him but it could not breach the emptiness. His body grew limp, and in that darkness covering his heart he caressed a small forgotten light flickering within its center.

An image of his mother came to his mind. The song she had sung to him surfaced in his memories.

"With an unsung song upon thy heart,
Might light steps ever mark thy start…"

OVERSHADOWED

Ellendren flew on Laureniel, Viren close behind. Another volley of arrows came at them, and Ellendren's ongoing attempts to embrace the erendinth against them still futile.

She had heard that wielding was impossible in Lankor, but she had never given the rumors any credit, assuming that it was really a case of anyone caught wielding was either arrested and sent to Yanil's prison camps or killed on the spot. She had never thought that wielding just wouldn't be possible, that the erendinth just didn't respond. Lankor was not the Temple of Ceur—there was nothing sacred about this city. It didn't have the Chamber of Light and whatever ward that prevented wielders from embracing the erendinth when in the temple.

Laureniel dodged yet another volley, her brilliant wings a clear target in the dawning sun. Viren slashed stray arrows away with his sword. He was a surprisingly capable swordsman even when astride. His crystalline sword glinted in the orange glow of sunlight. Ellendren tried to embrace the erendinth again, struggling to understand why she couldn't wield.

There wasn't any logical reason. If she hadn't been focused on finding her sister while dodging arrows just now, she would definitely be trying to solve the mystery. That the enemy had found a ward or something that prevented wielding did not bode well. She had no doubt that shadow elves were spread among the archers, waiting for her to draw near. Were they expecting her? Had the Judges of Yanil betrayed them?

Ellendren wanted to believe that. She didn't need a reason to doubt Ange's duplicity. Her dislike of the woman was enough. But Kaela trusted Ange. How had her sister grown to trust that woman after only a week? As much as it bothered Ellendren, she discarded those thoughts. Despite Ellendren's feelings about Ange, the judges had been nothing but courteous hosts and trusted allies through all of this. They had had plenty of opportunities to betray them. There was no need to deliver Devlyn and his escort to Lankor to prove their loyalties to the Erynien Empire. No—all they would have had to do was send a message to Broid and a shadow elf, a Deurghol, or Aren would have gladly come to collect them while they slept unaware.

Ellendren ground her teeth at that possibility. None of them had taken any precautions to ward against that. *How foolish could we possibly be?* she thought, urging Laureniel past another volley.

The archers had no way of knowing that their arrows were directed at a Guardian. They doubtless had grown up with tales of the superior capabilities of Guardian knights. Every child dreaming of knighthood in Eklean envisioned themselves as a Guardian. If they had known who they were shooting at, they would have likely reconsidered whether maintaining their posts was the wisest choice. Few would stand long against a Guardian.

Peering along the keep's battlements, Ellendren searched for Kaela. They had agreed to meet on the roof of the keep just as the sun rose. Ellendren couldn't help a tiny mental snort at the poetics of the time and place. They were Luminari after all, elves of the dawning sun. Granted, the plans might have changed if they had known that the Yanilean's Keep would be on high alert, awaiting Devlyn's retrieval of the lucilliae from beneath the murky waters of Lankor Bay.

Not seeing her sister anywhere, she swerved upward and away from the keep, trying yet again to embrace the erendinth. As Laureniel flew them higher, Ellendren felt a trickle of her power return. The sweet rivulets of the erendinth seeped through her and she started a wield of aquaeys. There was plenty of water to supplement her wielding. But, as she dove toward the keep intending to flush the archers off the battlements with a wave from the bay, the erendinth slipped from her grasp, like sand through her fingers. Her dismayed groan was forgotten when she spotted a flash of yellow on the far side of the keep, away from the archers on the opposite battlements. Ellendren didn't know whether to thank or curse Kaela for wearing such a bright dress. Blessedly, she was alone, none of the judges present. Their hands would remain clean for now. Hopefully, no one would link their arrival in Lankor with Kaela's escape.

Kaela's silken dress flapped in the breeze. Viren must have also seen her, for he urged his griffin forward just ahead of Ellendren and leapt off his mount in a graceful flip, quickly dispatching the few soldiers who had tried to reach Kaela before Ellendren or Viren could. Even with her anxiety over their dangerous situation, Ellendren gaped at Viren's fluid movements, his sword disappearing in flashes of light as it swung at his opponents. A few arrows flew past him, forcing him to divide his attention. Between every flash of his sword against his adversaries, he slashed arrows from the sky to protect Kaela, standing behind him. Ellendren's heart screamed in a panic as an arrow passed Viren and tore through Kaela's skirt. Laureniel landed in a flurry of white feathers and Ellendren reached out to Kaela who hopped onto Laureniel behind Ellendren with a swish of her dress, apparently unscathed.

"Are you okay? That arrow…"

"I'm fine, it grazed my leg, nothing more." Her gaze was on Viren's blade. "Who's that?"

"Now is clearly not the time," Ellendren bit off, nudging the alicorn to take flight.

"You could have let him carry me away as my knight in shining armor."

"I also could have left you with the Yanilean as his distinguished guest. What in Anaweh's name are you doing here anyway?"

Kaela didn't answer. Instead they watched Viren remount the griffin, leaving the incapacitated soldiers behind. Despite her assumptions, they hadn't come across a single shadow elf on the keep's battlements. Then just as Ellendren encouraged Laureniel to leap into the air and away, the alicorn screamed, jerking suddenly and drawing Ellendren's attention even as they rose. Ellendren looked down Laureniel's right side searching for the wound, anxious it might be fatal. Seeing nothing there, she looked down her left side, and saw an arrow embedded into Laureniel's hindquarters. Tamping down her immediate frantic response, Ellendren tried to embrace the erendinth to heal the alicorn, frustrated when she still could not.

Instantly, inspiration struck. Something about the Yanilean's Keep was preventing her interaction with the erendinth! Her only option was to get them away from this wretched place. "Back to the boat," she urged Laureniel.

The rescuers flew swiftly away, dodging the continuing barrage of arrows, Viren slashing those that came too close until they were finally out of range. A low mist clung to the water, hovering over Lankor Bay. That was a good sign. A Deurghol or shadow elf on a dragon would have no difficulty seeing the Salty Mermaid from above, but it would be difficult for anyone trying to locate the Salty Mermaid from another boat through the rather dense mist. With those thoughts, Ellendren looked for Devlyn, and knew that Viren searched too. But Devlyn was nowhere to be seen.

They landed on the Salty Mermaid, Viren just behind Ellendren. Ellendren and Kaela dismounted carefully, and Ellendren immediately looked at Laureniel's wound. The arrow hadn't gone too deep, but blood stained her pearly coat. "This is going to hurt, Laureniel," she said soothingly and pulled the arrow out.

Laureniel let out a scream, then turned her head to look at Ellendren with an apologetic snort. Ellendren embraced the erendinth, thankful that whatever had blocked her at the Yanilean Keep was gone. Even as she exhaled a relieved sigh and wove a healing wield into Laureniel's wound, her inspired thought that it was the keep itself came to mind. Something to think about further, but now was not the time. The wound was not serious, and luckily the arrow had only bit into flesh and not near any internal organ. As the healing wield went on, Laureniel's breathing steadied and she nuzzled Ellendren.

Ellendren hugged the alicorn and followed Viren into the captain's cabin.

———————————

Devlyn could not remember why that small light was familiar, nor why he should care about it. It began to grow, perhaps quickly, perhaps slowly; he could not tell, but nonetheless it grew. The small growing light tried to fill the oppressive emptiness consuming him, both within and without. The light grew warm, pushing the interior darkness away, and realization erupted. Aliel!

The merpeople must have grasped what was happening, for they released Devlyn just before golden wings of light exploded from his shoulder blades and the darkness dispersed to return to the watery depths where it belonged. Grabbing Wyn in a hug, he pulled them both from the water, directly in front of an ominous building of black stone, torchlight flooding from its windows. He gasped in quick breaths, welcome air filling his lungs.

But Wyn barely breathed, and in this moment, that was more important to Devlyn than keeping his presence in Lankor a secret. His luminous body shone its wondrous golden light just above the murky bay, a sight the Lankorans had never seen. In the growing light that meant dawn approached, he could see the merpeople floating at the surface of the water below him.

Murmurs from the keep and the waking city reached his ears, then were lost in the whooshing sound of volleys of arrows directed at him. Comprehension struck: they had been waiting for him. Lankor had known they were coming.

Devlyn tried to press into the erendinth, but could not. Not understanding why, he was left with few options, and feinted to the left just enough to avoid the multitude of arrows soaring through the predawn air so that they landed in the water. The merpeople disappeared into the murky depths of the bay.

Wyn took in a shallow gasping breath, then began breathing more steadily; his eyes opened and then widened in shock when he realized that a golden Devlyn held him hundreds of feet above Lankor Bay. Still very weak, he managed to put his arms around Devlyn's torso, but without any strength to hold on.

Annoyed by the archers, Devlyn's greatest concern was that he was cut off from the erendinth. However that had happened, he needed to get Wyn to safety. Looking around, hoping to find a safe location to deposit his cousin, he was greatly relieved to see a griffin carrying Alethea flying toward him.

Alethea drew close, arms outstretched for Wyn and Devlyn gently placed Wyn astride just in front of the ancient elf who held him tightly in her arms, then flew off, Wyn slumping, still incapable of supporting himself. Devlyn knew full well that without Aliel and their ability to bond as a Phaedryn, he would be in the same predicament.

When he turned back to the oppressive building—realizing that he looked upon the Yanilean's Keep—he caught sight of a dark figure standing on the flat roof and with dismay, Devlyn recognized Aren. The imposing creature's shadow absorbed the early dawn's available light. Behind Aren, Devlyn saw the glimmer of pearly white wings. Ellendren and Viren were at the keep rescuing Kaela.

The air hummed around him, rising to an almost drumming sound, drawing his attention back to Aren whose wings of darkness were in stark contrast to Devlyn's wings of light. How could such a thing ever happen to a Phaedryn? Surely death was preferable to such corruption.

Devlyn could feel the destructive tenebrys lightning that Aren was forming in the distance and saw it streak uncontrollably toward him.

Pressing as strongly into the elemental erendinth as he could manage, he tried to form a defensive wield while also trying to submit simultaneously to the transcendental erendinth, hoping they would fill his being so that he could send a blast of energy against Aren's attack.

Nothing happened.

He was still cut off from the erendinth; there was nothing he could do to halt the chaotic lightning or protect himself. The two wields should have clashed in the air, creating an explosive noise that would have awoken anyone still asleep, the ear deafening collision causing every Lankoran to sweat in terror at the threat of Lankor's destruction yet again.

Devlyn could only dodge the tenebrys wield by diving toward the water.

Had he been permanently affected by the black box he had been kept in? Suddenly terrified that his connection to the erendinth had been severed, and relieved that neither Ellendren nor Viren had drawn Aren's attention to their presence on the rooftop. He didn't know whether they would manage to rescue Kaela. The only thing Devlyn could do was to give them as much time as possible.

Aren's dark wings lifted him from the keep; he hung in the air a moment then charged at Devlyn.

The air began to drum again, but it was not coming from Aren. Devlyn quickly looked around, his heart plummeting at the sight of a Deurghol riding a dragon, and the violent and direct streak of tenebrys that exploded from them. Chaos contained in a single force tore toward him. Devlyn didn't have time to consider whether it was the same Deurghol who had attacked them in the Freiton Wood. Did Deurghol look different from one another? Or did they all look the same, oozing poisonous shadow from their bodies, darkness taking an incorporeal form?

With a great thrash of his golden wings, Devlyn flew upward to avoid the devastating attack.

Chancing a look back, Devlyn saw that the Deurghol held a blade unlike anything he had ever seen. It had no hilt; it looked as though he clenched the raw metal. It had a corrupted quality that Devlyn could not identify, as if it should be something other entirely. It shifted, losing its physicality as if it did not belong in this realm. Whether it had been sharpened and drew blood was another question. Mesmerized by the blade, he lost himself in a trance, his eyes shifted between the blade and its owner. Time seemed to stop as Devlyn stared into the Deurghol's ethereal cowl.

"*Lorenthien*," the Deurghol hissed. Aren froze in the air, the name stopping him.

The Deurghol held them both with its power, paralyzing them from the back of his dragon. He spoke again. Devlyn didn't recognize any of the words and forgot them as soon as he heard them, but they held him. The shadowed dragon drew closer to Devlyn, engulfing his golden light even as it sent out dark tendrils to encase Devlyn. Unaware of the bindings, lost in the depths of Deurghol's cowl, Devlyn's hypnosis fell away when Aliel cried within his mind.

Coming to himself, Devlyn's eyes shot wide open, the Deurghol as close as the dragon's girth would allow. With a flap of his wings, Devlyn pushed himself away, noticing again the Deurghol's blade as it came arcing toward him, slashing through empty air with a demonic whine. Its residue hung in the air, as if it had cut the ether between realms. It had to be a corrupted verathn and he recalled the Myrish soldier who had been mortally wounded by one. That memory was enough to keep Devlyn as far away from that blade as he could get.

Weaponless, Devlyn panicked, and tried again to press himself into the erendinth to form a shield. Unable to, he dove toward Lankor's canals, and felt the air of the passing blade rush against his back as he lunged downward.

He felt Aren and the Deurghol race after him. Both tore through the sky, wielding their wretched lightning, the Deurghol's dragon roaring and breathing flames of tenebrys after Devlyn. Dodging as best he could, Devlyn wove through the canals and buildings.

Hundreds of people gawped as he flew by, standing just outside their doorways or poking their heads out the windows, hoping to catch a glimpse of the chaos. They swiftly rushed back into the supposed safety of their homes when tenebrys exploded against every building Devlyn passed, colorless flames setting the structures ablaze.

Behind him, Devlyn felt Aren and the Deurghol join their wielding, and the air thrummed violently with a terrifying lethal explosion directed at him. There was no side street or alley to turn into; his only possible direction for escape was up.

Striking into the sky, Devlyn exposed himself once again in the morning light just rising in the east. The awful sounds of the dragon followed him, shaking his bones as it roared more thunderous fire into the air. Barely avoiding the flames, Devlyn felt his heart, then his entire being go cold. He was falling, his golden light gone. Wind rushed against his naked body. *Aliel?*

Everything went dark, even the dawning sun.

His body struck the black stone of Lankor. Something had broken his fall; there were cracking and breaking sounds beneath him like wood snapping. He tried pushing himself to his feet but fell back as everything went black.

HERE ENDS THE THIRD PART OF

THE JEWEL OF LIFE:

FADING LIGHTS

LOOK FOR THE FOURTH PART OF
THE JEWEL OF LIFE:

BURNING DESIRE

APPENDIX A
GLOSSARY OF TERMS

ABBEY SCHOOL

The preferred system of education for children throughout Eklean. Those deemed capable are sent to higher studies, preferably at Gwilnor Academy.

AELISH

Native language of the elves. Largely forgotten, only used in academic circles.

AERYS

An elemental erendinth. The essence of air.

ALBIEN

One of the seven Schools of Septyl. Albiens focus on truth and care for many of Eklean's libraries. Motto: Truth is discoverable. Emblem: A naked male and female elf holding unraveled scrolls with an owl perched behind, cast in gold on a white field. The chair of Albien is known as the Seeker.

ALDARCH

Deific rulers of Aldinare who reigned from their sanctums.

ALDINARE

Western Skyland of the Aldinari, one of the four elven kindreds. Lost to the Darkness. Only a hundred Aldinari escaped the Skyland with their lives.

ALICORN

A legendary beast native to the Skyland of Aldinare. A winged unicorn.

ANADEL

Spiritual creatures that predate Teraeniel and Somnaeniel. Their native home is Lumaeniel. There are four known classifications of anadel: irythil, enthiel, lorendil, and naril.

ANACORDEL

Creatures of body, soul, and spirit.

ANAWEH

The Creating Light.

ANIMYS

A transcendental erendinth. The essence of spirit.

AQUAEYS

An elemental erendinth. The essence of water.

ARANTIULYN

One of the seven Schools of Septyl. Arantiulyns focus on strength and protection and oversee the Knights of Septyl. Motto: With fortitude, we will protect. Emblem: A naked male and female elf in a fighting stance with swords in hand with a lion prowling cast in gold on an orange field. The Chair of Arantiulyn is known as the General.

ARCANE GEMS

Sources of magic used by the Mages of the Kilnae Del.

ARCHSTEWARD

Part of the Ei'ceuril hierarchy, they are elevated wise ones. Before kien wielders were restricted to the Temple of Ceur, archstewards lived in every major city of Eklean tending to those faithful to Anaweh, the Creating Light.

ARENTHYLEAN BELLS

Twenty-four bells composed of four materials that ring every hour.

ARYL

The united head of an elven house composed of a king and queen or lord and lady.

AUBURNIS

One of the seven Schools of Septyl. Auburnises focus on inner peace. Motto: To love is our gift. Emblem: A naked male and female elf offering a garland with larks flying above, cast in gold on a brown field. The Chair of Auburnis is known as the Pilgrim.

AUREPHAEN

Feast day of the Luminari, commemorating Auriel and the dawning sun. Celebrated on the 15th of Aurenth, the spring equinox.

AZURELLE

One of the seven Schools of Septyl. Azurelles focus on the advancement and training of the erendinth. Motto: The zealous soul must be temperate. Emblem: A naked male and female elf wielding the powers with a dragon behind, cast in gold on a blue field. The Chair of Azurelle is known as the Blue Dragon.

Belin's Watch

An Evellion city in the Vespien Mountains comprised of humans and dwarves. Named for Belin, the dwarf who sheltered Thellion refugees in their greatest hour of need.

Borephaen

Feast day of the Eldinari, commemorating Boriel and the sleeping sun. Celebrated on the 15th of Borenth, the winter solstice.

Bowl of Theniel

Sea set apart by the merpeople as sacred. The place where Theniel brought the waters to Teraeniel.

Centaur

Anacordel dedicated to protecting the forests of Eklean, particularly the Illumined Wood. The upper body is like an elf's but broader and more rugged while the lower body looks much like a four-legged horse.

Ceurendol

The Jewel of Life. Created by the Luminari by placing their life essence within seven jewels of incredible brilliance which allowed them to share their immortality with every race in 1.3a (7085.3E). Also known as the Light Diamond, the Lieben Stone, and the Heart of Hearts.

Ceurendol War, the

A cataclysmic war instigated by the Erynien Empire which began over a philosophical difference over the Jewel of Life and whether immortal life was proper for the 'lesser races.' The war divided Eklean in two factions, those faithful to the Luminari and those subjugated by the Erynien Empire. As the fate of the war grew clear, emissaries and merchants from other continents withdrew from Eklean, fearing the Erynien Empire. 322-500.3a (7407-7585.3E).

Ceurenyl

City founded by the ei'ceuril. Home of the Temple of Ceur and Gwilnor Academy. The only city not to fall into Erynor's control when Krysenthiel was lost to the Shroud.

CEURTRIARCH

Leader of the ei'ceuril, known as High Archsteward and Arbiter of the Light.

CHANCELLOR

The head of Gwilnor Academy under the authority of and appointed by the Seven Chairs.

CHILDREN

When capitalized, refers to the proto-race.

COR'LERA

A small village in eastern Parendior and in disputed territory claimed by both Lucillia and Perrien. The vineyards of Cor'lera produce the coveted ice wine, the Cor'leran Blue.

CRIMSYN

One of the seven Schools of Septyl. Crimsyns focus on healing and run many hospitals and infirmaries throughout Eklean. Motto: Through healing, hope is given. Emblem: A naked male and female elf dancing with a dog, cast in gold on a red field. The chair of Crimsyn is known as the Physician.

CYNDINARE

Southern Skyland of the Cyndinari, one of the four elven kindreds. Lost to the Darkness.

DAERENETH

Continent south of Ogren and west of Ja'Horan. Tropical continent.

DEURGHOL

The Cyndinari directly responsible for the Shroud. They are neither living nor dead. Also known as the Deathless.

DRAGON

Legendary creatures bound to the erendinth.

DRUIDS OF KWEIL AITCH, THE

Secluded faction of humans who learned to walk Somnaeniel, the World-in-Between, early on.

DWARF

Anacordel who sought the deep roots of the mountains.

Ei'ana

An organized group of wielders. Since the Balance was lost during the Ceurendol War, there are only kiara wielders among the ei'ana. There has not been a kien wielder among the ei'ana for over a thousand years.

Ei'ana Counsels

A series of norms ei'ana are to follow in regards to wielding. The counsels prohibit men from becoming ei'ana due to their inability to wield safely after the Balance was lost. The counsels also require ei'ana to bring kien wielders to the Temple of Ceur for their own protection and the protection of their communities.

Ei'ceuril

A religious order, currently a majority of men, focused on serving Anaweh, the Creating Light. Because a kien wielder is not capable of wielding with control, every male ei'ceuril capable of wielding is confined to the Temple of Ceur.

Ei'denai

Elven lord serving as aryl with his spouse. Head of House.

Ei'ethil

Elven lord.

Ei'lythel

Elven lady.

Ei'terel

Elven lady serving as aryl with her spouse. Head of House.

Eklean

Continent where the anacordel first stirred as Children.

Eldin Wood, the

Home of the Eldinari.

Eldinare

Northern Skyland of the Eldinari, one of the four elven kindreds. Lost to the Darkness. The Eldinari were the first to evacuate their Skyland for the lands below.

Elemental Erendinth, the

Forces wielded to influence the elements. *See Erendinth.*

Elf

Anacordel who changed little when the different races were created. Because they wished to retain their original form, their immortality remained, and they were gifted the Skylands. There are four elven kindreds, the Luminari, Cyndinari, Aldinari, and Eldinari.

Elya

Powerful wielders born of any race who learn to wield instinctively and are not limited to the restrictions common to normal kien and kiara wielders.

Emradiel

One of the seven Schools of Septyl. Emradiels focus on beauty and life. Motto: Only the prudent thrive. Emblem: A naked male and female elf gesturing with open palms toward the beauty around them with a stag behind, cast in gold on a green field. The chair of Emradiel is known as the Tender.

Enthiel

Anadel dedicated to one of the seven irythil. The enthiel are very involved with the anacordel. A single enthiel guides an entire people.

Erendinth, the

The erendinth are the wielded powers believed to have created Teraeniel. Tradition says that there are seven powers, three transcendental: lumenys, animys, and umbrys; and four elemental: aquaeys, aerys, terys, and ignys. Much is forgotten or unknown about the full extent of the erendinth which are dependent on inner spiritual and emotional workings.

Erendinth Games, the

A game of wielding created at Gwilnor Academy, involving the wielding of all seven erendinth.

Faun

Short nocturnal anacordel with the hind legs of a goat from the navel down. Some fauns have horns.

Giant

Anacordel that were drawn to the frozen north. During the Great Blessing, their physical features became capable of withstanding the harsh tundra of Glacien.

GLACIEN

Northern frozen continent spanning the northern pole. Connects Eklean and Ogren.

GOBLIN

Anacordel native to the Kinzdol Islands. Known for their monetary shrewdness.

GOBLIN GUILD

Infamous bank and guild of Eklean. Regulates the majority of Eklean's currency. The Goblin Guild is based in the Kinzdol Islands with branches in every city and most villages.

GREAT BLESSING, THE

Event recorded in the Theseryn where Anaweh blessed the growing differences among the anacordel and solidified their choices by making each their own distinct race.

GUARDIAN KNIGHTS

Order of knights once based in Krysenthiel that served and protected all the land from injustice. The Guardian Knights were largely composed of Luminari and were defeated during the Ceurendol War.

GUARDIAN SENATE, THE

An international body, crossing countries and continents to ensure the wellbeing of Teraeniel. Disbanded toward the end of the Ceurendol War.

GWILNOR ACADEMY

The foremost school dedicated to the education of wielders, located in Ceurenyl.

HOLY TOMES

Volumes recorded by various ei'ceuril, some being prophets, and from which the ei'ceuril base their beliefs and practices.

HUMAN

Anacordel that differ among themselves more than any other race. They traveled the furthest from the Valley of Saeryndol, migrating across the entirety of Teraeniel.

IGNYS

An elemental erendinth. The essence of fire.

ILLUMINED WOOD, THE

A vast forest with mysterious qualities and inhabitants.

IMPERIUM

Selective school for Cyndinari youth. Its violent academic style educates the next generation of shadow elves.

IRYTHIL

The seven anadel who, under Anaweh's guidance, introduced the erendinth, thereby creating Teraeniel.

JA'HORAN

Continent south of Eklean. Inhabited largely by nomadic peoples.

JAHRO ISLANDS

Island chain in the Unarian Sea. Believed to be the home of pirates.

JUDGES OF YANIL

An order that once ruled beside the Yanilean. The judges are now a secret organization that strives to uphold law and order with limited influence.

KEEPER

Head of the time wardens and possessor of the time key.

KIARA WIELDER

A female wielder. Kiara wielders learn to control the erendinth easily but require a kien wielder to reach their potential strength. Because the Balance was lost, kiara wielders are not able to reach their potential strength.

KIEN WIELDER

A male wielder. Kien wielders reach their potential strength easily but require a kiara wielder to learn control of the erendinth. Because the Balance was lost, kien wielders are not able to wield safely, and if any male begins to show an aptitude to wield, he is sent to the Temple of Ceur where wielding is impossible.

KILNAE DEL

Order of mages native to Charren, headquartered in the Charrenese capital, Karithel.

Kinzdol Islands

An archipelago in southern Eklean, homeland to the goblins and Cyndinari.

Kweil Aitch

Island east of the Illumined Wood. The place where the veil is thin between Teraeniel and Somnaeniel.

Lay Votary

A non-clerical class of ei'ceuril.

Lorendil

Anadel that guard and protect individual anacordel. Some anacordel are known to communicate with their lorendil.

Lucillian Alliance, the

An alliance of the Eklean kingdoms established to return peace and order to Eklean following Emperor Erynor's disappearance.

Lumaeniel

The World-Beyond. Dwelling of Anaweh, the anadel, and those anacordel who have passed beyond.

Lumenys

A transcendental erendinth. The essence of light.

Luminare

Eastern Skyland of the Luminari, one of the four elven kindreds. Lost to the Darkness. The Luminari evacuated their Skyland for the lands below where they established Krysenthiel.

Mar'anathyl

City on the Skyland of Luminare. Governed by the Lorenthien aryls.

Masters, the (Seven Masters, the)

Vigyl Vyoletryn, Cyrelle Azurelle, Lanielle Emradiel, Lyon Arantiulyn, Mainor Auburnis, Caelyn Crimsyn, and Saeyrn Albien are the founders of the Seven Schools of Septyl and Gwilnor Academy.

Meridean Conclave

Governing council of the merpeople.

Meridephaen

Feast day of the Cyndinari, commemorating Meridiel and the noon sun. Celebrated on the 15th of Meridenth, the summer solstice.

Merpeople

Anacordel who longed for the depths of Teraeniel's oceans.

Miervae

Anacordel who longed to nurture Teraeniel's forests. Miervae are also referred to as Great Trees and begin their life as Settlings.

Minum

The least of Eklean's races. A short half-bred creature of goblin and human origins. Before the elves migrated to Eklean, they were enslaved, sold by goblins to humans.

Naril

Anadel reminiscent of the seven erendinth. There are seven types of narils and they are commonly known as nymphs.

Nymphs

See Naril.

Observant

Non-wielders who have dedicated themselves to one of the Seven Schools of Septyl.

Ogre

Brutish anacordel covering the vast majority of Ogren. Half-bred creature of giant and human origins.

Ogren

Continent east of Eklean and west of Qien. Mountainous land with a mixture of forests and deserts. Inhabited by giants, humans, and ogres.

Phaedryn

Those bound with a phoenix.

Purged Desert of Dwonia, the

A vast wasteland in western Eklean that was rumored to have at one point been fertile. Home of the Twelve Tribes of Dwonia.

Return

The final stage of formation of an ei'ceuril toward becoming a steward. Often occurring in the Illumined Wood.

Sanctum

Expansive complexes housing the aldarchs and their courts on Aldinare.

Schtach

Language of the dwarves.

Schtam

(1) A dwarven people. (2) The dwellings of the dwarves.

Schtamite

The eight dwarven Schtams.

Seguian

A portal created to traverse space and time. Traversing time is restricted and only the keeper can use the time key to traverse time.

Septyl

(1) The Order of Ei'ana composing the Seven Schools of Septyl. (2) The city of the ei'ana in Krysenthiel and now lost in the Shroud.

Septyl Knights

Order of knights dedicated to Septyl. The knights receive their training at Gwilnor Academy and vow to serve one of the Seven Schools of Septyl.

Servants of Shadow

Secret organization carrying out the orders of shadow elves and, in some instances, the orders of the Deurghol.

Settling

Tree-like creatures that wander about in their youth until finding an appropriate place to settle their roots and grow into a Miervae, also known as a Great Tree. Settlings have unique vitality qualities.

Seven Chairs of Septyl, the

The leaders of the Ei'ana. Each of the Seven Schools elects its own Chair who leads his or her particular School and participates in the leadership of Septyl. Responsible for admitting student wielders into Gwilnor Academy and selecting a chancellor.

Seven Schools of Septyl, the

The order of Ei'ana, composed of Albien, Arantiulyn, Auburnis, Azurelle, Crimsyn, Emradiel, and Vyoletryn Schools.

Shadow Elves

Cyndinari who consume the spirit of others to prolong their own life.

Shroud, the

A diseased-looking fog placed by the Cyndinari over the entirety of Krysenthiel. It severed the Luminari from the Jewel of Life, cutting them off from their life essence and making them mortal, as well as any others who had benefited from it. An unanticipated result was that the Cyndinari also lost their immortality with that placement of the Shroud over the Jewel of Life. The Shroud's mysterious origin is one reason no one has been able to remove it.

Skylands, the

Four island countries, Aldinare, Cyndinare, Eldinare, and Luminare, floating in the clouds thousands of feet above the ground. The dwelling places of the elves before they were forced to evacuate to the land below.

Sojourners

The exiled of Dwonia who sought reentrance after forming an allegiance with the Erynien Empire.

Somnaeniel

The World-in-Between. A realm visited by dreamers. Gateway between Lumaeniel and Teraeniel.

Star Warden

An elven military unit, typically ensuring the protection of their lands.

Steward

A clerical class of ei'ceuril with the ability to wield.

Stewards of Shadow

Ei'ceuril stewards who forsook Anaweh to support Ramiel.

Temple of Ceur, the

Home to the ei'ceuril and pilgrimage site for the faithful. It is impossible to wield within the temple walls. All kien wielders are confined to the Temple of Ceur.

Temple Knights

Order of knights dedicated to protecting the Temple of Ceur and the city of Ceurenyl. Some of the temple knights are men who were brought to the temple when it was discovered that they could wield. These temple knights are prohibited from leaving the temple.

Tenebrae

An unrecognized School of Septyl intended to replace the other seven Schools. Its adherents focus on power and dominance. Motto: Might conquers. Emblem: A naked male and female elf standing triumphantly on seven broken emblems, cast in gold on a black field. The chair of Tenebrae is known as the Conqueror.

Tenebrys

A corrupted form of the erendinth, unrecognized by the Ei'ana of Septyl as one of the erendinth and absolutely forbidden to wield. The essence of Darkness.

Teraeniel

The World-Below. Composed of the continents Daereneth, Eklean, Glacien, Ja'Horan, Ogren, and Qien.

Terys

An elemental erendinth. The essence of stone.

Theseryn

Holy tome recording the creation of Teraeniel and the anacordel, written by the first Ceurtriarch of the Ei'ceuril. The Theseryn states that seven irythil, under Anaweh's guidance, introduced the erendinth thereby creating Teraeniel.

Time Key

An artifact created by the Luminari to restrict the ability to traverse space and time. It was entrusted to the minums, the least of Eklean's races.

Time Wardens

A select group of minums entrusted by the Luminari with the ability to create seguians, allowing them to travel to any place and any time.

Transcendental Erendinth, the

Wielded forces to influence the ethereal realities of lumenys, animys, and umbrys. The ability to wield the transcendental erendinth is forgotten.

Tree Spirits

Narils who agreed to bond with the trees under Sariel's guidance.

UMBRYS

A transcendental erendinth. The essence of shadow.

VAER

Fruit native to the Illumined Wood.

VALLEY OF SAERYNDOL

Birthplace of the Children, the first anacordel.

VERAKRYL

A crystalline tree within Mount Verinien which brought life to the world and is connected to Anaweh. Also known as the Tree of Life.

VERATHEL

Sprouts of Verakryl, the Tree of Life.

VERATHN

Weapons of power.

VESPEPHAEN

Feast day of the Aldinari, commemorating Vespiel and the setting sun. Celebrated on the 15th of Vespenth, the autumn equinox.

VYOLETRYN

One of the seven Schools of Septyl. Vyoletryns focus on justice and diplomacy. Motto: With justice, peace. Emblem: A naked male and female elf holding a staff with an eagle soaring above, cast in gold on a violet field. The chair of Vyoletryn is known as the Watcher.

WIELDERS

Anacordel capable of wielding the erendinth.

WISE ONES

(1) Part of the Ei'ceuril hierarchy. There is no certainty how many are among the ei'ceuril. (2) Part of the Ei'ana hierarchy. There are seven wise ones for every School of Septyl.

YANILEAN, THE

The undisputed monarch of Yanil, always male. Used both as the monarch's title and as his name during his reign.

DAYS OF THE WEEK

(Based on the seven anadel involved in the creation of Teraeniel)

Gwynthaen–Thenaen–Uraen–Ramaen–Lerenaen–Saraen–Karaen

Months/Moons

(Based on the anadel attached to the elves)
Spring – Marenth, Aurenth, Delenth
Summer – Dynenth, Meridenth, Reventh
Autumn – Kyrenth, Vespenth, Orenth
Winter – Estlenth, Borenth, Lierenth

Currency

Goblin Guild currency – 16 iron angots for a copper lewt. 9 copper lewts for a silver jent. 13 silver jents for a gold crown. 3 golden crowns for a lumol.
Luminari currency – 8 kenols for a narol. 4 narols for a lumol.

Appendix B
Dramatis Personae

Aaron Roendryn

Luminari. Prince of Lucillia, brother of Ellendren. Ei'ceuril.

Abbie Wintyr

Human with emerald eyes. Student at Gwilnor Academy. Druid of Kweil Aitch.

Aen Finamarc

Half elf and half human from Cor'lera, squire to Alex Vaerin.

Agnelle Phanstienne

Luminari. Ei'ana and Chair of Auburnis.

Alesei

Queen of Tiel. Of the Royal House Ziera.

Alethea Lenwyn

Eldinari. Emradiel ei'ana and former Lenwyn aryl.

Alexander (Alex) Vaerin

Human from Perrien, whose family migrated to Cor'lera. Devlyn's cousin on his father's side.

Aliel

The first phoenix born since the fall of Krysenthiel, bound to Devlyn.

Amry Thellion

King of Evellion. Married to Queen Lara.

Andrew

Human from Sudern. Student knight at Gwilnor Academy.

Angennia (Ange) Soricci

Human from Yanil. Judge of Yanil.

Arbol

A faun searching for settlings.

Aren Lorenthien

Luminari. Led a rescue party to Aldinare and did not return. Now a Dark Phaedryn in service to Erynor.

Arlyn

Ei'ceuril steward from Cor'lera. Devlyn's uncle on his mother's side.

BERNARD

Human from Perrien. Ei'ceuril, librarian, and magister at the abbey school of Cor'lera.

CATALINA TURLAN

Human from Yanil. Supreme Judge of Yanil.

CLARA

Aldinari. Ei'ceuril, steward and abbess of the Monastery of the Poor Ladies in the Ashton Wood.

DANIELLE AEQUIN

Luminari of House Aerquin. Student wielder at Gwilnor Academy.

DANYOL

Eldinari. Assistant magister to Yvonne.

DAPHNE ASHTON

Human from Mindale. Lady of Ashton Wood. Emradiel Ei'ana.

DEVLYN TELVIN

Ward of Cor'lera's abbey school. Physical features indicate Lucillian ancestry.

DOLAN TELVIN

Father of Devlyn, Leilyn, and Liam. Husband of Evellyn. *Deceased.*

EAGAN WINTYR

Human. Druid of Kweil Aitch, and Abbie's brother.

EALYNDOL ROENDRYN

Luminari. Ceurtriarch.

ELLENDREN ROENDRYN

Luminari. Princess of Lucillia. Student wielder at Gwilnor Academy.

EMDIAN

Human from Sudern. Ei'ceuril steward.

ENRICO DESILLIO

Human from Yanil. Noble in the Yanilean's court.

ENTIEL TELVIN

Human from Perrien. Ei'ceuril, steward, and abbot of the abbey school of Cor'lera. Devlyn's uncle on his father's side.

ERYNOR MERIDEN

Emperor of the Erynien Empire. Disappeared after Lucillia gave birth to the twins, Roendryn and Feolyn in 7857.3E. First Cyndinari born on Eklean.

EVELLYN TELVIN

Luminari from Cor'lera. Mother of Leilyn and Devlyn. Wife of Dolan.

FERINN

Merperson. Currently resides in Myrium.

FYONA ORENDI

Luminari. Student wielder at Gwilnor Academy.

FYREH GLAEDA

Eldinari. Azurelle ei'ana and magister at Gwilnor. Twin brother to Myrah, husband to Suella, and father to many children.

GORDON CARVIL

King of Torsil. Of the Royal House Carvil. Supporter of Erynor.

HANNAH TORIN

Human from Mindale. Azurelle ei'ana and chancellor of Gwilnor Academy.

HARNYL ROENDRYN

Luminari. Aryl of Lucillia. Married to Queen Vernal. Father of Prince Aaron, Princess Kaela, and Princess Ellendren.

INDRYL

Luminari. Tenebrae ei'ana, once believed to be a Vyoletryn ei'ana.

JAEROL SOLARIS

Cyndinari. Former Erynien emissary.

JAX

Minum and time warden.

KAELA ROENDRYN

Luminari. Princess of Lucillia, sister to Ellendren and Aaron.

KAEYTH ILLIERO

Luminari. Ei'ceuril novice.

KAI

Human with physical features that suggest an origin other than Eklean. Azurelle ei'ana and magister of politics at Gwilnor Academy.

Karina Lariviere

Queen of Sorenthil. Widow of the late King Dorian. Mother of Myranda.

Karl Olney

Human from Perrien. Observant of Vyoletryn.

Kevn Weyvien

Luminari. Student at Gwilnor Academy. Previously studied to become an ei'ceuril.

Kiara

A mythical woman believed to be the first female wielder.

Kien

A mythical man believed to be the first male wielder.

Lacus

Human from Torsil. Ei'ceuril steward.

Lara Thellion

Queen of Evellion. Married to King Amry. Azurelle ei'ana.

Lawrence Maroven

King of Mindale. Of the Royal House Maroven. Supporter of Erynor.

Leilyn Telvin

Sister of Devlyn, believed to be living in the Illumined Wood. Daughter of Evellyn and Dolan.

Lenora Hanaryld

Human from Ceurenyl. Ei'ana and Chair of Arantiulyn. *Deceased.*

Lex Telvin

General from Perrien, key player in events surrounding Devlyn's family. Devlyn's uncle on his father's side.

Liam Telvin

Son of Dolan. Half-brother to Devlyn and Leilyn.

Lillianna

Human from Mindale. Ei'ceuril and formerly an Emradiel ei'ana.

Loretta Javie

Human of Sorenthil. Ei'ana and Chair of Crimsyn.

Lucillia

The woman who gave birth to the twins, Roendryn and Feolyn.

MELANIE BIRKWELL

Human from Mindale. Ei'ana and Chair of Arantiulyn.

MYRAH GLAEDA

Eldinari. Albien ei'ana and magister at Gwilnor Academy; twin sister to Fyreh.

MYRANDA LARIVIERE

Queen of Sorenthil. Student wielder at Gwilnor Academy.

OLIVER PENAULT

Human from Perrien. Septyl knight of Vyoletryn.

OMA

Dwarf of the Oern Schtam. Stone seer.

ORANNA

Luminari. Azurelle ei'ana and chancellor of Gwilnor Academy.

ORENIEL

Centaur of the Illumined Wood.

PAUREL ROENDRYN

Luminari. Ei'ana and Chair of Azurelle.

PHENDIEN SHENDIELLE

Eldinari. Ei'ana and true Chair of Emradiel.

RAMIRA BIR GINTHOL

Human from Yanil. Supreme Judge of Yanil at the time of Nauto's Wrath.

REIA

Luminari. Arantiulyn ei'ana.

RUSYL

A free dragon of the Blue Flight.

SAENDRE

Luminari. Student wielder at Gwilnor Academy.

SANJIN AL'SANHIR

Human from Charren. Crowned Prince of Charren of the Royal House Irithru.

SARA

Human from Briel. Auburnis ei'ana.

Selenya Waeyn

Luminari. Ei'ana and Chair of Albien.

Skimp

Minum and time warden.

Taen Taerinior

Luminari. Ei'ceuril novice.

Therril

Ei'ceuril magister of theoreticals at Gwilnor Academy.

Tiera Weldon

Luminari. Ei'ana and Chair of Emradiel.

Tindol

Human from Dwonia. Member of the Sojourners.

Trethien Narielle

Luminari of House Narielle. Student knight at Gwilnor Academy.

Tye

Human from Dwonia. Member of Tribe Fendur.

Velaria Treyven

Cyndinari born in Lucillia. Ei'ana and Chair of Azurelle.

Vernal Roendryn

Luminari. Aryl of Lucillia. Married to King Harnyl. Mother of Prince Aaron, Princess Kaela, and Princess Ellendren. Direct descendant of Lucillia.

Vine Vaerin

Human from Perrien. Mother of Alex. Devlyn's aunt on his father's side.

Viren Dekenurel

Luminari. Guardian Knight.

Waleisius

Merchant in Cor'lera, more commonly known as Walei.

Wyn Lierafen

Eldinari. Grandson of Dalenya and Fendryl. Star Warden. Emradiel ei'ana.

Yelaris

A free dragon of the Blue Flight bound to Velaria.

YVONNE KARDOL

Human from Yanil. Crimsyn ei'ana and Magister of the art of wielding at Gwilnor Academy.

THE SEVEN IRYTHIL AND THEIR ASSOCIATED ENTHIEL

URIEL – Lord of the Stars, whose name means Anaweh is my Light. Irythil who brought Anaweh's Light to Teraeniel.

AURIEL – The Dawn Star. Guardian of the elves of Luminare.

MERIDIEL – The Noon Star. Guardian of the elves of Cyndinare.

VESPIEL – The Evening Star. Guardian of the elves of Aldinare.

BORIEL – The Night Star. Guardian of the elves of Eldinare.

GWYNTHIEL – Lady of the Lorendil, whose name means Strength of Anaweh. Irythil who brought Anaweh's spirit to Teraeniel.

RAMIEL – Lord of Death, whose name means Arrogant toward Anaweh. Betrayed Anaweh and all creation. Irythil who brought shadow to Teraeniel.

THENIEL – Lady of the Seas, whose name means Anaweh Heals. Irythil who brought water to Teraeniel.

NAUTO – Guardian of all humans living along the coasts.

AQUAE – Guardian of the merpeople.

SARIEL – Lord of the Land, whose name means Command of Anaweh. Irythil who brought substance to Teraeniel.

TERA – Patroness of harvest and nourishment. Often referred to as Mother Tera.

MUNDI – Guardian of the dwarves.

LERENIEL – Lady of the Winds, whose name means Friend of Anaweh. Irythil who brought air to Teraeniel.

KARIEL – Lord of Peace, whose name means Who is Like Anaweh. Irythil who brought fire to Teraeniel.

Aldarchs of Aldinare

Gael of Quel'anir – The Reverent Mother, also known as the Nurturer. Her followers dedicate themselves to nature and caring for the ilithae trees, native to Aldinare.

Orien of Eln'dinai – The Just Father, also known as the Judge. His followers focus on upholding law in Aldinare.

Nialth of Dur'linos – The Philosopher, also known as the Learned One. Her followers dedicate their life to study.

Theseryn of Thas'thallas – The Faithful Servant. His followers devoted their lives to the worshipping Anaweh, the Creating Light. Theseryn left his sanctum of Thas'thallas to establish the Ei'ceuril order and became the first Ceurtriarch.

Lerathel of Val'quin – The Artisan. Sister to Nialth. Her followers are practitioners of the arts, and designed the great cities and sanctums of Aldinare.

Endruil of Kir'enon – The Shepherd. His followers are caretakers of the alicorns native to Aldinare.

Aeryth of Ai'lyr – The the Rogue. Her followers prefer the to hide in the shadows and wield the fabled Aldinari bows.

Irithel of Mel'inor – The Smith. His followers develop advanced weapons and tools, often forged from aldaryl.

Appendix C
Civilizations of Teraeniel

Aldinare

Remnant of Aldinari rescued from the Skyland Aldinare by Aren and accompanying Phaedryn. They are considered part of Krysenthiel.
Race: Elf
House/Aryl: Avign, Eraen, Kenoril, Threilen

Audun

One of the eight Schtams composing the Schtamite. Situated at the westernmost edge of the Laudien Mountains.
Head of State: Patriarch Dridn IV, son of Dridn III
Race: Dwarf

Briel

River valley kingdom situated between two rivers forming the River Reifen and the slopes of the Dead Wood.
Capital: Briel
Head of State: King Irvienne of the Royal House Haert
Motto: Seek the message
Sigil: Black raven on a yellow field
Race: Human

Brunst

One of the eight Schtams composing the Schtamite. Situated within the Vespien Mountains. Close friends with the Eldinari.
Head of State: Patriarch Thraen, son of Anuun
Race: Dwarf

Charren

A kingdom spanning across two continents, Ogren and Daereneth.
Capital: Karithel
Head of State: King Sanhir al'Gahnir of the Royal House Irithru
Race: Human

Daer Empire

Oldest continuous human empire in Teraeniel and advocate of slavery and colonialism. Situated on the continent of Daereneth.
Capital: Daer
Head of State: Body of the Daer Senate

Race: Human

DWONIA

Desert country once controlled by the Twelve Tribes of Dwonia. Only two tribes refused to ally with Erynor and remained in the desert.

Heads of State: Chief Kodin of Tribe Fendur and Chief Genin of Tribe Vadir

Capital: Nynev

Sigil: Red lion on a yellow field

Race: Human

ELDINARE

Eldinari society secreted away in the Eldin Wood.

Head of State: Aryl Fendryl and Dalenya of House Lierafen

Capital: Stellantis

Houses/Aryls: Aeris, Allandis, Glaeda, Illia, Jamsyl, Lenwyn, Lierafen, Nyen, Oreleste, Shendielle, Rudyn, Taureh

Sigil: White tree on a green field

Race: Elf

ERYNIEN

Cyndinari empire founded by Erynor Meriden, its sole emperor. Responsible for the Ceurendol War and enslavement of the Luminari.

Capital: Broid

Head of State: Emperor Erynor Meriden

Sigil: Bronze sun on a red field

Race: Elf

EVELLION

The mountain kingdom where the Laudien and Vespien mountain ranges meet. Original inhabitants were the refugees of Thellion.

Capital: Everin

Head of State: King Amry and Queen Lara of the Royal House Thellion

Motto: The pure will soar

Sigil: White eagle on a blue field

Race: Human

FRIETON

The free city-state of Frieton. Given to the minums on their release

from slavery.
Capital: Frieton
Head of State: The Keeper (identity unknown)
Race: Minum

GESTORIA

Fallen kingdom situated on the Plains of Orithil. Once great allies to Thellion and Krysenthiel. Obliterated during the Ceurendol War.
Capital: Quellion
Motto: Will triumphs pride
Sigil: White gold winged lion on a blue field
Race: Human

GLYOL

One of the eight Schtams composing the Schtamite. Easternmost and only schtam in the Illumined Wood.
Head of State: Matriarch Vylma, daughter of Toreldn
Race: Dwarf

HAROL

One of the eight Schtams composing the Schtamite. Situated in the Laudien Mountains.
Head of State: Matriarch Loewn, daughter of Brenola
Race: Dwarf

JA'HORAN, TRIBES OF

Nomadic civilization on the continent of Ja'horan.
Race: Human

JA'NALIHN

Short lived kingdom covering all of Ja'horan.
Race: Human

JOPHT SCHTAM

One of the eight Schtams composing the Schtamite. Southernmost Schtam in the Vespien Mountains and staunch defenders against the Shadow Schtams from northern infiltration.
Head of State: Patriarch Oerth III, son of Oerth II
Race: Dwarf

KRYSENTHIEL

The kingdom of the Luminari. Currently lost within the Shroud. Translates to land of the golden flowers, named by a human trying to speak Aelish, the language of the elves, to describe the countryside.

Capital: Arenthyl

Head of State: Exalted Lorenthien Aryl

Houses/Aryls: Aerquin, Clarion, Ginielle, Lauriel, Lorenthien, Narielle, Reyndien, Taerinior

Sigil: Seven golden kryseniels blossoming from a larger central kryseniel on a white field.

Race: Elf

LUCILLIA

Kingdom of the Luminari after gaining their freedom from the Erynien Empire. Named after Lucillia, the woman who gave birth to the twins, Roendryn and Feolyn.

Capital: Lucillia

Head of State: Aryl Vernal and Harnyl of House Roendryn

Race: Elf

MINDALE

A kingdom east of the southern Vespien Mountains.

Capital: Binton

Head of State: King Lawrence of the Royal House Maroven

Motto: Mind over body

Sigil: Brown ox on a green field

Race: Human

NUNSTOL

Shadow Schtam that was cast off by the Schtamite for their actions in Mount Cyngol.

Head of State: Patriarch Uriden, son of Urodrn

Race: Dwarf

OERN

One of the eight Schtams composing the Schtamite. Belin belonged to Oern Schtam and sheltered Evellion and his people as they fled Elothkar.

Head of State: Patriarch Forvl VIII, son of Forvl VII

Race: Dwarf

PARENDIOR

A hilly country north of the Laudien Mountains and west of the Illumined Wood. Most Parendians are farming folk, and when Perrien invaded, they had no means of defending their land.

Capital: Gneal

Head of State: Perrien Council

Motto: Protect the harmony

Sigil: Purple doe on a beige field

Race: Human

PERRIEN

A kingdom north of the Laudien Mountains where the citizens over-threw their monarchy and replaced it with a council and doubled their territory by invading Parendior.

Capital: Gneal

Head of State: Perrien Council

Motto: Swift to action

Sigil: Grey rider and horse on a white field

Race: Human

QIEN EMPIRE, THE

Empire of the Hundred Kingdoms on the continent of Qien, west of Eklean.

Capital: Zhongshi

Auxiliary Capitals: Beishi, Dongshi, Nanshi, and Xishi

Head of State: Empress Qien Wei

Race: Human

SORENTHIL

A kingdom along the River Meyien.

Capital: Myrium

Head of State: Queen Karina of the Royal House Lariviere

Motto: Flow with the waters

Sigil: Blue dolphin on a light blue field

Race: Human

SUDERN

A city state on the Dagger's Point peninsula. After a bloody civil war with Josque, the inhabitants declared themselves independent.

Capital: Sudern

Motto: Hidden daggers

Sigil: Red ship and dagger on a white field

Race: Human

Thellion

The fallen Eklean kingdom covering all the lands east of the Vespien Mountains. Met its downfall through a civil war relating to succession.
Capital: Elothkar
Motto: Eternal wisdom
Sigil: Silver winged horse on a white field

Tiel

A southern kingdom bordering the Erynien Bay and the Unarian Sea.
Capital: Josque
Head of State: Queen Alesei of the Royal House Ziera
Motto: Eternal wisdom
Sigil: Orange serpent on a blue field
Race: Human

Torsil

A weak kingdom with little influence on its neighbors.
Capital: Trest
Head of State: King Gordon of the Royal House Carvil
Motto: Stronger together
Sigil: Grey wolf on a red field
Race: Human

Undol Schtam

One of the eight Schtams composing the Schtamite. Deeply religious and situated in the Laudien Mountains surrounding Lake Saeryndol. They have strong ties to the Luminari.
Head of State: Matriarch Miurel IV, daughter of Miurel III
Race: Dwarf

Vorn Schtam

One of the eight Schtams composing the Schtamite. Situated at the northernmost edge of the Vespien Mountains.
Head of State: Matriarch Tiltha, daughter of Tilma
Race: Dwarf

Yanil

Southern kingdom along Erynien Bay. Yanil was once jointly ruled by the Yanilean and the Judges of Yanil.
Capital: Lankor
Head of State: The Yanilean

Motto: Deep as justice
Sigil: Black castle on a blue field
Race: Human

ZORIK

Shadow Schtam that was cast off by the Schtamite for their actions in Mount Cyngol.
Head of State: Matriarch Jiora, daughter of Jiorza
Race: Dwarf

About the Author

Ryan D Gebhart first started writing the Jewel of Life series in 2012 in Philadelphia, PA, shortly after concluding his undergraduate studies in philosophy. This unexpected passion evolved over the years and has remained a constant companion through his career changes, from a Franciscan Friar, to a Claims Processor, receiving a Graduate Degree in Architecture, and now working at an Architecture Firm in Washington, DC. Ryan D Gebhart is originally from Wilmington, DE.

Keep up with Ryan D Gebhart at www.RyanDGebhart.com